Satan's Petting Zoo

Brian Koscienski   Chris Pisano

an imprint of Sunbury Press, Inc.
Mechanicsburg, PA USA

an imprint of Sunbury Press, Inc.
Mechanicsburg, PA USA

NOTE: This is a work of fiction. Names, characters, places and incidents are the product of the author's imagination or are used fictitiously, and any resemblance to actual persons, living or dead, business establishments, events or locales is entirely coincidental.

Copyright © 2020 by Brian Koscienski and Chris Pisano.
Cover Copyright © 2020 by Sunbury Press, Inc.

Sunbury Press supports copyright. Copyright fuels creativity, encourages diverse voices, promotes free speech, and creates a vibrant culture. Thank you for buying an authorized edition of this book and for complying with copyright laws. Except for the quotation of short passages for the purpose of criticism and review, no part of this publication may be reproduced, scanned, or distributed in any form without permission. You are supporting writers and allowing Sunbury Press to continue to publish books for every reader. For information contact Sunbury Press, Inc., Subsidiary Rights Dept., PO Box 548, Boiling Springs, PA 17007 USA or legal@sunburypress.com.

For information about special discounts for bulk purchases, please contact Sunbury Press Orders Dept. at (855) 338-8359 or orders@sunburypress.com.

To request one of our authors for speaking engagements or book signings, please contact Sunbury Press Publicity Dept. at publicity@sunburypress.com.

FIRST VERBOTEN BOOKS EDITION: March 2020

Set in Adobe Garamond | Interior design by Crystal Devine | Cover design by Lawrence Knorr | Cover art by Dirk Shearer | Edited by Lawrence Knorr.

Publisher's Cataloging-in-Publication Data
Names: Koscienski, Brian, author | Pisano, Chris, author.
Title: Satan's petting zoo / Brian Koscienski Chris Pisano.
Description: First trade paperback edition. | Mechanicsburg, PA : Verboten Books, 2020.
Summary: A group of college students deal with bullying through sorcery and suffer unintended consequences.
Identifiers: ISBN 978-1-620063-93-4 (softcover).
Subjects: FICTION / Fantasy / Humorous | FICTION / Mythology | FICTION / Fantasy / Dark Fantasy | FICTION / Humorous / Black Humor | FICTION / Horror.

Product of the United States of America
0 1 1 2 3 5 8 13 21 34 55

Continue the Enlightenment!

CHAPTER 1

Kyle pissed his pants. Right outside of the Student Union Center, in broad daylight with people milling about. Luckily, only Chad noticed.

Over the past month, part of Chad's weekday morning ritual was looking over the papers attached to the bulletin board before entering the Student Union Center. This was a part of the college experience, over-romanticized by the countless movies and television shows depicting magical events happening at the college bulletin board. They showed that anything he needed could be found hanging from the cork background by a pin or staple: from furniture to computers; lessons on how to play guitar or get into yoga poses; support groups for all kinds of loss or addiction; clubs and meetings. The most popular were want ads for carpooling or roommates. As a townie who still lived with his parents four blocks from campus, Chad didn't need that. In fact, Chad really didn't need anything that the flyers had to offer. Clearly, bulletin boards held the heart's desire only for television and movie characters.

Real students casually skimmed and moved on, if they even noticed the bulletin board at all, too focused on their phones while moving from class to class. Those who found something interesting pulled off one of the precut tabs from the flyer of note, or wrote down pertinent information, or took a picture of it with their phone. No one lingered like Chad. Still, if it happened in the movies and television shows, then it *could* happen in real life, since those scripts had to be based on *something*. The "something" Chad hoped for the most was the random encounter with the future love of his life.

Chad had always fantasized about meeting a girl at the bulletin board. He would reach to rip off the last tab from a flyer advertising a movie discussion group when another hand, one delicate and lithe, would reach for the same thing. Their hands would touch. They'd laugh. A conversation about their mutual admiration for the big screen and small screen would start, and a lasting, undying love would ensue. Instead of getting the girl of his dreams at the bulletin board today, he got a friend who became spontaneously incontinent.

Shifting himself closer to obscure his friend from curious eyes, Chad looked around, hoping for reinforcements. Found them. Turning the corner from the one sidewalk to this one came Cooper and Heston. A cold sweat forming along his hairline, Chad waved for them to hurry. Tall and lanky, Cooper scampered like an uncoordinated weasel and made it to Chad and Kyle first. Fancying himself a smooth talker, Cooper always had a smile while effervescent words bubbled quickly from his mouth like poured champagne. "Greetings and salutations, gentlemen. How goes it on such a glorious and wondrous da—whoa."

Chad had moved enough to show Cooper the emergency. Cooper put a hand on Kyle's shoulder and, in a soothing tone, asked, "Hey, Kyle. How are you doing, buddy? What's going on here?"

A tremble to his words, Kyle whispered, "That could have been me."

Cooper looked to Chad for an explanation. Shrugging his shoulders, Chad didn't have one. He had no idea what Kyle freaked out about this time.

Kyle had always been a bit of a bird—skittish and flighty—as long as Chad had known him. Once in kindergarten class, Chad had to console Kyle for over an hour after he broke a crayon. When they were ten, they listened to their first heavy metal cd together. Afterward, Kyle broke down into tears, afraid that his parents were going to punish him for listening to such music. They didn't, but Kyle's fears had always inhibited him in certain aspects of his life and manifested themselves in curious ways. Just last year, Chad, Cooper, Heston, and Kyle smoked pot for the first time. Kyle became so paranoid about the government listening to his thoughts that he wrapped his head with aluminum foil. But now? To wet himself in public? Chad was stumped. Right now, he just wanted to help his friend. "Cooper? You have any classes?"

Cooper understood exactly what Chad was asking. As nonchalantly as possible, Cooper removed his sweatshirt and tied it around Kyle's waist, making sure the sleeves draped in front of Kyle's crotch. Using his shoulders to steer, Cooper guided Kyle away. "Okay, Kyle. We're just going to call it a day and get you back home, okay?"

"That could have been me," was Kyle's only response.

Heston finally made it to the bulletin board. As big as an ox, his overweight frame made his run look more like a flustered waddle. Even his acne tipped cheeks bounced with every footfall. Trying not to sound out of breath, Heston asked, "What's up with Kyle this time?"

A secret agent exchanging classified information, Chad whispered, "I don't know. Kyle came over to the bulletin board, and then all of a sudden, he pissed himself."

"Really? That's extreme even for Kyle."

"I know. He said something about 'it could have been me' while looking at the bulletin board."

"Do you think he was talking about that?" Heston pointed to the one flyer that Chad hadn't noticed. The sheet of paper didn't make any promises or offer any invites. It asked for a favor. It asked for help. "Do you think he knew the kid?"

The "kid" was a black and white photo under the word "missing" and only two years younger than either Chad or Heston. He was a junior at South Bend High School. Chad and his friends had gone to East Bend High. There was a West Bend, but no North Bend. The locals referred to the trio of towns as "The Bends," and all the high schools were considered local, but East Bend High was just right down the road from the college. "He might have. You know Kyle. He's willing to go anywhere for gaming. Maybe that's how he knew him?"

"He still hung out with high school kids?" Heston asked.

Chad scowled a deep eyebrow furrow. "Don't be like that."

"Sorry," Heston said, lowering his gaze to his feet. "Just upset. They never found the kid from our old high school who went missing right before graduation."

"I know. Or the guy from West Bend four months before that."

"Yeah." Heston shook his head. "Poor kid."

Chad chuckled. "Kid? You know we were in high school just four months ago, right?"

Heston's shoulders slumped as he sighed. "I know. I thought things would be different now that we're in college."

"Well, that's the downside of being a townie. We're not the only ones who stayed after graduation."

"It just sucks to still see some of the same assholes who've picked on us in high school. Brittany's actually in my English 101 class."

3

Chad put a hand on Heston's shoulder. "Hey, at least she's not a cheerleader anymore, so she won't be following that herd of sheep."

"No. She'll just join a sorority and bleat along with a different flock. And she's still Mason's girlfriend."

"Yeah, I see that meathead around campus, too. But the good news is no more Ink Stains."

Heston's posture snapped to as straight as it could be. His eyes widened as he gasped. "Dude. Don't say their name."

Chad laughed. "Seriously. They're not going to suddenly appear just because I said their name. They're not like Voldemort or Hastur."

Heston leaned in closer so no one other than Chad could hear him. "You're right. They're worse."

"You don't seriously believe those rumors about them, did you?"

"Don't you? The Ink Stains are some seriously scary mother fuckers. Piercings. Tattoos. I'm not talking about some random skank getting a tramp stamp or douche bag getting a small tribal on his shoulder. The Ink Stains are hardcore. Why were they always hanging around our school?"

The redness of Heston's face deepened as he talked. Not wanting to upset his friend any further, Chad held out his hands in silent surrender. "Yes. Yes, they were. But that's my point. They hang around the high school selling drugs. We graduated, so we don't have to see them anymore."

Inhaling big gulps of air, Heston took deep breaths to calm himself down, his cheeks returning to their natural shade. "Yeah. You're right. Okay."

"I know I'm right. How about you grab a Red Bull to make yourself feel better. We'll get together later with Cooper and Kyle. Okay?"

"Yeah. Yeah, that sounds good. Later," Heston said as he ambled his way into the Student Union Center.

"Later," Chad replied, turning his attention back to the bulletin board, to the flyer with the missing boy. After doing a glance over each shoulder, he snatched the flyer from the bulletin board, leaving behind a fingernail-sized scrap of paper under the pushpin. He knew he shouldn't have done that, but this was the first thing he had ever taken from the bulletin board. One large sheet of paper instead of dozens of itty-bitty tabs. He studied the kid's features as he walked away.

Chad had been going to college for only a month, but he could walk the thin macadam path with his eyes closed. As intently as he studied the flyer, his eyes might as well have been closed. The boy looked familiar. He even sort of looked like Kyle. They both had freckles roaming the boundaries between their eyes and cheeks. They both had lighter hair, this kid's a mess. Kyle tried to make a smooth swoop with his long bangs, but it looked more like a bowl-cut gone awry with the unevenness in length and lack of direction other than straight down. How long was he going to keep trying that style before he gave up? Of course, with his hair, Chad had no room to judge. Thanks to the miracle of genetics, his hair had length without being straight, curl without being curly. He tried to say that his hair had waves, but the reality of it was in that ocean of chestnut brown, the waves were tumultuous and haphazardly crashing into each other. Sometimes he thought Heston had the right idea—put the clippers setting to "one" every two weeks. Cooper didn't have that problem; having black hair so malleable, he would change his style every month to match the current trends. Chad had only one style: moppy. His mother told him repeatedly that he would look so much more handsome if he'd cut it, but he refused. If a woman other than his mother told him that, then he'd do it. Until then, moppy it remained.

The kid on the flyer had been missing for a week. Was there any connection with the other disappearances? This would make three within one year. He knew the boy from East Bend. Not well enough to call a friend, but they had plenty of conversations with each other at the comic book shop or gaming store. What about the boy from West Bend? Chad had heard through the grapevine that he was of similar ilk, all things sci-fi and fantasy. Ponderous.

Chad glanced up at the perfect time just as Brittany crossed in front of him. As inconspicuously as possible, Chad snuck glances at her ass, perfectly round and offering just the right amount of jiggle in her gray yoga pants. After a few steps along the grass of the quad, she stopped and bent over at the waist. Already a second layer of skin, the color of her pants diffused enough to show that she wore a black thong today. Chad ran into a trashcan.

The base of the trash can was stone, but Chad hit with enough force to cause the metal lid to clang. A future bruise claimed its stake on Chad's thigh by sending a message of throbbing pain throughout his whole leg, a knot forming in his stomach from the intensity. All of that quickly dissipated, though, when he realized that Brittany had witnessed his indiscretion.

So did Mason.

"What the hell was that about?" Mason asked, voice like a quarry explosion.

"The perv was checking me out. Dumbass actually ran into a trash can," Brittany replied.

Fists clenched, Mason started to storm his way over to Chad, stomping like a giant ready to crush a village beneath his feet. Brittany followed. Within a few steps, Mason pulled up with a look of recognition upon his face. "Is that Barelli?"

Chad had hoped that Mason had matured over the last four months, leaving the pettiness of high school behind and embracing the adulthood that came with attending college. Instead, Mason cracked his knuckles as his frown deepened. "Still lookin' at Brittany, huh Barelli?"

Out of reflex, Chad glanced into the trash can, looking to see what was in it and calculating the best way to bend his limbs if Mason decided to stuff him into it. Then, somewhere in the most primal part of his brain where the survival instinct was paramount, he remembered an important piece of information. "Your scholarship. You wouldn't risk losing your football scholarship, would you?"

Mason stopped and looked down at Chad. Almost a foot taller, his iron forged chest threatened to smack Chad in the face with every angry breath. Mason's rage was a tangible thing. Chad felt it, felt the heat emanating from his bully, bloodshot eyes bulging out of his erubescent face. Then it stopped, the anger, the emotions washing away.

Chad first thought that maybe logic seeped into Mason's thick as a brick skull until he noticed that Mason was no longer looking at him. Eyes wide, the football player sneered and backed away. He almost looked afraid; Brittany looked terrified. The icy strings of fear laced their way through Chad. There was something behind him that scared the largest human being he had ever met.

No longer able to tolerate the fear of not knowing, Chad peeked over his shoulder. He suddenly struggled not to piss his pants like Kyle.

CHAPTER 2

The Ink Stains were the personification of fear. There were only four of them, and they had hung around his high school parking lot, or behind the school by the dumpsters, or skulking about the nearby woods. They were spotted other places around The Bends, but sleazy places Chad would never visit. Each Ink Stain had some form of tattoo. Each of them had some form of piercing. And each of them held the look of murder in their eyes. At least that was what the rumors said.

Killed a man. Been in jail. Ran a drug ring. Killed a woman. Satanic rituals. Underground fight clubs. Killed children. Burglary. Rape. Murder. All rumors. Hearsay passed down from a friend of a friend of a cousin who heard a story from someone they knew. Chad knew these rumors weren't true; they couldn't be. Over the years, his intellect disproved each rumor. How could they be allowed in public if they'd done even half the stuff the rumors suggested? His fear had a different interpretation, though. His fear believed every word spoken about the malevolence of the Ink Stains.

And now they stood right behind him.

A million little ants scurried through his body, agitated and electric, crawling under his skin. Just as many thoughts crashed into each other and piled up in his mind. Why were they here? Why weren't they in jail by now? Why were they on campus? Why couldn't Chad just be left alone? Why was this high school all over again? Why were they here? Why? Why? Why?

Hunter, the leader of the Ink Stains, spoke, his voice possessing an animal's growl. "Let him go, Mason. He's ours."

There was one rumor that Chad had heard last year, one that he thought might have held a modicum of truth, one that he desperately wished was real, the rumor about Hunter and Mason getting into a fight. A fight that Hunter won.

Mason's expression held no fear, not a single hint upon his face. Being one who lived in the clutches of fear for so long, Chad could see the fear *behind* Mason's mask of anger. Men like Mason had a difficult time coping with fear, so he took a step forward and barked, "What'd you say?"

"Hunh," Hunter grunted. "I guess 'roids make you hard of hearing as well as shrivel your sack. I. Said. Let. Him. Go."

The three other Ink Stains laughed.

Mason looked down at Chad and scowled. "I don't know what you did to them, loser, but I sure wouldn't wanna be you."

"Don't you have something to squat? Or press? Or jerk?" Hunter asked.

More laughter.

Mason took a few steps away and grabbed Brittany's hand. As they retreated, Mason mumbled, "Whatever, dude."

"Hey, what's your forehead doing later? I have some beer cans that need to be crushed."

"Freak!" Mason shouted as he raised a middle finger in the air.

"So clever," Hunter yelled back. "Don't be late for your creatine enema!"

As the quartet of laughter died down, so did Chad's hopes of getting out of this situation unscathed. All he wanted was to start anew in college. On a campus of over ten thousand students, he had hoped that he would never see familiar faces again, other than those of his friends. After a month, he found himself with the same anxieties, the same feelings of weakness. The same lack of control over his own life.

As if reading his mind, Hunter said, "Aren't you tired of being stuck in high school?"

Chad opened his mouth to answer, but it triggered an all too familiar sting behind his eyes, the warning of imminent tears. Standing on the macadam path, Chad studied his surroundings beyond the trashcan. He assumed that he still might gain intimate knowledge of its confines, but rumors told far more pernicious tales of what to expect from the Ink Stains.

He was going to get his ass kicked. Hell, he might even get sent to the hospital. That was his lot in life, being on the bottom of the food chain. But would the Ink Stains do that right here? Students flowed along the quad to the right while people moved up and down the sidewalk to the left, Chad equidistant between them and very visible.

"Come on, Chad, you're in college now." Hunter moved around Chad, so they now stood face-to-face. He was taller than Chad and more muscular, but that was quite an easy accomplishment. Mason was bigger by far, but Hunter's muscles were corded, each striating under his tight black shirt and pants as he walked. His black hair looked like a styled mess, one that implied natural wildness. Even though his words held compassion, his golden eyes sent an opposite message. A predator could never sympathize with prey. "You shouldn't let Mason scare you anymore."

Mason? Chad wished he was brave enough to let Hunter know that at this moment, it wasn't Mason who had him petrified. Instead, he swallowed a dry lump and nodded his head.

Hunter gave a quick lick of his bottom lip. Chad couldn't tell if that was a nervous tic, or something more sinister. "See? That just isn't right. You're not in high school anymore, are you?"

Chad shook his head.

"You shouldn't be stuck in your high school persona."

Chad wondered if Hunter knew that his words wove a tapestry of irony. Talking about leaving high school behind, there was nothing about the Ink Stains that were any different now than the last time Chad saw them four months ago in his high school's parking lot.

Katrina was as sexy as ever, showing off her taut body with minimal clothing, a tight black skirt, and a black lace top. If there were any differences between then and now, the number of piercings might have increased. Six tight hoops through each ear, a small barbell through her nose just above her philtrum, a hoop through her right lip, and a row of small, metal studs dolloped from between her cleavage down to the top of her skirt. Because his life most certainly depended on it, Chad tried not to stare, but still counted five visible studs.

Dylan was as large as Chad remembered, large chest, large waist, large facial features on a large shaven head. And a large black duster to cover it all.

Viper had always been the creepiest one. Chad wasn't too sure if "Viper" was his legal name or not; he doubted it, but it wouldn't surprise him if it was.

Viper was the most inked of the Ink Stains, two full sleeves of colorful scenes that Chad was too afraid to look at, and malachite snake scales running the full length of his neck. Viper was tall and thin, and his smooth movements gave him a slithering look as he walked.

Chad focused on his breathing as the four Ink Stains stood in front of him. In through the nose, deeply, slowly. He had never interacted with them in his four years of high school, never came in contact. He would go out of his way to avoid every one of them whenever he saw them skulking around his school. He was surprised and disturbed that Hunter knew his name.

Hunter sighed dramatically, disappointed. Chad almost believed the sincerity, if not for the way the other three Ink Stains smirked. "Why are you afraid of Mason?"

The reason was painfully obvious in Chad's mind. He didn't even think the question deserved to have an answer voiced, but if Hunter was *conversing* with him, then Hunter wasn't hurting him. "Because . . . because he's bigger. Stronger."

Hunter chuckled, causing muted laughter to ripple through his friends. "He's bigger. But he is not stronger. His refusal to grow beyond his current limits, his current mindset, is what makes him weak. That attitude is what weakens the whole human race. That weakness, that disease, needs to be culled from the herd."

"The herd? The . . . human . . . herd?"

Hunter squinted and smiled. Nodding, he said, "Yeah. The human herd. You feel it, right? You're not letting yourself grow beyond who you are. Your friends aren't letting themselves grow beyond who they are. Hell, even Brittany is still a mindless puppet. And why?"

"Mason?"

"Exactly. His weakness is affecting you all."

Chad mulled over Hunter's words, the validity of them. He altered his life because of Mason, made choices to avoid Mason, felt worthless when Mason would shove him into trashcans or lockers. Chad knew that his friends felt the same way, but he never took into consideration the amount of potential being inhibited because of Mason. Because of *one* person. He mumbled, more to himself, "He's not allowing certain members of the herd to grow."

With a conspirator's tone, Hunter said, "Now you're getting it. Now you understand."

A weird sensation passed through Chad. He was no longer afraid. He was smiling. Had he been avoiding the wrong people all these years? Should he have tried to make inroads with the Ink Stains in high school by being like the cool kids with their clandestine meetings in the parking lot and behind the dumpsters? The thought of donning a tattoo amused him, but the idea of piercings made him shiver hard enough to snap himself out of his self-conjecture. "So . . . now what?"

Hunter stepped closer to Chad, his soft gold eyes glowing. "You want to grow, right?"

"Yeah." The word fell from his mouth as if it had been dangling from his lip, waiting for the right moment.

"You want the herd to be stronger, right?"

"Yes," he said with more confidence this time.

"You want to escape from out of Mason's shadow, right?"

"I do." What little moisture that had come back into Chad's mouth was now gone. The rush of blood between his ears was almost deafening. Images of changing his wardrobe to all black danced through his head while he debated about what kind of tattoo he wanted.

"Good," Hunter growled. He turned and started to walk away, his friends joining him. Chad stood confused, uncertain if he should follow or not. Hunter and the others paused just long enough to look back. "Meet us on the hill near the forest by the football practice field tonight. We'll have some fun with the meat-heads."

Chad didn't like the sound of that, yet . . . he *did* like the sound of that. He had questions, but he kept them to himself because, as the Ink Stains left, Viper flashed a smile. His thin lips spread to show that he had filed some of his teeth to points.

CHAPTER 3

"After our conversation, Hunter told me to meet him and the Ink Stains after football practice tonight, and then . . . then they left." Chad marked the end of his story by shoveling french fries into his mouth.

"No. Fucking. Way," Cooper replied, the straw of his thirty-two-ounce cup an inch from his mouth, where it had been for the duration of the story.

"Dude," Heston added, burger particulate falling from his mouth in-between chews. "Thaff infane."

Chad leaned back in his chair and looked around at the dozen bustling mini-restaurant fronts of the mall food court. He had eaten there at least once a week for his entire life, seen old restaurants fail and new ones eager to take their places, sometimes less than a month between death and rebirth. But that was how fast life moved, wasn't it? Last month, he was merely a high school graduate, today, a college student. Death and rebirth. Last month, the knowledge of the Ink Stains still being in the area would have terrified him, today he contemplated meeting up with them. Death and rebirth? "I swear that's what happened. I swear on a stack of Pokémon cards."

"Fascinating. Utterly fascinating," Cooper said. He took the final pulls from his drink, not concerned that the slurping noise his straw made inside the Styrofoam container. "So, I must ask, how pray tell did you squirm your way out from an invitation such as that?"

"Ummm . . . I didn't."

Heston coughed out half of the food in his mouth, mashed burger and bun plopping onto the tray in front of him. "Dude. You can't be serious. Tell me you're joking."

"I'm serious. The Ink Stains hate Mason as much as we do. The enemy of our enemy is our friend, right?"

"That quaint idiom is hardly a placard to hang upon the wall of life choices," Cooper said. "Honestly, Chad, what could you possibly, or *think* you could possibly, gain from this rendezvous? I find it highly unlikely that the Ink Stains will just let you join whatever little club they have. What if Hunter doesn't show up, and then Mason and his Neanderthal friends see you?"

Chad looked away. He never thought about the Ink Stains standing him up, but he couldn't admit that out loud. He felt stupid for not thinking of something so obvious. What if Cooper was right? Trying to think of a clever response, he let his gaze drift to the far end of the food court to the corner where Wanda lurked. Whacky Wanda, as the locals called her, in her faded camouflage jacket, jeans, and black boots, her long, gray hair wild, looking as if it had never been introduced to the bristles of a brush. No one knew her story, how she came to be the local crazy woman. No one knew where she lived, or even if she had a home. Of course, no one knew because no one asked.

Occasionally, Chad would wonder about her situation, what she had gone through to get to where she was. Was she a townie, like him? Had she been on a set course in her life to become like this? Did she eschew opportunity when it presented itself like the one presented to Chad? Chad turned back to his friends. "The Ink Stains will be there. I can feel it. They're planning something, and they're going to do it whether I'm there or not. If it's something that will get revenge on Mason for all the times he's tormented me . . . tormented *us* . . . for every time he's given a swirly or pantsed one of us in a crowd, I have to be there to see it."

"It seems completely unlikely to me that the Ink Stains are a group of individuals altruistic enough to be doing this for you or any of us. No one in their right mind would mistake us for being their friends. I'm beyond the realm of surprise that they knew your name."

The all too common sensation of impending tears stung Chad's eyes. He pushed them back and fought through a cracking voice to make sure his lifelong friends understood. "At least they never beat on us. They never pushed us around, never even made fun of us. All through school, all the way back to elementary school, Mason and his friends have belittled us, made us feel worthless, and made us feel like we can't do anything about it. Now we're in college. Now is the time when all that shit should be over, but it's not. I can't do it for another four years. I'm sick of it. You may not like me going tonight, but at least I'm exploring ways to make things different."

Chad turned away again, nonchalantly swiping his thumb under his eyes, checking for any tears that might have escaped without his knowledge. On the other side of the food court, Wanda sat alone at a table with a cup of chain-restaurant coffee. Staring at him. The warmth of a blush bloomed within his cheeks. Embarrassed, exposed, confused by her unwavering eye contact. Chad blinked and glanced around from storefront to meandering patrons to the nearby fountain, finally back to his friends. He did what he had always done his whole life—ignore what made him feel uncomfortable. "So . . . umm . . . how's Kyle?"

"S'Okay," Heston mumbled as he pushed the last bites of his burger into his mouth.

"Good grief, Heston, chew your food. My concern for your eating habits is the reason why I took CPR and Heimlich classes," Cooper said, using a napkin to brush crumbs from the table into his hand.

"You went becauth your mom made you."

Brushing his hands together over his tray, Cooper replied, "Well, I was thinking of you the whole time, wondering if I ever needed to use these newly learned skills to one day dislodge an errant chicken wing or whole slice of pizza from your gullet."

Heston responded by opening his mouth to expose the horrors within. Cooper squirmed and sneered. "I've always said that you're a paragon of maturity."

Chad chuckled. Going to college meant starting the next phase in the journey to a new life, one more step away from the old one. But he still enjoyed being with his friends, being a part of these antics that had defined him over the years.

Still giving Heston side-eye, Cooper addressed Chad. "About Kyle—By the time I got him home, he seemed to be doing better. I had no opportunity to garner further details about his micturition mishap. He just kept muttering, 'It could have been me,' repeatedly. Neither of his parents was home, so he took one of his mom's sleepy-time pills, went cross-eyed, and then passed out."

"Hunh," Chad grunted. "I wonder what he meant?"

"We all do," Heston answered.

Chad was being rhetorical, but he didn't want to make Heston feel bad about not picking up on that, so instead, he stated what everyone was thinking. "We'll text him and then call him tonight after he's calmed down. If he wants to talk about it, that's great. If not, we can't force him."

Chad expected Heston's typical smile, warm and trusting. Instead, he received a look of wide-eyed surprise. Cooper frowned deep enough to crinkle his nose and asked, "Can we help you?"

Behind him. Someone was behind him. Chad looked over his shoulder and jerked so hard he almost fell out of his chair.

Whacky Wanda. Standing close enough that Chad could now smell her, a surprisingly nice aroma of vanilla. He had always imagined that she would smell of stale coffee and recently smoked cigarettes, possibly even whiskey on her breath. "What are . . . wha . . . what?"

Without warning, she leaned in close to Chad and sniffed, a long inhale meant to capture his essence. He did not smell like vanilla. He wasn't entirely sure what he smelled like, depending on how much deodorant, shampoo, and body wash was still noticeable, and he hoped that affected her judgment favorably. "Are you one?"

"Dude!" Heston yelped.

"Ma'am? Do we have to call security?" Cooper asked.

Chad didn't know much about crazy, or any form of mental illness found outside his textbooks, so he didn't know what to expect when having it so close to him. He didn't expect this. His ideas of Wanda scratching fitfully or swatting invisible bugs from her body while mumbling a conversation with herself were all shamefully prejudiced, but he expected at least something stereotypical of the town crazy person. He didn't expect clear, focused eyes, or a nice fragrance emanating from a body that lacked any form of tremor. He didn't expect such a concise question.

"One of what?" Chad asked.

"Of them. You smell like them."

"I . . . I'm trying a new body wash. It's called Man-cano. It's supposed to give me an eruption of manliness, a nine point oh man-gnitude on the Richter scale."

Cooper stood up and repeated, "Do you think you know him? I'm pretty sure he doesn't know you, so I will get security if you don't stop harassing us right now."

Wanda straightened and suddenly pointed to the other two at the table, causing Heston to jolt in his chair. "You don't want to know me."

"Of that, I'm certain," Cooper said. He flicked his hand dismissively, to shoo her away. "So, why don't you head back to where you might call home, and we'll all forget this ever happened."

Wanda backed away, but as she left, she pointed to Chad and asked, "Who are your new friends, Chad? Who are your new friends?"

The trio breathed a collective sigh of relief when she put her hands in her pockets and left the food court, a hastened pace as if late for an appointment. Panting as if he just sprinted a 5K, Heston looked from Chad to Cooper and back. "That was really fucked up."

"I agree," Cooper said, looking around. "It doesn't appear that we garnered any unwanted attention. No one's even looking in our direction after that interaction. The town crazy woman verbally assaults three innocent young men in public, and no one cares? What a bunch of fucking sheeple."

Chad didn't say anything as he left the table and emptied his tray. He couldn't articulate how unnerved he was that she knew his name.

CHAPTER 4

Who are your new friends?

Whacky Wanda's question haunted Chad for hours. The words slithered around his mind, discontent snakes looking for the perfect rock to hide under. Right now, the question should be, "*Where* are your new friends?"

Football practice hadn't ended yet, and Chad watched the jocks from the edge of the forest. The practice field was located at the far corner of the campus, a moderately manicured patch of grass that the college's sports teams took turns using. The field was even open to the public, not that Chad had any use for it during his lifetime as a townie. An open patch of grass shared by picnickers and dog walkers did not make a good environment for twelve-hour *Dungeons & Dragons* marathons.

"Good practice, men!" the coach yelled after giving the whistle three blows. "Hit the showers!"

Chad hid behind a tree close enough to hear everything. The whoops and hollers. The crack of helmets hitting each other. The manly ass smacks. Chad could almost smell the cloud of testosterone from where he stood.

"Hey," Mason said to two of his teammates, getting their attention by slapping each of their asses. "Let's go over the routes again."

Numbers 87 and 82 showed their agreement by each smacking his ass and putting their helmets back on. Chad chuckled to himself about the ridiculousness of their rituals. But were they so different than the ones he shared with his friends? How excited he got when they complete any role-playing quest, no matter how trivial. How Heston had a twenty-sided die custom made, the "twenty" replaced with a middle finger. How Cooper displayed sick breakdancing moves anytime he rolled "the finger" for a critical hit. How Kyle had flames emblazoned on his inhaler, which he always needed after laughing himself into a wheezing fit from Cooper's sick breakdancing skills. And that wasn't counting the thousands of dollars they all invested in the latest and greatest video gaming systems and accessories. There were definite comparisons between Chad's life and Mason's. Too bad Mason could never see that.

Instead, Mason and his athlete friends would harass Chad and others like him. Without mercy, without end. That was the whole reason why Chad waited for the Ink Stains, wondering where they were.

Not sure how much longer he should wait, Chad checked the time on his phone. He tried to do it as stealthily as possible, only pulling his phone halfway from his pocket. He was a prey animal, a creature of paranoia and suspicion. The only way Mason and company could see him behind the tree was if they had a reason to look, but Chad still took precautions. Sometimes as a prey animal, precautions just weren't enough, and luck would intervene. Bad luck, in Chad's case, as the snap of a large branch disrupted the forest.

He looked toward the noise. Nothing more than a patch of leaves fluttering to the ground. No danger from that, but it did result in a different form of danger.

"Looks like we got a new cheerleader," Mason yelled, deepening his voice for added masculinity.

Chad ran. He didn't need to look behind him to know that he was being chased, an inherent instinct shared by all prey animals. He was always surprised by how fast the predators moved.

Deeper into the forest he went, sprinting as fast as the terrain would allow him. He always found the effects of adrenaline fascinating. Ten strides into the gym class mandatory mile, and his muscles burned while his lungs tried to escape his body, but every time Mason and friends chased him, his legs churned like well-lubricated pistons in the revving engine of fear. But adrenaline wouldn't be enough to help him escape this time.

The forest played tricks with Chad, distorting sounds, making the gleeful whoops and hollers sound as if they were everywhere, beside him, in front of him. The words, though, were what told Chad he was losing this race.

"Always knew you were a sissy, Chad!"

"Wants to be a cheerleader!"

"Yeah!"

"Let's see what cheers he knows!"

"See where he's hiding his pompoms!"

"Yeah!"

Every word was like an arrow whizzing through the air, getting closer with every taunt. As Chad tried to run faster, he couldn't help but think about how Cooper would lord this over him, an "I told you so" that would forever be said. The pain of that would last longer than the pain of getting his ass kicked, a pain much more imminent.

The impact from Mason's tackle knocked the wind out of Chad, dirt and dead leaves filled his mouth, the taste of his grave. The good thing about dying now would never be having to hear Cooper say those words.

Chad clawed at the ground and squirmed, desperate for any kind of purchase to wriggle from under Mason. His attempts at escape were as effective as doing nothing at all. Mason flipped Chad on his back and knelt on him, knees digging into arms. "Well, boys, I got the new cheerleader."

The other two football players stood over Chad, looking down at him as if he were nothing more than a captured fly ready to have its wings ripped off.

"Not as pretty as the other cheerleaders," number 87 said.

"Yeah!" number 82 shouted, adding a fist-pump for emphasis.

Mason thrust his crotch toward Chad's face. Unable to do anything else, Chad turned his head as best he could. "May not be as pretty, but look! Just like the other bitches, he's trying to suck my dick."

"Just like the other bitches."

"Yeah!"

Mason thrust again; this time closer. Chad pulled his lips into his mouth and clenched his jaw. He started to squirm again, even though it did no good. "Whoa! Look at him bucking, trying to get my cock in his mouth."

"Hungry bitch."

"Yeah!"

Chad closed his eyes as Mason's crotch rubbed against his face, the hard plastic of the cup hurting his cheek. Mouth and eyes closed didn't help with the smell. The musk of excitement mixing with hours' worth of sweat. "Well, boys, since he's so hungry, I might as well feed him, right?"

"Me next."

"Yeah!"

Chad squeezed his eyes closed, tighter to shut down the burgeoning tears. Crying would only add fuel to their fire. He thought about going limp and opening his mouth; no fight meant no fun, right? That was a dangerous gambit with the possibility of them accepting the invitation. Was Mason really intending to go that far? In that past, Mason had made Chad eat mud, paper, and grass, so why not his dick today? Chad struggled again; Mason's cup digging into his other cheek.

"How many times do I gotta tell you meatheads that Chad is ours?"

Hunter's voice was deeper and scratchier than usual, more like the rough growl of an extreme hangover. Right now, it sounded like the voice of an angel.

Mason leaped off Chad and stood in between his friends, fists clenched. Chad rolled over and got his feet under him. He wanted to stand, to run, but the sight of the Ink Stains surprised him. They were shoeless and shirtless. Even Kat.

"No!" Mason yelled, his voice almost doing the pubescent frustration squeak. "Not this time, you freaks. I'm gonna rip out every piercing you got and use them to give you a few more tattoos."

"That doesn't even make sense," Kat laughed. She shifted her hips from side to side as she wriggled her way out of her leather pants. "Do you guys understand what he's trying to say?"

Viper stepped out of his pants with ease to expose dozens of piercings. Glittering studs embedded in his flesh created two paths leading from the hoops in his nipples and converged at the base of his sternum. The path of studs continued downward to the shimmering silver hoop peeking out from under his foreskin. "Sorry. I don't speak imbecile. Or is he speaking moron? Daft dolt, possibly? I just don't understand his language."

"I only understand pain," Dylan said as his pants fell to the ground. Black hair covered his whole body, making his bald pate look out of place. Even his penis had hair on it, which hung almost to his knees and as wide as Chad's forearm. Chad wondered if Dylan was going to use his baseball bat of Cthulhu to administer the pain.

Once Hunter stripped naked as well, he and his friends spread out. Chad knew something big was going to happen, knew that this was far from normal and safe, but . . . Kat was *naked*. Hunter stalked around Mason and friends to get behind them. Chad's gaze drifted back to Kat and her perfect body. Tattooed cat paws padded across her hairless vagina to her left hip. On her right thigh was a thin, black cat with gold jewelry, like one worshipped by ancient Egyptians. Fear squeezed Chad's chest as Viper flanked the footballers from the other side, his body moving strangely, more slithering than walking. Fear told Chad to run, but Kat's nipple piercings told him to stay. He had never seen a naked woman before. Well, not one that wasn't on a computer screen. Both his conscious mind and the parts of his pre-evolution brain designed for primal survival knew very well that his priorities were askew now, both telling him to pay attention to Dylan as he lumbered closer to Mason and planted his feet, but . . . tits. They jiggled slightly as Kat brought a cupped hand to her ear and said, "Could you repeat that, jocko, but talk English this time?"

"Yeah? You don't scare me, you goth-girl eyeliner witch! You freak! I got no problem hitting girls. And wait until you see what I'm gonna do to you after we mess up your freak friends." Mason shouted with such intensity that spittle dripped from his face mask after his tirade.

Kat brought both hands to her cheeks and ran her fingers over her mouth and chin, a sexy tug at her full, bottom lip, and down her neck. Her hands continued downward, cupping her breasts before gliding over her waist and stopping between her legs, all the while her hips swayed from side to side. "Oooooh, that sounds sooooo sexy . . . meat."

Chad still had a difficult time focusing on anything other than Kat, his peripheral vision reduced to blurry suggestions of the world around him until she sprouted fur. A coat of soft golden fur now covered her entire body, and her face changed. Her ears thinned and grew upward as her nose receded into her face. Full lips flattened and spread into a muzzle as whiskers grew. Kat was now a cat. A bipedal, anthropomorphized cat, still possessing enough humanity in her face to smile. A quick lick of her fangs, and then she pounced on Mason.

The pads of Mason's uniform did nothing to protect him from Kat. Chunks of plastic and foam twirled through the air with each swipe of her claws, soon followed by gobs of sinew and bits of bone. Mason's screams stopped once she ripped into his crotch and shoved his pulpy genitals into his mouth. To ensure silence forever, she dug out his lungs and tossed them over her shoulder.

The other three Ink Stains transformed and attacked as well. Hunter turned into a wolf—a werewolf just like in all those movies that Chad would laugh at with his friends, but then secretly had nightmares about. Dylan turned into a bear, his transformation the subtlest. The biggest difference between start and finish was the bald head replaced by a snarling bear face, and his body wasn't that of a floppy fur-covered grizzly, but a muscle chested, trimmed waist man.

Hunter came up from behind number 87 and grabbed his arms, claws digging into biceps, and tore both limbs from the football player. Dylan's clawed hands were thick but nimble enough to get a firm hold on the helmet's face mask. The bear yanked number 87's head from his body in one pull and shoved his muzzle into the open end. Face dripping with blood; he looked up. "Hard shell on the outside, tasty on the inside."

"I prefer the creamy nougat center," Hunter growled. Still holding the player's arms like an afterthought, the wolf used his teeth to dig into the fallen player's belly to get to his entrails.

Of all the horrors Chad witnessed, the one that burned indelible images into his brain was Viper. The thin, hairless man grew taller as a membrane ran the length of his legs, connecting them together and tapering to form a tail. His nose disappeared into slits as his pupils sickled in his yellowing eyes. His arms and torso remained human while a cobra-like hood flared from behind his neck. The space between his piercings spread as he transformed, yet the silver of the studs stood out even more against the malachite scales forming over his skin.

The snake creature slithered to number 82, his serpent tail long enough to wrap around the screaming football player multiple times from shoulder to thigh and thick enough to crack the shoulder pads as he constricted. 82's eyes bulged until they shot from his head with a slurping pop, the nerves flopping behind them like crimson streamers. Viper removed the helmet and then tore off 82's head. The man-snake shifted his jaw from side to side, his face going slack from unhinging it. Slowly, Viper stuffed the football player's head inside his mouth.

This wasn't real. Chad told himself that he was getting molested by Mason and his friends, and this was just an illusion, a mental defense mechanism. A twisted wish to keep him from having to deal with reality. He wanted to run, but his brain spent all its energy trying to process what his eyes were seeing, so it had nothing left for his legs, now cramped from crouching for so long.

This *was* real. The pain from dry and cracked lips told him so. So did the burning muscles in his legs. The coppery smell of the slaughter intensified and triggered a twist in his guts. He retched.

All four Ink Stains, in human form now, sauntered over to Chad. Viper had the least blood on him. Dylan's face was a mess of red, but his body was relatively clean. Hunter had random streaks of red splatted about himself. Kat made them all look spotless in comparison. Chunks of meat oozed from her matted hair and down her blood-soaked body, the pieces making sloppy splats on the forest floor when they finally fell away. Hunter crouched in front of Chad and asked, "So . . . what'd you think?"

Chad didn't answer, couldn't answer. His jaw jiggled while his bottom lip repeatedly slapped against his top, an impotent scream that would never come while trying to awaken from a nightmare.

Hunter still held 87's right arm and used it pat Chad's head, palm rubbing against his curls the way an older brother would lovingly dishevel the hair of a younger sibling. "Hey, Sport, how ya doin'?"

The quivering spread from Chad's face to his chest to his whole body. He could only quake. Still no words, no use of his legs. Hunter used 87's hand to gently slap Chad's face a few times. Still no change in response. "Hello? Chad? You still with us?"

It was Kat who distracted Chad. He couldn't pull his eyes away from her. Blood still flowed over her naked body, as if she just stepped out of a macabre bathtub. She stood behind Hunter and took long licks of her forearm, swallowing what her tongue collected. Hunter followed Chad's gaze. "No wonder Chad's all squirrely, Kat. You're a mess."

Looking down at herself, Kat chuckled. She ran both of her hands from her pelvis to her chest, cupping and lifting her breasts. They bounced as she released them and tossed away two handfuls of gore. "Yeah, I guess so."

Chad shook even more, a low moan formed in his throat as his mouth desperately tried to form words. His eyes rolled up into his head as he finally uttered, "Tits," and passed out.

CHAPTER 5

"Tits!" Chad yelled as he awoke in his bed. A sense of panic ran through him instead of relief. So many questions jumbled around in his mind; he couldn't have articulated any one of them if someone had asked. Someone? Was someone in his room with him? He checked. No. He brought his hands to his face and ran them through his sweaty hair and then threw off his sheets. Wiggled his toes. Patted the rest of his body. He was still clothed and seemingly uninjured. That answered a few questions, but he still had more, still had to look himself over.

He leaped from the bed and ran to the full-length mirror on the back of his closed bedroom door. So far, so good. Shirt off, pants off, boxers off. Even socks off. Turn, twist, bend. The purple bloom of a bruise started on his right hip from where he landed after the Mason tackle, but no other injuries. No bite marks. He gently tugged at the bottom lids of his eyes to expose the slimy red barrier of the eyeballs and then stuck out his tongue. No idea why, just because he had seen this action so often in television and movies anytime the protagonist woke up concerned. Then his computer beeped.

In his current state of confusion, the noise he had heard thousands of times before seemed so alien that he created a mental checklist of where it could be coming from after creating a mental checklist of what he could use as a weapon. Both lists evaporated when he realized it was just a call coming in.

Too jittery to sit, he moved his desk chair out of the way and answered the call. Cooper's face filled the screen. "Greetings, missing adventurer! Where have—*oh my God, your dick!*"

Cooper pressed his hands against his screen, his fingers covering his camera and taking over Chad's monitor. "Why the hell did I see your dick, Chad? In what universe could there be a possibility of reasonable explanation?"

Chad looked down, not registering that he was naked until now. "Dude. Settle down. We've taken gym class together."

"Circumstances beget choices and consequences. I never felt the need to look down during post-gymnasium shower time, and I certainly never had the desire to have it exposed to me so close to my face."

Cooper's comment acted like a syringe injecting the memories of last night directly into Chad's brain. Mason's dick against his face, then severed and in his own mouth. Mason's guts flying through the air. Mason's blood covering Kat's body.

"Ummm, dude?" came from Chad's computer. Cooper's eye peeked out from a small gap made from his intertwined fingers on the monitor. "I can still see Little Chad, you know. Have you mysteriously and unexpectedly found yourself in a world with no pants?"

"Yeah. No. Yeah," Chad muttered as he shook his head, physically trying to shake the memories from his mind. "Sorry. Yeah, they're right here."

Chad found them on the floor by his door and bent over to pick them up. Cooper screamed, "Aaaah! Chocolate starfish! Brown eye! Chasm of Cthulhu! In the name of all the dark lords, why am I being subjected to this? I just wanted to make sure you were okay!"

"Make sure I'm okay?" Chad asked Cooper's hand. "Why?"

"Ummm, maybe because Heston and I hadn't heard from you all last night? We thought the Ink Stains sacrificed you to whatever malevolent being of pure evil they worship."

"Last night? What time is it?"

"Pants o'clock!"

Chad put his pants on and pulled up his chair. 7:05 A.M. He opened his mouth to let Cooper know what happened, but a thought slammed into the front of his head so hard that he winced, *Is that a good idea?*

What was he going to tell Cooper? That the Ink Stains were a group of . . . of . . . lycanthropes? How would Cooper react when told that these creatures shredded and ate three members of the football team? Maybe he'd be more susceptible to believe if the dead football players made the news. "Did anything weird happen last night?"

"Yes. Yes, something weird happened last night. You went off to meet up with a biker gang and then disappeared."

"No, I meant, did anything make the news?"

"Well, there was more unrest in some country no one can pronounce, some celebrity ate mushroom ice cream, and the world can't stop talking about it, there was a scandal within a scandal among the ultra-rich who control the world, and—oh yeah—*one of my best friends ignored our desperate texts and phone calls about his safety!*"

Phone. Did he lose his phone? Another round of panic exploded within his chest but dissipated to warm tingles down his spine as he reached into his pocket and pulled out his phone. He went to the local news app, but nothing more than articles about local businesses and upcoming town events. Of course, there wouldn't be mention of the dead players if their bodies hadn't been found yet. Someone needed to discover the bodies, but they were in the forest. Not many people just happen to wander around in the forest for no reason. He'd have to find them, bring the media attention to them. If he brought it to the media, then his name and face would be better known to the public. If the public eye was on him, then it would be much more noticeable if he died in some bloody, gore-bath party. Finding the football players meant he would be safe from the Ink Stains!

Chad turned to the monitor and looked at Cooper. "Okay, I'm sorry about last night, but I can't explain now. I gotta go do something that I'll tell you about later." He turned off his computer right as Cooper started a string of expletives.

Shirt, socks, shoes, out the door. It was a typical Thursday morning; both of his parents were off to work, and he was left to fend for himself. No breakfast, not in the mood. His first class was at 10:00, so he had plenty of time to get to the forest and contact the authorities after finding the dead bodies of his "beloved" classmates. His heart would go out to their families—well, that was what he'd tell the news crews. He might even blog about it, the first interesting thing to happen to him worth blogging about. Now the cover story. Out for a morning jog and found the bodies? Okay, no one would believe he jogged in the morning or any other time of the day. Morning stroll? That could work. A stroll sounded more believable despite that concept being a fiction as well. By the time Chad made his way to the slaughter site, his legs hurt, and it was more of a morning trundle. And there were no bodies.

There was a bare patch where it had happened, minimal leaves scattered about doing nothing to cover the dirt. The area looked slightly suspicious, but no evidence of the massacre. Was this the right spot? Chad looked around, wondering if he made a wrong turn or got confused. This was the spot; he recognized a small grouping of trees too unique to be found anywhere else; some of them had strips of bark missing, possibly where blood had splattered. *What the fuck?*

Chad walked in circles, kicking around clumps of leaves, looking for . . . he didn't know what. A splash of blood they might have missed? A bit of bone or chunk of an organ? A strip of skin or football jersey? Nothing. A small dirt mound looked a little out of place, and as he debated about digging into it, a rush of wind blew over his cheek. The sound of something hitting a tree. An arrow. Chad was looking at an arrow sticking out of the nearest tree, mere inches from his face. "What the—?"

For the second time within a day, Chad got tackled on this same spot in the forest. This time it was by someone smaller, but it hurt just as much to be driven to the ground. At least dirt and leaves didn't get shoved into his mouth. Slapping. Someone slapped him. Repeatedly. This time, though, when he struggled, he was able to move the other person, but he wasn't fast enough to get away.

He pushed against the ground and kicked his legs, but his attacker shifted to counter his escape attempts. Instead of tossing his assailant as he had hoped, he ended up on his back, grunting from the pain of having knees pinning his arms to the ground. Another fight lost, another crotch in his face, and Chad couldn't even see who manhandled him this time. Her chest was in the way.

"Who are you?" she asked.

"Chad. Who are *you*?"

She shifted, to sit on his chest and lean forward a bit. Now that he could see who kicked his ass, he fell in love. A girl, maybe around his age. Pretty, yet her face had no one feature that commanded attention. Her eyes were neither too big, nor too small; her cheeks weren't round; her nose could go unnoticed; her lips thin; her chin tapered, but not pointed. The color of her eyes, though, such a pale shade of green that they bordered on yellow. So intriguing that Chad forgot that he just got thrown around by this woman. "Wow."

She cocked her head as if trying to understand the meaning of his word. The moment passed, and she scowled. Shifting her hips further down his body, she leaned forward more and grabbed two fistfuls of his shirt. "I know who you are. You're one of them, aren't you?"

At first, Chad didn't want to answer, enjoying how her straight, auburn hair flowed over his cheeks, a soft tickle. Her question then struck him as odd. Not only did she say she knew him, she asked a question he had heard before, heard from Whacky Wanda. This time, he understood it and knew the answer. "No."

She shifted further down his body again, her ass on his crotch, and leaned even closer. Annunciating every word so her lips could reveal perfectly white and clenched teeth, she said, "I smell them."

"They were here last night." Trying to sound tough, he deepened his voice but wasn't sure how well he did. The scent of cinnamon on her breath was too distracting, as were the subtle movements of her hips. So distracting that he couldn't halt an erection from forming.

"How did you—?" she stopped midsentence and then jumped off him, looking at his crotch as if it were a snake ready to strike. She wore a simple blue hoodie and stood beside a crossbow on the ground. That was the last thing Chad noticed about her before she punched him in the dick.

For a moment, he thought he passed out, his world spiraling into blackness, but as the darkness gave way to pops of random colors burst like a fireworks display just for him, he wished for unconsciousness. Fighting through the pain, he flopped around on the ground, unable to stand, but desperate to protect himself.

Gone. She was gone.

Curling up into the fetal position, he waited for the throbbing to recede as a few streams of pain-sweat rolled over his forehead. He was looking forward to going back home for a shower and then going to class so he could pretend none of this ever happened.

What the hell was he going to tell his friends?

CHAPTER 6

"So, guys, you know how we get wedgies because we spend most of our lives lost in a fantasy world populated by mythical beasts like werecreatures? Well, they're real. They're real, and they're horrible. Any questions?"

Chad played that scenario through his mind again and again. There was no better way to tell his friends. He had to tell them, but there was no way they'd believe him. First, he had to make them believe he witnessed the grisliest of massacres in recorded human history; then he had to make them believe something even more farfetched—he met a girl. A beautiful one at that. Did he *really* have to tell his friends?

He didn't know what he was talking about. Literally. All he knew about lycanthropes came from games and movies, works of fiction. He knew nothing about werecreatures . . . *real* werecreatures. *Jesus, God. I'm thinking about the motivations of real werecreatures.* What were their motivations? They could have killed Chad at any time. Not only did they not kill him, but they also returned him to his bedroom completely unscathed. As much as he wanted to ignore the problem, he couldn't. There was more to the situation, and there was more to come. Was he willing to face it alone?

Cooper, Heston, and Kyle were his friends. They had been through everything together. First this, first that, first everything. Hours of comradery. Secrets shared and kept. Helping each other through the aftermath of a run-in with Mason and his jocks. Chad's friends would believe him, and they would be willing to help him through this. But, seriously, how the hell was he going to convince them that he had met a girl?

The activity around him pulled Chad out of his own head and back into the real world. People shuffling around, mumbling to each other. Class had ended. And he missed most of it.

Chad sighed. He'd have to go online to get the notes because he didn't take any. Instead, his subconscious doodled while his conscious pondered how to handle this new situation. Class was over, and he had no more for the day. Heston and Cooper would undoubtedly be standing outside the building, waiting for him right now. He sighed again and started to pack up until he looked at his doodle.

In his notebook was a sketch of Kat, naked, standing on a pile of severed limbs. Her breasts were each three times larger than her head, face sized areolas, and great gouts of blood sprayed from the mountain of arms and legs. He wondered if he needed to seek professional help, either for his witnessing violence that would forever haunt him or his unhealthy obsession with breasts.

"Dude. That's really dark."

Self-conscious, Chad started to shut his notebook, but a hand slipped in between the pages and forced Chad to reopen it. Tyler sat next to Chad every class and never said anything until now. He nodded soulfully and repeated, "Really dark."

"Umm . . . thanks?"

Slouched forward to the point of looking like he started to melt on his desk, Tyler looked up from the notebook. "So, what's it about?"

Chad had always assumed Tyler was a stoner—half-shut eyes, boneless posture, straight hair cascading to his back, Errol Flynn facial hair—yet Tyler's grades were never lower than an "A," and the only people he conversed with were gorgeous women. Tyler seemed to have life figured out and made it look easy. Chad wondered if he could learn a thing or two from Tyler. The earnestness, the focus in Tyler's gaze, as if he talked directly to Chad's soul, demanded truth. "A dream I had. More like a nightmare."

"Demons?"

Between the enigmatic questions that had been asked by Whacky Wanda and those by the mysterious nad-puncher, Chad didn't know how to interpret Tyler's. "Excuse me?"

Tyler sat up straight and crossed his arms. His smoldering eyes were slits; Chad couldn't tell if he ever blinked. "It seems like you have some demons that you're trying to deal with."

Under the crushing weight of Tyler's perpetual stare, Chad felt young, guilty. "Yeah, I guess so."

"What happened?"

"I did something that didn't turn out the way I expected."

Tyler nodded again with that soulful stare implying a depth beyond his years. "I get it."

Chad believed him, believed those eyes that he could barely see. "Yeah?"

"Totally. That happened to me. Got into something that I thought would lead to happiness, take me away from my miseries, but it didn't turn out like that. Not at all. Didn't answer any of my big life questions; just gave me more questions. I figured it out, though, and got my answers. It's all good now."

Answers. There was something about Tyler's quiet confidence that made Chad want to befriend him. Confide in him. Chad knew little about Tyler, but he truly believed he had answers. That was all Chad wanted right now, just a few answers. "How?"

Tyler leaned in, put his hand on Chad's back, at the base of his neck, a weird spot where either a hug or a head slam against the desk was imminent. "Twelve steps. I found these twelve simple steps to happiness."

Something inside Chad withered, hope escaping from him like air from a deflating balloon. Not the answers he was looking for. Tyler reacted to Chad's body language. He gave a slight pat on the back while standing up. "Hey, no worries. No pressure. You're not ready. I get that. I can't sell you something you're not buying. I'm right here when you're ready. I like to hang out at the organic café on Third Street if you need me after hours."

Turning away, Chad closed his notebook and grabbed his satchel. "I appreciate the invitation, but I'm—"

Chad turned back, and Tyler was gone. ". . . apparently talking to myself like a crazy person."

As Chad predicted, Heston and Cooper were waiting for him outside of the building and intercepted him at the bottom of the steps. Cooper was the epitome of cartoon anger—arms crossed, hip cocked, jaw jutted, the scowl of a worried father. "And?"

Now was the moment . . . but not the time. He wanted to tell them the truth, but he had no evidence. He hated lying to his friends, so he convinced himself that he was merely postponing the truth.

"Sorry for being so shitty, guys. I was just trying to process what happened last night. The Ink Stains showed up and things . . . things got violent, so I ran."

The best lies contained the most truths. It was easy to believe that Chad ran. Hell, he had wanted to run, but everything happened so fast that fear temporarily petrified his muscles, and then he passed out.

Heston's face went ashen, and Cooper's eyebrows furrowed. "When you say things got violent, was there . . . ," Cooper paused to look around as they walked. Satisfied there were no eavesdroppers, he leaned in and finished his thought as a whisper. ". . . blood?"

Chad had worried about concocting a story, but they were offering their own story. He had no intention of ruining it. "Yeah. There was."

Cooper's tone changed from angry to sympathetic. "Oh, shit. That must have been quite the sight. No wonder you ran. I don't believe I would have the wherewithal to stay either."

"Yeah, that's crazy," Heston mumbled, still visibly shaken. Chad felt bad for him. Even though he was big and had the best chance of surviving a fistfight out of the three of them, he was always the quickest to drop to his knees and cover his head. That exposed him to wedgies, the torment of choice by Mason and crew during the public-school years.

Cooper looked around again, a coconspirator assessing his surroundings. "Was it like a high school fight where it's really just shoving and loud profanities masquerading as bravado, or was it actual fisticuffs?"

"Worse. Much worse."

"Was there an involvement of . . . weapons?"

"Yeah."

"Will this be something that we'll see on the news?"

"I don't know. Look, I'm sorry, but I really didn't see a lot. Shit got real, and I ran."

They walked by two more campus buildings in silence. Chad felt awful for creating the awkwardness, for lying to his friends. He was able to dance around the truth, but he had to end the conversation before he tripped up. Maybe someday he could tell them the truth, but why burden them with the same questions that weighed on him now? "Anyone hear from Kyle?"

"No," Heston answered. "He hasn't been answering our texts."

Chad felt doubly bad now. Two of the four all but disappeared on them, so he could hardly blame them for being angry and confused. He decided that his best course of action with the Ink Stains is no action at all. If they wanted him dead, he'd be dead. If they wanted him to become one of them, then he failed their test. No one who passes out would be welcomed into a gang of murderous lycanthropes. If they contacted him again, he'd pass out since it worked so well last time. There was no reason for them to be in his life anymore, and if he kept the Ink Stains out of his life, then that should keep the nut-puncher out of his life as well. Now that he figured out how to help himself, he could now help his friend. "Oh shit. Okay. I'm gonna head over to his house now."

The trio stopped halfway across the quad. Cooper and Heston still had a few more classes, and Kyle lived in the opposite direction. Cooper smiled. "That sounds great. Now that you're okay let's figure out what's going on with Kyle. You act as reconnaissance, and then we'll reconnoiter and develop a plan of attack with the information you garner."

Heston smiled too. "Yeah!"

Chad gave a fist-bump to each of them, and they turned to each other to perform a fist-bump / high-five celebration so involved and needlessly intricate that Rube Goldberg himself would have been jealous. Every time was a new routine, this one involving spins and behind the back handclaps.

Chad laughed to himself as Cooper and Heston walked away. His mirth was fleeting, though, as a strange sensation overcame him. A minor worry, a precursor to something bad. The innate warning system that came equipped in all prey animals. Danger was near, and Chad needed to find it, to run from it. Were the Ink Stains around? The enigmatic junk-puncher? None of the above. Worse. Football players.

Brittany was at the far corner of the quad, talking with three football players. Why do they always travel in threes? Two of them were monstrous. As tall as Mason, yet somehow bigger. These two probably weighed the same; however the one kept the weight in his obscene muscles while the other stored it in his waist. The third was taller than an average human but not as tall as the other two, nor as large. Thinner, wiry. Now that he identified the danger, time to move away from it. Head down; Chad started toward the neighborhood next to the campus.

The football players paused from their conversation with Brittany. All four of them stared at Chad.

They watched with anger and suspicion in their eyes. Well over a hundred feet away, Chad swore he could see the veins along the one player's arms. Why were they always watching him? Mason was gone, but more took his place. Was this to be Chad's life? Always hunted?

Chad hastened his pace.

But they were faster.

The predators were always faster.

"Hey! Hey, you!" one of them called out.

Chad kept walking.

"Chad!" barked the same voice.

This time, he stopped. He didn't turn around yet, taking a moment to observe his surroundings. Plenty of people milling about the quad, the nearby buildings. Through a tight line of pines and down a small hill was Main Street. Lots of witnesses on the sidewalks and plenty of storefronts to run into. He twitched and almost ran to the trees when the football player yelled, "We need to talk!"

The trio and Brittany surrounded him. A fear lump formed in the back of Chad's throat, and an all too familiar tingle danced around his bladder, the same sensations when dealing with Mason. Chad tried a recent tactic. "If you hurt me in front of all these witnesses, you'll lose your scholarship."

Head like an angry bullet, monster muscles leaned down to address Chad. "Might be worth it if you had something to do with this."

Genuinely confused, Chad reeled back. "What are you talking about?"

"Our friends missed morning prep today. They never miss morning prep."

Not sure what else to do, Chad turned to Brittany. She frowned and said, "Mason. Brick is talking about Mason and a couple of their teammates."

Chad never had good acting skills. The few times he tried to lie to his parents, his eyes got wide, and his voice cracked on every other word. Fear had a similar effect on him, so it seemed appropriate that his eyes widened as he said with a cracking voice, "Mason's missing?"

"Yeah. Brittany said she saw you with him. You and your friends, the . . . the . . . what'd you call them, Britt?"

Never taking her eyes off Chad, she said, "The Ink Stains."

Brick shook his head. "You fucking townies and your stupid fucking names."

Brittany's expression finally changed. Confused. Hurt. It was fleeting, and she went back to glaring at Chad, wordlessly accusing him.

"The Ink Stains," Brick continued. "She saw you and The Ink Stains fucking with Mason. Then Mason disappears. You're our number one suspect."

A tiny portion of Chad's brain, the part that recognizes irony at the most inappropriate times, thought about how funny it was that he was being accused of harming someone who had tortured him for more than a decade. He didn't laugh, but the notion did calm him, allowing him to deliver the line, "I have no idea what happened to Mason."

"You better not," Brick growled. "Tell your friends that we're looking for them."

With one last snort to remind Chad of his masculinity, Brick turned and walked away. The other three followed, Brittany offering a glance back, a look of mixed emotions. Fear? Concern? Chad didn't know if it was a message to him or about him. He didn't understand women. But he did understand predators, and he was being hunted again.

CHAPTER 7

"Chad, it's so good to see you!" Mrs. Sedgeweck grabbed Chad and smothered him in her copious bosom. It was just a regular hug for her, but all he could feel were her breasts trying to devour him. And her hair smelled nice.

Kyle's mom never showed this kind of affection before. Sure, when they were kids, she doted on them and fussed to make sure they were all safe and having fun, having *safe* fun, but she never once hugged him, or any of her son's friends.

Mrs. Sedgeweck had been a model in her younger days, one known for her obscenely large chest. But men controlled the modeling world, especially the subcategory of the industry where she had found her success. Men were callous. Men were abusive. Men were voracious. Not able to cope with men being in power anymore, she quit the industry and got married.

Kyle's father was a nebbish man, the kind of fellow who had a job where he needed to wear suits and carry a briefcase, quick to analyze bar graphs and pie charts. He worshiped the ground Mrs. Sedgeweck walked on and never hit her, or raised his voice. Of course, life took advantage of people like Mr. Sedgeweck. Chad recalled a story Kyle told about a kitchen remodeling project that cost three times as much as estimated because all the contractors price gouged the Sedgewecks knowing full well that they would do nothing to stop them and pay the inflated bills. Kyle was a prey animal, too, just like his father. Just like Chad.

Chad admired Mr. Sedgeweck, though. Even though he was a prey animal, he still did well for himself with his career and found a woman like his wife.

Sure, she was old, late forties, and she carried more weight than when she modeled, but she was still rather attractive. And very caring, even if, at times, she crossed the line into the over-protective territory. Chad hoped that he could find a woman like that someday, no matter what her past, even if there were pictures online.

Kyle *never* talked about his mom's modeling. A simple internet search garnered a full page of thumbnails, images of her younger days. She was clothed in those, but a deeper dig yielded much more salacious results. Chad had never looked for those, choosing honor over curiosity. He'd at least wait until he turned twenty-one, then he could blame getting drunk if anyone ever found out about it. None of Kyle's friends had looked either, but Chad had his suspicions that Cooper might have peeked at least once.

Chad needed to move away from Mrs. Sedgeweck before he presented physical evidence that he had just thought about her naked. Plus, he couldn't breathe, her breasts quite literally smothering him. "It's good to see you, too, Mrs. Sedgeweck."

"Oh, Chad, I'm so happy you're here. Kyle's always been moody and a little withdrawn, but he's been like this for two days now. Paul and I have been giving him various medications, and nothing seems to be snapping him out of this. I'm so happy you came to visit."

Chad chuckled a little. "Just because we're in college now doesn't mean we're going to stop being friends, Mrs. Sedgeweck."

The slightest hint of pink blushed her cheeks. "I know, I know. I'm just such a worrier. He's in his room. I'm going to go get his meds ready."

Chad admonished himself for letting his gaze linger on Mrs. Sedgeweck as she walked away, but he couldn't stop himself.

In powder blue pajamas, Kyle sat cross-legged on his bed and played a game on his tablet. He barely blinked, and his eyes seemed unfocused as he slid his finger across the screen in broad swipes. Chad knocked on the door frame and then sat in the office chair by Kyle's desk. "Hey, Kyle."

"Hey." Kyle tossed the tablet aside and slouched forward, not looking at Chad.

"So . . . how's it going?"

"I don't know if I'm ready to talk about it yet."

"We're all worried about you."

Kyle sighed and finally looked at his friend. "I feel . . . stupid."

Chad rolled the chair closer to the bed. "There's no reason to feel that way."

Kyle sat on his bed and drew his knees to his chest, arms wrapped around his shins.

"Let's just take one thing at a time. That kid on the flyer. You knew him?"

Kyle nodded into his knees.

"What happened? Why'd you get so upset?"

Kyle drew in a deep breath; his exhale was slow and shaky. A fat tear rolled down his cheek, but he wiped it away before it could hit his chin. "I'm afraid. I'm afraid of what happened and of what might happen. I'm afraid of tell the group because you guys wouldn't believe me. I know I wouldn't. I don't. I don't believe me."

"Well, how about you tell me. Instead of telling three people, you tell one person. We'll go from there, okay."

The tiniest glimmer of light sparked within Kyle's eyes. He sniffled, wiped his nose with the back of his hand, and nodded again. "Yeah. Okay. Yeah. You'll think I'm crazy for being scared, but I . . . I just can't help myself."

"You're not alone."

Chad thought his comment was too open-ended and he was worried that he might have invited questions, but his friend missed the inference. Instead, Kyle accepted it as an invitation to share. "Thanks. So, the kid on the flyer. His name is Justin Butera."

"A junior at South Bend, right?"

Kyle remained in a seated fetal position but kept his head lifted as he spoke. More engaged now. "Yes. I met him over at Boards & Bytes, the gaming store off Market Street at the beginning of summer. He and I had a lot in common. We both loved the gaming mechanics in certain card games, hated first-person shooters, and had over-protective parents. He was the 'me' in his group of four at his school. Why do people like us always travel in fours?"

Chad had never given it any thought before and chuckled at the notion. "Good question."

"Anyway, we'd meet up here and there and played a few games that I knew you guys didn't like. He said it was fun playing without the 'Cooper' of his group, making sarcastic comments the whole time. But last week, when we met, he . . . he . . ."

Chad was losing him! He wheeled the chair closer to the bed. "It's okay, Kyle. I'm right here, been with you the whole story. It's all right."

After another sniffle and cleansing breath, Kyle continued. "We shared some stories about being bullied. He was sick of it. I was sick of it, just some usual complaining, you know? Well, it took a turn. He must have trusted me because he told me about a group of thugs who hung out at his school. They'd sell drugs and bought booze for anyone willing to pay. Justin said one day they approached him. They offered to help him with his bully problem."

"Help him? Help him how?"

"I asked him that, and he said . . . he said . . . oh, God, this is so stupid . . . they would turn him into a lycanthrope."

Chad slipped into an icy tunnel, cold and darkness surrounding him. Every thud of his heart echoed louder in his ears. Afraid the word would trigger an avalanche, he whispered, "Lycanthrope?"

Kyle chuckled as more tears formed. "I know, right? I laughed. I felt bad right after I laughed, but I couldn't help myself, you know? Justin insisted it was for real, said they showed him. One turned into a wolf. Another guy turned into a bear, and there was a snake, and a girl was with them. She turned into something too, but I can't remember."

"She was a cat." The words fell out of Chad's mouth.

Kyle looked at Chad with bloodshot eyes. "How'd you know?"

After having to lie to Cooper and Heston to get them off his back and then to Brick to save his life, Chad was starting to become good at it. He shrugged a shoulder. "Just seemed logical that the girl turned into a cat. You know, Natasha Kinski, *Cat People*, 1982 movie."

"Yeah. Yeah, that makes sense. You're right, that's what Justin said the girl turned into. I didn't laugh again, but I certainly didn't believe him. I felt bad for him because I could tell he believed in what he was saying. He believed that this group of people would change him into some form of were-creature so he could take care of his bully problems."

Kyle looked away, and the tears stopped. He stared at his wall as if it were a movie screen showing events only he could see. Chad moved the chair a bit closer and asked, "Then what?"

"Then he asked me to come with him."

"Wow. What'd you tell him?"

"No, obviously. But afterward I did think about it. How could I not? The ultimate fantasy, you know? Becoming a were-creature—a wolf, a bear, something—and getting back at Mason and his friends. It was hard not to think about it. The next day I couldn't stop thinking about it so much that I think I started to believe it. Justin was so into it, that I *almost* changed my mind. If I had . . . I'd be on a missing person flyer too."

Chad knew it was the Ink Stains. But what did they do to Justin that they didn't do to him? Did they turn Justin into one of them? If so, then why did Justin disappear? If not, if something worse, then why was Chad still alive? "Do you think these . . . thugs . . . did something to him?"

"Yeah. I mean, they had too, right?"

"Did Justin say who there were? Any names?"

"No. I didn't think to ask at the time. I was just so surprised that he believed them that I forgot to ask him anything like that. I just . . . I wish I would have asked, so I could tell someone *something* to help. I can't tell anyone *this* story."

Chad shoved personal need aside. Asking any more questions wouldn't help Kyle. "You told me, and I believe you, Kyle. I know Cooper and Heston will believe you, too. You can tell them, and I'll be right there with you."

Kyle smiled. Tears welled in his eyes, but none fell this time. "Yeah?"

"Yeah."

A knock on the door interrupted them. Mrs. Sedgeweck entered, beaming and holding a pill bottle and a glass of water. "It's so great to see you smiling again, Sweetie."

"Yeah," Kyle mumbled as embarrassment shaded his cheeks pink. "Chad helped a lot."

"Wonderful!" She popped open the bottle and shook out one red pill. "Here, I found this in my collection. I think it will help take the edge off. Might make you sleepy, though."

Chad stood while Kyle washed down the pill. "That's okay. I'm gonna head out. I'll text you later, Kyle."

"Sounds good."

Mrs. Sedgeweck shut Kyle's bedroom door and escorted Chad to the front door. Before he left, she gave him another hug. "Thank you, Chad."

Chad's eyes crossed, unprepared for the boob attack. And how nice her hair smelled. "You're welcome."

As he left, thoughts of ditching his mission to go home and spend some quality time on the internet bounced through his head. He pushed them aside, reminding himself that there was something much more important going on, and he needed to stay focused. He needed to find the Ink Stains.

CHAPTER 8

Chad didn't know what the hell he was drinking. It reminded him of the last time he saw Mason, getting his face shoved into the ground. This concoction tasted of dirt, branches, dead leaves. In such a hurry to add five packets of sugar, he almost forgot to rip them open. Not that throwing some paper into this tea would make it any worse.

"Great stuff, right?" Tyler asked.

Chad had a difficult time keeping his tongue in his mouth, as it wanted to escape. The taste of this tea coated his teeth and the roof of his mouth. "It's . . . certainly something else."

Tyler laughed, one of victory and camaraderie. "Yeah, man. Something else. I call it God juice because it cleanses the soul."

Four more packets of sugar and a splash of milk. He seriously thought about dropping the paper in as well, but he already felt awkward in front of Tyler. It now tasted like tree flavored melted ice cream. "I'm sure it does."

"Step number two, brother. Believe in a power greater than ourselves to restore us to sanity." Tyler lifted his cup of "God juice" and smiled. "I'm totally addicted to this shit."

While Tyler tilted his head back to chug his remaining tea, Chad slid his cup aside and wondered what addiction Tyler had that he needed twelve steps to break. Draining his cup, Tyler plunked it down in the middle of the table and then did a shimmy, his long hair rippling. Chad assumed it was a spasm caused by his body adjusting to the nastiness that had just been put into it. "All right, my brother, I'm ready to fight some demons. Since you sought me out, I'm guessing you are too."

"I am." Cooper and Heston were still in class, so Chad hadn't talked to them about Kyle yet. In the meantime, he needed some help finding the Ink Stains and had no idea where to begin. On a lark, he decided to try the organic café Tyler had mentioned. He didn't expect him to be here, so long after their last meeting. Maybe he lives in the apartment above? Hell, he could be living in the alley around the corner for all Chad knew. If he was going to hunt down lycanthropes, he needed help. He had immersed himself in enough fiction to know that in these situations, he needed a contact person who always seemed to have the right answers at the right times. It seemed fated that Tyler was going to be that person. What else could he be? Chad hoped Tyler wasn't going to be a plucky sidekick because he certainly didn't want one of those. Who was he kidding? If there was a plucky sidekick at this table, it was him. He didn't like that idea either.

Tyler leaned back in his chair and ran a hand through his hair to tame it, getting it out of the way of his steely gaze, hard eyes set in his squinting scowl. "Excellent. How about friends and family? What do they know of your demons?"

"Nothing. Well, one of my friends knows a little, but he doesn't know what they are."

Tyler nodded, processing Chad's words. "Your demons are affecting other people. I get it. You don't feel like you're in a good place to talk to them about it."

Chad nodded, trying to mimic the same cool way that Tyler did it but felt like he was just bobbing his head like a cartoon pigeon. He then felt extra stupid nodding yes while saying, "No, I'm not in a good place. I need to do something first before I can tell my friends and family what's going on."

"Okay. I can respect that. Getting your words ready before you speak them minimizes misunderstandings. That's cool. What is it that you need to do?"

"I need to find someone. A group of someones. They're the reason why I have my demons in the first place."

Tyler frowned and leaned forward, placing both elbows on the table. He pointed to Chad and said, "Hey, man, the twelve steps are all about personal responsibility. These people may have helped you feed your demons, but they didn't give birth to them. Only you birthed your demons, not them."

This was pointless. Chad wanted to get up and leave, wanted to forget ever meeting Tyler. None of this was Chad's fault. He didn't "birth" these demons. Or did he? No, he didn't know that the Ink Stains were going to turn into nightmare murder beasts and tear apart a few football players, but it was his history with one of those football players that caused them to do so. A history he could have changed. He could have gone to the gym and bulked up. He could have taken martial arts classes to protect himself. He could have gotten his friends together to stand up for themselves. He did none of that; instead he would bitch about Mason after every tormenting incident, and soon things would go back to the status quo. Even though Tyler didn't know what he was talking about, he did give Chad a sense of clarity. Something to think about, if nothing else. Maybe Tyler was his spirit animal? "Yeah. Okay, yeah, you're right, that makes sense. I'm the demon birther. But I still need to find these people first. Still need to confront them before I can confront my demons."

Tyler nodded again and leaned back in his chair. His look softened from super intense to regular intense. Chad had never been to a psychiatrist before but assumed this was what it felt like. Being studied. Being judged. "These people. Who are they?"

Chad wasn't sure if it was the tea or Tyler's influence, but the café around him faded away during this ersatz therapy session. There were no other customers, no other chairs or tables, no counter with disenfranchised employees behind it. Just Tyler and his piercing eyes. "People from my past infiltrating my present. People who have been barely props in my play of life now trying to upstage me and become the stars."

"These people, do they have names?"

Why not? The conversation was therapeutic, so why not say their names out loud. "Hunter. Kat. Viper. Dylan."

"The Ink Stains? Yeah, I know them."

The world suddenly reappeared around Chad in a flash, and he grabbed onto the table as if he had been dropped into his chair. Voices talking with other voices, utensils against plates, chairs sliding against the floor, fingers poking laptop keyboards, all the noises returned, louder. All the people returned as well, more than before, closer to him. Tyler could not have just said what Chad thought he said. "You . . . ? What?"

"Yeah. I mean, I don't party with them or anything like that. But I know who they are. You say *you* are looking for *them*?"

Chad didn't know what to say. He thought he'd ask Tyler if he knew the Ink Stains and hoped for a vague, "Kind of." He wasn't expecting first-name basis. He didn't want to *meet* them again, maybe spy on them to learn about who they were and what they wanted. Chad wanted to run from this conversation. Run from Tyler. Run from the Ink Stains. No! It might just be the "God juice" talking, but Chad was tired of running. No more running!

Chad answered Tyler with a soft, "Yeah."

Tyler offered a morbid chuckle and a shoulder shrug. "Your life, man. They usually hang out at Clinty's."

"Clinty's?"

Chad could only repeat the one word, focusing too much of his attention on trying to stave off an aneurysm that wanted to explode from his brain. He didn't entirely know what an aneurysm was, but he knew that they were caused by referring to the Ink Stains as demons to someone who knew them.

Tyler mistook the tone of Chad's question as one of ignorance. "You're a townie, right? You know McClintock's bar on Mill Road in West Bend, don't you? The place that serves minors on the down-low? You have to know about that place."

Chad was familiar with the place, that neighborhood. After telling someone who knew the Ink Stains that he was looking for them, there was no turning back. He was going to have to face a lot of fears today.

CHAPTER 9

McClintock's was a neighborhood corner bar. No parking lot, just an uneven sidewalk between it and the road. It was next to a three-story duplex and shared the same block with a grimy convenience store that had a faded sign advertising that they sold lottery tickets, probably their bestselling item. Both establishments had bars over the windows and a sliding gate to go over the door during non-business hours.

Chad didn't belong in this neighborhood, and it felt like everyone was watching him, a set of eyes peering out from every window in each row home along the street. The rational side of his brain told him he was an idiot, and no one cared that he was there. As proof, two gray-haired men engaged in conversation walked along the sidewalk across the street and took no notice of him, never even glancing in his direction. However, the rational side of his brain did agree that he would eventually draw attention to himself if all he did was stand in front of a bar and stare at it all day. He swallowed down the lump in his throat and opened the pockmarked door.

Dark. He paused to let his eyes adjust, coming into a wooden cavern from a sunny day. At first, he felt the heavy stares of a hundred eyes upon him, but as distinct shapes started to form, he realized there were only six other eyes in the place, and none seemed to care about him. The bar was on the right and shaped like an upside-down "L." Chad walked past the lone patron sitting at the bar, in the very first stool. He paid Chad no mind, too engaged in conversation with the bartender.

There were two small tables to his left, and in the back of the room were six more tables, but they were bigger, each able to seat four people. The third person in the bar sat at one of those tables—an old man, white hair tinted yellow, no discernible teeth, and muttering to himself. Chad made a very special note in the forefront of his brain not to make eye contact with the man, no matter the circumstance. At the far corner of the bar, Chad took a seat on a wobbly stool.

The bartender paused his conversation with the other patron and strolled over to Chad. This was it, the moment of truth, the moment Chad needed to step on his instinct to run and elevate himself as a person. He knew the process—he was to say that he left his I.D. in his car when the bartender asked for it—he just needed to execute.

The bartender stared at Chad for a long moment with judgment in his eyes. Finally, he growled, "What do you want?"

Chad knew nothing about beer. He remembered his parents talking about one the other night. What was it? Oh yeah! "Do you have a mango infused double wheat pale ale?"

"Sorry, all out. But I got a stout that tastes like a jelly donut."

"Really?"

"No. Now get the fuck outta here, kid."

"I left my I.D. in my car."

"I didn't ask."

"If you did, I have it in my car. Left it in my car."

"Get out."

Chad didn't like it here but didn't want to leave yet. Even if nothing came about from him sitting here for the rest of the day, he still felt like he was trying to do something, trying to take some form of control in his life, trying to change his status from prey animal. He had spent much of the day lying, so he decided to try some truth right now. "Please. I had a rough couple days."

The bartender sighed and pointed to the three tap handles between Chad and him. "These are what I got. What do you want?"

Chad's knowledge of beer had not changed one iota, but he recognized these three, having seen television commercials for them. He pointed to the one on the right.

"Got any I.D.?" the bartender asked as he filled the mug.

"I left it in my car."

"Well, I tried." The bartender grabbed a coaster from the nearby stack and placed the mug on it. He went back to the patron he had been talking to as if Chad didn't exist.

A sense of accomplishment bloomed within Chad's chest as he contemplated about what just happened. The thrill of blatantly disobeying a law raced through him like a hamster on amphetamines. This was no gateway to being a career criminal, but now he had a greater understanding of the rush that accompanied such behavior. He did this on his own, with purpose, and succeeded. He didn't cry. His voice didn't crack. *Within victory lives opportunity*, he cheered to himself and took a big pull from his mug.

For the second time within an hour, he wanted to spit out an offensive liquid he willingly put in his mouth. He forced himself to swallow, but halfway a cough shot some of the carbonated liquid up his nose. More coughing followed as he swallowed the rest in a painful gulp and gasped for air. Even though there were only three other people in the place, the establishment became noticeably quieter when they stopped talking and turned their attention to Chad.

In between the last few coughs he tried to stifle, he said with a raspy voice, "I'm good. I'm fine. All good." To demonstrate, he took another swig of beer. It didn't taste any better, but it went down with no issues. The bartender and patron went back to their conversation with each other, and the old man at the table went back to his conversation with himself.

Satisfied that he could go back to congratulating himself, he slouched and stared at his beer. Now what? There was nothing to do except wait. No wonder the old man at the table was talking to himself. Chad shuddered to think about what the old man was waiting for.

There were plenty of unusual knickknacks on the shelves behind the bar mixed in with the half-empty bottles of liquor. A few strands of beads dangling from the top shelf; polaroid pictures of the bartender in his younger, long-haired days posing with feathered-haired women; three taxidermy blackbirds frozen in mid-squawk; dust-coated shot glasses advertising foreign alcohols; small signs using pithy jokes to assert the bartender's authority; beer advertisements from the 70s, some containing feathered-haired women. Yes, there was plenty to look at, but not enough to pass the time.

Getting a crick at the base of his neck, Chad sat straighter. He took another sip, and it went down easier, not sure if the beer was getting better or if his taste buds were giving up. Coughing fit aside, he still felt proud of himself, overcoming all kinds of fears. Fear was limitation. Such a simple life rule. Throughout his life, he limited himself with many of his decisions. Now that he pushed himself to do this, he felt great about it. He had no idea what he'd do if the Ink Stains showed up, but he felt ready.

Physical strength was built by pushing the muscles beyond their current boundaries. Mental strength was built similarly, challenging the brain to work harder and faster using puzzles. Maybe emotional strength was built the same way? Chad willingly put himself in a situation that his current emotional state was incapable of handling, but he survived and felt better for it. He flexed his emotional muscles by taking another drink. His emotional muscle suddenly cramped when *she* walked into the bar.

The ball-basher from the forest sidled up the bar and ordered a beer. Chad squirmed. He started looking around for a rear exit and feared for the health and wellbeing of his penis. To defend against more attacks, he grabbed a coaster and shoved it down the front of his pants. Too panicked to even think, he remained perfectly still. This tactic sometimes worked for other prey animals, so why not him? It didn't work. After she received her beer, she looked right at him and frowned.

Leaving the bartender to return to his conversation with the patron, she aimed for Chad. Not knowing what else to do, he grabbed more coasters and crammed them down the front of his pants. Her expression changed from anger to disgust by the time she claimed the stool next to him. "What kind of weird sicko fetish is this?"

"Fetish? This is *protection* in case you feel like punching me again."

"Well, keep your dick away from me this time."

"I wasn't the one who put my dick near you last time." Chad realized he might have said that too loudly when the old man stopped talking to himself and chuckled.

The girl rolled her eyes and took a drink from her beer. After a moment of awkward silence, Chad did the same thing. The beer still tasted awful, and that only added to the awkwardness of the silence. He returned his mug to the bar; a bit disheartened that he only finished a quarter of it. A lot of swill left to get through. Then what? Another beer? Or two? How many would he have . . . *could* he have before it started to affect him? How long . . . ?

"Natalia," the girl said, interrupting Chad's thoughts.

"Excuse me?"

Natalia sighed and took another drink. She turned in her stool to face Chad, devoting her attention to him. She still looked pissed at the world but showed no signs of aggression. "My name is Natalia. I need to know what you know, so I guess it'll be easier if we tried civilized conversation."

"Chad." He thought about putting out his hand to shake hers but stopped as his mind flooded with images of her either yanking it from his body or pulling out a knife and stabbing it to the bar. Either way ended with pain and blood, so he opted to do nothing. He also opted to say nothing beyond his name, but that seemed to agitate Natalia.

"I already know that," she huffed.

"Oh, yeah," Chad mumbled, wondering how she knew who he was and why. Another sip of beer as he silently mulled this over.

Her frown deepened, pinching her features. "So?"

Not sure about her question, Chad decided to keep his follow-up question short to stymie her obvious anger. "Ummmm . . . ?"

It didn't work. She clutched the corner of the bar and gave a quick huff to the ceiling as if losing a battle with internal demons of her own. A hint of a frustrated growl to her voice, she asked with a clipped tone, "So, what do you know?"

Chad decided that if there was one time in his life to pull his head out of his ass, now was that time. He connected the dots and made assumptions. Looking around at the other patrons to make sure everything was status quo first, he leaned closer and whispered, "About the . . . werecreatures?"

Natalia leaned closer as well. "Yes."

"Nothing."

Chad felt the heat from her erubescent face wash over him in pulsating waves. He sensed pain coming. Sitting straight, he raised his hands in front of him as a form of early surrender. "Whoa. I know they exist. I know the names of four of them. I've seen them . . . ," a tiny bit of rationalization remained in Chad's fear-addled mind, reminding him to be careful of what he shared and with whom. ". . . transform. I don't know where they came from or what they want. I heard a rumor that they hang out *here*."

Natalia relaxed, her whole body unclenching. She turned back to the bar and took a drink. More awkward silence. Chad took a drink as well and debated about using his phone to do an internet search on how to break awkward silences. That and how to make beer taste better. "Hunter and his friends?"

Blood sloshed around the inside of Chad's head just at the mere mention of Hunter's name. "Yes."

"Why are you looking for them?"

"I don't know. To follow them? Spy on them? Learn about them?"

"Well, that's stupid."

"Oh yeah? Then why are *you* looking for them?"

"To confront them."

"How the hell is that any less stupid?"

Natalia turned again in her stool to face him, but she didn't look angry this time. "Because I'm a hunter."

"A hunter?"

"Yes."

"You're hunting him."

"Yes. I hunt lycanthropes. Werecreatures, as you call them."

"So . . . you're a hunter hunting Hunter?"

Natalia closed her eyes in inhaled deeply through her nose, nostrils flaring to take in as much air as possible. The next priorities on Chad's internet search list were lycanthrope hunters and how to talk to women without pissing them off. When she reopened her eyes, she said, "Go home, Chad."

In a day of facing his fears, he didn't like being told what to do anymore. "But, I—"

Chad jumped when she held her hand up for him to stop talking. Clearly, there were still plenty of fears left that he needed to face. She attempted a smile, but it looked pained. "Chad, you seem like a nice guy. I got everything out of you that I need, and I've concluded that this isn't for you. If Hunter or any of his friends show up, you'll be a distraction. I can't have that."

"But—"

Her other hand shot up, palm out. Her eyes went wide, and her smile grew. She looked maniacal and more than ready to push him off his barstool if necessary. "Chad. I said, go home."

He did as he was told. After digging out a crumpled five-dollar bill from his pocket and putting it on the bar, he left with less than zero fanfare. Not a single person in the bar paused from what they were doing as he left. His impact on their lives was nil.

Like a salt-covered slug, his bravery shriveled as he crossed from West Bend to East Bend. The farther away he got from Clinty's, the more his desire to go back and tell Natalia off wilted. She was right. He had no idea what was going on and his attempts to change that were clumsy at best. Research. He needed to research this some more. And questions. The next time he saw Natalia, he wanted to have a list of intelligent questions to ask so he didn't sound like a bumbling douche. This was a good plan. So excited by it, he ran into his house and straight up the stairs to his room. He opened the door and . . .

Froze.

On his bed, looking every bit as gorgeous as he remembered her, was Kat.

CHAPTER 10

"So, I heard you were looking for us."

Us. The only word of her sentence that resonated with Chad—us. More than just her. Panicked, he looked behind his door for the others. No Hunter. He opened his closet and rifled through his clothes. No Dylan. He dove to the floor and checked under his bed. No Viper.

Just Kat.

On his bed.

Running her fingers through his hair. "Hey, Stud. I'm right here."

Electricity skittered from the base of skull down his spine, a lightning strike right to his groin. Still on all fours, he couldn't feel the floor beneath his knees, the carpet digging into his fingers. They curled when Kat added, "Why don't you come up here and join me?"

Chad didn't know what she meant. He knew what it meant if he were someone else, someone like Hunter. It couldn't mean what he thought it meant, not for someone like him, not from a woman like Kat. But why not?

There were all kinds of crazy fetishes in this world. A quick search on the internet could prove that within seconds. Maybe her fetish was wussy kids with no discernible muscle tone? Maybe she was tired of being with men like Hunter and wanted to try something completely opposite? Maybe he was looking for ways to convince himself that the most gorgeous woman he had ever seen in his life wanted him to join her in his bed. Just as he was about to believe the lie, the tips of her nails glided over his delicate skin. His cheek. His neck. His throat.

Every protective sense kicked in, and he jumped to his feet, leaping halfway across his room.

Kat laughed, a throaty noise that implied hunger, power. "Don't you think I'm pretty?"

"Fuck yeah! I mean . . . yes, but . . . why . . . I mean . . ." *Stop being the prey*. If he ever wanted to stop being a prey animal, he needed to stop acting like one, thinking like one. He pushed himself to go to a bar illegally in a scary part of town in search of the Ink Stains. One of them was right here, right now. "Stop fucking around and tell me why you're here."

Kat's expression changed. She tilted her head, clearly not expecting those words. Chad surprised himself, too. He stood straight, to remain stalwart against whatever came next. She moved off the bed, her tight muscles rippling under black leather pants and a white half top. No bra to buffer her piercings as they rubbed against the thin fabric. Those piercings were an indelible image burned into Chad's brain. *No! Stop thinking about her tits*. Prey animals never thought about their predator's tits.

To show strength, Chad didn't avert his eyes from her gaze. Her eyes. So amber that they almost glowed. She sauntered over to him, her hips rolling like ocean waves, her pupils changing with every step. Going from round to sickle-shaped. Human to cat. *Don't look away. Don't look away.*

Only one part of his body was able to move, and it had limited mobility in one direction. Arms by his sides, he was powerless against her mystique. Had she hypnotized him? Probably no more so than any other woman slinking her way toward him. He licked his lips, a futile effort to preserve any form of moisture receding from his parched mouth. Focusing hard to make sure his voice didn't crack, he asked, "What do you want?"

Fingertips gliding across his chest, she stepped around him and pressed her chest against his back. She was a couple of inches shorter, but her lips still lined up perfectly with his ear as she whispered, "You."

She slid her hand down his chest and over his pants, her breath hot against his neck. Her hand stopped, and she pulled away from his body just enough to look over his shoulder. The façade of sexiness dropped, she reached down the front of his pants and pulled out five coasters. "Huh. You're weird little guy, ain't ya?"

"It's not what you think." Chad had no idea why he said that, just an excuse that flowed from his mouth every time one of his parents caught him in a precarious situation. The time his dad came home from work early to the vacuum cleaner running in his room. The time his mom found a copy of one of her cooking magazines in the bathroom. He had hoped that thinking of embarrassing moments with his parents would have been enough to break the spell, but his boner raged on thanks to the goddess of all things sexual pressing up against him.

"It never is, Sweetie." She slipped back into seductress mode with zero effort. If her pheromones were fire, Chad would have been a pile of ash.

"What do you want?"

Chin on his shoulder, she slid her hands over both of his thighs. "I already told you, smart guy. You."

"For dinner? Like Mason?"

"He was a piece of shit who got what he deserved. We knew how he treated people. We did it for you."

"I didn't want him to die."

Her lips brushed over his lobe as she whispered directly into his ear again, this time with a touch of anger in her voice. "Didn't you? Are you sure about that?"

Chad had a difficult time connecting with his thoughts about the situation. Any time he got stuffed into a trash can or had to put medicated lotion on the burns around his groin after an atomic wedgie or needed fistfuls of paper towel to dry his head after a swirly in the school bathroom, he'd tearfully wish Mason dead. After the pain faded from those events, he'd wish to be left alone, to be forgotten by Mason. He never truly *wanted* him dead.

Did he?

Every time he thought Mason had forgotten about him or moved on with his life, he was there to shove, trip, push, throw. Every new school year, Chad convinced himself that things would be different, that everyone matured. Things were never different from year to year, including this one. Mason was never going to stop. Ten years from now, Mason would have come to Chad's office wherever he worked to piss in his coffee mug and flip over his desk.

Mason was dead now. That was the *only* way to stop him.

"You're happy he died." Kat's lips moved from his ear to his cheek, his jaw, his neck, gliding over his skin with the slightest flick of her tongue along the way. An angel's touch with the devil's words. "I can smell it on you. I can taste it on your skin. Your happiness every time you think about Mason dying. You sooooo wanted him dead."

Chad was back in the forest, watching as Kat slaughtered, watching as she chewed on an indiscernible chunk of meat, watching her dance in a rain of blood. "So much blood."

"Blood is power."

Chad gulped; his breath shaky. Rushing blood pulsed between his ears, the primal drumbeat of his body warning him of danger. "You still haven't told me why you're here."

Kat slid her left hand over his crotch, and he almost went cross-eyed. She then extended her right hand and transformed it. Fingernails extended into claws, the skin on her palms thickened to padding, a wave of golden fur washed along her arm. "To offer you power."

"Me?" Chad's voice squeaked.

"Yes. We . . . what does everyone call us? Oh yes, the Ink Stains. We Ink Stains talked it over, and we'd like to give you the gift of our power."

For the first time in Chad's life, a woman was touching his dick. The same woman also terrified him by wiggling the clawed fingers on her mutated cat hand. The one thing he knew he shouldn't do was to say anything that could piss her off. Yet, "Is this what you offered Justin?"

Chad tensed and held his breath, readying himself to experience pain he couldn't imagine. Instead, the fur and claws faded back into her skin, and she removed her other hand from his crotch. Her lips left his ear. Her chest stopped pressing against his back. He stood perfectly still like an ancient terracotta boner soldier as Kat walked to the center of his room. She stood stiff with her arms crossed over her chest. "You know about Justin?"

"I know you offered him the same gift, and then he disappeared."

"What he decided to do with his power was his choice. He chose not to use it properly."

"You think I'll choose more wisely?"

"I hope you do."

"Why would I need power? You took care of my problem for me."

"Oh, Chad. Dear, sweet, lovable, goofy Chad." Kat moved her hands to her hips and looked at the ceiling as she turned in a circle. Stifling a laugh, she finished her turn and held up her index finger. "We took care of *one* problem. People have noticed that Mason and the other two idiots have gone missing. He has friends."

Chad frowned. "Yeah, but I'm not going to kill to solve my problems. I'm not going to kill an entire football team all by myself."

Kat chuckled. "Killing isn't the only option, you know. We killed Mason and his friends because we wanted to have some fun and we were hungry. You don't have to use your power to kill. Accepting our gift will give you a little advantage. Sometimes when you show someone that you have a little advantage, they assume you have a big advantage."

Being able to turn into an anthropomorphic killing machine *is* a big advantage. And she was right. There were more Masons in this world. Chad's run-in with Brick and Brittany earlier today proved that. The Masons of the world weren't going to stop once he graduated from college. They'd still come after him. Maybe not with wedgies and swirlies but turning him into a cuckold with his wife or stealing a promotion he should have had at his job.

Kat's tone softened, threaded with hints of sympathy. "You wouldn't be by yourself, Chad. You'd have us. Your own community."

A community. Chad had a community already, but they were just as weak as he. They had the same problems he did. They had no solutions like the one Kat was offering. Wait . . . what if he could be their solution? If he joined the Ink Stains, then he could protect his friends. Better yet, he could learn how to give his friends the same power, the same opportunity to be in control of their own lives. He could merge the two communities. "Where and when?"

Kat smiled. Her fangs glistened as she ran her tongue over them. "How about tonight, 10:00? Where you last saw Mason? In honor of his memory."

This was his last chance. If he declined, he might get eaten, or he might go back to his normal life. If he accepted, then there would be no backing out. He would totally be eaten if he tried to back out after accepting. His heartbeat rolled through his whole body, through his fingertips and down to his toes. Never had a decision this big been thrust upon him, yet it felt like it was the only option. "Okay."

"Excellent choice," Kat purred as she sauntered to the bedroom's window.

"So . . . ? You're not going to stay?"

"I will . . . when you become a part of my community."

Kat leaped out the window.

Chad ran to the bathroom to finish what Kat had started.

CHAPTER 11

"The members of your party lie unconscious, defenseless, and unable to protect themselves from the werewolf standing between you and them. Saliva pours from his mouth in anticipation of devouring them, and you. A mere hit point keeps death at bay and gives you hope. What would you like to do?" Heston asked, dice clacking between his hands as he rubbed them together.

Adding to the drama of the situation, Cooper stood. "I, Floridian Musk, the greatest warrior in the lands, shall add to my legend with this attack!"

Dice clatter across the tabletop.

"You hit!" Heston slid the twenty-sided die to Cooper. "Now roll for damage. The werewolf has twenty hit points left. You, Floridian Musk, must now defy the odds, lest the adventure ends before it even begins."

With a flick of his wrist, Cooper rolled the die, putting a spin on it. He placed both palms on the gaming table and stared at the fate deciding tool. "Come on. Come on."

Heston leaned back as Kyle and Chad leaned forward. The die slowed enough to flash numbers within the blur of color. Nineteen was equally as useless as one.

The die stopped.

The finger.

Floridian Musk slayed the werewolf to save the party.

Cooper did a backward summersault and jumped to his feet, both middle fingers flailing about. He then did the wave with his arms and body, his lanky frame exaggerating the ripple effect. The others laughed, but Chad just smiled, a bittersweet flavor of emotion flowing through him. He loved being with his friends, but their limitations frustrated him. This was the only time Heston felt comfortable enough to string together more than a few sentences. This was the only time Kyle felt comfortable enough to follow his instincts and be cunning. This was the only time Cooper felt comfortable . . . well, he'd feel comfortable acting like this anywhere, but he lacked opportunity and any other form of an appreciative audience. A situation like this was the only time they were allowed to be themselves without the constant need to keep their guard up, to wonder when and from where the next attack came. This was why Chad had to go through with meeting the Ink Stains tonight, had to gain their power, their abilities.

"What's all the cheering about?" Mrs. Sedgeweck announced her presence as she descended the stairs with a plate of freshly baked cookies to the finished basement, a game room decorated to Kyle's tastes. It was a shrine to gaming with two floor-to-ceiling bookcases stuffed full of tabletop games, framed posters on the wall, and replica props atop any surface that could support them.

Cooper stood soldier straight, hands behind his back as if hiding something, years of training turned this action into a reflex. His rigidity melted away with every step Kyle's mom took down the stairs, but he kept his posture straight as he made his way over to her. "Here, let me take that from you, Mrs. Sedgeweck."

She looked surprised as Cooper took the plate of cookies from her. He had always helped Mrs. Sedgeweck over the years—he had helped *all* the parents—but this time, as he took the plate, his fingers brushed over hers.

Chad rolled his eyes and prayed to God that Kyle didn't notice. Luckily, Kyle was too busy trying to get Heston to slip up and give information about what might be in the next room of The Demon Orc's Dungeon.

Cheeks blushed; Mrs. Sedgeweck went back upstairs. Chad punched Cooper in the shoulder to keep him from staring. His punch was a bit off, so he ended up aggressively swiping his forearm across Cooper's shoulder, but it had the intended effect. "Ow! I hope in your mind the potential consequences of me dropping the cookies was worth your unexplained actions."

Chad reached for a cookie as a distraction technique, turning his back to the others and leaning in close to Cooper so the other two couldn't hear his angry whisper. "Dude. What the fuck is wrong with you? You're being extra creepy, and you need to stop."

Cooper took a step back, and he put his free hand on Chad's shoulder. A look of guilt swept over his face. "You are correct, my friend. My actions were vulgar, and I appreciate your forthcoming. You hit me with a lot tonight, and I'm afraid I'm not processing it well. I assure you that I'm focused enough to enact your plan. This, I promise."

After giving Chad's shoulder a reassuring squeeze, Cooper delivered the cookies to the gaming table. Chad had zero doubt that Cooper would follow through with the plan. It was simple enough. It was what would happen afterward he was concerned about.

When Chad first arrived at Kyle's house, he had time to pull Cooper aside while Heston and Kyle set up the game. He told Cooper about his visit with Kyle. Of course, Cooper's takeaway from Chad's story was, "You hugged her?"

"Yes. I then went to Kyle's room—"

"How did you survive?"

"Dude. This is our friend's mom. A woman we've known for most of our lives."

"Who is a *woman*. And *she* hugged you, right?"

"What? Yes."

"You didn't intentionally or unintentionally initiate the hugging process."

"No. How could I have unintentionally initiated the hugging process?"

"I don't know. You're a particularly clumsy individual. Studies have shown that for some people, their coordination levels drop when subjected to extreme stress. Maybe the extreme guilt you were surely feeling about exposing your naked ass to me mixed with your worry about our mutual friend, Kyle, and as you were approaching the house, it all became too much for your body to handle, then . . ." Cooper's actions mimicked his words. His exaggerated loping ended with a controlled stumble toward Chad. To stabilize himself from his mock fall, he put both hands on Chad's chest.

"Dude!" Chad pushed his friend away again and then repeatedly swatted the air in front of him. "It wasn't like that! What the hell is wrong with you?"

"In the entire history of us being sentient organisms, she has never displayed such a greeting. Maybe this means that she is finally viewing us *adults*. Maybe . . . ," Copper gasped and looked away, covering his mouth with his hand. ". . . Maybe Mr. Sedgeweck is no longer capable of satisfying his end of the marital agreement? Or maybe she no longer seeks refuge within her husband and/or his loins."

"What? Loins? Gross! She hugged me. It's not a big deal. Stop being a creeper."

"Mrs. Sedgeweck's bosom is the first thing that greets you after you fist-bump St. Peter and stride through the pearly gates of Heaven!"

"You have a unique and distorted view of Heaven."

"I'm a unique and distorted person. You know this."

"I do, which is why I came to you about this situation with Kyle."

Cooper ran his hands through his hair as if trying to brush away his lascivious thoughts. After a long exhale and resculpt of his hairstyle, he said. "Yes. Yes, you are correct, my friend. You are correct. My thoughts and questions were wildly inappropriate."

"Okay." Chad cleared his throat. "So, you and Heston talked to Kyle about what happened?"

"We did. We did, indeed."

"What do you think?"

Cooper ran a hand through his hair, this time taming it. He shook his head. "I don't know. I want to believe him, and I certainly believe that he believes his story. But . . . lycanthropes? If the whole story isn't a manifestation within his mind as a way to deal with Justin's disappearance, then Justin had some deep-rooted issues. I mean, if he *truly* believed in werecreatures and that he met one willing to cast upon him the power of lycanthropy, that's some serious fodder for the Satanic-panic of the earliest days of D & D."

"I agree. But what caught my attention was the person making the offer."

"The individual who belonged to the group of pernicious rapscallions?"

"Yes. The people offering up the power to Justin. Don't they sound familiar?"

"You have someone in mind, maybe?"

"The Ink Stains."

"That is one hell of a leap in logic, Chad."

"Think about it. A group of thugs hanging around a high school. Mason and a couple of other football players are missing the very day after they had a run-in with the Ink Stains. They're just the latest in a string of disappearances. The leap in logic isn't all that big."

"If these mysterious and yet unnamed individuals from Kyle's story are the Ink Stains, what pray tell do you suggest we do? We certainly can't involve the authorities. We don't have enough evidence . . . redact that . . . we have zero evidence that the Ink Stains are involved with these disappearances."

Chad smiled, trying hard to make it as cool as the unlikely heroes in the movies make it look. "I'm going to find some."

"Oh, Dear Lord of all things earthly and divine, you're going to come up with a ridiculously stupid plan that makes you like some unlikely hero in a movie."

"It's not that stupid."

"You're going to tell me that you're going to go looking for the Ink Stains, aren't you?"

"Yeah, but you didn't have to kill my mood about it."

"I did. I did because I'm your friend, and you're about to verbalize a proposition akin to suicide."

Chad hated to lie, but his sense of justified righteousness urged him on. "I just want to observe them. Simple recon, nothing more."

"Simple recon? You don't even know where to find them."

"I heard a rumor about where they're going to be tonight."

"A rumor? Seriously? Where have you been lurking to hear such rumors?"

This was it. This was the moment that would go down in the history of their friendship, a turning point. Either Cooper would think he had gone too far and end their lifelong friendship, or he would view Chad's act as one of courage and resolve. "I went to Clinty's. While there, people talked, and I overheard a conversation about them, about the Ink Stains."

"You went there without me? I thought we said our first time venturing into the legendary Clinty's we would do it together."

"I know. I'm sorry about that, but I had to go. I heard a rumor that's where the Ink Stains liked to hang out."

"What? *Another* rumor? Where are you getting all these rumors from? Have you turned into Lord Varys from *Game of Thrones*? With your own network of ne'er do well children giving you information about everyone in town?"

Chad closed his eyes and pinched the bridge of his nose to keep his throbbing eyeballs from popping out of his skull. "There are no children, ne'er do well, or otherwise. It's Tyler. Tyler Manchester is the one who told me they would be at Clinty's."

"Tyler Manchester? The stoner who got forcibly and permanently removed from our high school for dealing drugs?"

"I don't think he's into that anymore. He keeps preaching twelve steps."

"How in the name of all things holy and unholy is Tyler Manchester one of your information gathering ne'er do well children?"

It was Chad's turn to run his hand through his hair, mussing it to distract from his rising frustration levels. "He's not . . . I ran into him in Psych class . . . We met at . . . You know what? It really doesn't matter. There's a rumor that the Ink Stains hang out at the last place I saw them, the last place I saw Mason and his idiot friends."

"Chad, you cannot be serious. The Ink Stains have always had a reputation for varying levels of bad-assery, but if you really think they're involved with people disappearing, then what you're suggesting is flat out dangerous. You have no idea what they're capable of. Unless you've been taking secret ninja classes that I don't know about, your idea is really bad."

Yes, this was a bad idea, and what they were capable of was constantly at the forefront of his mind. "That's why I'm telling *you*. Kyle would probably have a heart attack or slip into a coma, and Heston would sweat through his clothing. Look, I know it's dangerous and stupid, but we can't just sit back and do nothing. We've done that all our lives and nothing will change unless *we* make it change. I'll be careful, I swear."

Hands clasped behind his back; Cooper paced in small circles again. "Do you need me to accompany you?"

"No. The less people, the better."

"What if your skulking skills are just as lacking as your sports-ball skills, and they catch you?"

"Then I'll tell them I was looking for them to apologize for running away when they got in a fight with Mason and his crew."

"Promise me you'll run at the first sign of the first inkling of the slightest bit of danger."

"Promise."

"Okay. Is there any way I can assist?"

"Actually, there is. . . ."

Chad knew that his actions as of late had been suspect at best. His erratic behavior and questionable choices shined on him like an unwanted spotlight. He came over to Kyle's tonight to play a little D & D with his friends, to act as if everything were normal. But he needed to leave now. If he were to leave early tonight, there would be way too many questions, too many more lies. But Cooper did exactly as requested. As the clock embedded in the Pac-Man on the wall struck 9:30, Cooper clapped his hands and said, "Well, gentleman, I hate to pause the adventure, but our characters could use a much-needed respite."

"Really?" Heston asked. "It's so early."

"Sorry. Big test tomorrow."

"Look at you being mature," Kyle said, laughing.

Cooper puffed out his chest and started toward the stairs. "We shall see who laughs the loudest as my GPA crushes all of yours."

Kyle escorted everyone to the front door. Heston and Cooper said their goodbyes first, a fist-bump, high-five fiesta that concluded with them hopping around on one leg. Chad hung back a bit and whispered to Kyle, "Are you sure you're okay?"

Kyle nodded. "Yeah. It felt good having you guys around."

"Okay. Contact me if you need anything."

Kyle nodded again and gently shut the door.

CHAPTER 12

Music.

The drums were faint at first but became more distinct as Chad got closer. Fast guitars and screeching vocals soon followed. Chad was worried about wandering through the forest at night. Even though he had grown up in the area and now used the flashlight function on his phone, the constant fear of unseen rocks and branches teased him, images of *127 Hours* dancing through his head. The music helped push down those fears. Getting lost was no longer a concern now that all he had to do was follow the music.

The growling, barking vocals, and machine-gun drums led him right to the site. By the time the guitar solo started, Chad stepped into the light.

Thick candles slowly melted upon moss-covered rocks. Oil lanterns hung from branches. Strings of tiny white lights flowed from tree to tree. A full-length mirror framed with ornate swirls of gold rested against a large tree. Chad couldn't see the speaker but assumed that it was close to the duffle bag resting empty at the edge of the light's reach. Plus, Kat was topless, so Chad had no care about the speaker.

"Chad's here!" Viper yelled, victoriously thrusting his hands into the air above his head. He was naked, and his body piercings glimmered in the different types of light.

Kat sauntered over to him, her leather pants low on her hips. As soon as she was close enough, she grabbed the bottom of his shirt, lifted it over his head, and tossed it to the ground. No permission sought after; no resistance given. "Hi, delicious."

The amount of effort he put into thinking of a cool rejoinder almost gave him an aneurism. Over the years, he had learned that if he couldn't think of anything awesome to say, then it was best to keep his mouth shut. Sure, that sometimes led to awkward silences, but awkward was better than stupid. Chad remained silent, but there was no chance for the situation to become awkward thanks to Hunter.

Chad jerked as the leader of The Ink Stains appeared from out of nowhere next to him. He, too, was shirtless; leather pants the only thing between him and nature. Hunter put his arm around Chad and smiled. "Hey, no need to be so jumpy. Soon, you'll be like us." He gestured to everyone else in the small clearing. Amber liquid splashed around the bottle in his hand.

"Truth," Dylan said as he walked by and gave Chad a fist bump.

Hunter took a gulping swing from the bottle and handed it to Chad. "Here. You'll need this."

This was it. The moment of truth. The moment that would change his life forever. This ceremony would help him transcend. He'd gain great powers and be freed from weakness. All he had to do was drink from the bottle. "This . . . is this what will change me?"

Hunter laughed. "No. It's just whiskey. But you'll need it for the pain. Now get naked unless you want to ruin your clothes."

Fear crept back into his mind. What if this was some elaborate hoax? They get him naked and steal his clothes and turn on industrial-sized spotlights, and the whole school was there to point and laugh? Stupid thoughts. This was not high school anymore. Mason would have been more likely to try a stunt like that, and he was now dead, eaten by these people . . . no, not people . . . these *powerful* creatures. Embarrassing others was not how these creatures did things, how they settled scores. If they had something untoward planned for Chad, then it wasn't embarrassment, and they would have done it before now.

Chad dropped his pants and took a chug from the bottle.

The other four cheered.

The liquid burned. Chad doubled over in a coughing fit after three gulps, whiskey spraying from his lips and dribbling down his chin. No! He was not going to fuck up an opportunity like this because he couldn't handle his alcohol. He straightened up and wiped his forearm across his face. Better prepared this time, he downed three more gulps. He took one more mouthful and leaned back. With purpose, he sprayed the whiskey in the air, the alcohol misting his face and chest. He howled. The other four howled with him.

Kat tossed another bottle to Hunter while she kept one for herself. They got naked as well and started dancing, aggressive jumps and fist pumps, shaking their heads to the beat of the music. They passed the bottles to Viper and Dylan, both dancing as well. All five moved around in the clearing, around the perimeter, across the center, back and forth. The music got louder and the dancing faster.

All five laughed and cheered and howled with each other, with the music, with the voices of nature only they could hear. Chad drank again and again. He lost count of the songs after four, but he didn't tire, he just kept dancing and jumping, moving about the space. All he focused on were the others. Their moving bodies. Their tattoos.

Hunter had traditional black tribal markings, jagged curves on his left shoulder, and part of his chest. Viper had snakes that wriggled as he moved his body. Kat's were various in size and style. A skull just below her sternum, roses flowing from behind it as if the flowers were cupping her breasts. An Egyptian style cat on her left thigh. Vines around her right foot and calf. A flaming ankh on her right hip. Dylan had only one—a blackbird peeking through the natural brush of his chest hair. A lone blackbird. That struck Chad as odd, but he noticed that the other three had a blackbird on their bodies as well: Kat on her left hip, Hunter on his ribs under his tribal work, Viper above his pelvis. Was this their brand? Would Chad have to get one too?

Chad emptied the bottle and found himself standing in front of the mirror, wondering where to put his impending blackbird tattoo. The whiskey blurred his vision and made the inside of his head fuzzy, but he saw his reflection. He wasn't as skinny as Kyle or lanky like Cooper, but he had no muscle tone, just a quick sketch of "young, human, male." That observation was exacerbated when Hunter again appeared out of nowhere and put his arm around Chad's shoulders. His skin was pulled taut over rounded muscles and changed the reflection to an image of "before" and "after." Chad so desperately hoped that he was the "before" and would look like Hunter after this. "Are you ready? Are you ready to say goodbye to this person?"

Chad still had enough wherewithal to register Hunter's words. "Fuck yeah, I'm ready."

"Then drink this. *This* is what will change you."

A glass vial. The liquid inside was such a dark red that it shimmered purple when the lights touch it in the right way. "This?"

"Elder blood. Drink it and let out your inner animal."

Chad was ready. Ready to change, to be something else that would allow him to be someone else. Someone strong. Someone in charge of his own life. Someone who had enough power to go an entire day without feeling fear. He swallowed the liquid in one gulp.

The others cheered, and Chad howled. Kat sauntered forward, her sweat-sheened body glistening in the confluence of light. She smiled and scraped her tops fangs over her bottom lip hard enough to draw blood. Chad thought the move was badass, but before he could express his thoughts, she kissed him.

Her tongue was moist, yet sandpaper rough, swirling her blood around in his mouth. At first, he thought tasting someone else's blood might be gross, and then admonished himself for not thinking about that before this moment, before changing himself into a creature that craved fresh meat. It wasn't bad. It was better than he expected. He enjoyed it, felt the sustenance it contained. He liked it so much that he wrapped an arm around Kat and pressed her body against his.

Then the first wave of pain hit.

A freight train of razor blades chugged from the base of his skull and ripped its way through him all the way to his toes. The kissing stopped. He let go of Kat and doubled over.

Bones shifted. Muscles rearranged themselves. Tendons pulled, and ligaments pushed. Hunter was correct with his advice about alcohol. The buzz was gone. Chad went from tipsy to sober as his ribs shifted around his changing spinal column. His fingers became stubby and pulled close together. Pain from his legs changing tore through him as his feet grew longer, and his knees rearranged themselves while his hips cracked and reformed. Yet, it was his ears that he felt the most. A constant pull, they kept stretching throughout the entire process no matter how the other parts of his body changed. Finally, it ended. The pain. The confusion. The waiting. He had been transformed. He was now a lycanthrope. Panting, he gazed upon the mirror to see what beast had been unleashed.

A rabbit.

A fucking rabbit.

All his life Chad had been a prey animal. Now to see himself as a rabbit turned his stomach. He was almost human-sized, but still a rabbit. He should have known this was the animal he was fated to be, that this was what was burrowing within him. Did the Ink Stains know? Did they sense that Chad would transform into a rabbit? He looked to the others but didn't need to ask the question.

The salivating maws of four predators answered his question for him.

CHAPTER 13

Why?

Why did they do this to him? Why go through the trouble of befriending him to betray him? Why was he always destined to be a prey animal? The only good thing about being a prey animal was he knew how to react. He knew how to run.

Even though he had never been a rabbit before, never had to sprint on four legs, he allowed instinct to take over. The slightest sliver of thought that passed through his mind was one that reminded him evolution designed rabbits for this, so he should let this body do what it was built for. Run!

Chad kicked with his back legs and launched himself farther than he thought, right at Dylan in bear form. Reflex kicked in, and he kicked away, narrowly avoiding the swipe of the bear claw, and he leaped toward the mirror. It was leaning against the tree and formed the closest form of cover. Green scales flashed nearby as Chad ran between the mirror and the tree. Viper attacked but crashed into the mirror. Chad sprinted away from the sounds of breaking glass and hissing.

Chad looped around the tree to find Hunter, the wolf, waiting for him. He didn't know how—a form of extrasensory perception? A new ability to detect the slightest twitches in Hunter's muscles? Timing? Luck?—but he turned ninety degrees just as the wolf pounced. Not only did the wolf miss, but he crashed into the bear that had been behind Chad. There was a meaty smack followed by the two predators growling and gnashing their teeth at each other.

Kat dropped out of the sky and landed right beside Chad, forcing him to turn back toward the small clearing. She swiped a claw, but missed, giving him a half step advantage. The clearing offered no shelter, no obstacles for him to use. The lights!

The candles and lanterns would start a fire, potentially burn down the whole forest. His life was on the line, but he still couldn't bring himself to wreak that level of damage. But the strings of white lights? He jumped. He cleared the strands. Kat did not. Feline yowls and hisses chased Chad into the forest.

The ground rumbled around him as Dylan picked up the chase. Chad swore rabbits were faster than bears, but he felt Dylan's presence behind him. No matter how fast he weaved around the trees, or how many branches he ran under, he couldn't separate himself from the bear. He had seen something earlier, knew it had to be around here. A zig. A zag. A dash between two trees. Found it!

A tree. Two distinct prongs grew away from each other about halfway up the tree. When he had first seen it, he found it interesting that it was shaped as if it were ready to catch something. Aiming for that tree, he slowed just enough so Dylan would focus on him and not what lay ahead. Chad felt the hungry breath of the bear right behind him. Sticking as close as he could to the tree, he ran around it, finding exactly what he had hoped for. Approaching from the angle he did, the Y shaped tree obscured the other tree, the one that had fallen months ago and now rested between the two arms. Sprinting, he turned and ran under the fallen tree. Dylan did not.

The impact was devastating enough to dislodge the half-fallen tree. Branches snapped and leaves rained down as the dead tree crashed to the ground. Chad hoped that Dylan had been crushed underneath it, but he knew deep in his heart that that was not the case. Luck had a special way of spitting on him when he needed it the most. Now proved no differently.

Chad hoped he was far enough away from the Ink Stains, the predators, the absolute assholes trying to eat him, to get his bearings and formulate a plan. Nope. Luck hocked a loogie on him in the form of Hunter jumping out from behind a tree. Foam spraying from his snapping jaws in time with growling barks. Chad jerked to the side out of reflex, but his momentum was too great to turn. He slammed into Hunter and kicked out in a panic. His rabbit hind legs connected squarely with Hunter's chest and launched him away from his attacker. Not fast enough. Before he could gain any speed, Viper shot out from behind another tree. Fangs and forked tongue obscured Chad's vision, and he turned again. This time into a tree.

Stunned from the collision, Chad's blurred vision came into focus just in time to see the wolf and the snake converge. Death in front of him, a tree behind him. Tears formed in his eyes as he quivered from fear. He wasn't sure if it was because this was the most terrifying moment in his life, or if it was one of the new effects that came along with being a rabbit, but he felt like his heart had hummingbird wings, beating faster than he thought possible. He was going to die. Not just die but get eaten like an animal on a nature show. Not "like" an animal; he was an animal!

The wolf's body shifted as it stood, bones and muscles adjusting to accommodate standing on hind legs. His front paws extended to clawed fingers. His muzzle altered just enough for Hunter to move his lips to speak. "What do you think, Viper? Should we save a chunk or two for the others?"

Viper altered his form as well, arms sprouting from the snake body, his face showing signs of humanity. His forked tongue flicked as he spoke. "No. If they weren't quick enough to catch this one, then they don't deserve a piece of it."

"My thinking as well. This one put up a hell of a chase, so I think we deserve the whole thing for catching it. They always taste better in their real form, don't they? More succulent than humans."

Chad cowered, shrinking back against the tree. Escape was no longer an option in his mind as the wolf and the snake inched their way closer. Instead, he thought stupid things like hoping he would taste bad or that his fur would get stuck in their teeth. Scaled hands and clawed fingers reached for him. Then they reeled back as both creatures yowled in pain.

Chad wondered if it was something he did, some crazy super power that he attained along with the furry paws and cottontail. Viper and Hunter turned, exposing an arrow stuck in each of their backs. Still too panicked to think rationally, Chad's initial thought was to thank the great goddess Artemis for her miracle arrows from Heaven. They didn't come from Heaven nor a centuries-old mythical figure. Instead, they came from two women.

It was nighttime, but the moon was out, and there were very few leaves on the trees. There was no doubt in Chad's mind that the two women a hundred feet away wielding crossbows were Natalia and Whacky Wanda. A cable connected each of them to the canopy above. Chad would never have seen the cable if not for it yanking them off the ground as Viper and Hunter charged after them. The snake slithered up the tree Natalia had been pulled into while Hunter, still a wolf in humanoid form, climbed up Wanda's tree.

Branches shook from one treetop to the next. There was snarling and hissing, but no screams. Chad assumed the women were experienced enough to have an escape plan. This was no time to ruminate, though. An opportunity to escape presented itself, so he took it and ran.

CHAPTER 14

The forest went on forever. Chad had no idea how far he ran or even how long he had been running. Just tree after tree, a random rock here and there. He didn't even know if he was running in a straight line or in circles. The moon was still high in the sky, so it didn't help with his sense of direction. Even if the moon was setting, he wouldn't know which direction he ran, but it would at least be a good point of reference. Finally, as the last droplet of hope dripped from his body, a miracle happened. He found a stream.

Water splashed his entire face as he lapped at it furiously. His tongue had a mind of its own, darting in and out at incomprehensible speeds. The thirst hit him as soon as he saw the water, but now as it started to get quenched, he gained some control over his tongue. The speed slowed by a fraction, but the splashing stopped. Water in mouth. Better, much better.

Thirst quenched, he took a step back and brought his front paws up to clean his face. After a few quick strokes over his nose, he stopped and looked at his paws. Paws, not hands. Rabbit paws. He wanted to cry, but he wasn't sure if any tears came out. Could rabbits even cry? If there were tears, they were getting absorbed by his fur before they got too far.

Fur. Paws. He reached the top of his head and pulled down his long ears. Deep in the pit of his gut, a wave of anger grew, consuming everything in its path, from fear to confusion to frustration. The one time—the *only* time—in his life, he had an opportunity for power, *real* power, to change his fate, to be something more than he was. What happened? The universe dick kicked

73

him by making him a fucking rabbit! Panic blasted away his anger when he wondered if he still had a dick anymore because he knew zero about the arcane machinations of leporine anatomy. If he did still have a dick, it wasn't quite where it should be. Despair made its way back as his number one emotion. But at least it calmed him down enough to think.

He wanted his dick back. He wanted his arms and legs back. He wasn't handsome or the epitome of fitness, but he wanted his face and body back as well. This wasn't his body. This was some sick joke, and he was tired of being the punchline. He could get his body back. All four of the Ink Stains could transform at will, partially or completely. He didn't care about partial transformation. There was no way in hell he'd ever go back to being a rabbit

If they could do it, so could he. But how? Well, they had more experience than he did, so there was that. Years, maybe longer like decades. If any of the horror movies and fantasy games were remotely true, then possibly centuries or millennia. How could he get himself to do what they could do? Chad rationalized that they had to have started somewhere, right? There was a first time turning back to human for all four of them. If they could do it, he could do it.

Control. That was what Chad needed right now, control. He needed to push aside the betrayal, the attack, the unknown of what was going to happen next. Push all of that aside. Relax. He needed to relax. He closed his eyes and focused on his racing rabbit heart. A few years ago, he dabbled with hardcore techno music, some songs reaching three beats per second. That was too fast for him, like his heart right now. It needed to slow down. He needed to breathe deeper, slower. Deeper. Slower. Breathe. Heartbeat. Slower.

Chad curled his toes and flexed his fingers. Toes! Fingers! Dick! He had all his original body parts again. Human toes and fingers and dick. His dick! Chad covered his genitals with both hands and crouched down, his face burning from embarrassment. Some wild animal he was; ashamed to be naked even when no one else was around. Standing back up, he looked around to make sure he was alone. Now what?

The stream. It would lead somewhere, it had to, and he'd have a constant source of water if he got thirsty. He was wrong again.

He followed the stream for what he estimated to be about half an hour, but little by little, it narrowed and eventually disappeared. So did the forest. The trees became sparser and smaller until Chad found himself slopping around bushes and grasses that grew to his chest. The dark voices of fear began to whisper words of hopelessness, but he saw something spotlighted by the moon—a barn.

He knew it was a good thing but couldn't seem to formulate the best use of this information. Barns had horses! So, he'd take a horse and ride into town.

Dumbest.

Idea.

Ever.

What else? Okay, no one lived in a barn, but a barn usually meant a farm. A farm meant a farmhouse. House meant people, but he couldn't just knock on their door. Not many people would respond too well to a naked guy knocking on their door in the middle of the night. Maybe a blanket would help? If there were horses in the barn, there might be at least some horse blankets.

The grasses diminished in height as he made his way to the barn, ankle-high by the time he reached it. Red, but paled to a dull brown by the moon, the barn seemed well maintained. The large doors were open, and Chad crept inside. The moon's light helped, but couldn't reach everywhere, the center of the barn remaining a mystery because of the darkness. Except for one tiny orange glow that flared up. Chad stopped in his tracks. The glow dimmed but didn't extinguish. It just floated in the middle of the darkness. Chad felt a strange compulsion to go to it, but a bizarre fear of it. Was this how those little deep-water fishes felt when they saw the glowing tip of an anglerfish? But what was it? The answer came when the lights came on.

Tyler.

Two strings of round light bulbs dangled from the two sets of beams that formed the main aisle. Chad brought his hands to his eyes, shielding them against the sudden brightness. As the spots faded from his vision. He remembered his nakedness and brought his hands back down to cover himself. "Ummm . . . hey? Wassup?"

Tyler sat on a hay bale, one of many shoved and molded together to form an ersatz couch. His feet were resting on a couple more, a mockery of a coffee table. Hay bales formed the furniture of a living room. Rectangular blocks of straw were stacked together to form a half-wall. A giant wooden spool once used for industrial-sized cable was now turned on its side to become a table, but the chairs around it were strategically stacked blocks of hay. The only true piece of furniture was a refrigerator. If not for the bales, it would have looked like any other room unprepared for company—empty pizza boxes, crushed beer cans, a few articles of clothing piled in a corner. And there sat Tyler in the middle of it all.

The straw king in his hay domain leaned forward and took one last pull from his joint, the tip glowing amber, and then tapped it out in an ashtray on the hay coffee table. Chad got nervous about the tiny bits of ambers being so close to something so combustible, but Tyler showed no fear. Instead, he just stared through unblinking, squinted eyes at the interloper. Slowly, he stood and removed his shirt. "I had no idea you were into this, but, hey, okay."

"What? No! I'm not gay!"

"So, you play for both teams? I can dig it. Me, too." Tyler unfastened his belt.

"No! Stop taking your clothes off! I don't play for both teams! I barely play for one team!"

Tyler had his thumbs hooked inside the top of his pants, ready to pull them down at a moment's notice. "You don't have to be phobic about it. I mean, you have been finding ways to run into me, including coming into my barn all kinds of naked."

Chad squeezed his eyes shut so hard his whole face hurt. "I'm not phobic. I'm all for GLBTQA+ rights; I'm just none of those letters. Running into you is a coincidence. In fact, you came up to me in class, and then told me where to find you, and then I found you because I was looking for the Ink Stains and then I found them, but not before I found Natalia, and then, stop talking! Just stop talking!"

"Dude, you're the one talking, not me."

Chad inhaled, his breath quivering. He opened his eyes and released two streams of tears. "I know. I told me to stop talking."

Tyler sat down on his hay bale couch and leaned back. Like some form of reefer wizard, he reached behind the couch and conjured a tightly rolled joint and a lighter. He lit it and pulled deeply from it. Holding his breath, he extended it to Chad. The entire time, he never once blinked his squinted eyes, never once looked anywhere else other than into Chad's soul.

Chad waved off Tyler's offer. Maybe he should take a hit? That might calm him down a bit, but he was so uncomfortable right now. Having spent so much of his life being awkward, he thought he'd be used to it by now. Other than the time Mason yanked his pants down in eighth-grade gym class, he had never experienced humiliation like this. But that time was different. He had no control over the machinations of high school. This exposure right now, he felt like he had control over this, that he actively did something to lead him to this shame.

Tyler opened his mouth but didn't exhale. The smoke exited like a mythical creature made of mist escaping its confines. It glided over Tyler's face, rolling over the contours like a liquid spilling upwards. Tyler leaned forward, his face parting the thick cloud. "Do you believe in God?"

Chad was standing in a barn with both hands covering his nudity, yet he was somehow still surprised. "Wha . . . what?"

Tyler reached down and pulled a beer can from behind his hay bale coffee table. He took a swig and then continued. "So much of the twelve steps is built upon God. For those who don't believe in organized religion, it's about spirituality. How we fit into this world, this universe, with ourselves and each other. It's about believing that we're all pieces of a great puzzle. About taking ownership of being that piece, figuring out where we fit into the grand puzzle. So, I ask again . . . do you believe in God?"

"I did until maybe an hour ago."

"What happened?"

Chad shook his head. "I . . . I can't explain."

"Sure, you can. Any experience can be explained; some just take longer than others."

"You wouldn't believe me."

"You wouldn't believe what I wouldn't believe."

Frustrated beyond words, scared beyond belief, angry beyond reason, Chad decided to do it. It wasn't even an issue of trust. Up until today, he knew Tyler by name and reputation only. It was the same reputation that would keep this secret hidden in plain view. So, what if Tyler knew? So, what if Tyler told anyone, the whole world; no one would believe him. Whatever vice was crushing him enough to make him turn to a twelve-step program was enough to keep him from being a credible source of information.

Chad let his emotions flow through his body and change him. Much less painful and much easier than the first time, he turned into a rabbit.

Tyler took another long drag and then leaned forward, resting his elbows on his thighs, hands dangling by his knees. As before, he let the smoke leave his mouth at its own pace. Through a gray veil, he finally said, "Well, this is interesting."

CHAPTER 15

Chad paced along the path he had created in the straw and dust.

"Dude. You're making me nervous," Tyler said right after taking a swig of beer and before licking the rolling paper. Tyler had been gracious enough to allow Chad to spend the night. Chad had to use Tyler's phone to send his parents an email stating that he was spending the night at Cooper's. This was the third beer and second joint of the morning for Tyler.

"Are you sure it's not all the pot?"

Tyler laughed and lounged back on his hay bale couch. "This? This is the breakfast of champions. *You* need one to calm down."

"I can't calm down."

"Okay. I know what you need. You need a meeting."

Chad stopped pacing. "A meeting? Like an addiction meeting?"

"Yes, an addiction meeting."

"But . . . but I'm not addicted to anything."

Tyler took a drag. Without a single wisp of smoke escaping, he asked, "Aren't you?"

"What could I possibly be addicted to? No, I'm not addicted to anything."

"No?"

"No! The only things I do are go to school, game with my friends, and get my ass kicked by life. School is okay, and I love gaming, but I've never skipped class to play. I've never hurt myself in any way to spend one more minute with a game."

"What about the other thing?"

"Getting my ass kicked? I certainly don't enjoy that!"

Tyler sat up and regarded Chad with those eyes that bored into his soul. As he spoke, the smoke seeped out from his nostrils. "There are many theories about addiction, one being that we don't crave the highs, rather the lows. Alcoholics can have crippling hangovers, yet they start drinking as soon as one hangover ends to get to the next one. Overeaters sometimes keep eating past the point of pain. How often do you think in a gamblingaholics meeting someone shows up and says they're there because they can't stop winning? Hey, I knew the downside of what I was doing, yet I couldn't stop myself until I found the twelve steps."

That was the perfect invitation to ask Tyler about his addiction, but the stoner had struck a nerve. How could he possibly imply that Chad enjoyed getting bullied by Mason and company? *No one* could enjoy that! But what did he do to stop it? Sure, no one should be bullied, but the world didn't work that way, and Chad knew it. He never once went to a gym or even researched ways to gain muscle. The closest he came to a martial arts class was glancing at flyers or playing through the tutorial mode on a new video game. He never once tried to rally his friends to come up with a plan to strengthen themselves. Instead, they'd complain about how the strong felt entitled to attack the weak and never once explored ways to become strong themselves. The first time he decided to do something about it was to trust others, hoping they could turn him from weak to strong. Instead, they did what the strong always do—attack the weak.

As much as Chad hated to admit it, maybe Tyler had a point. Chad didn't like his station in life, but there might be some unconscious, compulsive need never to stray from it. Addicts needed to hit "rock bottom" before they could improve, so maybe this was his? If so, he would need help. Help from his friends. It was time to tell them the truth. As soon as he had woken up, he texted them to meet at Tyler's barn. The sounds of tires on gravel let him know they just arrived.

The trio got out of the car and walked toward the barn. Chad was happy to see Kyle out of the house but started to worry about how he would handle this news, the exact reason why he freaked himself out into a near coma two days ago.

"Chad?" Cooper called out as soon as they entered the barn. "What forms of mischief might you have planned that would involve the use of farm buildings?"

"Hey." Chad stood in the center of the area; his hands folded together in front of his body. He didn't know what else to do.

Heston laughed and pointed to a pile of straw in the one corner. "Chad said, 'hay.'"

Tyler laughed as well, but it was halfway through a pull, and he coughed smoke out of his nose. Once finished, he shook his head and lounged back on his couch. He gave a single wave of his hand as a salutation. " 'Sup?"

Cooper looked around Chad to address his host. "Tyler, correct? Thank you for your hospitality and for offering our friend sanctuary."

"*De nada*." Tyler smiled and took another drag. He extended his hand to offer his joint.

"No thanks. That stuff makes me paranoid."

Heston ambled over and sat on the other end of the couch. He accepted what Tyler offered. Holding his breath, he shrugged his shoulders in response to the looks of surprise he received.

Cooper looked Chad from head to toe with the over-exaggeration of a stage actor. "So . . . is this why you summoned us? To participate in some form of barn pot party? Is this your new lifestyle now? No wonder you can't locate your phone. Probably lost it while wondering through a purple haze."

Heston laughed, noises quickly turning to snorts and wheezes. Once finished, he said, "Pottery barn."

Tyler laughed as well and handed Heston a can of beer.

Chad was wearing a white t-shirt with a large green cannabis leaf on it, and black nylon shorts, the only clothes Tyler deemed clean enough to lend to another human being. "No, this isn't my lifestyle. I lost my phone because of what happened last night, and no, I wasn't wandering through a haze, purple or any other color. I've . . . I've been lying to guys recently."

"Obviously."

"You . . . you may want to sit down for this."

Kyle accepted the offer and sat in an armchair, the size of the hay bales making it more like a throne for a giant. Cooper refused and assumed the stance of a jilted party demanding answers, frowning with his arms crossed over his chest. Chad nodded and then started to pace the small circle he had created earlier. "Okay, so I met with the Ink Stains a couple nights ago."

"Yes, this we knew. Or is this a part of your lies?"

"Sort of. The part about the fight was a lie."

Cooper sucked his teeth and threw his hands in the air. "So, what happened? Did they pants you like the football players would have?"

"No. The fight was a lie. It was *more* than just a fight. Much more. The Ink Stains killed Mason and the other two missing football players."

Kyle drew his knees to his chest, and Heston muttered, "Whoa."

Cooper became more agitated. "Wait . . . what? Did you witness this? Were you a *witness* to a homicide? If you were, then you should have contacted the authorities."

"It's not that simple."

"Not that simple? It. Is. Murder. I wholeheartedly understand you being in a complete and utter state of shock from being a part of such atrocity, believe me, I know I would be, too, but contacting the authorities is the only option."

"Well . . . it wasn't technically a murder."

"Okay, Chad, now you're not making less sense than the fourth edition of *Dungeons & Dragons*. How was it not murder? Did the Ink Stains end the lives of Mason and his friends or not?"

"They did. But then they ate them."

Kyle shrank further in on himself, and Heston gasped again. Cooper's face became a stage; every facial feature engaged in a performance of confusion. "They're . . . cannibals . . . ?"

"No. Lycanthropes." Chad hurried to get the word out of his mouth, any form of hesitation, and he would have lost the nerve to say it and fumble around trying to concoct an improbable lie. Silent tears rolled down Kyle's cheeks, and Chad felt awful about being the cause of them. He knew what he had to do next and the heavy guilt of how that would make Kyle feel hung around his heart and dragged it down to his gut. He took off his shirt and stepped out of his shorts.

Despite his initial bout of speechlessness, Cooper found his voice long enough to blurt, "Dude! Why have you been so eager to show me your naked ass these past couple of days?"

"Because I need to show you something. Something you wouldn't believe otherwise. The Ink Stains are all lycanthropes. They all changed into different animals and attacked, killed, and ate Mason and his friends. They offered me their power. They offered to make me one of them."

Kyle trembled, shaking harder and harder after every word Chad spoke. Chad wanted to stop, but he had to do this to make sure his friends understood. After showing Tyler last night, he changed back and forth a few more times. It hurt less each time; weird aches replaced the extreme pain. He didn't need to concentrate as hard either, a conscious act, but no more difficult than squatting or making a fist to start the process. The tingling started as his internal organs moved about, and then intensified as the fur poked through his skin. The transformation took less than a minute this time, and the unpleasant sensations passed just as quickly. He hopped a few times in a circle and changed back into his human form. "I accepted their offer."

CHAPTER 16

Chad stepped into the shorts and slid the t-shirt back on. His friends reacted just as he suspected they might. Kyle buried his face behind his knees and sobbed. Heston and Cooper offered gape mouth silence. Tyler lit another joint.

"Wha . . . ? Wha . . . ? What . . . ?" Heston tried to ask but couldn't make it past the first word. Tyler passed over his joint, and Heston took a big puff from it. Releasing a cloud of smoke, he finally finished. ". . . the fuck?"

Cooper turned his body just the slightest bit, enough to make the fastest escape possible if events led to that need. He ran his teeth over his bottom lip and squinted. "I don't think I could arrange my words quite as eloquently as that, but I certainly do share the same sentiment."

"Sorry for not giving you enough warning, but you wouldn't have believed me if I didn't show you."

"I would have believed you," Kyle spoke into his knees, his voice small and timid, a terrified child trying to be brave in a dark room.

Chad looked at his friend, curling in the corner of the hay bales as if they could offer any form of protection. "I know. I know you would have, and I know I should have told you sooner. About all of it. About how this is probably what happened with Justin. The Ink Stains turned him."

"Into a rabbit? Like they did with you?" Cooper asked.

"I don't know. Maybe something different. All the Ink Stains were different. Hunter is a wolf, and Dylan is a bear. Viper and Kat are what their names are."

"So, why in the name of all that is holy did they choose to turn you into a rabbit?"

"They didn't choose. I think . . . I think this is who I am. What's inside me or my spirit animal or whatever."

"You chose to be a rabbit?"

"It wasn't like they handed me a character sheet and some dice where I could roll for traits. They performed a ritual, and I turned into a fucking rabbit."

It was Chad's turn to strike the cross-armed pose of a jilted party. "This was why I didn't want to tell you."

Cooper exhaled and ran both hands through his hair. "You're right. I'm being an asshole, and I apologize. I'm having a hard time processing that one of my three best friends turned into a rabbit. I just can't . . . my eyes took in the sight of you turning . . . it's all so . . ." Cooper placed his hands on his knees and exhaled again. "Okay. They transformed you. Are you the newest member of the exclusive Ink Stains club?"

"No. After I turned into a rabbit, they tried to eat me."

Kyle squeaked and buried his face again.

Heston moaned, "Fuck."

Cooper straightened his posture and clenched his fists. "What? They changed you just to eat you?"

"They're predators. Evolved predators. They liked the thrill of the chase. Hunter even said something about me tasting better as a rabbit. I don't really know."

"What course of action did you take next?"

"I ran."

"Straight to Tyler's pottery barn?"

"No." So caught up in the situation, Chad had almost forgotten what happened next. "They chased me, and I ran. Hunter and Viper had me cornered, but I was sort of rescued by . . ." Chad chuckled and shook his head. "Okay, you might not believe who saved me."

"Oh, I think we would believe you if you said the Pope rode in on his holy unicorn to save you. Who was it?"

"Whacky Wanda."

Cooper started to walk in a circular path. "Wow. You're right. That is certainly quite a large, scratchy pill to swallow. You're saying that the town derelict swooped in and rescued you?"

"I don't know if she intended to rescue me, but she shot Hunter with a crossbow. Natalia shot Viper."

Everyone snapped to attention. Even Kyle lifted his head and asked, "Who's Natalia?"

"She's a girl I met the other night. She's a lycanthrope hunter. And she punched me in the dick."

"So, you turned into a rabbit, and this girl punched your dick?"

"No, she punched my dick the night before."

"Seriously?" Cooper stopped pacing and stood with his shoulders frozen at the highest point of a shrug. "Who is this mystery girl, and why all the dick punching?"

Heston sat back into the hay sofa again and took another swig of beer, but not before adding, "I'm mad that you didn't tell us you met a girl."

Chad closed his eyes and pinched the bridge of his nose. He reminded himself that he was tossing a lot of confusing and fantastical information at his friends all at once and doing a poor job of presenting it. Inhale. Exhale. Start from the beginning. "After the Ink Stains slaughtered Mason and his friends, I ran home and did nothing, hoping someone would find the scene of the attack. I realized that probably no one would, so I went back the next morning and discovered that all evidence of the night before was gone. I wasn't the only one looking for evidence. Natalia was there."

Heston raised his hand and asked, "Is that when she—?"

"Yes! That is when she punched me in the dick. Don't ask why, because it is not pertinent to this story." That, and he loathed to think about how Cooper would react if he mentioned that Natalia was so gorgeous that he couldn't control an erection, warranting the subsequent punch to it. Which was the same reason why he had yet to mention that he had seen Kat naked. "Anyway, I went to Clinty's looking for the Ink Stains, and that's when I met her again. She said her name was Natalia, she was a lycanthrope hunter, and she was looking for the Ink Stains, too. She warned me not to try to find them, but I . . . I just wouldn't listen."

"So . . . did you happen to get her phone number?" Cooper asked.

"What? No! I wasn't trying to hook up with her." Chad's response was almost shrill, way more defensive than he had hoped for.

"I didn't say that you were! It just made sense to exchange numbers. It seemed like you two were searching for the same thing."

"Well, we weren't." Why was he so upset by Cooper's accusations? It was a logical question that he would have asked in the same situation. Maybe he should have asked for her phone number?

"Obviously, she wasn't looking to get turned into a rabbit."

"Well, neither was I."

"Okay, so . . . now what?"

"Now? Now I need your help to figure out a way to go back to being human."

"What about the Ink Stains?" Kyle asked. He still had his knees pulled to his chest, but he was more attentive, looking at whoever spoke.

Chad looked away to wipe a stray tear from the corner of his eye. He had tried to ignore the thought of the Ink Stains knowing where he lived. His family could be in danger at this very moment, and he might have even put his friends in danger by telling them. No! There was safety in numbers. There were three football players from this town and one high school student from the town over recently missing. Killing Chad's friends and family would only attract attention, the very opposite of what the Ink Stains wanted to do. But if Chad figured out how to become human again, would that be enough to make the Ink Stains leave him alone? "I don't know."

"Let's find Whacky Wanda," Heston's voice came from within a cloud of smoke.

Cooper slapped both of his hands against his cheeks and slowly dragged his fingers down his face. "Find a known crazy person who we now suspect is hunting the very thing that Chad had just turned into. Are you stoned already? That suggestion makes no sense."

Kyle released his legs and scooted to the edge of the hay armchair. "Actually, it does make sense. It might solve both problems. If we go to her and tell her what happened, she might know a way to reverse what happened to Chad. If there's anyone who would know how to do that, it might be her. Plus, she's a hunter. We help her find the Ink Stains, and she'll take care of them for us."

Us. Chad liked the sound of that. He wasn't sure about the plan, but it made sense, and they at least had a logical place to start. And he was thrilled that Kyle was the one who came up with it.

Smiling, Cooper walked over to Heston and massaged his shoulders. "Excellent suggestion, my friend! Excellent suggestion, indeed. Shall we depart and track down Whacky Wanda, who is apparently our new savior?"

Chad looked down and grabbed two fistfuls of his t-shirt. "Is it okay if we swing by my house first to change?"

CHAPTER 17

Chad stared at himself in the mirror. Naked. This made him blush, uncomfortable with this. He wasn't a big fan of what he saw. He wasn't skinny like Cooper, and he was bigger than Kyle, but he couldn't help feeling like he was nothing more than clavicles, elbows, and knees. Especially if he thought about the naked specimens of the Ink Stains. Sure, Viper was thin, but he had very defined muscle tone, and an eight-pack worth of abs. Chad had none of that, and it became more obvious when he recalled how physically perfect Kat and Hunter were. Even though Dylan seemed overweight, he still had plenty of muscle to support his size and a snake between his legs bigger than what Viper could turn into. Chad wondered if "manscaping" would help better display his package to make everything look bigger.

Nope. Chad closed his eyes and shook his head. Comparing penis sizes with a man who could turn into a bear was not the point of this exercise. Control. He wanted to control his new ability.

He opened his eyes but couldn't keep his gaze upon his body. Instead, he looked everywhere except for his reflection. Behind him, his bedroom was tidy; clean clothes put away, dirty clothes in the hamper, bed made, the piles of papers and books on his desk stacked neatly. He looked for more ways to procrastinate. No! No more stalling. Not wanting to admit that he was a rabbit didn't make him any less so. This was the point. Facing reality, no matter how unsettling it was to behold.

First things first. Turn into a rabbit. He wanted to focus on what it felt like, what changed, what moved. He tried to watch the process, but it still hurt too much to keep his eyes open. Bones twisted at the joints, the shifting muscles pulling them this way and that. The itching. God, the itching as fur sprouted from his skin. A hundred times the annoying agony of letting his chest hair grow back after the only time he shaved it off.

Done.

The pain was minimal and subsided quickly. But a rabbit was within the mirror. Human-sized, but a bunny, nonetheless. Brown fur. Long ears, but not floppy. White puffed tail. A burn ignited behind his chest and climbed the ladder of his neck, stopping behind his eyes. No. No crying. Not this time. This wasn't the time for tears.

Chad tried to stand on his hind legs. At first, he thought it worked; his front feet were off the ground, but he realized he merely rested on his haunches. That was a start, he could stand from here. His legs shook, and he pushed with his feet. Bad electricity radiated from his knees and down his back legs. He dropped forward to his front paws, and the pain subsided. After a minute to collect himself, he tried again. Haunches. Balance. Push. Pain. Four more attempts yielded the same results. He changed back to his human form.

How did the Ink Stains do it? Each of them could control their transformation, stopping halfway to garner the best of both human form and animal form. Obviously, they had more time to learn all the ins and outs of the process. *More practice*, Chad thought. *More practice*.

Into rabbit form he went, much easier and faster this time. The process still created unusual feelings within him, but the numbing effect of experience kept everything within a tolerable discomfort. But try as he might, he couldn't get the creature in the mirror to become bipedal. He went back to human.

Twisting at the waist, he stretched sore muscles. How did they do it? Hand behind his back, he pulled his elbow. He then rolled his shoulders and shook out his hands. His hands. Maybe it wasn't so much trying to start at the end and move forward, but start at the beginning and move slowly toward his goal? Why not try to make the human more animal instead of the other way around? Chad liked this idea and decided to start with his hand.

He went to full rabbit.

Going back to human was getting easier and faster as well, so there was at least one benefit, but that was just a byproduct. This time he held his hand out in front of him and concentrated just on his hand. Just his hand. Change the hand. The urge to change consumed him, the same kind of desire to jump into a warm bath after coming inside from walking through snow. He fought it, muted it, forced the yearning to his fingers. The discomfort he didn't want, the itching he wished to ignore, he pushed it into his hand. His fingers thickened; his palm calloused to padding. Fur covered his arm, *only* his arm.

His arm went back to its human form as soon as he stopped concentrating. He did it! It wasn't impressive, but it was a start. Shifting his other arm was faster, but he still needed to concentrate. His legs were next. It hurt his head to concentrate so hard, but both thighs and downward changed, thickened, bent, angled. Like a bizarre satyr, he had rabbit legs. Excited, he hopped up and down on them, but misjudged his strength and smacked his head on the ceiling. One hundred percent human, he flopped to the floor.

Laughing, he stood and massaged the point of impact. Who he saw in the mirror was different now. This was someone who could take control of his life. This was someone who could change himself. He didn't become quite the form of superhero he had envisioned, but he was impressed with what he had been able to do thus far. Striking the pose of feet shoulder-width apart, fists on hips, he nodded to the person in the mirror. He then wondered if he'd someday be able to make positive modifications to what dangled between his legs. As fast as thought, his hips and surrounding areas turned to brown fur, and a puffy white tail burst from his ass. "My dick! Where'd my dick go?"

He transformed into rabbit mode.

But he went back to human just as quickly and grabbed his genitalia with both hands. "Oh, thank God. Thank God. Thank you, God."

As if to forever secure his most prized possession, he put on clothes. He then flopped down in his desk chair. He needed to meet with his friends soon to find Whacky Wanda. But first, he needed to search the internet to see if rabbits had dicks.

CHAPTER 18

"I wonder what his demons could possibly be?" Cooper posed the question to the group but stared at the thirty-two-ounce cup within his death grip.

"Who and/or what are you talking about?" Kyle didn't look around at anyone else at the table either, instead focusing on the patterns he made in the ketchup with a French fry.

"Tyler. Chad had mentioned that Tyler lives and breathes the concepts of a twelve-step program. After watching him share a few beers and a couple of joints with Heston in what he considers his abode, I can't help but wonder what habit he has that he feels is strangling his life to the point where he needs the assistance of others. Gambling? Internet? Sex?"

Chad was scanning the mall for Whacky Wanda. Any other time he and his friends take a respite in the food court, they usually had to pretend to be interested in something at the opposite end of the mall to avoid eye contact whenever Wanda meandered through. Now that they theorized she could be Chad's lone hope of going back to a normal life, she was nowhere to be found. They had been at the mall for two hours now with no luck. Scanning the sparse pockets of humanity took little brainpower, so he was able to pay attention to the conversations. The way Tyler had unwound last night was by playing poker for real money on his phone for an hour, so the addiction he was trying to kick was neither the internet nor gambling, and before that, he had tried to get Chad to explore the possibility of being bisexual. Chad had no desire to go into any of those details, so he just turned to his friend and shrugged a shoulder. "I don't know. Maybe one of those? Or none of those?"

"Dude." Heston nodded to Cooper's drink and timed his words with the lip-smacking mastication of his burger to minimize the spray. "You're gonna need a twelve-step program if you have another one of those."

Cooper's legs jittered, pumping up and down from the balls of his feet as if trying to keep the beat of bumblebee wings. "I'm nervous. My compulsion to fidget rears its ugly head when I'm nervous."

"That's your sixth one."

"I hardly believe anyone would think that's a quantity to get alarmed about."

"It's—*literally*—over a gallon of soda."

"The cola to ice ratio is always skewed away from the consumer's favor in these cups. I would challenge the validity of any claim that I ingested more than a pint and half of soda."

"That's what all addicts say."

Kyle smiled, and even Chad chuckled.

Cooper stood and tossed his cup into a nearby trashcan. "Okay, fine. Let's help me cleanse my system of this demon juice by doing yet another lap around the mall."

Hands in his pockets, Cooper led the way, Kyle and Chad close behind. Heston had to shove the remaining half of his burger into his mouth while hastily clearing the table of wrappers and napkins but caught up. While they walked by storefronts, Kyle and Chad stayed closely behind Cooper and slurped loudly from their drinks, giggling after each swig. Their fun was short-lived when Brick and two other football players turned the corner.

"Look who it is, guys," Brick said. "A group of suspicious characters."

Behind him were the same two from the last time. During the ride from Tyler's barn to Chad's house to the mall, Chad filled the group in on some of the side stories. Cooper and Kyle knew who these guys were. Emmanuel was the largest of the three. There were undoubtedly massive amounts of muscle hidden beneath his sagging chest and round belly, or else he wouldn't have been considered by college sports pundits to be the best nose tackle in the state. Orlando was a wide receiver, not an ounce of fat on his body to slow him down or hide his lean muscle. Brick was a defensive end, the new breed of monster designed to have the size to crash through the offensive line and speed to obliterate the quarterback. Chad still wasn't entirely sure what all those terms meant. After years of abuse from members of sports teams, he never learned anything more than the lone fact that most sports had some form of ball. Cooper loved fantasy sports—just another form of *Dungeons & Dragons*, he'd always say—and Kyle learned the rules by using console and controller to play them.

Heston slowly moved behind Kyle, as if he thought he could hide behind the smallest member of the group. The ever loquacious Cooper kept his mouth shut, his jaw muscles flexing. Chad's heart revved like a racecar engine, ready to zoom out of his chest at the first sign of green light. Brick was far more terrifying than Mason. Chad had grown up with Mason in his life. The football player's motivations for torment were flimsy, but Chad knew what they were, knew what to expect. Whenever Mason got bored or needed to assert himself, he'd deliver a few bruises or brush-burns to Chad. It was a shitty deal for Chad, but he knew Mason. He had no idea what lurked behind Brick's eyes. Whatever motivated him was far more pointed, the outcome far more dangerous. "What do you want, Brick?"

"What do I want? Well, I want to know where my friends are. They've disappeared, and they've been gone long enough for the police to finally open an investigation. Being the good, law-abiding citizens, the three of us did a little investigating of our own. A few of our teammates said they saw Mason and Billy and Spence run into the woods right by the practice field. We went to investigate. It took a while, but look what we found."

Brick pulled a cell phone from his pocket and showed the case to everyone. Lightning in the background with two twenty-sided dice set ablaze in the foreground. Chad's phone. He had thought about going back to that spot in the woods this morning to look for it but decided against it. That area now frightened him. Bad things happened there. He should have guessed that something bad was going to happen by not going back.

Brick turned the phone so everyone could see the screen. It came on with a push of a button, and access was granted with a single swipe of his finger. A dozen app icons hovered over an image of a grim reaper holding a flame thrower standing on a bed of skulls. Chad had hoped beyond hope that he would see something about this phone to prove that it wasn't his, but that hoped shriveled like a salted slug with every icon tap and screen swipe. This was a nightmare that his nightmares would have.

His contacts list had very few names on it, but each one had a picture. Brick identified Chad's friends by pointing at them and scowling. "The little one is Kyle. The tall, skinny one is Cooper. And moobs is Heston."

Still holding the phone for everyone to see, Brick continued to tap and swipe. "What else do we have here, Chad? Looks like a lot of texts between the four of you about meeting with the Ink Stains . . . about the Ink Stains fucking with Mason . . . about meeting up with the Ink Stains to fuck with Mason on the day he disappeared."

Chad felt his insides twist and wondered if he was subconsciously turning into his rabbit form. He couldn't take his eyes off his phone, so he ran his hand up and down his arm checking for fur. What if he did turn into a rabbit? Rabbits ran fast, faster than a bear, a wolf, a snake, a cat. He could grab the phone, turn into a rabbit, and run . . . or the phone would fall to the ground when his fingers turned into paws. And if he did miraculously figure out how to keep his fingers in rabbit form, then what? What would Brick do to his friends? How would Brick and his football buddies react to Chad being *more* of a freak than what they hated already?

"My phone?" Chad didn't plan on saying those words, let alone as squeaky-voiced as they came out.

Brick pocketed the phone and stepped closer to Chad. He could only stare at Brick's massive chest while the large man growled, "Yeah, I'm going to keep that. It might help the police in their investigation. If they find out that you were involved with the disappearance, then the police will be the last of your worries."

The football players walked away, mingling with the moderate flow of people strolling around the mall, leaving Chad and his friends to process what just happened. Police. More threats. Giant humans wanting to cause harm. These were all new flavors being added to his already piled high craptastic sundae. The cherry on top was now all his friends were involved.

Kyle and Heston each ran a finger along their bottom eyelids, swiping away tears just as they formed. Cooper's body tensed as his eyebrows pinched, and lips puckered. He was the first one to find his voice. "Why in the name of all the gods in all the pantheons did you not password protect it?"

"I did, but I got annoyed that I needed to change it every friggin' month, so I disabled it. I figured the worst things on it were some embarrassing pictures of us goofing around."

"Well, lucky for us, you figured wrong."

Heston put his hand on Cooper's shoulder. "Dude. You're not helping."

"He's right . . . ," came from behind them. All four jumped and jerked. Whacky Wanda.

". . . but I can."

CHAPTER 19

"Police. He's going to go to the police. I'm going to jail." Kyle sobbed, bottom lip twitching. He started crying as soon as Wanda led the foursome through an "employees only" door to a brightly lit, painted cinderblock walled hallway. Heston attempted to console him by rubbing and patting his back.

Thanks to his overly-protective parents, Kyle barely had the faculties to make it through regular, day-to-day life, let alone a large man threatening to expose a damning secret right after learning one of his best friends was a lycanthrope. Kyle sometimes needed to call a time out if a *D & D* campaign became too intense, so Chad was a little surprised that Kyle was handling things so well. He said the one thing he could think of to help, "The only person who would be going to jail would be me."

"Are you so sure about that?" Cooper asked. "All of our names and texts are in a non-password protected phone, readily available for all the world to see."

"All of the texts are of you and Heston trying to talk me out of going to meet the Ink Stains and conjecture about how Kyle was doing. Kyle, you weren't involved in any of those texts."

Kyle got his breathing under control, and the tears slowed. "No?"

"No. And the only texts that could be considered threatening toward Mason are the ones we sent to each other bitching about him after he did something dickish to *us*. Those texts would do more harm than good to Brick's case."

Cooper shook his head and waved his finger. "*Au contraire, mon frère.* If anything, those hateful texts would show motivation. That's even if those texts still exist anymore. Now that Brick has unfettered and unpassword protected access to those texts, he could just delete them."

"I can see why Chad kept secrets from us," Heston said.

"Wait? What?"

Heston squeezed Kyle's shoulder before he walked closer to Cooper. "He's our friend, and he made a mistake. Yes, it adds extra fear to each of our lives, but he had no way of predicting the course of events that led to this moment. He came to us for help, and you've been shitty about it this whole time. So, yes, I can see why he kept secrets from us."

Cooper turned his back and ran his fingers through his hair. By the time he turned around, his hands were sliding down his face, creating a caricature of himself. Finished, he put a hand on Chad's shoulder. "Heston, you are correct in the analysis of my shittiness. Instead of using the opportunity to build a bridge to be closer to my friend, I instead was selfish and constructed a moat to further the distance between us. For that, Chad, I am sorry. I will, from now on, be your humble servant through this crisis."

"Oh, Jesus Christ on a stick, what the fuck are you four going on about?" Wanda looked from one to the other until she got to Chad.

"We're upset that a few of the football players found my phone and might tie me to the disappearances of the other football players."

"Anywhere in your phone, does it say, 'I helped the Ink Stains murder and eat a bunch of jocks'?"

"No."

"Then you got nothing to worry about."

"But—?"

"Really? A bunch of knuckle-draggers hopped up on steroids is the threat? Not the group of people who can turn into real-life mythical creatures and eat you all in a matter of minutes? Morons versus monsters, and the morons are scarier?"

"But—?"

Wanda swatted the back of Chad's head. "You're lucky I don't put a spike through your heart. Is that what you want? I can do that, you know. I have my crossbow in my truck. You can wait right here while I go get it. Is that what you want?"

A billowy steam cloud moved through Chad's body from the ice of fear mixing with the fire of embarrassment. "No, ma'am."

"Okay. All of you need to quit bitchin' about what ain't important."

All four now hung their heads and said in unison, "Yes, ma'am."

"Good. Normally, I'd just kill Chad and get it over with, but since he's a rabbit, I don't see the harm in letting him go. For now."

"Actually, I don't want it."

Wanda scowled and moved closer to Chad. He still expected the stench of coffee and cigarettes, maybe even stale booze, not the softness of vanilla. She was a little shorter but loomed larger. The intense look in her eye. Her thick, frizzy hair liberally streaked with gray pulled back into a ponytail. Chad suddenly became afraid when her face was close enough to count each of her crow's feet. She even had a bit of a growl to her voice. "What did you say?"

"I don't want this . . . this . . . curse."

"Then what did you want?"

"I wanted . . . I wanted . . . strength."

"You wanted a different animal. You wanted to be one of them. You wanted to run around and kill and eat people with no regard for the morality of your actions."

"No! I just wanted to be stronger than I am now."

"Then hit a gym. You want to kill. You want to be like them."

"No! I . . . I . . . I would have been different than them."

"You wanted something, and when you received it, it didn't align with your expectations, and now you don't want it anymore. Sounds like every fucking person in this world."

Chad didn't know what to say. She was wrong, but she was right. He thought he didn't want to be like them, thought he didn't want to kill. But why have the power of the Ink Stains if he wasn't going to use it the same way? It was clear to him that she wasn't going to help him remove the curse, remove the rabbit from within. He would have to learn how to live with it. That thought made him want to cry right now.

"Wanda?" Cooper stepped forward. He reached out to touch her but pulled his hand back as if she suddenly burst into flames. "Wanda, please. Do you know how to reverse what happened to him?"

She chuckled. "Of course, I do. You can't be a hunter for as long as I have without learning how to do that."

"Can you . . . can you please help him?"

She squinted and stared into Chad's eyes. "Why should I do that?"

"He doesn't wish to be like them. He made a misguided attempt at trying to find an easy solution to a much more complex problem. He made a mistake."

"Some mistakes can't be fixed."

"You said this one can, and I believe you. Did he mess around with mysteries that should have remained unsolved? Yes. We all have, at some point in our lives, even you, right? Think about how different your life would have been if someone gave you the opportunity, gave you the desired assistance to fix the mistakes that were fixable. An honest mistake, that's all he did."

Wanda's eyes were the color of tombstones. Unblinking, she continued to stare at Chad, judging him, weighing his worth as a human being. Chad wondered if this would be yet another one of life's tests that he'd fail. "Okay. I'll help you reverse what happened to you if only to shut Cooper up. He talks so damn much."

"Amen to that," Heston said.

"Hey!" Cooper replied in mock indignation. "I resemble that remark very much, thank you."

Wanda turned away, and Chad inhaled. He hadn't realized he was holding his breath, the air now tasting sweeter with hope and possibility.

"So . . . ," Kyle started, his voice small again. "What do we do?"

Cooper started to pace, taking two steps to the wall, turning, taking two steps to the opposite wall. "Well, as I see it, we have two distinct and unsettling problems. Problem number *uno*—the jocks, as our esteemed guide to what lies behind the veil so succinctly put it. Even though it is doubtful that there is enough legitimate evidence on Chad's phone to get anyone in trouble with the police, Brick and his friends exist on a different plane of reality, where they feel the rules of normal law-abiding citizens don't apply to them. If they think that we're involved with the disappearances of their friends, then we could be in serious trouble. Problem number *dos*—the Ink Stains. They want to eat one of our best friends. Hmmm. Maybe . . . maybe we could get the two sides to fight against each other?"

Heston slapped his palm to his face. "What are you? The samurai from *Yojimbo*? Do you really think you have the skills to mastermind such a feat?"

"No, obviously! All we really have to do is let Brick and his friends know lycanthropes exist and let their blind ignorance and xenophobic nature take over. Like Yoda said—ego leads to hatred, hatred leads to the jocks fighting the Ink Stains."

Wanda stood next to Kyle and nudged him with her elbow. She pointed to Cooper and said, "See? This one talks too much."

Kyle smiled and nodded in agreement.

Heston face-palmed again. "Are you even hearing yourself? How are we going to do that? Let's say we even know where to find either Brick or the Ink Stains, which we don't, how do we get them to meet? Set up fake profiles on Tinder and trick each of them into meeting that way?"

Wanda stepped forward and held out her hand, signaling everyone to stop talking. "Okay, I've had enough. The Ink Stains aren't going to give a shit about your jock problem. They've already caused the disappearance of three jocks and few more people in this area and were taking a pretty big risk with trying to eat Chad, so it's highly unlikely that they'd kill three more people, even if provoked by them."

Cooper snapped his fingers. "Oooh! Maybe we could find a way to leverage that information to our advantage. Maybe—"

"No. Let me rephrase my earlier comment—*I* don't give a shit about your jock problem. I'll help Chad reverse his curse, and then I'm going to kill the Ink Stains and any others like them. I don't care about meatheads. That's your problem. Do we all understand?"

"Yes, ma'am," everyone mumbled.

"Okay. The first step is actually finding where their lair is."

"I think I can help with that, Aunt Wanda . . . ," echoed in the hallway after the entrance door slammed shut. Natalia. Ignoring everyone other than Wanda, she finished, ". . . I found their den."

CHAPTER 20

The oily stench of burnt carbon was still in the air. The fire happened over a decade ago, yet inside the building, the smell remained. Of course, after it had happened, no one came in to clean it up. The mining company that owned this place did what any other company in the twenty-first century would have done—left the structure as a monument to progress and relocated.

Chad had known about this abandoned West Bend coal depot, just as everyone in the area had. It sat just far enough off the two-lane highway between the mountain and the railroad tracks to be noticed, but not an eyesore. The structure was a simple one: four stories of graffiti-tagged metal and broken windows with a hopper in and a spout out. Once upon a time, trucks would haul coal from the mines to here, then it was loaded into train cars, and off it went. The fire was serendipity—or an insurance scam, depending on who told the story—for the mining company because it saved a ton of money by moving the operations to South Bend.

Someone still owned it, though, Chad reasoned, because it served as a dumping ground for trains and tracks. Every year or so, a stack of gnarled railroad ties or a dilapidated train car would appear during the cover of night. This made Chad feel uneasy about trespassing. There was a lot about wandering around this building at night to make Chad feel uneasy. It was dark. The moonlight pouring through the window openings helped, but it mingled with the shelving and conveyors to create paranoia-inducing shadows. This was also the enemy lair, and the enemy wanted to eat him.

According to Natalia, only Dylan and Viper were skulking about the depot. Hunter and Kat were off either getting food or fucking. Or both. Chad didn't like being here, but he was very happy that the two lycanthrope hunters were with him. He didn't like the plan either, though simple enough—sneak in, grab the Elder Blood, and get out. If they stumbled across any of the Ink Stains, then Wanda and Natalia would distract them while Chad took the prize, tossed it in his fanny pack, and ran. He had done hundreds of insert-steal-extract missions using a monitor and controller, or paper and dice. Now it was time to put that experience to practice.

"Ow," Chad yelped, as hushed as possible. Wanda and Natalia were in front of him and stopped. Both women wielded crossbows, now pointing at Chad. He held out his left hand. Barely audible, he whispered, "Splinter."

Wanda rolled her eyes and turned around. She continued to follow the massive shelves filled with charred wooden boxes and soot caked tools, damaged beyond value. "Sissy."

"It hurts." Chad moved his hand to the nearest beam of moonlight and dug at the wooden sliver.

Natalia moved close enough to him that the sweet scent of cinnamon overpowered the smell of burnt coal. He could also feel the anger radiate from her in hot waves. "Seriously?"

"Look, it's bleeding now."

"That's because you're picking at it."

"It's really deep."

Natalia grabbed his wrist, tight enough to cause more pain than the splinter, and angled his hand in the moonbeam to examine it. "Transform your hand. The padding on your paw will be thick enough to push it out."

"I'm . . . I'm not really good at that."

"Really? Why not?"

"Because I've been a lycanthrope for less than twenty-four hours."

"Shhh!" Natalia hissed.

Chad didn't realize that he had been getting louder. Why was she so mean? Didn't she understand this was difficult for him? Sure, she tried to warn him against meeting with the Ink Stains, but she couldn't have predicted this any more than he could have. She continued, "Just try it now."

He had hoped he'd never needed to try. He wanted to slip in, grab the Elder Blood, get out, and have Whacky Wanda mix up a cure. Life was never that easy, was it? All he needed to do was concentrate. No worries if he went full rabbit—he was dressed for the occasion. He wore baggy nylon athletic shorts that should stay on his body even after the change as well as a very oversized t-shirt. His shoes were old slip-ons that he wouldn't miss if they got left behind. Even if Brick somehow found them, he would need specialized equipment to match Chad's DNA. *Stop being distracted! Concentrate!*

Chad took a deep breath and focused on his hand. Like he practiced in his bedroom, he conjured the feelings he needed to change but tried to guide them, limit them to just his hand. The familiar tingle, the accompanying itch, ran from his shoulder to his fingertips. Sparks of pain popped throughout his hand from shifting bones. He was ready for it, though, willed it to continue. Brown fur sprouted from the back of his hand and forearm, golden in the moonlight. His palm turned to padding, and as Natalia predicted, the splinter popped out. "I did it."

"Shhh!"

"Sorry." Chad couldn't help himself. Even though he didn't want the ability to transform into a rabbit, he was delighted that he was able to use it with such a great deal of control. Maybe if this plan failed, there would be hope for him after all? Doubtful. If this plan failed, odds were he would get eaten within the next few days.

Natalia continued onward. Chad transformed his hand back to human form and followed her. He crouched as he walked, in a perpetual state of ducking. He had no idea why he was walking this way. He had no idea where they were going, or even what they were looking for. Head swiveling, he looked from side to side, up and down, all around the room and in every shadowy corner. He was so preoccupied with what was around him, he lost track of what was in front of him and ran into Natalia when she stopped.

"You're a pervert. You know that, right?" she whispered.

Chad removed his hands from her hips. "No."

"No, you don't think that you're a pervert, or no, you don't know that you are one? Either way, you need to seek psychiatric assistance."

"Shhh!" Wanda hissed. She pointed to a small office about forty feet away, soft light emanating from inside. "That's most likely where they're keeping the Elder Blood."

Natalia punched Chad in the shoulder and then moved next to her aunt, "What's the plan?"

Wanda pointed to a workbench twenty feet away. "Chad, you hide behind that. Natalia and I will flush out Viper and Dylan. When we do, go inside and get the Elder Blood."

"Okay. Then what?" Chad asked.

He wanted to ask what to do if the Elder Blood wasn't there, or if he couldn't find it. But he was too afraid and hoped that Wanda would cover such contingencies in her answer. All she offered was, "Then you run."

Chad didn't like this plan, but it was the only one they had, and he followed it. He scurried over to the workbench, a massive piece of wood-topped steel bolted to the floor that could probably withstand a nuclear assault. It might have to, depending on how mad Wanda and Natalia made Viper and Dylan.

Crouching with his back against the bench, Chad tried to control his breathing. These missions were less stressful from the safety of his couch with a video game controller in his hand. Wanda and Natalia crept into the room where they thought Dylan and Viper were. They were right. All Chad could do was clutch his fanny pack with both hands and listen to the sounds. The distinctive twang of two crossbow bolts being fired. The crashing of two bodies flailing around a small space in surprise. The growl of a bear and the hiss of a snake.

The women ran past Chad on either side of the desk. Neither looked back; they just sprinted into the cavernous area and disappeared among the shadows. Dylan and Viper followed, both in their animal forms. Chad held his breath until he could no longer see or hear them. The building was quiet except for the sound of his heart drumming inside his head. It was a game of hide and seek that he was thankful not to be playing. If he wished to stay a nonparticipant, he needed to get his fear-petrified legs moving.

The office was small, a place for storage, not for sleeping. A few chairs were placed about old-style desks, lining three of the four walls, immense and crafted to last. The shelving of what was left of the charred credenzas were being used. One desk was almost overflowing with laptops, speakers, cell phones, tablets, all resting within nests of wires and cables. Two tablets atop the only cleared space on the desk were on, one in the middle of a mobile game, the other streaming a show.

Chad poked around the gadgets a bit and pushed some wiring around but didn't have high hopes that what he was looking for was on this desk. A desk against the side wall looked more promising. Chad didn't like the human bones piled on the one side, desperately trying not to think about how they were once inside of a person, maybe even Mason. Keeping his focus on the other half of the desk, he rummaged through goblets and medallions, rings and crowns and necklaces. A few flasks. There! Atop the credenza were two racks. They were wooden and had four layers, each layer with twenty-five holes in a five by five

Satan's Petting Zoo

pattern. One rack was empty, but the other had a liquid-filled glass vial in each of the hundred holes. Jackpot! Each vial looked like the one from his ceremony, the liquid just as familiar. Chad couldn't quite reach the rack from where he stood, so he cleared a small spot on the desk just large enough for his feet. Closer now, he grabbed the rack and lifted it from the credenza. Completely unprepared for how heavy it was, the entire rack slipped from his hands. It slammed against the edge of the desk and crashed to the floor. Broken glass and Elder Blood went everywhere.

Human heart racing faster than his rabbit heart; he jumped off the desk and prayed for a miracle. Amidst the shards slicked with Elder Blood, he found an unbroken, stoppered vial. As if holding an egg, he wiped the blood away and examined it for cracks. The vial in his shaking hand was the cause and solution to all his newest problems. He put it in his fanny pack and turned to leave.

Then stopped.

What if Wanda made a mistake while making the cure, and they had to do this all over again? What if the Ink Stains found more people much more worthy of becoming members of their gang, adding to the number of creatures who wanted to eat Chad? Chad ran a quick risk-reward ratio in his head and determined that he could spend one more minute to see if any other vials survived the fall. In the time it took him to count to sixty, he had found five more vials. He grabbed them, zipped up his fanny pack, and hurried to the door.

Ever so carefully, he peeked into the main room. He didn't see or hear anything. Tiptoeing, he made his way to the closest exit of the building—a doorway with no door attached to it, just a fallen beam leaning at a diagonal across the opening. One tentative step, then another. Nothing happened. He tried two more steps, then another two. The opening was getting closer. He just had to be careful of the beam once he got there. Licking his lips, he could almost taste freedom and debated about sprinting to his goal. Just as suddenly as that thought crossed his mind, the world changed.

The sound of clanging metal reverberated through the building. Chad rushed to the nearest work table and ducked behind it. Something large was slamming against the grated concourse that lined the wall ten feet above the ground. Hungry growls mixed with the steel squeaks. The growls intensified, and Chad brought his knees together to stave off his bladder's wishes, but he looked out from behind the table anyway. A large figure and a smaller one on the walkway. Chad's eyes adjusted to the white light of the moon. He couldn't see the details, but he saw enough. Dylan and Wanda. The bear roared and lunged at Wanda. He must have connected—Wanda's scream overpowered the clanging metal. A second figure appeared and ran to Wanda. Natalia, her crossbow ready. The bear reared up again, massive claws ready to slash. Crossbow bolts! Both hunters shot Dylan. So close, each shot hit the bear. With little room to move or escape, Dylan flipped over the railing and hit the ground with an echoing thud. Dust billowed up around his body.

Natalia ran to Wanda, prone and holding her left leg. Arm around her shoulders, Natalia helped her aunt stand. "Run, Chad! Run!"

The command could not have been more simple or direct. He jumped up and aimed for the doorway to the outside once more. He was greeted by fangs and claws.

Viper, in half-human, half-snake form, lunged at Chad, but missed. Chad leaped completely over the table to the other side. Surprised he was still alive, Chad took a breath and looked down. His legs were rabbit legs, but everything above his waist remained human. He partially transformed without even thinking about it! No time to celebrate or mentally process what happened. Viper slithered around the table. Even his forked tongue looked ready to strike. One last thought zipped through Chad's mind—*rabbits have strong legs.*

Chad grabbed the table and kicked. Bracing himself against the table, he lifted both feet off the ground and put every ounce of energy, power, muscle he had into one kick. Both of his feet connected squarely with Viper's chest, launching his attacker across the room. Viper's arms flailed, and his tail spiraled into a coil as he flew through the air. One more metallic clang as he hit something across the room.

Chad smiled, proud of himself for overcoming his fear and fighting back for once. Despite his new abilities saving his life, he still wanted to be rid of them. His fanny pack had stayed in place, the contents safe. His shorts remained on as well, but his shoes were no longer on his feet. Wanda and Natalia were gone. They escaped. The only other possibility for their whereabouts was Hunter, and Kat had returned and caught the women unaware. That seemed unlikely. If that happened, there would still be a lot more noise. In any case, it was time to go.

Chad kept his rabbit legs for the entire run back to Tyler's barn.

CHAPTER 21

Chad looked out the barn window again. Cooper came up behind him and said, "Remember, Rome wasn't built by watching a pot that never boils."

"Yeah, I know. I'm just worried."

"About the lovely Natalia?"

Cooper's words had a suggestive tone to them, and Chad tried to dismiss them, but his cheeks warmed from a blush. "About both of them."

"I'm sure they're probably back at their secret lycanthrope hunter lair patching Wanda's leg. Those two are professionals. This is what they do."

Chad turned away from the window and walked to the hay bale coffee table, the only items on it being the six vials of the Elder Blood. Like the last visit to Tyler's barn, Heston sat on the couch with Tyler smoking pot and drinking beer, Kyle sat on the oversized armchair, and Cooper couldn't relax enough to sit down or even remain still. He looked out the barn window just as often as Chad. "I know," Chad said. " I'm just anxious to reverse the process."

"What are we going to do after that?" Kyle asked. He had returned to his default position of sitting with his knees to his chest and his arms wrapped around them.

No, Chad didn't want to talk about what was next. It wasn't good. There was so much "not good" happening in his life right now that he wanted to cling to the hope of Wanda making a cure, the one good thing that he could see come to fruition. *If* Wanda ever arrived. "Shouldn't we focus on curing my curse, first?"

"I think it would certainly behoove us to at least assess the different situations we find ourselves in," Cooper said.

"Cooper's right," Heston said, holding his breath to keep his recent toke inside his lungs.

"Okay." Chad acquiesced. His friends got sucked into his drama because he kept secrets and lied. He wasn't about to do more damage by arguing against something he didn't want to talk about. "What do we think comes next?"

"Well, first and foremost are the Ink Stains," Cooper said, strolling closer to the coffee table, looking at the vials as if he were addressing them instead. "They know you've absconded with their Elder Blood and destroyed whatever else they had left. That makes you, and potentially by extension, us targets for their wrath."

"That's what Wanda and Natalia are for. They hunt lycanthropes and know where the Ink Stains have been living," Chad said.

"What if the Ink Stains regroup and strike while Wanda is injured? Will Natalia be able to handle four bloodthirsty creatures by herself?"

"She seems capable."

"Other than punching you in the dick, have you experienced her lycanthrope fighting prowess?"

"A little. But I don't think the Ink Stains will do anything too crazy right now. Three college football stars disappeared in the same week that Justin disappeared, and that's after two *other* high school kids disappeared. We now have three neighboring towns on high alert. If something happens to us, anyone of us, the Ink Stains know I know where they're hiding out. I'm sure they don't want the cops involved more than they already are."

"Speaking of the cops . . ." Kyle's voice was fragile, almost too afraid to leave the safety of his mouth. ". . . what do we do when they question us about the disappearance of those football players?"

Chad kept his tone even, calm. He didn't want to spook Kyle any more than he already was. "You don't really think Brick would give my cell phone to the cops, do you?"

"Honestly, I'd rather him do that than think we were involved with Mason and the other two," Cooper said.

"What? Why?"

"Do you even know Brick? Or Emmanuel? Or Orlando? I never thought I'd utter these words, but I'd rather deal with Mason. Sure, over the years, he beat the shit out of us and humiliated us, but he had limits. Did you guys see the look in Brick's eyes? He. Is. Terrifying."

"We've accidentally replaced Mason with something worse," Heston summed up.

Chad sighed and ran his hand through his hair. "Okay. I agree that Brick is much scarier than Mason, but he's a potential problem that could go away if we ignore it. The police will be investigating for weeks. Brick threatened us to see if we knew anything. If we keep our mouths shut and stay out of his way, things will calm down, and he might move on with his life."

"Do you really think that will happen?" Kyle's voice warbled and cracked, tears imminent. "We all just agreed that Brick is *worse* than Mason. Do you think Mason would have let something like this go?"

Cooper reached out and grabbed one of the vials. Holding it in the palm of his hand, he stared at it. "During this entire conjecture, I've been hearing 'if' and 'might' and other non-concrete words. Intermingled with all those words of speculation were hopes of some potential outcome or another. Please let Wanda handle our one problem. Let's ignore our other problem. We're being passive in our own lives. There is one *known* factor right here, one *known* factor that would help us with our problems."

A chunk of ice dropped into Chad's gut. Did Cooper suggest this curse was salvation? Chad wanted his friends to help him out of this problem, not join him in it. He made a mistake, and Cooper wanted to fix it by everyone else making the same mistake. "No. No fucking way. You can't be serious."

Cooper's expression was hard, almost angry. "Why not? It took you less than a day to figure out how to use your ability, and you used it to *fight back*. Why is that you've ignored everything that you've actively done recently? You *sought out* the Ink Stains, you *met* Natalia, you *fought* Viper and won, you became *something more*, yet these are all details that you gloss over when talking about it. What you've focused on was that you ran from Mason, you ran away after you were transformed, you ran from the Ink Stains lair, and that you were tricked into this whole situation. Don't you understand? You're so used to being passive that you can't even consciously recognize when you do something active. I'm just as guilty. All of us are."

Chad's hands trembled. He folded his fingers together to make them stop. Cooper was right. Being tricked into the situation was what he focused on, what felt normal within his thoughts, as well as hoping someone else could solve his problems for him. Trying to take control of his life didn't feel normal, so he always assumed it would end badly because he had never tried it before. He wanted to better his life and viewed the failed efforts as mistakes. Maybe he was looking for an easy way out or some form of a quick fix, but at least he *tried* to do something about it for once. Maybe reversing his transformation wasn't the answer. Maybe having his friends join him was.

Cooper turned to everyone else and continued. "Look, I don't know what I will turn into. Even if I turn into a rabbit like Chad, it will elevate who I am, make me into something more than I am now. One cannot climb Maslow's pyramid by passively waiting around. And one cannot reach the top without assistance from those one loves and trusts."

Kyle got out of the chair and grabbed a vial. For once, he wasn't pale, wasn't wide-eyed, or on the verge of tears. "I'm scared. I'm scared of what will happen if I drink this. I'm scared of what happens if I don't drink this. I've lived my whole life not drinking this vial because I didn't know it was an option. For once, I want to drink this vial. For once, I want to make the choice to drink this vial."

Heston handed his joint to Tyler and set his beer can on the coffee table, took a vial, and stood with Cooper. "Same."

Everyone turned to Tyler. Through half-shut eyes, he offered a lazy smile. "I'm a no go, bros. I'm content being content."

Cooper, Kyle, and Heston unstoppered their vials and looked at Chad for guidance, for approval.

Chad nodded.

The three friends drank.

CHAPTER 22

"Okay. Anything?" Heston asked.

"No." Cooper looked down at himself and held out his hands, examining them. "Nothing for me either."

Kyle asked Chad, "How long did it take? Did you feel anything?"

Chad took the empty vials and looked at them as if one of them would have instructions. "It was instant. And it hurt."

"It hurts?"

"The first time, really bad. The more you do it, the easier and less painful it gets. You all should have changed by now. I don't get it."

"Okay. So, we drank the Elder Blood like you did. What else happened during the ritual?"

"Well, like I said, we got naked—"

"I'm not getting naked!" Cooper shouted.

"— and we danced and drank."

Tyler held up his can of beer. "Got plenty of booze here if you guys need any."

"Do you think that's the missing factor?" Kyle asked. "The alcohol, not the nakedness."

Chad nodded toward Heston. "I don't think so, because Heston's half drunk and he's just as unchanged as you and Cooper."

Heston responded with a lip-flapping belch.

109

Kyle waved his hand in front of his face to dissipate the cloud of Heston stench. Heston laughed, and he rejoined Tyler on the hay couch. "Okay. So, after the naked dancing and drinking—"

"Still not getting naked!" Cooper reiterated.

"—you drank the Elder Blood, and then you immediately changed."

"Yes, I—" Chad cut himself short, shaken by a memory punching his brain. "No! It wasn't immediate. First, Kat kissed me."

His three friends gasped in disbelief. Tyler whistled and laughed. "Grabbin' Natalia's ass, kissin' Kat while naked. You're a man-whore, dude."

"Kat's gorgeous," Heston said. "You're my new hero."

"Thanks. She is. But that's not the point of what I just said."

"Are you sure?" Cooper asked. "She is a rather incredible package of womanhood, and you not only got to see her sans encumbrances but got to exchange a rather intimate gesture. Why is it the most interesting things you've done in the past eighteen years of existence are the stories you fail to recount with the group?"

"Because, even though she's gorgeous and hot with amazing tits, she only kissed me as part of the ritual to turn me into a rabbit so she could eat me!"

"So . . . does that mean *we* have to kiss you to make it work?" Heston asked.

A flower of ice blooming within his chest, Chad shook his head and whined, "Oh, God, no. No. No. No. No."

"If that's the ultimate step to this process, then it must be completed," Cooper said.

"Who's going to go first?" Kyle asked.

Cooper closed his eyes and inhaled deeply. "I should go first. I have been less than a stellar friend and a constant source of turmoil to Chad throughout this process. It was my idea to do this, and I shall fall on my sword for it."

"Oh . . . oh, dear God, please . . . No . . . ," Chad continued.

"Dude, you shouldn't be so *phobic*," Tyler said as he lit another joint.

"Me? Cooper has been repeatedly screaming out about not getting naked in front of us ever since we got here."

"An individual's feelings about public nudity and discriminating against someone's sexual orientation are mutually exclusive concepts."

"Discrimina—? I've never discriminated against *anyone*, let alone someone with a different sexual orientation than mine."

"It's obvious you've never kissed another man before. Have you ever sat down and thought about it? Really searched your soul and wondered about any form of sexuality other than hetero?"

"Well, no, but—"

"Sounds pretty discriminating to me."

"Stop!" Chad held out his hands as if they would shield him from Tyler's words. This was all too much. It wasn't about sexual orientation; it was about crossing a line with his best friends, three individuals he grew up with, and had known since the earliest development of motor skills. Kissing Cooper would be a relationship altering act that couldn't be undone. Who was he kidding? Pretty much every event that had happened in the past two days created a relationship altering act. The fact that his friends had stuck with him through all the secrets and were willing to change their own lives in order to save his was a testament to their friendship. "Let's stop talking about it and just do it. Tyler, I promise I search my soul later, but for right now, this is an uncomfortable, yet necessary situation, so Cooper, let's just get this over with."

Tyler raised both hands in the form of surrender. "It's your truth, man, as long as you own it."

Cooper rolled his shoulders and bent his neck from side to side, limbering up for the task at hand. "I am of the same mindset as Chad. I find great discomfort with the task at hand, but not because of any form of phobia, for I am far more enlightened than to feel such useless emotions. I have explored and categorized every facet of id and ego to develop my own truth unique to myself. I will probably not like this."

"Ditto," Chad said, moving closer to Cooper.

Cooper shook out his hands and did one last full-body shimmy before approaching Chad.

The two stood face to face, as best as Chad could muster since Cooper was over four inches taller. He stood on his toes just as Cooper crouched down. Finding the stance awkward, he went back to flat feet, and Cooper adjusted accordingly. Neither of them could look each other in the eye; Cooper's gaze was downward while Chad stared at anything behind Cooper.

The men inched closer. Chad mustered every incident where he anticipated Mason hiding behind a corner or walking toward him in school. This dread had the same effects—racing heart, shallowed breathing—but somehow felt much worse, much more real. Chad parted his lips as Cooper puckered. Chad puckered right as Cooper parted his lips. Their mouths moved closer.

"Was there tongue involved?" Cooper asked, his face mere inches from Chad's.

Worms of disgust squirmed through Chad's belly. The intolerable situation just became worse. There was, but he just couldn't get the words out of his mouth. Maybe remembering that night was the best way to survive this? Kat, naked and approaching him, her hungry tongue running across her blood slicked lips. Her . . .

"Stop!" Chad yelled, jumping backwards. "Blood!"

Cooper ran the back of his hand across his lips and then looked at it. "Am I bleeding?"

"No, but she was," Chad answered.

"She? You mean Kat? Kat was bleeding?"

Chad laughed and grabbed an empty beer can from the floor. He pinched the center of it and folded it in half, one way and then the next. He repeated this, as he explained. "Yes. She bit her lip hard enough to draw blood before she kissed me. It was her blood that completed the process, not her kiss."

Cooper bent forward and placed his hands on his knees. "Whew. Thank God."

Heston got off the couch and approached Chad. Kyle joined them, too. "What are you doing?"

Chad folded the beer can faster, stopping intermittently to pull at the top and bottom. "We don't have anything sharp enough around here to draw blood, so I'm going to rip the beer can in half to create a jagged edge. I'll use that to make a controlled cut along my forearm and then—ow! Shit!"

The beer can separated into two halves but sliced Chad's palm as it did so. A small pool of blood flowed up from the cut in his skin.

Heston reached out and gently dabbed his index finger in Chad's blood. "Was there . . . Did she use a lot?"

"Ow, fuck! No. Just enough that I could taste it."

Kyle, eyes wide and skin pale, dipped his index finger in next. Cooper followed suit with no theatrics or rhetoric. Chad squeezed his hand shut and stepped back. All three of his friends looked to him, his blood slowly dripping down their index fingers. He wanted to say something inspirational, meaningful, or even something pithy like a movie hero would in this situation. Words failed him again, and all he could do was nod his head.

All three finished the ritual.

All three screamed in pain.

CHAPTER 23

A ferret.

A pheasant.

An ox.

The ox was a little smaller than what Chad imagined a full-sized ox would be, but the other two were much, much larger than what nature ever created as examples for these animals.

Chad didn't know how to feel. On one hand, he felt an immense form of solidarity as a member of a very exclusive club. It was an unusual club that he never wanted to join, but his closest friends decided to face an immense level of risk to join it with him. On the other hand, they were too similar to him—all prey animals. Sure, the ferret and pheasant fed on insects, and an ox had horns, but none of them were anywhere near the top of anything food-related—chain, pyramid, chart. Maybe the top of a menu. Chad was certain that the Ink Stains would prefer ox over anything else.

"Umm, dude . . . ?" Tyler interrupted Chad's train of thought. He stood on the couch and reached up to grab the bottom of the loft. With the expertise of a parkour master, Tyler flipped himself onto the loft above. From behind the safety of the banister, he finished his thought. "I don't think you thought this through."

Tyler was right. There were a hundred ways to have done this, and Chad felt like this way was the worst possible. First, they should have done this one at a time. Let one of them change, offer support, then wait for him to figure out how to shift back before moving on to the next member of the club. Second, a mirror. Even though Chad had been severely disappointed in becoming a rabbit, it helped to know what had happened. Third, create a relaxing environment, because focus was needed in mentally processing what had just happened and figuring out how to change back. Panic was the last thing needed for the situation, but since Chad completely botched steps one and two, panic was all his friends had.

Cooper, as a ferret, spun in circles to get a look at himself until he sat upon his haunches and twisted his flexible back to look at his tail. Pointing at it with his front paw, he squeaked and hissed. He twisted the other way to look at the same spot and hissed again.

The angry noises from Cooper must have upset Kyle because the pheasant fluttered its wings and jumped backward. Wings spread out, he continued to run backward while staring at his clawed feet as if trying to flee from them. As expected, he backed into a wall. This startled him, and he launched forward with enough force and wing flutter to leave the ground. Warbling in fear, he flew right at Heston.

Much like Cooper, Heston craned his neck to see his hindquarters. The large pheasant flapping his direction caused him to release a high-pitched moo and rear up on his hind legs. When he came down, he ran away from Kyle. Right toward the hissing Cooper. Heston turned, his hooves tossing up dust and hay as he clomped along the floorboards, and ran right into one of the hay bale armchairs. Through an explosion of straw, Heston sped up despite his face being covered in hay.

Until he crashed headfirst into a support beam.

The entire barn shook from the collision as Heston dropped to the ground.

Chad ran to his friend but didn't know what to do other than impotently watch. Lying on his side, all four of Heston's legs twitched. His head bobbed up and down as he made a throaty noise, a cross between a pained snort and a moo.

"Heston!" Cooper, in human form, started to his friend but stopped next to Chad.

"Oh my God, he's having a seizure." Kyle was in human form as well and stood on the other side of Chad. "What do we do?"

"I . . . I don't know." Chad had to deal with a lot of feelings these past few days; many were ones he never experienced before. But this feeling of helplessness was the worst. His friend lay twitching on the ground, possibly dying, and

Chad had no idea what he could do to make the situation better. "Heston? We're here. We're all here."

Kyle's voice cracked, and Cooper ran his hands through his hair, but they both added words of encouragement. Chad tried to remain positive, but tears threatened to form at any second. But they could be tears of joy as Heston's front hooves turned into hands. His back hooves transformed as well, giving way to stubby-toed feet. The bulky body of the ox slowly gave way to the bulky body of a human. On his side, Heston's right arm covered his face, and his whole body jiggled as he sobbed.

Guilt hung from Chad's heart like an albatross, dragging it down into his gut. He should have thought this through. He should have made them do this in a more controlled way. He should have stopped them. It was because of his shortsightedness that his friend hurt himself and was lying on the ground crying. No . . . wait . . . not crying? Laughing?

Heston sat up as his belly shaking laughter died down to wide-grinned chuckle and wiped away a stray tear. "That. Was. *Awesome!*"

"You scared the shit out of me!" Cooper yelled as he helped Heston to his feet. His frown didn't last long and gave way to a smile. Chad and Kyle laughed as well, joining Heston and Cooper. The four friends shared a group hug. Until Cooper jumped away from the pack and used both hands to cover his crotch while looking skyward. "Naked people!"

Both Heston and Kyle pointed to each other and shared another round of laughter followed by a round of howling. Chad wasn't as uncomfortable as Cooper, but kept his eyes above the horizon, fully expecting Tyler to lambast him for being phobic. Instead, the owner of the barn peeked over the edge of the loft and asked, "Everything okay down there?"

"Yep!" Heston called out, "But I think we made a mess. I broke one of your chairs. Sorry about that."

"No worries, dude. I keep all the important stuff up here. Including . . ." Three t-shirts, along with three pairs of nylon shorts, came flying over the banister.

Chad distributed clothing but noticed that the t-shirts displayed the name and wild artwork of different heavy metal bands and snorted. "They get the cool shirts while I got one promoting pot, which I am very not into."

"Don't be phobic!" came from the loft above.

"How can I be phobic about pot . . . ? I'm not phobic! I'm not phobic about anything, other than maybe dying."

"If you're really afraid of dying . . . ," came from the entrance to the barn. Natalia.

She was pointing her crossbow at him and looking none too happy. ". . . then you better tell me what the fuck is going on here."

CHAPTER 24

"It's not what it looks like!" Chad stepped forward and held out his hands.

The butt of her crossbow snug against her shoulder, Natalia growled, "No? Well, it looks like I have to kill you all for lying to my aunt and me and tricking us into *risking our lives* to get the Elder Blood so your idiot friends could become the vilest creatures on the planet."

Heston raised his hands over his head as if on the wrong side of a bank robbery. His shorts fell to the ground and caused Cooper to cringe.

"We didn't lie," Chad said, stepping between Natalia and his friends.

Natalia squinted, anger clipping her words. "Hmmm. I guess, technically, you didn't lie to us by withholding that you wanted the Elder Blood for your friends. That just means you manipulated us to do your bidding."

"No! It wasn't like that at all."

"It sure seems like it is. My aunt took a claw swipe to the leg for you, Chad. And for what? To start a little army of Lycanthropes?"

"No. Quite the opposite."

"Sorry, Chad, I'm just not seeing the picture you're trying to paint."

"You and Wanda . . . We just . . . Okay, can you put that down? You're making me *really* nervous."

The light in the barn caught the green of her squinting eyes, setting them ablaze with an ethereal fire. She stared at him hard, weighing her options. He had no idea what emotions they were hiding. They didn't have the contempt of Brittany's eyes, or the hunger of Kat's, or the pity Mrs. Sedgeweck usually reserved for him. Or it was a mixture of all those emotions?

Natalia lowered her crossbow, but kept both hands on it, implying there was no amnesty yet. "Paint me a picture, Chad."

Chad exhaled. "Thank you. We were waiting for you and Whack . . . your aunt Wanda. We were getting nervous for you two. Scared, even. We wanted to wait, wanted to take our minds off what might have happened to you, so we started talking about our other problem with Brick and his friends. I know, I know, that doesn't mean anything to you and your aunt, but they are a problem for us. A real, legitimate problem. We started to speculate what would happen if Brick took my phone to the cops or if Brick decided to dish out his own brand of justice. We don't know what he's going to do next. So, we started talking about how our friendship carried us through a lot, through hard times because of people like Brick. We got into a 'safety in numbers' mindset. We wanted to protect ourselves against those who had power over us."

Chad's words had an impact, though he wasn't sure what kind. Natalia's expression softened as he talked as if she were watching a four-year-old struggling to open a jar of pickles. When he stopped talking and allowed her to process what he said, her expression went harder than diamond. "How the fuck does turning yourselves into abominations help your situation with the police? Are you planning on killing them if they start to investigate you?"

"What? No!"

"Sure. I can see it now. A detective starts asking too many questions, then chomp, chomp, swallow. Then they send a couple more to find out where he disappeared to, then yummy, yummy cop in your tummy. Then they send more, and you kill more. Where is it going to stop, Chad?"

"Nowhere!"

"So, you're just going to be a bunch of indiscriminate killing machines?"

"No! Stop! We don't want to kill anyone. We just wanted to protect ourselves against Brick. That's all. He's a psycho, and we wanted to make sure we could survive if he physically attacked us."

"By becoming animals?"

"By becoming animals."

"You can't fight the nature of the beast, Chad. You may think you're in control, but sooner or later, you will become the thing that you turn into."

Natalia was no longer yelling, and Chad took that as a minor victory. She saw his point but didn't understand it. How could she? She was strong, capable.

Being weak was such a foreign concept to her. If there was a threat to her wellbeing, she'd kill it. He just had to prove to her that they weren't threats. "Why do you hate lycanthropes so much?"

Reeling back as if he had thrown a bucket of ice water in her face, she spat, "They're dangerous killing machines!"

"You've seen what I turn into. Do I remind you of a dangerous killing machine?"

"No, but you're still an abomination. You are going against the natural order separating man and beast."

"Not all people are the same. Not all animals are the same. Doesn't it make sense that not all lycanthropes are the same? I mean, am I like all the other lycanthropes? Am I anything like the Ink Stains?"

Natalia gripped the crossbow tighter, not because he posed a threat, but because he was making her think, making her doubt something she had believed in. Her voice held the apprehension of someone who knew a request for a favor was coming, like a ride to the airport or a kidney. "No. . . ."

"Do *they* seem like any kind of lycanthropes that you've known before?" Moving aside, Chad gestured to the trio standing behind him. Cooper had his arms crossed over his chest but still flashed the peace sign. Heston smiled, then sneezed, then wiped his nose with his forearm. Kyle stood between them, but a little further back and waved.

"No. . . ."

"Because we're not. We're not bloodthirsty beasts. We're not like the Ink Stains or all the other lycanthropes you and your aunt have hunted down." It dawned on Chad that maybe she and Whacky Wanda had hunted down others like him and his friends. How many pheasants and oxen and ferrets had they killed? How many rabbit's feet did they have as trophies? "Please. Please look at us differently."

Natalia continued to regard everyone in silence, her jaw muscles flexing. Suddenly, her body went lax, as if her anger had been giving her form, and it suddenly disappeared. Crossbow dangling from her hand like a prehensile appendage, she walked closer to them. "Your motivations for doing this better be what you said they were."

With a grand wave of his hand, Cooper bowed. "I assure you, milady, our intentions are the purest of heart, merely a means of protection."

Natalia sneered. "Okay. Then change."

"Excuse me?"

"I didn't get a good look at what you three are when I first got here. All I saw was a bird, something shaped like a furry turd, and a cow running around."

Heston elbowed Cooper. "Fur turd."

"I choose to believe I transform into a much sleeker, majestic creature than something resembling a 'fur turd.'"

"Quit yapping and change," Natalia demanded.

The trio moved behind the hay furniture and disrobed; Kyle and Cooper were slowly inching their way behind Heston as they removed their clothes. Cooper looked skyward as he dropped his shorts and mumbled.

Natalia addressed Cooper while gesturing to Chad. "Just make sure you have better control over yours than this one has over his. Don't forget, I still have a working crossbow."

"Hey! I have control over my . . . it was . . . a weird situation . . . and . . . context . . ." As Chad stammered, he lost faith in his own words and just let them die in the air as soon as they left his mouth. As he tried and failed to think of something clever to salvage any form of dignity, his friends changed.

They controlled the situation much better this time. No panicking, no impotently racing in circles. Just three animals were standing around: a large pheasant, large ferret, small oxen. Natalia crinkled her nose. "Ugh. What a menagerie. Throw you into the mix, Chad, and I'd be looking at Satan's petting zoo."

"Hey!" Chad barked. Even though she was the most beautiful woman he had ever seen in real life didn't give her an excuse to treat his friends the way Brittany did. "There's no need to be mean."

Natalia huffed and waved her hand in front of herself as if trying to erase away the last words she said. "You're right. That was mean. I'm just trying to process how to tell Aunt Wanda."

"Okay."

The trio changed back to human and put their clothes back on.

"I don't know if she'll be as understanding as I am, but I'll just let her know how non-threatening you four are."

"Hey! Being mean again."

Natalia walked toward the door. "Sorry, Chad. That wasn't mean. That was the truth. You say you guys did this for self-defense, but I've never heard of a chicken, a weasel, a cow, and a rodent successfully defending themselves." With those words, she disappeared into the night.

Cooper gazed upon the ground with a slump-shouldered stance. Heston slouched as well, making his belly look even bigger. Kyle used the back of his hand to wipe away a tear that escaped from his reddening eyes. Chad dug deep. The right words had to be within his soul somewhere, incubating for all these years, waiting for the right moment to hatch.

He opened his mouth.

Nothing came out.

Natalia was right.

"Natalia is totally wrong," Tyler said, climbing down the ladder from the loft. "You guys have a strength that she has never seen before in her life, which is why she didn't recognize it as a strength. The strength of friendship. She had to be cold and closed off because of her lifestyle. There is a certain weakness in that, weakness in blindly fighting something because someone told you to, blindly fighting for something that you don't understand. You guys know why you're fighting and what you're fighting for. Friendship. Each other."

Heston stood straight. Cooper pumped his fists in the air. Kyle smiled. Even though he didn't think of them, the words did make Chad feel better.

Tyler held a beer in one hand and a joint in the other. "Feeling better? All right. Rock on. Anyone want to party?"

The quartet laughed. Chad felt confident enough to speak for all four when he said, "Thanks, but not tonight. It's been a long day. I think we all need a good night's sleep."

Tyler held his beer up in a solo toast. "Very nicely put, Chad. May the lands of Morpheus empower you."

Chad so wished that was an option. He was tired and desperately wanted sleep, but when he finally made it to his house, he found three slaughtered cows wearing football jerseys on his front lawn.

CHAPTER 25

Chad took a swig of his root beer. Flavorless. It wasn't that it didn't taste like anything; it just tasted like any other root beer. This brand was no longer his favorite. How could it be after he had real beer?

Over the years, he and his friends refined their palates with regards to the "sophisticated sodas"; the carbonated beverage flavors ignored by the major soft drink corporations as they battled for the cola and lemon-lime market share. Root beer, birch beer, cream sodas. Even though none of them truly liked ginger ale, they respected it enough to become experts on that as well. Coke vs. Pepsi was a non-issue to Chad and his friends. Snyder's birch beer brewed in town versus Mamma Q's birch beer made one county over? That was a yearlong debate. But after *sitting in a bar*, drinking real beer, the answer to that debate was now a moot point.

The Two Trees Company root beer used to be Chad's favorite. They got their ingredients from two different types of trees, and Chad trained his taste buds to recognize each of the main flavors. He enjoyed how they worked together and played off each other. Now, as he took another swig, it tasted like any mass-produced excuse for root beer that he could buy at a bulk goods store for half the price.

Chad had not particularly liked the beer he drank at Clinty's, but he knew that people held similar debates over which brands were better, which styles were more pleasing. It was one of those situations in life that was a step forward, and one that an individual could not step back from. Heston noticed it, too.

Chad could tell by the way his friend would take a drink and then examine the bottle, sometimes holding it inches from his face as he read the fine print. Chad wanted to tell him that it was the same root beer that he loved for so many years, but it was he who had changed, his psychological ingredients that had been mixed in different proportions because of a new recipe. It was because he took a step forward in life by drinking beer and smoking pot with Tyler. Chad didn't share that information with Heston, though. Sharing conjecture about the different one-way doors a person had to go through in life wasn't why he and his friends were in his basement. They were trying to figure out what to do next. Finding slaughtered cows on his lawn wasn't something Chad had ever thought about until recently.

"So . . . ," Cooper started as he set his bottle of root beer on the table that they had gamed on for over a decade. Round with built-in cubby holes on the underside. Cooper had pulled out his specially made twenty-sided die and absently played with it, spinning it on the table for a few seconds, then stopping it with his index finger, only to repeat the process. "Is Veronica McMasters as hot in real life as she is on television?"

His question was met with three separate sets of glares.

"Oh, come on. I was making a feeble attempt to break the tension and create the opportunity for meaningful conversation. Sitting around in gloomy silence will not solve any of our problems."

Chad almost chuckled. Cooper was right, so Chad played along. "Actually, no. She was wearing so much makeup; it looked like she was a victim of a freak baking accident."

"Did you talk to her at all?" Kyle asked.

"No." His father had told him not to talk to anyone other than the police until the situation was under control. So, when local news reporter Veronica McMasters approached him with a microphone in hand, the best he could offer was a wide-eyed, opened-mouthed, "Uhhhh." The news crew had spent the entire night at the house and were currently still parked out front, but they opted to use the clip of Chad as well as a panoramic shot of the slaughtered cows. "Well, other than my most stellar interview with her."

Cooper chuckled. "Oh, I saw that travesty of an interview, accompanied by the perfectly timed zoom in as well. It was quite meme-worthy. I might just have to make the GIF myself if it hasn't been made readily available yet."

"I was overwhelmed."

"I get that, but that was an epic fail of massive proportions. If you were impersonating a politician getting caught *en flagrante* with a porn star, then you nailed it." Cooper widened his eyes to the point of bulging and lolled his tongue out the left side of his gaping mouth while moaning, "Uhhhh."

Heston smacked Cooper's shoulder. "Don't be a dick."

"Ow! Okay, okay. I'm sorry. I get it. I'm just trying to make the best of a bad situation while simultaneously compensating for my own new and complex levels of fear."

"We're all experiencing these same new and complex levels of fear. Don't be a dick."

Cooper held up his hands and bowed his head. "Yes. Yes, you are correct. Again, I apologize profusely."

"The news segment was pretty short," Kyle continued. "Even though they're still camping outside your house. It was weird knowing I was being filmed while coming here."

"The news crew magically appeared right after the police showed up. My dad told me and Mom not to say anything, so I *technically* didn't say anything."

"Ugh. Your parents," Cooper moaned. "Your dad eyed me like I was the one who put the cows on their lawn. How are they doing with everything?"

Chad inhaled and held his breath. His heart beat slower, yet harder, each second he kept the air prisoner in his lungs. The police stayed for hours. They brought a special crew to examine the disemboweled cows and ultimately took the carcasses away as evidence. After the police left, it was one argument after the next with and between his parents, accusations piling up on top of each other until they came crashing down in the form of tears. His dad asked Chad a hundred different ways what he did to warrant this. His mom reminded his dad that this was the act of a bully. Of course, his dad reminded her that there was always a reason behind bullying. Life didn't occur in a vacuum. Everything that happened to everybody happened for a reason. If Chad was getting bullied, there was a reason behind it. In his father's mind, Chad did *something* to someone somewhere to end up with three dead cows on the front lawn. "About as well as expected."

"It must be hard having a star high school quarterback as a father," Heston mumbled.

Heston's father was no joy either, but Chad raised his root beer as a mock toast. "One that ran for three touchdowns during the state championship."

"At least your mom saw your side of the story," Kyle said.

After a big, boring swig of his drink, Chad raised it in the air again. "The cheerleader who got knocked up by the quarterback her senior year and had nothing else in her life for the past eighteen years other than her son."

"What have you told them?"

"As little as possible. My dad thinks you guys are involved."

Cooper took a long pull from his root beer bottle and placed it on the game table. "No wonder he glared at me like I was his arch-nemesis the entire way from the front door to the basement."

A smirk tugged at the corners of Chad's mouth. "Well, that's because he doesn't like you. Never has."

"Ha, ha."

"It's funny because it's true. He doesn't like any of us," Heston said.

Chad leaned back and stretched. The stress from last night carried through to this morning, and the lack of sleep didn't help. His dad said, "No," to having friends over, but acquiesced when his mom pointed out that Chad needed his friends for support, and it would not do him well to leave and have the news crews follow him all over town. "It's not that he doesn't like you. He does. He said on multiple occasions that he wished the four of us would work harder to release our full potential."

Cooper held up his right hand. Brown fur sprouted from the back of the hand and along his arm as claws grew from his fingers. His palm thickened to padding. "I wonder where this falls within his grand desires for us?"

Chad snapped forward and leaned on the table. With an angry whisper, he admonished, "Dude! We promised never to do that here."

Shaking it as if flicking away water, Cooper's hand went back to normal. He had practiced all last night and most of this morning. "You're correct. We did agree, and I apologize. We, collectively, have a lot going on and are lacking any good ideas regarding how to solve any of our dilemmas."

Still keeping his voice low, Chad said, "Well, at least the cops shouldn't be an issue for now."

"Yeah?" Kyle asked, perking up. "What'd they say?"

"Not much, really. They had already received calls from two of the local farmers. They each reported the missing cows, and then when they looked at their security videos, they saw animals take them."

"The Ink Stains?"

"Almost certainly. The one said he saw a mountain lion, and the other said it was a coyote or wolf."

"Farmers have security cameras?"

Chad shrugged. "Welcome to the twenty-first century, I guess?"

"But the cops didn't ask about . . ." Kyle paused and looked over his shoulder, toward the stairs. ". . . the disappearances?"

"They did."

Kyle gasped, but Chad hurried to finish the story, so his friend didn't pass out. "They asked if I knew why the perpetrators put jerseys on the cows that were the same numbers as the missing players. I told them I didn't know. He asked me a few more questions about our history. I gave him simple answers, that I had known Mason since elementary school, but had zero social interactions."

"Plenty of anti-social interactions, though," Cooper muttered.

"*That* information I did not share. I may be a doofus, but I'm not stupid."

Kyle smiled. "Okay, so at least that dilemma is solved, right?"

Chad sighed. "At least for now. Brick still has my phone with our suspicious texts. If he gives that to the police, then the whole cow situation could become worse."

Kyle's smile faded as he brought his feet to his chair and hugged his knees to his chest. "Oh. I didn't think of that."

"What is the likelihood of that, though?" Cooper asked. "Brick just doesn't seem like he possesses the type of personality where he would seek justice through proper channels. Are we confident that Brick wasn't the one who did this in a misguided attempt to make us 'slip up' in some way?"

"Chad said that the cops said that the farmers said it was animals."

"True. Maybe it's two separate forms of intimidation and threatening behavior? Maybe the Ink Stains slaughtered the cows and put them on Chad's lawn as one message, and the Brick saw this somehow and added the jerseys as another message? The police never said that the jerseys on the cows were the actual jerseys of Mason and the other two."

"Maybe Brick and the Ink Stains are working together?"

"That's not very likely," Chad said. "The Ink Stains hate the jocks as much as we do, which is why we're in this mess, to begin with. And Brick isn't a townie like us, so he barely even knows who they are."

Kyle moved his feet from the chair to the ground. "Okay. Yeah, that makes sense. It'd be horrible to think about them working together. But Cooper's right. Brick doesn't seem like the person who'd just sit back and do nothing, especially now that the jerseys of his missing friends were found on Chad's lawn. I think we need to focus on him first."

"The Ink Stains are more deadly, though," Heston said.

"They are, but Brick could be a more immediate problem," Chad said.

"Guys!" Cooper slapped his hand on top of the spinning twenty-sided die. "I have devised a solution for one of the problems. We *confront* Brick and get Chad's phone back."

"Dude. There are better ways to commit suicide," Heston said.

"No, my dear friend, we will be doing no such thing. Thinking like that is for those who are less than ordinary. Have we forgotten already? Each of us has been imbued with some very extraordinary abilities. We can take him!"

"Our abilities match what's inside of us," Kyle said, his voice quivering. "We're still weak."

"I greatly disagree. We can turn into human-sized animals. Brick may be able to handle all four of us as is, but when we transform, we transform into something he has never seen before. Hell, Heston alone could now take Brick out all by himself. At the very least, we will be aided by the element of surprise."

Kyle and Heston looked at each other, their wide-eyed expressions showing they did not like this plan. "Guys," Chad said, "Cooper's right. The whole reason why I did this was to get an advantage over those who have bullied me. It's the same reason why you did it as well. We may not have become the lycanthropes we hoped, but we're still lycanthropes. We are now creatures that most people on this planet think are fictional or can only be found in legends and myths. We are *strong* now. We just have to stop stopping ourselves."

Kyle's expression softened as he nodded his head. "Yeah. Yeah, Chad, you're right. I may be a bird, but I'm a damn large bird."

"And I'm an ox. I'll stampede him," Heston said.

Laughing, Cooper held up his custom made twenty-sided die. "I shall roll for bonus courage."

He flicked his wrist, and the die bounced to the middle of the table and stopped on the seventeen. All four young men erupted with cheers.

"Hey, guys?" came from the top of the stairs.

Chad and his friends all froze in whatever position they were in when they heard his mother's voice. Terrified by what she might have heard, Chad did his best to keep his voice from cracking. "Yeah, Mom?"

"I just wanted to let you know that the reporters have moved on. You know that set of abandoned rowhomes at the edge of town?"

Chad relaxed, delighted that the local news no longer found any interest in his house and overjoyed that it seemed like his mother didn't hear anything she wasn't supposed to, but he was curious as to what new story could steal the spotlight from cattle mutilation. "Yeah?"

"They're burning down. The fire companies from all three towns are involved, and they seem to think it might be arson."

"Wow! That's crazy."

"What's crazier is the half a cow that they found in one of the units."

"Did . . . did you say half a cow?"

"A whole side of beef. The police are investigating. The good news is you four aren't suspects now."

The foursome participated in a chorus of fake and nervous laughs. "Thanks for letting us know."

"You're welcome. Love you."

"Love you, too."

No one breathed until the door at the top of the stairs closed, and even then, no one spoke. After the minutes of silence caused Chad a pain behind his ribs, he decided to listen to his own hype about being more active in the role of their fates. "Well, I say our primary mission is to get my phone from Brick. However, it now appears that a side quest has been placed before us."

"Side quest?" Heston asked.

"The fire, right?" Kyle added.

"Yes," Chad answered. "I don't know what the cow means, but it can't be a coincidence. I hope it is, but it seems suspicious that someone set fire to an abandoned set of row homes with a half cow in it one day after dead cows appear on my lawn."

"Okay, boys, it looks like we're going to investigate a fire after the authorities get it under control. I shall now roll for luck."

The die landed on the middle finger.

CHAPTER 26

One more minute. They had to wait one more minute before they could investigate the burned-out buildings.

The firemen had put the fire out before the six-unit row homes lost any structural integrity. The left side had been burned down to the studs; the right side had merely been repainted in a layer of oily, black smoke. However, the fire didn't detract from how the building looked mere hours ago.

Located at the end of a cul-de-sac, the building originally started as the first set of townhomes meant to populate the street, and that was meant to be the harbinger to a fantastic neighborhood with office buildings and a mall and more houses. As with any Icarus, the real estate developer's wax wings melted as the bankruptcies, depositions, and lawsuits burned all involved. The townhomes were abandoned before they were ever inhabited, now occupied by the occasional squatter brave enough to chance the drug dealers. The rare time that there was a murder in the tri-town area of The Bends, it was usually here and because of a drug deal gone wrong. The place was so haunted by the ghosts of dead junkies, that the local teens opted for other remote places for secret parties. In a week, adults would whisper under their breaths that this fire was a blessing.

Ready? popped up on Kyle's cell phone.

He typed back, *one more minute*.

Anal retentive was Cooper's response. Chad and Kyle looked at each other and rolled their eyes. Chad agreed with Kyle. The four of them devised a plan, and they should follow it. If specifics weren't important, then why come up with them?

After Chad's mom shared the news about the building, the quartet waited in Chad's basement for four more hours. The building took an hour to get to by foot, and when they arrived, the news crews were packing up to leave, but the police were still around, putting up the yellow tape and doing last-minute evidence gathering. There were no witnesses to interview, but like they did at Chad's house, the police removed the partially cooked side of beef to examine in a forensics laboratory.

Splitting up to get the best vantage points, Chad and Kyle hid in the copse of trees on the left side of the street while Heston and Cooper prowled about in the forest along the right side of the street. After a text conference, the group decided to wait for *exactly* thirty minutes after the cops left.

Chad and Kyle casually walked among the trees toward the building. On the other side of the street, Cooper and Heston attempted stealth and failed miserably. Cooper dashed from one tree to the next, stopping behind each one until Heston caught up using more of a tip-toe technique. Not only were their efforts more visually noticeable than Chad's and Kyle's, but they were also somehow louder.

There were no other houses around, but behind the burned rowhomes was a fifty-foot slope down to the main two-lane highway leading to and from West Bend. Directly across that small stretch of highway were the railroad tracks and the abandoned coal depot that the Ink Stains called home. This fact was not lost on Chad and his friends, as they spent most of the four hours in the basement debating if the rowhome fire was a setup for an ambush. If it was *someone* sending an invitation, then the most likely culprits would be the Ink Stains. The four decided to accept the invitation anyway. This was the time for them to step up and stop being the cowards they thought of themselves as. If this was a trap, then they were armed with the element of surprise. Only a few people knew that Chad was a lycanthrope, and even fewer knew about the other three.

The four met up in front of the building, Heston tripping over the uneven sidewalk. Looking much like a video game hero, Cooper stood with his shoulders rolled forward and a slight bend in his knees and elbows. He balled his left hand into a tight fist while he kept his right-hand fingers splayed wide. "Okay, now what do we think we should do? Do we still think someone is trying to lure us here?"

"Yes," Chad answered. "I overheard the police. They said arson. It seems like someone simply poured gasoline and lit it. Plus the dead cows. After someone put dead cows on my lawn, this arson really seems like a message to me."

Looking at everything from the early evening sky to the shadows on the ground, Cooper nodded. "Okay. Very well then. This was obviously no accident, and there are better ways to destroy a place for insurance purposes. The only option before us is to discover if this was a message to us or not."

They crossed the lawn to the corner of the building where the fire started, but Kyle stopped at the police tape. "Guys. I mean, the police were here. Officers of the law put this tape up. This is serious."

Heston grabbed the caution tape and snapped it in half, letting each end flutter to the ground. "What police tape?"

The four crossed the perceived Rubicon, entering the building through the gutted far wall. Most of the studs remained, but a few had fallen, creating an opening for them to exploit. The sun barely hovered over the horizon, but still cast plenty of light.

"I've never committed a B & E before," Kyle whispered as he turned on the flashlight function of his phone.

"Technically, we didn't break anything," Cooper replied. "It was like this when we arrived."

The first housing unit was the most devastated. They walked through the living room and investigated the gutted kitchen. They could see into the nonexistent second floor while being wary of the detritus scattered about. The far wall separating this unit from the next had been burned to the studs as well, but Heston knocked one of the studs down with a simple push. The second unit looked almost as bad as the first, and they moved into the third unit using the same process as before.

Chad felt a little safer when they walked through the kitchen to the back door. The third unit still had enough sheetrock covering the studs to keep them out of the fourth unit. They exited via the back doorway and entered the fourth unit the same way, all of the doors long gone before the fire.

Cooper and Heston used their phones as flashlights, but Chad had no idea what to look for. Each unit was the same. A large living room in the front, a kitchen and dining room in the back with a powder room built under the stairs to the second floor.

"Should we go upstairs?" Kyle asked as they made their way through the fifth unit, the first unit with a staircase that looked sturdy enough to use.

"No," Cooper answered. "If this is a trap, then it would be sprung upon us during the course of a logical path. No one sets an ambush in an area they *hope* their adversary will go. An ambush is always set up along a predetermined path."

Chad kept that in mind as they crept around the sixth unit. His pulse heavy, the pounding was slow but slammed between his shoulders, the punch radiating up to his ears and down to his gut. The smells from the chemicals used to help extinguish the fire were thick and all around him, contributing to the pastiness forming on the back of his tongue. His fingers trembled. This was the last unit. If the Ink Stains were going to attack, it'd be here. Now.

A floorboard creaked, and Chad spun. No Hunter. No Kat. No death—yet—just Heston mouthing the word, "Sorry," as he crept along, the board offering another creak as he stepped off it. Chad doubted he'd hear the attack anyway. He and his friends had the same abilities as the Ink Stains, but none of the experience. If there was an ambush, they wouldn't survive.

There was no ambush to be sprung. Only debris and walls with smoke stains and graffiti for the cellphone lights to shine on. Chad didn't care about the cause of the fire or what it had consumed. That was for the police to sort out. He focused on potential hiding places, where the enemy might be lurking. Would they jump from the half-bath under the stairs? Were they biding their time in the kitchen? Would they come bounding down the stairs any second now? No, apparently not.

A squeak from the middle of the living room and Chad jerked again. Kyle. His wheezing echoed through the room as he reached into his front pocket and pulled out his inhaler. "Sorry. The smells are messing with my asthma."

Chad walked to the front door and opened it. "Com'n guys. It looks like even though this was done on purpose, it wasn't meant for us."

Alas, he was wrong.

Veins snaking along his crossed arms, Brick stood on the lawn with Emmanuel and Orlando on either side of him. "Oh, it was for you, all right. It was definitely for you."

CHAPTER 27

All the blood in Chad's body rushed to his face, his heart a hyperdrive system delivering pulsating heat to his neck and cheeks. Sweat rolled down his face, in front of his ears, along his jaw to his chin. Earlier this week, he stood face-to-face with creatures that wanted to eat him, yet now he found himself more terrified by the football players in front of him. Maybe because he had successfully fled from the Ink Stains on more than one occasion? Maybe because he had been hunted by lycanthropes for less than a few days while athletes had been chasing him for all his life? It was easier to fear horrors he knew to be true than ones he could only guess at.

He had a limited time before something bad was going to happen, so he slid from the doorway to the lawn, increasing the number of potential escape points. Luckily the football players turned to keep facing him. This allowed Cooper and Kyle egress from the house, and they stood next to Chad. Heston made it no farther than the door, stopping cold when he saw the football players.

"Brick? Did you just say that you did this? You set the row homes on fire?" Chad asked.

The large man extended his arms and gestured to the burned husk of a building. "This piece of shit? I've heard around this lame fuck town that this place was a pimple on its ass. I should be considered a hero for doing this."

"So . . . you burned this place down because you wanted to be the town hero?"

All three of the football players laughed. "You really are a fucking idiot, aren't you? Let me spell it out—after I saw your house on the news and the jerseys of our missing friends on your lawn, it made me want to talk to you, but there were way too many news vans around. The best way to get rid of them was to make another news story. This was it."

"And to lure us here."

Brick smiled, and Chad discovered a new source of nightmare fuel. "Yeah. We grabbed a side of beef from that butcher at the edge of town and tossed it in the fire."

"Why?"

"There were cows on your lawn, so we figured a cow here would be a nice invitation."

"Invitation for what?"

"To talk."

"About what?"

"About the dead cows on your lawn."

"Yeah?" Cooper jumped in, voice cracking as if adolescent. "How do we know that *you* weren't the ones who put the cows there?"

"Sorry, Puberty, it wasn't us."

Cooper shrunk back after the insult, and Chad went back to being the representative. "How do we know that? What proof do you have?"

"Proof? What the fuck proof are you talking about? We didn't fucking do it. *Why* the fuck would we even do that?"

"I don't know. Why would I put dead cows on my own lawn?"

"I know you didn't put dead cows on your lawn. Someone else did. We wanna know why that someone put the jerseys of our missing friends on those dead cows. What do you know that we don't?"

"We don't know what you don't know!"

"We think you do know."

Fists clenched, the three football players advanced on Chad, Cooper, and Kyle.

This was it. Chad had never once tried to stand up to Mason, and Brick was larger and scarier. He had always run away. Not this time! He had power now. The playing field was finally level. This was his chance to take control of his life, to take it back!

Chad slipped out of his shoes while he took his shirt off and dropped his shorts. Brick stopped in his tracks and twisted his face with a look of someone watching the corpse of a loved-one get defiled. But he was close enough to strike.

Appreciating the role-reversal of trying to defend against an ambush to springing one of his own, Chad turned his back to Brick and dropped to all fours. The Neanderthal growled, "What kind of gay stuff are you—?" It was Chad's turn to cut him short by turning into a rabbit and slamming both of his hind feet into Brick's chest.

Satisfaction bloomed within Chad, a tingle of pride and excitement skittered through his whole body. He envisioned sending the mountain of a man into orbit, but he was happy with him going air born for a few feet and then hitting the ground with a thud. It blossomed, even more, when Cooper shifted into a ferret, and Kyle turned into a pheasant. But their attacks weren't quite as effective.

Orlando kept yelling, "What the fuck?" over and over, but he was able to tap into the quickness and speed that made him the team's star receiver. Kyle pecked at him, and the football player jumped away from the beak and dodged the flapping wings.

Cooper, as a weasel, went after Emmanuel. Hissing and chittering, he ran in circles around the lineman. Every other pass, he reared up on his hind legs and swatted with his front claws, his tongue flopping from his mouth. Emmanuel started wide-eyed, mumbling profanities to himself, but his slack face tightened with focus, determination. He no longer just watched Cooper; he was studying him. Cooper went on his hind legs and flashed his claws again. This time when he came down, it was to Emmanuel's fist in his gut.

"Ow, fuck!" Cooper yelped as he fell on the ground and curled himself into a ball. "Mother . . . Fuck!"

Emmanuel strode over to the writhing lump of fur. Chad couldn't believe that Emmanuel had the wherewithal to stand against a human-sized animal and fight it. He also couldn't believe that they hadn't tried to speak in their animal forms until now. "Cooper! Look out!"

The ferret stopped squirming just in time to avoid Emmanuel's foot stomping down. He scurried around the large man again, but this time he swiped his claws with purpose. Emmanuel swore anytime Cooper slashed his skin.

Kyle still had no luck with his attacks. Dirt caked his face from repeatedly pecking the ground, grass blades stuck in the corners of his beak. Small feather tufts floated about as he fluttered his wings, trying to connect with Orlando. The football player finally struck back, an open-handed slap across the large bird's face. Kyle squawked and fluttered again, snapping his mouth closed. The tip of his beak scratched Orlando's arm. The football player yelled and used his other hand to hit the bird.

This wasn't going according to Chad's plan. The extent of the failure became obvious when Brick tackled him. First pain, then the taste of grass and dirt, a flavor he was all too familiar with. He twisted and turned, Brick's fingers squeezing his neck. No! Chad was not going to lose this fight, not going to have his fantasy shattered. There had to be a way out of this.

Feet kicking faster than anything human, he couldn't connect with Brick, but he broke free from Brick's stranglehold. The much larger man kept his weight on Chad and grabbed at any body part he could get his fingers around. Chad just needed to get his back feet to touch the ground. Another twist of the waist, a pull of his hips, and success. He pushed himself up from the ground, but for only a moment. Brick wrapped his arms around Chad's waist and drove him down again. Chad had Brick where he wanted him. Right at his tail.

Chad wasn't proud of himself, but this was a fight for survival in a war, so he turned human. Brick's nose was right between his cheeks.

The football player let go and jumped to his feet. "Fucking fuck!"

Back to rabbit and Chad kicked Brick in the chest again.

No time to rest. He had a moment to help either Cooper or Kyle, whoever Heston wasn't helping. Wait. Where was Heston?

Still in the doorway, Heston hadn't moved. He stood shaking, a look of impending tears on his face. He was the strongest of the four, and he wasn't even in the fight. Chad yelled at him, "Heston! We need your help! Change!"

Heston didn't blink, didn't breathe. He only shook his head.

In between swatting his claws and avoiding Emmanuel's fists, Cooper tried. "Com'n, buddy. We could use any and all assistance you can muster."

Heston transformed. Snorting, the ox stood in the doorway.

The rest of the fighting stopped. Emmanuel and Orlando kept an eye on the small ox in the doorway while they inched toward Brick. The large man stood and used his forearm to wipe the blood from his nose and mouth. "Fuck this freaky shit. Let's go."

The three football players backed away, and when far enough, they turned and jogged.

Chad and his friends had won. They finally won.

Why didn't it feel like a victory?

CHAPTER 28

"Yeah, baby!" Cooper yelled as he jumped mid-step to slap a patch of dead leaves from a branch overhead. The frail leaves exploded into confetti. Kyle laughed as he shook his head to clear them from his hair. Chad ran his hand through his hair twice, not overly concerned if he got them all. Heston just kept walking with his hands in his pockets, shoulders slumped, head down. "The emotions flowing through me are intense and positive and intensely positive."

This wasn't the first time Cooper had expressed his glee. He even used those exact same words. For the past fifteen minutes of walking through the forest, Cooper had been unable to control his outbursts. Chad hadn't been able to muster quite that level of excitement. He had hoped for a more definitive outcome, a true and solid win. It didn't feel right to burst Cooper's bubble, so he walked along with a smile on his face.

Cooper skipped over to Kyle, and play-boxed his shoulder. "That felt incredible, right, Kyle?"

Kyle laughed again and then returned fake punches. "It did. It really did feel good."

"We had and maintained an element of control for the first time since bullies were introduced into our lives."

Fist pumping in the air, Kyle became more animated. "Yeah!"

A branch fell in the distance, but it was loud enough for Cooper to stop his antics and transform his hands into claws and his face to that of a ferret. Everyone stopped as well while he swayed, nose twitching in the wind. After a few seconds of quiet, he changed back to fully human and laughed. "Nothing. I smell not one iota of a living creature even near us."

The four continued to walk. Cooper ran a circle around the other three and stopped with his arm around Chad's shoulders. "Of course, if there were other living creatures, no matter what form or breed, we'd be able to thwart their nefarious plans. Right, Chad?"

Chad's smile faded, and he shrugged his shoulders. "It's certainly a possibility."

Cooper let go and went to the front of the group, but walked backward, an exaggerated bounce with each step. "Oh, come on. We successfully stood up to bullies for the first time in the history of us walking the Earth."

"True. But . . . we didn't exactly kick their asses like we wanted to."

"No, maybe not, but it was, without a doubt, a victory."

"Are we so sure?"

"They fled with their tails between their legs. Metaphorically, of course, because *they* don't have tails; *we* do!" Cooper high fived Kyle; Kyle laughed.

"They really didn't do that. They were surprised at first, but then they grew angry. If they had any fear, they hid it or moved past it. We barely touched them with our attacks, and they fought back."

"Those are all valid points, Chad, but I'm not saying it was a flawless victory. Sure, you could have kicked harder, and Kyle could have been a little faster, and Heston froze, but the fact of the matter is—we won."

"Don't be mean."

"It's true," Heston mumbled. "I froze."

"See?" Cooper loped over to Heston and put his arm around his shoulders. "He knows his performance was lacking. All of ours were. We'll get better in time, with more experience."

"You mean the next time we run into Brick? We've lost the element of surprise," Chad said.

Cooper moved closer to Chad. Walking backward, he looked squarely into Chad's eyes and said, "God damn it, Chad. If you're always looking for defeat, then you will never find victory."

Cooper hurried ahead, grabbing Kyle along the way, pulling him to the front of the small group. The two laughed and shared embellished memories of an event that never really happened. Or did it? Chad wasn't too sure anymore. Was he being so pessimistic that he was ignoring the fact that one of his greatest fantasies had come true? He had always dreamed of finding the necessary bravery to stand up to bullies and possessing the required skills to beat them. No, he and his friends certainly did not kick ass, but they did precisely what he dreamed of. They *did* stand up to bullies. They *did* win. Why was he so determined to find fault?

Maybe because not everyone participated in the win. Cooper was right—Heston froze. Arguably the strongest of the four, he didn't do anything until the very end. Yes, he was the reason why Brick and his friends left, but he could have done so much more. He could have turned the tables much sooner in the fight and ended it before it began. He could have provided the fear that Chad so desperately wanted Brick and the others to feel for once in their lives. Frustrated, Chad couldn't tell if he was upset with Heston for not being able to help, or for Cooper not noticing how upset Heston was at himself for dropping the ball, or himself for expecting so much from Heston. Either way, he would have to work through these feelings later; their destination was in sight—the barn.

Even though it smelled of marijuana, the barn was becoming quite a sanctuary for Chad. He felt safe here. Neither the Ink Stains nor the football players knew of its existence. Having Tyler's wisdom helped, as well. It sometimes made him mad, but there were truth and honesty within Tyler's words. And, as with most times he entered the barn, Chad had no idea what to expect.

Tyler was practicing some form of martial arts using a staff. Masterfully. Well, Chad couldn't attest to how masterful Tyler was, just that his movements were crisp, precise, and fast. Dancing with an implement of potential death, Tyler moved about the center of the barn combining graceful leaps with spins and flips. The rare moments where it didn't seem like he found a way to break free from the tethers of gravity, his feet slid across the ground as if gliding on ice. His hair was tied back in a ponytail, and even that moved in coordination with Tyler and the staff, elegant and purposeful.

John Williams led the orchestra playing in Chad's head, scoring the one-man fight scene playing out before him. Tyler concluded the exercise by lunging toward the hay bale coffee table and striking it with the tip of his staff, near an opened beer can. He hit with such force that the beer can jumped, but just high enough for him to catch it with his staff. Perfect balance, Tyler used the staff to bring the can closer to him, hand over hand, without spilling a single drop. After a long chug, he held it up as a toast to his guests. "Hey, guys. How'd the expedition go?"

Cooper had texted him asking him if they could meet back at the barn after they visited the burned down townhomes. Tyler had replied with, "*Mi casa es su casa.*"

Cooper stepped forward. "Glad you asked, Jedi Master Tyler. It went splendidly. The jocks were there to ambush us, but we ambushed them."

"We won!" Kyle added, voice more like a squeal.

Tyler finished his beer and tossed the can aside. He leaned on his staff, the third leg of a tripod, and looked at Chad. "Really? I thought there would be more jubilation."

"It wasn't quite the decisive win that we were hoping for," Chad said.

"Oh, Christ, must we revisit this again and again and again and ad nauseum? A victory is a victory, no matter how infinitesimal the winning margin is."

"I froze," Heston mumbled, still looking at his feet.

Kyle put his hand on Heston's shoulder. "But you came through at the end."

"It was obvious that we could all use a little practice," Chad said.

Tyler nodded, slow and rhythmic as if deep in contemplation. "Okay. I'll help. I'll train you."

"You will, will you?" Cooper asked, puffing up his chest while strutting toward Tyler. "Out of the goodness of your heart?"

Tyler's squint became more pronounced as he stood straighter and adjusted the grip of his staff. "Something like that."

"What if I believe that all of your fancy moves are nothing more than pale reproductions of a fanboy spending too many hours watching *Cirque du Soleil* videos on the internet?"

"Then I would let you know that the twelve steps encourage modesty and admission that there are greater powers than the individual at play."

"Okay, I must traverse into a social taboo, but I can no longer exist without knowing this answer—what are you addicted to? What was your great vice that forced you into a twelve-step program?"

"GMOs."

Cooper's face went slack, and his eyes went wide, the accompanying blinks slow and pronounced. "G . . . MOs? Did you just say that you were addicted to GMOs?"

"I did. Is there something wrong with my addiction?"

Cooper's laughter was like a newly freed caged animal, tentative at first, but then rushing out in full force. "Yes! Yes, there is absolutely something wrong with your addiction. First of all, I would wager that's it's an impossibility to be addicted to GMOs. Second, you really can't cut GMOs out of your lifestyle, unless you become a Tibetan monk, and even then, I'd be a little suspect, because I have zero idea how often they interact with the outside world. Ninety percent of the United States corn, soybeans, and cotton crops are GMO. The clothes on your back are from GMOs. Whatever soy substitutes you ingest probably have more GMOs in them than whatever it is you're substituting. Even if you try to cut out corn from your diet, then it's being used to feed tasty, tasty livestock."

Chad had seen only two emotions from Tyler since meeting him—enchanted stoicism and detached bemusement—and usually, the only way to tell them apart was how he was smiling. There was no smile on his face now, and upon careful inspection, Chad believed he saw what might pass as a frown. Yes. Yes, it was definitely a frown, getting deeper the harder Cooper laughed. The frowning stopped once Cooper turned to everyone else. "Can you believe it? Can you believe he thought he was addicted to GMOs? Too much pot and beer must have rewired his brain, because that—"

Tyler stopped frowning so he could focus on his attack, a smack of his staff to the back of Cooper's thighs. It was loud enough to cause everyone else to wince and hard enough to make Cooper fall backward. But he didn't hit the ground. Tyler stopped Cooper by planting one end of the staff in the ground and using the rest of it to catch him mid-fall. Using the perfect blend of strength and leverage, Tyler lifted Cooper back to his feet and pushed him forward.

"Dick!" Cooper yelled as he extended his hands to buffer the impact. He didn't hit the ground this way either. Again, Tyler had stopped him, balancing the weight of Cooper on his staff. With a push and a reposition, Tyler sent Cooper falling backward. Halfway through the arc, Tyler repositioned himself and sent Cooper aiming face-first to the ground again.

"Enough!" Cooper changed into his ferret form and used his claws to gain purchase on the floor. He scurried away from Tyler, then turned and rushed him. Tyler backed away while tapping one of the staff's ends on the ground in front of Cooper's hissing face. Cooper swatted the staff, but Tyler just brought it right back to the tip of his nose. Hissing and swatting the staff, Cooper charged. Tyler spun the staff in small circles and planted his feet.

Chad knew very well that it was an illusion, a weird effect of his brain trying to make sense of the information assaulting it through his eyes. To him, it looked as if Tyler spun Cooper around using his staff like a fork twirling spaghetti, then flung him across the barn. Everyone winced as Cooper slammed against the far wall. Back to his human form, Cooper landed upside down against the wall, lanky arms and legs akimbo. "I am sorry. I was wrong about everything that spilled out of my mouth since stepping foot into the barn tonight. It is your human right to be addicted to whatever you would like and to thwart that very addiction by any means you deem necessary. Please find it in your heart to forgive me. My friends and I would absolutely love for you to train us, Master Splinter."

Tyler smiled the lazy, squint-eyed smile of a stoner a few joints into the night. "No worries, brother. Training will begin tomorrow."

For the first time since the fight with the football players, Heston smiled. Cooper righted himself and got to his feet. More comfortable with his nudity this time, he limped his way over to the hay couch and collapsed on it after tossing down a nearby blanket. Chad felt good. He now had a sensei, one who showed a new emotion today. Chad decided to call it "effervescent annoyance."

CHAPTER 29

The two weeks since Tyler started training Chad and his friends went quickly. Two weeks of going to classes, spending some quality time with his parents—although the discussion about Chad getting a job to pay for the new phone was quite a formidable one, even with his mother defending him—and then heading over to the barn for training. Chad almost forgot that there was a secret race to see who could kill him first happening among a group of four bloodthirsty lycanthropes, a trio of vengeful jocks, a couple of hunters who disapproved of his lifestyle, and a partridge in a pear tree. He certainly didn't forget about any of the race participants. A week ago, Natalia had come by the barn to update Chad. Aunt Wanda was *pissed* that Chad had created three more lycanthropes. Chad offered their services to aid the hunters in tracking down the Ink Stains, but Natalia declined his offer, stating that while her aunt was healing, she was keeping tabs on them, and they had been laying low. She gave him her cell number and left. He texted Natalia once a day, and she'd reply with "not now" or "stay low." Today had been the first day that his situations hadn't weighed on him.

Chad finally understood the concepts of "good pain" and "positive burn," thanks to Tyler. One to two hours of martial arts training—a style Tyler defined as one meant to use the world's energy to defend against it, while Cooper referred to it as bong-fu—every night was more exercise than Chad had done on his freewill ever in his life. He was sore every day, but in ways that let him know that he was improving, getting better as a human being. He now knew the benefits of push-ups and pull-ups, squats, and planks. He understood the need to focus and visualize. Over the past two weeks, he had gotten so much better at transforming into his rabbit state as well as various partial stages. Heston and Cooper were gaining more control over their abilities. Not Kyle.

Calling upon his rabbit legs to sprint or kick became as natural as breathing for Chad. Cooper could transform into any stage of "wereweasel," as he called it. Heston could become quite an impressive minotaur but couldn't hold it for long. Any form of stress or anxiety sent him back to human form. Kyle learned to change into a pheasant as quick as a thought, but that was it. He couldn't stop anywhere in between. No wings upon command, no talons only. His options were either Kyle or large pheasant. Tyler assured him the power was within him, within all of them. They just needed time, perseverance, and training. Time and perseverance were easy. It was the training that left knots in Chad's muscles.

Today after class, Chad wanted a flavored coffee before heading to the barn as a small reward for his hard work and dedication. While waiting in line at the coffee shop, the muscles between his shoulder blades tightened down his spine. Keeping his left arm straight, he pulled it close to his chest and slowly twisted at his waist. He repeated the process with his other arm. However, this time, he poked Brittany in the back of the head.

"Oh my God, I'm so sorry," came out of his mouth as he turned around, but he completely froze in wide-eyed fear when he saw who he hit.

Chuckling while rubbing the back of her head, Brittany was turning around as well. "No problem, I was—" Her face went expressionless. "Oh. It's you."

His training went out the window. His encounters with the Ink Stains, meaningless. His fight with the football players never happened. The depths from where a woman could pull scorn were endless, the imagination of their wrath, limitless. "I'm sorry. I'm sorry. I'm so, so sorry."

Chad expected her head to split in half to release a demon made of fire and teeth. Instead, she gave a half shrug and said, "S'okay. My fault. I was looking out the window to the shoe sale across the street."

Silence. Chad responded with stunned silence, which soon morphed into an awkward silence. He thought about leaving, finding another coffee shop on the other side of the state to get his morning fix of caffeine, but the line moved, so he used it as a chance to retreat from her withering gaze. He turned back around and moved with the line as if nothing had happened.

"Sorry, I didn't recognize you."

Chad heard Brittany's words, but it took almost a full minute for his brain to recognize that she was talking to him. "I have a very forgettable face."

Brittany chuckled as if it happened by surprise. "We've known each other since second grade, Chad. I know your face. You do look a little different, though. Are you working out?"

Chad had heard that line used a hundred times in a hundred different movies and television shows, but he never heard it said to him. Of the hundred possible responses, he forgot them all, never expecting that a situation would present itself where he would need to recall one. He went with his default response to any question he didn't know how to handle. "Ummm . . . ?"

Brittany laughed and shook her head. "I'm sorry. That came out so wrong. It sounded like a cheesy line, right?"

Chad gave a fake laugh, still having no idea what the heck was happening or how he should react to it. Seeing her started his instinct engine to run, and the longer he stayed, the faster it revved. It would be rude to look around for an exit, so he tried to recall one from memory. He had a good idea of which direction to flee but had no clue how many chairs, tables, patrons, and other potential instruments of calamity lay in wait between him and the door. The tiny part of his brain dedicated to helping him be a civilized human adult male reminded him that she asked a question. He answered, "Yeah."

Brittany crossed her arms just under her chest as if hugging herself because no one else would. "It's just . . . it's been weird since Mason disappeared. It's scary. And I really don't have a lot of friends. Well, I mean, I do, but none from high school. None who knew Mason."

"Really? What about the other cheerleaders?"

"None of them are at this college. All the ones that graduated with me all go to different schools. Sure, we talk and text and I.M. each other, but it's not the same as seeing them face-to-face, like this."

"Oh."

"I guess I've been feeling nostalgic. Missing the good ol' days. Missing Mason."

"Good ol' days" was just a reminder about the inequity of perception. Chad had zero concept of which "ol' days" were good whatsoever, especially about high school. "Frustrating ol' days" didn't have the same panache, and Brittany had no concept of what that would mean anyway. Even though Chad couldn't fathom what she meant by "good ol' days," he did recognize that she was lonely. So astute to the concept, he often wondered if this college offered a doctorate program in loneliness. Her loneliness was legitimate, and she was turning to him for help. There was only one thing to do—help her. "What about Brick?"

Brittany twisted her face as if Chad had used an orifice much lower on his body than the one on his face to ask the question. "Brick? Why Brick?"

"Well . . . he . . . ?" *Has the same penchant for sadistic torture of anyone smaller than him!* ". . . plays on the same team. I mean . . . I know he's not a townie, but he did know Mason. And you know him. It's not the perfect solution, but it's probably the best one available."

Judging from her frown, maybe that wasn't the best suggestion. "It's interesting that you bring him up. He soooo does not like you. Heard he has your phone."

Chad wanted to tell her that he kicked Brick's ass, wanted to parade around and strut. And with only two weeks of training, he felt much more confident about tangling with Brick again, even if the jock knew what to expect. "Yeah. He thinks I'm involved with Mason's disappearance."

"I know. I told him repeatedly that there was no way someone like you could do anything like that. You just don't have it in you. But he just won't listen. He's gotten so weird and obsessed with you and all the weird things happening around The Bends."

"Weird things?"

"Yeah. The dead cows on your lawn and then the fire at those abandoned rowhomes right after that and then the bizarre footprints on the football practice field."

"Footprints?" Chad hadn't heard anything about unusual footprints on the practice field. Were the Ink Stains messing with Brick and his teammates? Did Brick start his own form of investigation into lycanthropes and stumble upon the Ink Stains' secret?

Brittany cocked her head, the inference being he was an idiot. "You haven't heard? There are all kinds of footprints all over the field. Big round ones, like a herd of zoo animals, escaped and rampaged all over the place. Let me see if I can find the article."

Brittany tapped away at her cellphone. While she was distracted, the guy behind her leaned to the side and faux-whispered to Chad, "Dude. Stop trying to get in her pants and place your order."

Chad had no idea he was now at the front of the line. The disenfranchised teenager behind the counter stared down at Chad and mumbled, "She's way outta your league, dude. What do you want?"

Chad jumped out of line and said to Brittany, "Sorry, gotta go."

"Where?" she asked, but he didn't answer. He rushed out the door, in the direction of the barn. Coincidentally enough, the practice field was on the way.

CHAPTER 30

The practice field. Where it all started. It had been half a month but felt like a lifetime ago since the Ink Stains tricked Chad into coming here to be bait. Nothing more than a piece of meat to lure more meat. Chad shook his head, trying to dislodge the meat analogy. He was still meat to the Ink Stains.

There was one person still on the field. Brick.

Tucked in the corner of the campus, the practice field had a row of fir trees leading to it. From the cover of the trees, Chad crept closer to the field. At first, he hoped that no one would be using the field, but now he saw an opportunity.

While sneaking along the tree line, Chad took a moment to change into his nylon shorts and an oversized t-shirt. He always carried a set of "rabbit clothes" in his backpack. Now at the last tree in the line, he watched Brick on the field. Shirtless and barefoot, he would get in a three-point stance, sprint ten yards, and then repeated the same process in the other direction. Chad hardly understood the purpose of his practice or why he was doing it wearing only a pair of shorts, but that didn't matter. He placed his backpack against the tree trunk and stepped out from his hiding place.

He was going to talk to Brick.

It was crazy, he knew this, but being afraid was exhausting. There was no one else around, so no outside pressures for either party. Just two men who had a problem with each other. This was an opportunity to work things out, come up with a diplomatic solution. If not, if Brick continued to threaten, or make accusations about Mason's disappearance, or attack, Chad would change into rabbit form and run. Maybe even fight back?

Chad reminded himself of the last time they met. Brick was strong and durable, raw power in the shape of a human being. But he had been practicing martial arts under Tyler's tutelage. Balance. Opportunity. Control over his lycanthropy. How to slow the situation down and think during times of stress. Brick might be better prepared than last time, but so was Chad. He was very prepared.

Chad walked toward the field as Brick was sprinting away. By the time Brick pulled up and turned around, Chad was on the field. Brick crossed his arms over his chest and frowned. "You."

"Chad. My name's Chad."

"Yeah, I fucking know."

"Brick, right? Is . . . that your birth name? Or a nickname?"

"Why do you even fucking care?"

"Sorry. Just trying to connect with you on a personal level."

Brick dropped his hands to his side and clenched his fists. He moved five yards closer. "Are you hitting on me?"

Chad took a step back and put his hands up. "Whoa! No! No, no, no. I'm not like that at all."

Brick stopped his advance, and his face softened from anger to confusion. "That's a pretty extreme response."

Chad squeezed his eyes shut and pinched the bridge of his nose. "I'm just trying to connect with you on some human level because we have a lot to talk about."

Brick snorted and started to pace back and forth for a few yards. "Human-level. Yeah, we got a lot to talk about. How about we start with *human* level. Are you even human?"

"I . . . I think so? I feel human. I mean, you know what I can do."

"I do."

"Even when I do that, I still feel human. I'm cognizant of my actions, and I still think like me, so I'm pretty sure I'm still human."

Brick took a few steps closer, but Chad didn't back away. This made him nervous, but he went back to Tyler's training. *Expect a sucker punch*, he reminded himself. *I think he's right-handed.*

"So, why do you wanna talk?"

Chad gestured, repeatedly pointing between Brick and himself. "Because of whatever's going on between us. It's not good for anybody, and it should stop. I don't want a repeat of what happened at the row homes. Do you?"

Brick squinted. "No. No, I do not."

"Okay, then. Let's talk this out like rational adult human being people."

Jaw muscles worked as if Brick chewed his words before he let them out of his mouth. "Tell me what you know about Mason's disappearance."

Be ready for anything, a simple and logical teaching from Tyler. Chad had heard those words all his life from parental guidance to fortune cookies to pithy click-bait internet headlines. His brain understood the concept, but it took a stoner sensei to repeat it before Chad's soul caught on. Now he understood. Now he was ready. "I do not know anything about Mason's disappearance."

Nailed it! There was no warble in his voice, no twitch in his face. If he could have lied this well when he was younger, then maybe he wouldn't have been the rule-following nerd that he was today. He didn't want to lie to Brick, but there was no way he wanted to tell the scariest human being ever to walk the planet that a pack of bloodthirsty lycanthropes ate his friends.

Brick twisted his lips, his jaw muscles still working. And then shook his head as if disappointed. "You know, I gave you a chance. I *really* gave you a chance. *Then you lied to me!*"

Chad wasn't ready. He wanted to be. He thought through different scenarios, many including Brick taking a swing at him, but he never expected Brick to turn into a rhino-human hybrid.

In the time it took Chad to curse his luck, Brick's nose hardened and extended upward into a massive horn, while his skin went gray and calloused. His body became even more muscular as he charged at Chad with his head down, pointed horn leading the way.

Jump! Chad's survival reflexes kicked in, rabbit legs propelling him straight up. He easily leaped over the charging beast, but as soon as his feet touched the ground, he had to jump again, Brick being quick enough to stop himself before he ran too far. This time as Brick charged, Chad jumped away instead of straight up in the air, but he was still nowhere near any form of real protection. The tree line wasn't dense enough. There were sets of small bleachers, rickety wooden constructs, six benches high. The forest was the only option, on the other side of Brick.

Chad decided to go full rabbit. Clearly, Brick had enough mastery of his ability to attack while semi-transformed, but maybe that meant he wasn't comfortable being fully changed. One more jump over Brick and Chad sprinted for the forest. Brick chased but quickly gave up. Chad was a dozen trees deep into the forest, and Brick was still on the practice field. Turning his attention away from the forest, the football player changed back into his human form and walked back across the field to the line of fir trees with a definite purpose to his step. At first, Chad deemed the escape from the giant football player a victory, until he realized what Brick was aiming for—his backpack

Thanks to Brick's ambush, Chad's desire to live took priority over everything else, including remembering his backpack, which included his brand new phone. He could *not* lose another phone to Brick!

Still in rabbit form, Chad loped through the forest and sprinted back onto the field, toward Brick. Discovering Brick was a lycanthrope threw him off his game, but thanks to Tyler's training, he had a plan.

As soon as Brick noticed that Chad returned, he changed back into his partial rhino form. "I'm going to crush you into a pile of bloody fur."

Chad ignored the threat. Focus. He needed to focus and time his actions perfectly. A few steps away from Brick, he hopped, a small one barely leaving his feet. Brick jumped upward, leading with his horn. His feint worked! Chad dropped and slid on his back, passing under Brick on his downward arc. Chad kicked with his back legs as hard as he could.

Despite the size difference, Chad sent Brick tumbling end over end across the field. He knew his window for success was small and closing by the second. Getting to his backpack was easy. He went human just enough to slip it over his shoulders. He was able to carry it in rabbit form, though it did slow him down a bit. Now, to escape.

He thought about running straight down the tree line, but the fir trees were close enough together that he wouldn't be able to run at full speed without getting impaled by a low hanging branch. That and the trees led to the campus, to people and civilization. No one would react well to a rhino-thing chasing a human-sized rabbit wearing a backpack. The forest.

Brick righted himself and charged, this time as a full rhino. Chad was no expert on African animals, but he knew that rhinos could run faster than what most people think. Much faster.

The bleachers. They weren't large enough to stop a strong wind, let alone a rhino in psycho-kill-charge mode, but Chad hoped they would at least provide some form of a hindrance. He ran behind them, over and under the wooden crossbeams lending support. The bleachers exploded behind Chad, a chunk of wood smacking his haunches. Adrenaline fueled his muscles to run faster as Brick reduced the bleachers to tinder. Chad prayed as he sprinted through the shrapnel and then thanked every god he could think of once he escaped the bleachers with no blood loss.

Rhinos were fast, but rabbits were still faster. Chad easily outraced Brick for the remainder of the field to the forest. Without looking back, he just kept running through the woods in rabbit form, all the way to Tyler's barn.

CHAPTER 31

Sweating in his human form, Chad ran into the barn. Gripping both of his backpack straps for no other reason than an attempt to contain his nervous energy, he blurted, "Guys! You're never going to believe this, but Brick is one of us! Not one of us, like cool and awesome, because he's still a jock, but he can transform. He's a rhinoceros, and he tried to kill me on the practice field, the one at the corner of campus."

As he was rambling, both Cooper and Heston ran to him and blathered on in unison. While Chad was rushing to tell them everything, he was able to pick out a few words like "attacked" and "bull" and "greyhound."

"You got attacked, too?" Heston asked just as Chad finished.

Tossing his backpack aside, Chad ran his hands through his hair, hoping it would help him sort through all he just heard, his mind buzzing like a hive full of discontented bees. He addressed Heston's question. "I was. By Brick at the practice field. Wait . . . were *you* attacked?"

Heston's eyes bulged as his head bobbled in short, quick nods. Cooper looked panicked as well and said, "Yes. We both were. I received a text from you to meet at the Riverside train trestle, posthaste, and when I arrived, I thusly learned I had been set up for an ambush."

The Riverside train trestle was a stretch of train track that had been decommissioned decades ago in favor of building new and upscale developments on either side of the small valley that the trestle bridged. "I texted you? I didn't—"

Cooper raised his hand, palm out. "I fully understand that now. Due to the nature of your text, I failed to notice that it came from your old phone number."

"What did the text say?"

Cooper sighed and rolled his eyes in homage to self-disgust. "It stated that the Barbareau twins were sunbathing, and you had a perfect vantage point from the trestle into their backyard."

"Seriously? I understand forgetting that was my old number, but you should have realized that even though it's a nice day out, it's still October. No one sunbathes in October."

"Clearly, our enemy has found the weakness in my armor!"

"So, what happened?"

"Orlando sprung the trap he laid for me. He was fast. Extraordinarily fast. He, too, was like us, but only in the manner of being more than human."

"What kind of animal can he turn into?"

"A canine, but not like the wolf you described Hunter to be. More like a greyhound. Long and slender was his head, his body cords of lean muscle."

"Wow. How did you get away?"

"It was no easy task. Getting over my initial surprise, I remembered my training and focused. It was a fight, one that could be lost if I succumbed to panic, so I tried to remain calm and tap into my inner warrior as best I could. After a few attacks of my own, I realized my chances of survival increased with the option of retreat. Luckily, Orlando is not a townie, so despite his speed, I was far more elusive. I owe my escape, and possibly my very life to our ultimate sensei guru master Tyler." As a form of gratitude, Cooper turned to Tyler, pressed his palms together, and offered a deep bow. Tyler took a puff from the joint in his left hand while giving devil horns with his right. He then opened the mini-fridge and pulled out a beer.

"How about you, Heston? What happened?" How the story was going to go was obvious, but Chad needed to hear it anyway, to get all the information possible to piece together the puzzle labeled, "What the hell is going on?"

Heston had calmed down, no longer bug-eyed with worry, but now pink-cheeked from embarrassment. Gaze dropping to his feet; he shrugged a shoulder. "Kinda the same thing. I got a text from you to meet at Faraday Park. I missed that it was your old number because the text said that Mr. Freezey-Frozen Treats ice cream truck was doing one last run for the year. I was ambushed."

Chad wondered if his friends had enough common sense to make a dollar, but it would do way more harm than good to bring up that no ice cream truck would run in October, no matter how temperate Autumn was being. Instead, he asked, "Was it Emmanuel?"

Heston nodded. "He was a bull. A minotaur, really. A better one than I can do. And . . . and he was really, really big."

Chad was confused. He knew Heston was sensitive, but he hadn't said anything to warrant the level of social discomfort he was displaying. "How did you get away?"

"I . . . umm . . . ran. Well, first, I turned into my ox mode when I saw him. I didn't even think about it, and I changed. But . . . I wasn't wearing the right clothes, so they all got ripped up. Then he changed, and I knew I didn't stand a chance. I needed to get to the woods because he's not a townie either. But . . . umm . . ."

The park had a simple design, a patch of lush green between a large stream and the woods veined with paved walking paths and freckled with stone benches. The park was large enough for two pavilions, a fenced-in dog park, and a sizable playground. Chad assumed that Heston was ambushed someplace secluded, by the stream. The woods were on the other side of the park. If Heston had to run the entire length of the park naked, then his embarrassment was understandable. "Were there a lot of people?"

Heston gave a small shoulder shrug again. "Enough. Unfortunately, that was what I was hoping for. Emmanuel was at least smart enough not to chase me as a bull or minotaur or naked football player."

"Wow. But you're both okay. Kyle? Were you attacked at all?"

Kyle was sitting on the oversized hay armchair, back to his usual pose of arms-wrapped-around-legs, head-buried-between-knees. This concerned Chad, even though Kyle answered, "No."

"Okay, well, that's good. It seems like it's just those three, and they didn't bring in anyone else, like the entire football team."

"I agree that the new members of the menagerie seem to be limited to those three, but I think it's fairly obvious that they had help. They couldn't have done this by themselves," Cooper said.

"The Ink Stains?" Heston asked.

"There's no other possibility."

"But I don't understand how," Chad said. "Even if they convinced one of the Ink Stains to give them their blood, there's the issue of the Elder Blood. I took all of the vials that I didn't destroy."

"They must have gotten more," Cooper suggested.

"Even if that happened, how would Brick and Orlando and Emmanuel know that the Ink Stains were werecreatures? And then convince them to go through with the ceremony?"

While they were debating, Tyler wandered over to a closet-like pantry and opened it. "Hey, guys. The rest of the Elder Blood is missing."

"What?" Cooper yelled. "What in the hell of hells do you mean?"

Tyler stepped aside to reveal the contents of the pantry. No vials.

"How?" Heston's voice cracked as he spoke faster, his flailing hands matching the increased speed as he paced in a small circle. "How is it possible that Brick and Orlando and Emmanuel found this place? How did they break in? How did they even know? How are they always ahead of us, beating us?"

Cooper inched closer to his fretful friend. "Hey, Heston. Easy, buddy. We'll figure this out together."

"How? How are we going to figure this out?"

This wasn't good. Heston was freaking out, and Kyle was slipping back to his old tactics of putting his head in the ground. Then Kyle took the problem from bad to worse to awful to cata-fucking-strophic. "It wasn't them."

Chad moved next to his friend and crouched down. "What did you say, Kyle?"

Voice muffled by fighting through tears and speaking into his knees, Kyle said, "They didn't take the vials."

"Kyle?" Cooper whispered. "You can't be serious. You cannot be serious."

Fat tears rolled over Heston's round cheeks. "What are you saying? What are you saying?"

Kyle didn't say anything. He couldn't from crying too hard, his whole body rattling from the sobs. Instead, he pointed. On his floor, beside the chair. His backpack.

Chad picked it up and unzipped it. Books. Notebooks. Crushed on one side were two large wads of thick paper. They were what Kyle wanted him to find. He knew it. He pulled them out, and Cooper took one.

Crumpled paper, thick and glossed. A small poster that had been rolled up and folded a few times. Cooper held the same thing. They both unfolded and unrolled the posters. They were of Kyle's mom.

Topless.

From her younger days of modeling, no crow's-feet, hair bigger, face a little less full. Her pillowy lips were parted, just enough to hint at whatever word the viewer wanted to hear her say. She was holding her breasts, each twice the size of her head and spilling over her hands, pie-plate areolas dominating the picture.

"Whoa," Cooper whispered.

Kyle lifted his head, his eyes glowing red from tears. "They . . . they approached me about a week ago. I was walking home from school, and they cornered me. They didn't attack, didn't hit me. They said they wanted to do what we did; they wanted to know how we did what we do. At first, I didn't tell them anything. I tried to stall, to look for a way to escape. Then they pulled out those posters. They said they would hang them up all over campus. They said they found a website with hundreds of her pictures and they had the means to make dozens of copies, of poster-sized, and banner-sized, and bigger . . . and . . . and . . ." Kyle's whole body trembled as his words gurgled out, "It's . . . it's my . . . mom."

Tyler walked to Chad and took the poster. He crumbled the poster into a tight ball and threw it into a small trashcan. Chad thanked him and then said, "It's okay, Kyle."

Cooper ogled the second poster for a few seconds more and then rolled it up. He placed it in his back pocket. "Chad is correct."

Tyler walked behind Cooper and snatched the poster from him on his way to the trashcan. Cooper scowled.

"No!" Heston yelled. "No! This is not acceptable!"

"Dude," Cooper whispered. "They blackmailed him using nudes of his mom."

"Then he should have come to us. I'm tired of his secrets fucking us over."

"Heston?" Chad made his way to his friend, his steps slow and deliberate as if approaching a cobra with flared hood. "This isn't Kyle's fault."

"Isn't it? Isn't it? He literally gave the potential for our enemies to win without telling us. That's after trying to team up with some kid from a different school to get supernatural powers."

"Heston, what happened with Justin has nothing to do with this."

"No? Do you remember that day at all? Kyle pissed himself in public, and we rallied around him like we always do when something like this happens to him. If *that* hadn't happened, then *you* wouldn't have run into Mason and gotten yourself in the crosshairs of the Ink Stains."

Brittany's ass was the reason why Chad ran into Mason that day, more specifically, his inability to control himself when she bent over. Correcting Heston now would serve no purpose, and as much as Chad didn't want to admit it, Kyle's piss-fit that day did change up his routine. "Heston—"

Walking toward the barn door, Heston gave a dismissive wave. "No, Chad. I'm not cleaning up Kyle's mess this time."

No one said a word as Heston walked out of the barn.

Cooper sighed. After one last glance to the trashcan, he jogged toward the door. "I'll talk to Heston to see if we can't get him a little calmer to help us deal with this new problem."

Chad walked over to Kyle and put a hand on his shoulder. "Let's get you home."

"No!" Kyle snapped and swatted away Chad's hand. "Heston's right. You're always cleaning up my messes, always escorting me back home. I don't want to go home. I want to be left alone."

Chad didn't know what to do. Heston flipped out and left in a rage he never displayed before. Kyle was so hurt and frustrated that he was lashing out blindly. Back at the pantry, Tyler waved Chad over.

"I'm so sorry about this," Chad whispered.

"No worries." Tyler sifted through a box filled with tiny bags of dried leaves. He pulled out three bags. "Just looking for something to help Kyle. Ahh, these will do the trick."

"Umm. I don't think Kyle smokes."

Tyler looked at Chad with those soulful, squinted eyes. His face was alive with emotion, but Chad couldn't identify which one. Annoyance? Disappointment? Sadness? "This is tea. Don't walk under chickens unless you want egg on your face, dude."

"Chickens? What do—? Never mind. You're going to make him tea?"

"Yes. And you're going to leave."

"Wait. What?"

"I may not have the addiction I thought I had, but I know enough about enablers to know that they sometimes need to be removed from a situation."

"Enabler? I'm an enabler?"

"You all are. There's a false perception among the four of you that Kyle is the weak one. The fragile one who needs to be protected, cared for, dealt with in an overly sensitive manner. He's an adult who is perfectly capable of making it home all on his own. All I'm going to do is make him some tea, give him a chance to chill, and treat him with respect."

"Ummm. Okay." Chad had no other response, so he just left, dumbfounded and confused.

The day was young, and he didn't know where to go. He wondered what time Clinty's opened and started to weigh the pros and cons of being a teenage derelict. Home. He should go home and formulate some form of a plan as well as do some soul searching about enabling Kyle to be weak.

Tyler's barn was only a half-mile from civilization. Within twenty minutes were sidewalks and nicer houses with small, manicured lawns. Some had gates, Some had shrubs taller than Chad. He assumed that since it was a sunny day that he'd be safe from another attack from Brick and his cronies, so he didn't pay much attention to his surroundings. He should have. By the time he heard the rustling from within the bush he passed, he had a hand over his mouth and a knife to his neck.

CHAPTER 32

Chad wondered if he could turn into a rabbit fast enough to escape from the clutches of whoever was holding him at knifepoint. If not full rabbit, then maybe just his legs to kick? At first, he was a little proud of himself for his initial thoughts being more aggressive and proactive than usual, but the metal of the knife was cold against his throat. Despite having power and better knowledge about how to wield it, he still needed to be passive in this situation.

He offered no resistance, allowing the knife-wielder to guide him backward, deeper into the alleyway of hedges. The hand over his mouth was soft and smelled oddly familiar, a hint of cinnamon. Right when his brain fought through all the fear and confusion to identify who the aroma belonged to, he stopped moving, and the hand released his mouth only to grab his shirt sleeve and spin him around. Natalia.

"Why are you pointing a knife at me?" Chad whispered.

"Because it's clear to me that I can't trust you." Even though she was whispering as well, Chad could feel the anger propelling her words.

"What? What are you talking about?"

"You promised that it was just going to be the four of you, and then as soon as I leave you morons alone, you turn more of your friends into damnable creatures."

"We didn't turn any of our friends into creatures like us."

"You did. The rhinoceros, the greyhound, the bull."

Chad relaxed, no longer concerned about the knife tip inches from his face. "Oh. Them."

"Yes, them, your friends you completed the ceremony with."

"They're football players. They're no friends of ours."

"I'm sure they are."

"Seriously? In what universe do jocks and nerds get along? Haven't you ever gone to high school?"

Natalia's face softened, her bravado bursting like a popped balloon. "I . . . I was home-schooled."

"Oh." Pity weighed upon the word, more than he had intended.

"What does *that* mean? Just because home-schooling isn't the norm, doesn't mean the education I received is any less viable or meaningful."

"I know that, but since you didn't have the same social environment, it's no wonder that you don't understand that jocks torment nerds."

"I had access to just as many extracurricular activities and clubs as you did."

"Did you actually participate in any of them?"

". . . no . . . but that's not the point."

Chad reached out and gently placed his hand on hers, guiding the knife away from his face. "That is exactly my point. You don't need the knife. You can trust us. Those three are *not* our friends, and they threatened and bullied one of us into changing them. Quick rundown of how our peer groups work in Western civilization— Jocks torment nerds. My barn friends and I are nerds. The guys who made us change them are jocks. They abuse us, and we are powerless to stop them, which is why we're in this mess to begin with because we were trying to find a way to stop the torment and abuse."

Natalia sheathed her knife and crossed her arms over her chest. Turning her back to Chad, she said, "I understand different social groups not liking one another. You didn't have to be so pedantic about it."

Chad couldn't win with this conversation. He tried so hard to be informative that he didn't realize he had been patronizing. "Sorry. It's just frustrating to be under someone's thumb for my entire life, and when I finally get out from under that thumb, I find myself underneath a bigger and worse thumb because of the way I got out from underneath the first thumb."

Natalia remained silent, arms still crossed, back still facing him. Lack of experience was a weakness for Chad, especially in his social game. Especially with women. He didn't know how to read her reaction or lack thereof. Did she need a moment to herself, or was she waiting for him to say something? If so, what?

He crossed his arms, too, but that didn't feel appropriate. Hands in his pockets didn't last long either. He reached to put his hand on her shoulder as a supportive gesture but thought better of it as images of bloodied dismemberment danced through his head, so he decided to scratch an itch that didn't exist on his elbow. The idea of running away from the awkward silence moved to the top of the possibility list until thoughts of her chasing him down and beating the crap out him claimed the top spot. Maybe sliding into the bushes? Both sets of hedges were well-manicured and at least seven feet tall. Although, what kinds of neighbors grew hedges this tall at the same time? Was it one-upmanship? Or did they both really hate—

"How did they get ahold of the Elder Blood?"

"The details don't matter. What matters is they forced us to change them, and we want to stop them just as badly as you do."

"It does matter, Chad." She turned back around, but now her hands were on her hips. Chad had enough in his limited repertoire of body-language assessment to know she was being earnest. "You're asking me to trust you after you blatantly did the opposite of what my aunt told you to do right after seeking her help. You need to give me all the details."

The anger flowed from her like ocean waves crashing against him. Attempting to flee became a viable option again, but he decided to try the truth first. "Kyle. He—"

Natalia cut him off with a snap of her hand. "Which one is he?"

"He's the smallest of the four of us and—"

Another hand snap. "No. I mean, what is his true form."

Chad took great exception to her label. There was no way his true form was a rabbit. It may have been a manifestation of how he felt over the years, but it was most certainly not his "true form." He knew what she wanted, though, so he just gave it to her. "The pheasant."

She nodded. "Okay, continue. How did the pheasant screw things up?"

Again, her words rankled him, but he hid his frustration as he told her the story, including the posters and the threats of how they would be used. After he finished, he assumed that she would belittle him some more. Instead, she looked away and mumbled. "The children must always pay for the sins of their parents."

Unsure of what she meant, Chad answered with, "Umm, something like that."

"So, what's your plan now?"

"I don't know. Kyle's still at the barn, and Cooper went after Heston."

"Who?"

Chad rolled his eyes. She was quickly becoming worse than the jocks. "The pheasant is still at the barn while the ferret went to go talk to the ox."

"You don't need to be so huffy. I'm not the one who released your true selves. And that's not much of a plan."

"Not our true selves," Chad muttered as he ran his hands through his hair. Natalia opened her mouth, but he cut her off with, "Okay, so what do you suggest?"

Natalia sneered. "I don't see any other choice. We have to talk to my aunt."

CHAPTER 33

The trailer park scared Chad. He had neither issues nor prejudices with trailer parks in general and knew plenty of kids from school who grew up in parks and were fine young citizens, graduating from high school with top grades. West Bend had one trailer park, and South Bend had two. Those three would be considered upscale compared to the one in East Bend.

This was a trailer park that gave a bad name to this type of living arrangement. No paved roads, just bare and packed dirt lanes winding among the trailers culminating to one access point to the main road. Weeds grew along the chain-link fence perimeter of the park, some areas of the fencing buckled and collapsed. Whatever grasses grew between the trailers were dull green at best, mostly faded yellow from exhaustion and apathy. Just like the people.

Chad and Natalia walked along the main road through the center of the park. A shirtless old man sat in a half-rusted lawn chair. White hair grew over his chest and shoulders, thick enough to give the illusion that he waded through a field of dandelions. Four full beers by his feet, seven crumpled cans spread around, and one in his hand. He made no attempt at couth, blatantly staring at Natalia as she walked by. Another trailer had a toddler clad in only diapers using a stick to repeatedly smack the banister of the wooden steps leading to the front door. Unlike the old man, he paid no heed to either Chad or Natalia. The trailer next to the toddler shook in rhythmic quakes while sexual grunts emanated from the opened windows. Chad blushed and glanced at

Satan's Petting Zoo

Natalia from the corner of his eye. No reaction from her at all, just clenched-jaw determination.

Wanda's was the trailer on end, the one right after the trailer that had a kiddie pool filled with scum-coated water. As Natalia walked to the trailer's door, she said, "This is it."

Chad couldn't tell what color the siding started as, but it was a sun-bleached mixture of green, yellow, and brown. The inside was worse.

The smell of smoke was a living thing, a hungry creature that consumed him as he walked through the door. Chad needed a time limit in this trailer lest he be digested and shit out as one of the lost souls meandering around the fenced-in property.

A small kitchen was to the right. Despite the cabinet doors being closed, the sink being empty, and no stray eating implements anywhere, it still felt dirty. All the corners in the trailer were peeling; the stained linoleum, the threadbare carpet, the faux wood paneling, the worn furniture. Even Wanda sprawled along the couch—her left leg in a cast on the couch, her right leg on the floor—seemed to be peeling at the edges as well. "I knew I smelled an animal. What the fuck is he doing here?"

"He's one of the good ones, remember?" Natalia said as she shut the door, adding to Chad's burgeoning sense of demise.

Wanda spat—actual sputum flew from her mouth—on her floor while locking eyes with Chad. "Bah! The only good one of you animals is a dead one!"

"Aunt Wanda!" Natalia snapped. "You know that's not true!"

Squinting, Wanda draped her left arm over the couch. "My crossbow is inches from my fingers, boy."

Natalia moved closer to Chad, the smell of cinnamon simultaneously exciting and relaxing. She whispered, "This is as nice as she's going to get. Here, have a seat there."

Chad would rather not, the armchair was a shade of fester that implied a constant swarm of flies hovering around their territory. However, there were no flies, and he sat because Natalia told him to.

Wanda glared at him; he felt the full weight of her body behind that stare. So many questions, on either side of the silent exchange. Who? When? How? Yet it was Chad who finally acquiesced and let one brave word slip over terrified lips. "Why?"

"Because your kind is an abomination."

"My kind? I'm a prey animal."

"Even prey animals have abilities that help them live and thrive. Your abilities, whether you believe they do or not, give you an unfair and *unnatural* advantage."

"Men like those football players are bigger, stronger, faster than most humans. They have an unfair and unnatural advantage."

"They *worked* for that advantage. But instead of working, you tried to take the easy way out."

"And I paid the price."

"And you got your friends involved and made things worse!"

"And you haven't been able to kill the Ink Stains yet."

The mood shift in the room was just as palpable as the oppressive smoke smell. Chad felt bad for snapping like that, speaking without thinking first. Wanda looked away. Natalia's gaze dropped to her feet, looking as sad and guilty as Chad felt. He felt guilty because what Wanda said was right. He had caused a lot of these problems. So, why did Natalia look so guilty? Why did Wanda suddenly seem less abrasive? Unless . . . ?

"You created the Ink Stains, didn't you?"

"No," Wanda answered quickly.

"Not how you think," Natalia said.

Wanda whipped her head around to glare at her niece. Eyes shimmering from the start of tears, Natalia said, "We may as well tell him."

"Tell me," Chad said. "How did you make them?"

Wanda sighed. Her expression softened while her gaze still lingered on Natalia. "We didn't make them. Hunter did."

"Hunter? The leader of the Ink Stains?"

"Yes. He's just another lycanthrope that we've been tracking for decades now. He's an old one, well over a century. Hunter isn't his real name. We don't know what it is. He's chosen 'Hunter' to mock us. Natalia and I come from a long line of hunters; our knowledge and skills were passed down from generation to generation. Every time we find Hunter, we're able to kill off his pack, but never him. He just moves on and makes another pack. We do try to kill him, but with this pack, there is . . . an encumbrance."

"Encumbrance? You mean one of the other Ink Stains."

"My sister. Natalia's mother."

"Kat? You mean Kat?"

Both women winced at the mention of her name.

"Kat's your mom? But . . . how?"

Natalia kept her head low and showed no response to Chad's question, so Wanda continued, "Her mother, Katrina, and I hunted together, have ever since we were children and our parents taught us everything they knew. It was Hunter . . . he was going by Darius at the time . . . we had been hunting him for so long, following him, watching him, studying him, we were beginning to get to know him. Natalia's father died shortly after she was born, and Katrina snapped. She blamed this lifestyle, our family, me. She was in a weakened state, one of doubt and anger. This allowed Darius to seduce her with power. With love. With life. Hundreds of years are nothing to lycanthropes, and if an attack isn't a killing blow, then wounds heal so very quickly."

"So, at the coal depot . . ."

"Viper and the bear moved just in time for our bolts to miss their heads. We put two in the bear after he did this to my leg. It probably took less than an hour for his wounds to heal."

"With Kat, have . . . have you tried to . . . you know . . . ?"

"Kill her? We've debated the topic. We both know we should, but she's my sister, Natalia's mother —"

"Even though I don't know her," Natalia interjected.

"—and have determined that we need to go after Darius first. We've always killed the pack first, believing it was best to kill the pawns to get to the king, but that was flawed logic. Darius used his pieces well and fled his hunting grounds before we could get to him. This time, we'll change tactics. It may be more dangerous to try to get to Darius with his pack around him, but that's why Natalia and I are keeping you and your little friends alive, to help us kill Darius and reverse the curse on my sister."

"Hunter," Natalia growled. "His name is Hunter, and I want to whisper that into his ear as my blade pierces his heart."

Natalia's icy words chilled Chad's spine. It was his turn to look away, too afraid she might take her revenge out on him. Instead, he asked Wanda, "So you think killing Hunter would reverse the effects of Kat, because . . . ?"

"It was his blood that was used to turn her."

"She was the one who turned me, so do you think if she gets turned back to human, then I would get turned back, too?"

"That is what we believe will happen. It's possible that everyone who had been turned because of a direct or indirect result of Hunter will turn back to human."

Even though he and his friends would revert to human, this meant that he could take power away from Brick. That also meant that there would be no more Ink Stains, either. This would be a huge step in getting things back to normal. Excited, he turned to Natalia and said, "That would solve everything from getting rid of the Ink Stains to taking this power away from the jocks."

"Jocks?" Wanda asked. "What jocks?"

Judging from the pure anger in Natalia's glare, Chad was confident that he moved up on her death-kill-murder-revenge list. It was going to be a long day.

CHAPTER 34

"We close in ten minutes, sweetie, so you gotta make it quick." The clerk's tone was bored and sympathetic. *Why does everyone talk to me with a sympathetic tone? If anything, I should feel a little sorry for her.*

The clerk's nameplate read, "Shelby Blonsky," but in Chad's mind, there was no way "Shelby" was the birth name of a woman at least five years his mother's senior. Combined with her mid-nineties "The Rachel" hairstyle, he assumed that she attempted to grasp at her long-gone youth. Her shimmering red blouse was too small, unintentionally accentuating the wobble of her arms and the rolls of her waist. However, it did accentuate what it was meant to—her breasts. They weren't as large as Mrs. Sedgeweck's, but they deserved the right to be considered substantial. Her cleavage was copious and demanded attention. Chad couldn't help but pay tithing to her church of exposed skin any time she looked at something other than him. "I . . . ummm . . . I'm doing a project for one of my college classes on local war heroes, and I was wondering if—"

"If I could supply you with the name of the oldest grave of a war veteran?"

Chad wondered if she could read his mind, and if so, did she happen to hear his thoughts about her cleavage? Just in case, he glanced at the ceiling behind her in such a quick and jarring way, she turned around and looked at the ceiling as well. The way her blouse moved, Chad almost gasped as he looked back at her chest. He went back to looking into her eyes by the time she turned around. "How . . . how did you know?"

"Because I can read your mind."

All the blood retreated from his face, his cheeks and fingertips and toes now cold. What was he going to do? He thought about turning into a rabbit and sprinting out the door of the municipal building. Oh no! He *thought* about turning into a rabbit! "Shelby Blonsky" was now another name on the list of people who knew about his inner animal. She laughed, hard enough to create ripples in her breasts. Waves of skin clapped, and Chad almost passed out. He was embarrassed on so many different levels.

Shelby's laughter slowed as she brought her hand to her mouth in the act of fake modesty. "Oh, sweetie, you should see your face. Trust me. I don't need to read your mind to know what you young men think about all the time. The reason why I knew what you were gonna ask was that it's the second time someone asked for the same information today."

"Second? Really?"

"Yep. Young man and woman came in a few hours ago. Real sexy couple, too, all in leather. She was a hot little number, and he . . . oh, he was so handsome. So *dangerous* looking." As she spoke, she lowered her hand to her chest, her fingers playing across her skin.

"Kat and Hunter," Chad whispered to himself.

"Hunter? Oh, Hunter is such a *wonderful* name. Oh, that name suits him just fine," Shelby said, a soft pink blooming along her cheeks as her index finger disappeared into her flesh-walled gully. She then stood up and grabbed her nameplate to hide it away in her drawer. "Sorry, sweetie. The office is closed."

"I thought you said ten minutes—"

Shelby came around her desk and placed her hand on Chad's shoulder, gently turning him toward the door. "Closed. It's closed now."

Chad offered no resistance as he was being escorted to the hallway. "Did you give them a name? Which graveyard? Which plot?"

"Seamus McClintock. He actually fought in the Revolutionary War. Died twelve years later in a tavern fight. Fascinating and tragic."

"Where—?"

"The church on top of Cherish Hill. It's a tiny cemetery. You're a smart young man, so you'll be able to find it."

Chad turned to thank her and say goodbye but received a closing door to the face. The smoked glass with the word "Records" on it did nothing to hide the silhouette of Shelby's jiggle. As he walked down the hall of the borough building, he replayed the last few minutes in his mind, but couldn't move past the power of Shelby's breasts. Luckily, Natalia was waiting for him outside, her presence a cold shower for his soul. Everything about her was a hunter. The way she moved to him, her every step a potential attack. Even her words felt like an ambush. "Well, I checked the library, and their 'local history' section was pitiful. I found nothing of use. How did you do?"

"Well, I have good news and bad news."

Chad waited for her to choose which she would like to hear first. A blank stare was her only response.

"Okay, good news first. The oldest soldier buried nearby is Seamus McClintock, in that small cemetery on Cherish Hill. Ready for the bad news?"

Same answer as before.

"Okay, now the bad news. Hunter and Kat were in the office a few hours ago."

Even though she frowned, Natalia's eyes widened. "Is everyone in the borough office dead?"

"What? No. In fact, the clerk seemed . . . ummm . . . seemed to imply that they were rather charming."

Natalia relaxed, her face settling into her natural scowl. "Well, that's my mom."

"Your mom?"

"Yes. From what I've been told, she's much more dangerous than Hunter. She's smart and a strategist. She can be very, very charming. But, if they were here earlier today, then maybe they haven't gotten to the grave yet. How exposed is the cemetery?"

"It's beside a church right along Cherish Road. It's a country road, but it's one of the main ways into West Bend."

"Good. That's good. They won't try to defile a grave during the day time."

"So . . . we'll get there around dusk and wait?"

"Yes. I'll drive. I'll meet you at your house in two hours."

"Well, I don't have any plans for the next few hours, so . . . if you want . . . we could go someplace and come up with a plan."

"No."

Before Chad could make a feeble attempt to save face, she was already gone. He looked around to see if anyone had witnessed him getting shot down. No one to the best of his knowledge. No laughter. No pointing. No pain. This was by far the best shoot down yet. Things were looking up! Chad was so happy that he decided to spring for the sporty model as he ordered a share-a-ride through his phone. Within minutes the powerful engine of a muscle car rumbled through the streets and pulled up next to Chad. The trip to his house was fast, just long enough for him to think about what he had to do—help a hunter stop a pack of bloodthirsty half-animals from digging up the remains of a centuries-old corpse. The driver wasn't interested in conversation, so Chad took a moment to review what he had learned from his visit with Wanda.

After Natalia informed Wanda that there was a third group of lycanthropes, sparing no detail, of course, Chad learned more about the Ink Stains.

"You say that there is no more left? The Elder Blood is gone?" Wanda asked.

"All of it. Gone."

"So, we now know what their next move will be."

"To get more Elder Blood," Natalia said.

"How are they going to do that? It's been two weeks since we destroyed it all. Wouldn't they have gotten more by now?" Chad asked.

"It's not an easy process," Natalia answered. "I've been watching them while Aunt Wanda recuperates. After they figured out there were a few vials left, they were planning a way to get them back, but you turned your friends, so they needed to rethink their plans, and then you ruined those plans by turning the football players—"

"Not on purpose!"

"—and now that they've figured out there is no Elder Blood left, they have no choice but to get more. By calling an Elder, of course."

Chad turned to Wanda for a more direct answer. She adjusted her position on the couch, sitting as best as her cast would allow. "The Morrigan. Matron goddess of shape-shifters. The triple goddess with lore so old and deep, there are great debates as to who she is, what she means to the world. One book gives her a set of three names; another gives her a different set of three names. There are theories that she is Morgan of Arthurian legend."

"Really?" Chad almost squealed. "If the goddess that the Ink Stains are trying to call forth is Morgan, then there's a chance that . . ."

"You're not King Arthur, Chad," Natalia said. "Now focus."

"Sorry. So, if the Morrigan means different things to different people, what does she mean to the Ink Stains?"

"They," Wanda corrected. "The triple goddess is comprised of three goddesses. War. Death. Earth. To call them forth, they must perform a ceremony offering those three things."

"War, death, and Earth? I'm guessing it's not as easy as tossing a few dead mice into the mud."

Wanda chuckled. "No, it most certainly is not."

"Do you know what they need?"

"I do. One of the three items they need is easy to find, so easy they already have it. The slaughtered cows on your front lawn? They were missing organs, right? Undoubtedly their hearts were among what was missing. They would be perfect for the 'death' aspect of what's needed for the ceremony."

"If that's the easiest, then what's the hardest?"

"That would be a freshly bloomed Queen of the Night."

"So, who is she?"

"Not a who. A what. The Queen of the Night is the flower of a plant found in the south that blooms once a year."

"Well, it's fortunate that we live in the North East United States, and even if they found one, it's a zero point two seven four percent chance that it'll be the right night. So, what's the third item?"

The third item was the War item. Natalia had been spying on the Ink Stains, and it took them all this time to determine the specifics of what they needed—the bones of the oldest soldier in the area of the ceremony. Task completed. Well, not completely completed, because there was still the task of *stopping* the Ink Stains from getting those bones. That wasn't for another few hours, though.

Chad missed most of the ride in the badass muscle car because of his overactive brain. He still tipped well, though, and entered his house. No one home. He'd fix himself an early dinner in a bit, but first, he wanted to do more research on both the Queen of the Night and the Morrigan. That would have to wait, though, because he needed to figure out why Kat was naked in his room.

CHAPTER 35

"What do you want?"

Kat laughed, deep and throaty. "Why do you always ask such stupid questions, Chad? You have a naked woman on your bed, and you're asking why she's there."

"A naked woman who wants to kill me, and—in a very literal sense of the word—eat me."

"Things have changed, Chad."

He liked the way she said his name, added a little more to the "a" to make it sound sexy. So many people say it as if they were talking to a child. There was no pity in the way she said it.

Even though it rarely worked for him, he tried to play it cool, keeping his answers short. "Really?"

"Yes, really." She stood from his bed and walked toward him. The word goddess couldn't even begin to describe her. All of her piercings jiggled with every step, in time with her rolling hips. Her tattoos danced rhythmically to their own slow, seductive music. A lock of her black hair fell over her left eye, her right eye yellow with a slit pupil. She ran her teeth over her bottom lip, her fangs scraping over the metal hoops. Chad's erection began to hurt. "So much has changed."

"Like finding out that Natalia is your daughter."

He wasn't sure what reaction he was hoping for, he just desperately wanted some form of power, some upper hand, to do something unpredictable.

It backfired. As soon as he said the words, he could see all the resemblances. The same ferocious look in their eyes. The same small noses and full lips, even though Kat smiled all the time, and Natalia smiled never. Despite the difference in the level of nudity between the two women, Chad could identify the same drastic curves from thighs to hips to waist to breasts. The main difference between mother and daughter was their fingers—Natalia's were always curled into a fist to punch Chad while Kat used hers to run them gently over his cheeks. Chad liked Kat's fingers so much more than Natalia's.

He hoped his statement would have acted as a palisade against her vehicle of seduction, but it wasn't even a speed bump. Her right hand ran through his hair while her left explored his chest. "Ah, yes. My dear, sweet daughter. Corrupted by the overly-simplistic and backward ideals of my sister. I smelled her on you a mile away. I'm surprised and disappointed that it took you this long to make the connection. I thought you were smart?"

"I thought you used to share the same ideals as your sister." That got a reaction.

Kat tightened her grip of his hair and pulled his head back. For some reason, his erection got impossibly harder. Wave after wave of arousal flowed through him from her lips, brushing over his neck and cheek as she talked. "You once believed in Santa Claus until you learned that no creature, magical or not, could sustain life at the North Pole, nor visit seven billion people in a twenty-four hour span of time. Trying to rid the world of our kind is just as ridiculous as cows trying to rid the world of humans."

"What changed your mind?"

"There is no one on this planet that wouldn't evolve if given a chance. Hell, you made the same decision I did, so don't you dare pretend you're taking some high road."

"I don't have a daughter."

She squeezed her hand tighter and ran her tongue from the base of his neck to the tip of his chin. He had no idea the message she was sending. It felt too good to be torture, yet too painful for seduction. "You've had my daughter. No . . . wait . . . you haven't. I can still smell that you're a virgin."

Chad tensed as a burst of heat engulfed his cheeks. He desperately tried to think of a rejoinder, but how could anyone have a comeback for being called a virgin? Especially since it was true. "You said you would change that once I was no longer human."

He felt her smile against his cheek, the hoops in her bottom lip tickling his ear. She almost deflowered him as she slid her hand down his pants. "I did, didn't I? We're so close, Chad. There's still one thing left to do."

"Summon the Morrigan?"

Her laugh was deep, reverberating through his whole body, her hand touching parts of him that had never experienced anything other than his own hand. He tried to stave off the inevitable by closing his eyes and imagining her with blood flowing from her mouth and viscera dangling from her teeth. He wasn't sure if that made him less turned on, or more. "Hmm. You *are* smart. I was actually talking about you killing Hunter."

That did it.

That was the bucket of ice water he needed.

Somehow calling upon the skills of a trained contortionist, Chad extricated himself from her clutches without receiving a single scratch. "Wait—what? What the hell are you talking about? You never mentioned that before."

"You can't tell me you haven't thought about it."

"Thought about it? Yes. Actually, *thought about it*, thought about it, no."

Kat squinted and shrugged her shoulders. "Why not?"

"We talked about this before, remember? Same bedroom, same sexy you of sexiness. We talked about Mason and how I *didn't* want him dead, and how, when I became a lycanthrope, I *didn't* want to kill anyone."

"It's the next logical step, Chad."

"Then, you do it!"

Finally, the conversation shift he was hoping for, but after he said those words, he immediately felt bad for saying them. Kat crossed her arms under her chest, a comforting self-hug. She lowered her head and stood still for a few heartbeats and then walked to her clothes, piled on the floor by the bed. Still only leather pants and tiny white top, they seemed to weigh a ton as she picked them up and held them. After swiping her thumb under each eye, she mumbled, "He needs to die, but I can't kill him. I can't *bring myself* to kill him. The people I've killed were just food. He . . . he is emotion."

Human or lycanthrope, the machinations of women confounded Chad. He thought about trying to comfort her with a hug, but his raging hard-on reminded him that gesture could be misconstrued. And why would he want to comfort her anyway? She was using her sexuality to manipulate him while she was in love with another man. "Why do you want him to die?"

"He's taking things too far. We should have moved onto new hunting grounds long ago, but he's fascinated by how many of our kind there are. He still wants to eat you and your friends and triple the size of our pack."

"You and Viper and Dylan don't want to eat me?"

"I don't. You really impressed me, Chad. No one has ever gone through the transformation and escaped from us before. Viper and Dylan are simple guys who will follow whoever is in charge. If Hunter's gone, then that'll be me."

"What about Brick and his friends?"

Kat rolled her eyes and smiled, the sour act of knowing she was the punchline of a twisted joke.

"Hunter wants to eat them, too. Just another challenge. We want to get the Elder Blood first. If you hadn't noticed, we heal faster than any other animal, but Elder Blood heals us almost instantly. Hunter is anticipating a need for Elder Blood when we hunt the football players. I don't want that. I want to use the Elder Blood to change them back."

Chad ran his hands through his hair, hoping to pull the thoughts out of his head that no longer wished were there. He always daydreamed about getting revenge on Mason, leading to his ultimate demise. But they were always full-blown impossible fantasies, usually in a faraway future where Mason met his death at the other end of a laser blaster or falling from the top of a tall peak, thrown by Chad wearing his cybernetic exoskeleton. Sometimes the impetus would be to save Brittany, the damsel. Kat was no damsel, but she was asking for help. A simple task that would solve a lot of problems. On the other hand, a quick-fix solution was how he got most of these unsolvable problems in the first place. Or was he being asked to be the hero?

The death of Mason was still fresh in Chad's mind. He was able to call forth the memories with such acuity that he could hear the exact pitch in Mason's screams and feel the splashes of blood against his skin. Could he do that to Hunter? Even if there were a way to do it with less gore, could he go through with it? "So, if Hunter is . . . gone . . . you'd change Brick and his friends back to human?"

"Yes. Your friends, too, if they'd like." She was suddenly next to him again, her hand on his cheek, but she was now wearing clothes. Even though they did little to hide her body, Chad was still extremely disappointed. "With your help, we can make a lot of things right."

Kat kept her eyes in human form, rings of piercing green cutting through him to his soul. The same color as her daughter's. Wait . . . Natalia! Natalia would be with him tonight, and she'd be primed to kill. Kat never said that he specifically had to kill Hunter, just that he had to die, and she couldn't bring herself to do it. "Okay. Tonight, at McClintock's grave."

A smile formed on Kat's face, broad and beaming. "So, you've learned about that, too, huh? Very smart, Chad."

"Thank you." He had no idea what else to say.

Unfortunately, it wasn't enough to get her back to being naked, nor did it entice her to stay. She sauntered to the window she had used last time. "I'll guess I'll see you tonight."

Chad didn't want her to leave, but the only thing he could say to stop her was, "Hey."

It worked, but he needed a follow-up. Her eyes turned his insides into bubbling magma, and he could think of nothing better than, "Why'd you put dead cows on my lawn?"

"That was Hunter's idea. He was pissed that you stole the Elder Blood and wanted to spook you. He thought it'd be funny if we put the dead jocks' jerseys on them. Just another example of him taking things too far and why he needs to die. Our survival depends on people not knowing we exist."

"Apparently, farmers have security cameras on their farms now."

"I know, right? What the heck are they keeping an eye on?"

"I guess they're looking for the aliens that keep making the crop circles?"

Kat laughed again, genuine and alluring. "You're pretty funny, Chad."

As she opened the window, a legitimate thought struck him. "When Hunter dies, won't that change everyone back to human? The ones he's changed?"

"Depends."

"Depends on what?"

"If you believe in stupid fucking fairy tales."

Kat was gone.

Chad shut and locked the window, more from routine than thinking it would protect him from anyone who wanted to get him.

CHAPTER 36

Who was older? Obviously, Kat was older, but when did she turn? When did time stop for her? Chad studied Natalia's face and wondered how old she was. She was drinking at McClintock's, but that didn't mean anything; maybe she had the password, too. Even though she was beautiful and intelligent and more than capable of taking care of herself, Chad felt bad for her. He couldn't imagine a life never having a father in it and having his mom as his mortal enemy.

"Stop staring at me. It's creepy."

Chad looked away, an all too familiar warmth rushing up his neck and settling within his cheeks. "Sorry. I was . . . I was trying to think of a compliment."

"This isn't a date, Chad."

"If it was, I'd take you someplace nicer than a graveyard." Chad laughed, a burst to get the ball rolling. Natalia responded with a stoic coldness that made the headstones of the graveyard look inviting, and the pink warmth of his face burst into a raging red inferno.

Thankful for the cool fall breeze that the sunset brought with it, Chad went back to watching the graveyard and reviewed the plan. It was a simple one. Natalia hypothesized that a two hundred plus-year-old corpse would not be very well preserved. Depending on how well the coffin was constructed, the bones would be dust brittle, if not gone. Natalia and Chad decided that they had the same obstacle stopping them from digging up the body as the Ink Stains did—daylight.

The Cherish Hill church was small and community-run with no official diocese affiliated with it, used twice on Sundays and occasionally for a wedding when the bride and groom found everything else booked. Despite its minimal use, it was located along a nicely maintained two-lane road. Not a main thoroughfare by any stretch of the imagination, but a road used enough that digging up a grave would not go unnoticed. Natalia and Chad decided to let the Ink Stains dig up the remains and steal them. Plus, if the Ink Stains discovered the soldier too decayed to be useful, then Natalia and Chad had no reason to engage. They arrived an hour before sundown and waited.

Across the street was a small cornfield surrounded by forest. That was the escape plan. Chad and Natalia hid five trees deep in the forest behind the church, downwind and far enough away not to be seen, but close enough that they had a clear line of sight to McClintock's grave. Once the Ink Stains had the remains in a container, Natalia would create a diversion, and Chad would rush out, grab the container, and cut through the cornfield. Hopefully, there would be enough surprise and confusion for escape. They assumed that the Ink Stains would use something with handles for the remains, but just in case they didn't, Chad had his messenger bag slung over his shoulder. All that was left to do was sit next to a gorgeous woman in awkward silence for an hour.

Seventy-five minutes.

Ninety minutes.

One hundred minutes.

Two hours.

Two full hours of Chad wracking his brain trying to come up with any form of conversation. This embarrassed him. Alone with a woman, and he couldn't think of a single talking point. Sure, she wasn't a normal girl, but that was what made her interesting, made all kinds of questions stack up in his mind. She was homeschooled and raised by her aunt! Plenty of non-threatening questions from those two facts alone. By the time he decided to form a question around that, rustling came from the cornfield across the street.

An hour after sunset, two shadows emerged from the corn and strode to the grave, one large and lumbering, one thin and quick. Dylan and Viper. They were carrying things, but Chad couldn't make out the details. He whispered, "What do they have with them?"

Natalia watched them through night-vision binoculars. She didn't answer Chad with words; instead she handed him the binoculars. Through a green world, Chad watched Dylan and Viper use shovels to dig up the grave. After a few minutes, they fussed with whatever they found in the hole, and Dylan pulled out a stick. It wasn't until it crumbled within Dylan's hand did Chad realize it was once a bone. The small chunks fell into a box that Viper held. The two continued to scoop from the grave and put into the box. "Well, it looks like they found—"

Chad was a little surprised when Natalia stood and took aim with her crossbow. "Get ready."

He set the binoculars down by her feet and put one hand on the messenger bag to make sure he was prepared. He put his hand over his pocket to make sure his emergency plan was still with him.

Natalia fired her crossbow.

A hand grabbed the arrow.

Hunter stepped out from behind the last tree of the forest line. In human form except for his sharp teeth glinting in the minimal moonlight. "Now, now, now. I can't have you two interrupting such a delicate operation. My associates are in the process of honoring a fallen war hero by moving him from such an inglorious location to someplace he could be more appreciated for his efforts. We have to—"

Chad kicked him.

It was obvious that Hunter had not read enough comic books or seen enough movies to know that the hubris of a monologue could lead to disaster. Chad was excited that he finally timed something perfectly. In full rabbit form, he hopped a few yards and planted his front feet. Just like he did with Brick, he slammed his back feet into Hunter's chest.

Hunter bounced off the nearest tree and landed with a thud. Natalia reloaded and shot, but her target was too fast. He moved just enough to take the bolt in his arm instead of his heart. Glowing eyes regarded Natalia as he stood and yanked the bloodied projectile from his arm. Natalia wasn't one for posturing, and she quickly reloaded. Hunter changed into a werewolf and disappeared into the forest. "Go, Chad!" Natalia yelled. "Get the box!"

Chad raced from the forest and aimed for Viper holding the box, but Dylan in bear form charged. A crossbow bolt whizzed past and struck the bear in the shoulder. Dylan stumbled and let loose a devastating roar. That cleared the path to Viper.

Even though he lost the element of surprise, Chad tried what he did before, planting his front feet and kicking with his rear. He missed. Expecting as much, he calculated the way Viper would dodge. Chad guessed correctly, but underestimated Viper's speed in his half-snake form, and missed again. Now it was his turn to dodge attacks.

Left, right, back. Chad jumped all around. He ducked away from claw swipes and evaded every bite, but he couldn't avoid getting repeatedly hit with Viper's tail. Each smack stung, the pain getting cumulative. He was getting tired, fear and fatigue seeping into his muscles. Then he heard Kat's yowl.

In her half-cat, half-human form, she raced out from behind the church on all fours. When she got close enough, she pounced. Chad was confused—she could have killed him if she hadn't commanded his attention, and she was moving slower than he expected. It dawned on him that she must have been telling the truth in his bedroom because he parried her attack with ease, and she went careening into Viper. The impact was hard enough to get him to drop the box.

Perfect! The turn of events sent a burst of adrenaline through Chad's body. He made his hands human long enough to scoop the box into his messenger bag. He sprinted across the street and got to the cornfield when he heard, "Chad!"

He stopped.

He knew he shouldn't have, but it was who called out to him that made him stop.

Hunter.

Standing behind Natalia, he held her by her hair with his left hand while his right was in werewolf mode, the tips of his claws around her neck. "You're a smart kid, Chad. I think you know what you have to do, or else you know what I'll have to do."

Natalia struggled and yelled, "Don't, Chad! Keep running!"

Chad had hoped he didn't have to activate his contingency plan, but he shifted back to his human state and reached into the pocket of his shorts. Now he needed to stall. The brittle stalks of unattended corn were tall enough to conceal most of his body as he walked to the road. Once out of the cornfield, he stopped at the edge of the road and held out the messenger bag. "Let her go, and I'll put it on the ground."

All four lycanthropes were in some hybrid stage between human and animal, and they laughed. Hunter said, "Chad with the jokes tonight."

With no other choice, Chad looked both ways and crossed the road, stopping at the edge. He didn't want to give up the bag, but he had to, and he needed more time. "This better?"

"A joke loses its impact the more you tell it," Hunter growled.

"I don't trust you."

"I don't care."

Chad looked at the bag in his hands and then down the road to his left and right. "I'm not coming any closer."

"Then I'll kill her."

The thin strands of blood running down Natalia's neck looked brown in the pale moonlight. "Then I'll run away with the goods."

"Then, we'll catch you."

"I'm faster, and I know the forest better than you do."

Fur bristled on those who had it as all four Ink Stains growled. Chad wasn't sure if either of his statements were accurate, but judging by the way the Ink Stains reacted, they certainly thought so. Hunter looked at Viper and nodded to Chad. The semi-snake creature slithered among the headstones.

Chad tried to think of more ways to stall, but nothing came to mind other than a classic game of "keep away," but he doubted there would be any outcome that didn't lead to his disembowelment. That thought made him paranoid. "That's close enough."

Viper stopped about ten feet away and hissed. Chad begged fate for another minute or two, but it just wasn't meant to be. He tossed the messenger bag to Viper.

"Chad! No!" Natalia yelled. "They're going to kill us!"

"No, they won't."

Hunter chuckled, a sick noise that made Chad's blood curdle. "Oh, no? Why is that?"

Chad reached into his pocket to pull out a small phone and then tossed it to Hunter. "I called the cops. It's a burner so they can't trace it back to me, but I'm sure they traced the call by now since they're undoubtedly pissed that I called and hung up on them three times. They're not far away, I'm sure."

Hunter crushed the phone. "We can still kill you. You'll just be two more dead bodies, and they'll never know to look for us."

Chad pulled out his cell phone and held it over his head. "They will after my friends show them the live stream that we're doing right now."

Natalia gasped as Hunter yanked her hair and growled, "I call bullshit."

"Then I must be a damn good illusionist to make those red and blue lights appear."

Everyone looked down the road. The lights were no bigger than Christmas tree lights, but they were coming closer. A growl rumbled deep within Hunter, culminating in a gruff bark. With that, he released Natalia, and all four Ink Stains sprinted to the forest.

CHAPTER 37

Natalia nibbled on her slice of pizza. Her teeth cut through just enough to be considered a bite; her lips pulled back as if contact with the food would melt them. She wasn't even halfway through her first piece while Chad was starting his fourth. Of course, if his friends were with him, there would be some debate if this was really his fourth piece or not since he didn't eat the crusts. Be that as it may, he was still a little dismayed that Natalia didn't like pizza.

While chewing, she set her slice back on her plate and grabbed a napkin to wipe her mouth, even though there was no mess to clean away. "You're doing it again."

"What?" Chad asked.

"Staring. It's still not a date."

"I know." He was about to tell her that if it were a date, then he would have taken her someplace nicer than Rocket Lizard Pizza but decided against it. Instead, he went with, "I've never seen anyone not like pizza."

Natalia's natural frown deepened. "I like pizza. I have no idea what the hell this is supposed to be. Let me try one of your crusts."

Chad slid his plate closer, and she snatched one. Clutching it the way she would wield a dagger, she took a bite. Nodding her approval, she took another bite while moving her remaining slice and a half to his plate. "Not bad. So much better without the greasy cheese and toxic sauce and whatever pitiful excuse of meat circles they consider pepperoni here."

Even though she trashed the pizza he so loved for over a decade of his life, Chad soaked in this moment. When she wasn't yelling at him, she was nice to be around. With confidence came a sense of comfort; she had the confidence to spare, and Chad felt comfortable around her. Almost relaxed. He found it endearing that they exchanged food with each other. "So, what's the pizza like where you're from?"

"Where I'm from? I'm from Delaware. Where the hell did you think I was from?"

Chad shrugged. "I don't know. Someplace a bit more far off and exotic, like Europe. Maybe Transylvania."

"Transyl . . . ? Do you really think all monsters and hunters are from the far off exotic land of Transylvania?"

"It's a real place, you know."

"I know. It's located in central Romania, bordered by the Carpathian Mountains on the east and south, the Apuseni Mountains to the west, has a population of about six point seven million people, and its most noticeable reference in pop culture is within the pages of *Dracula* by Bram Stoker."

"See? That response right there. That's why I didn't think you were from the United States."

"Because I know more about Transylvania than you?"

"I knew all that . . . you know what? Not important. I'm talking about the way you presented the information. Like you're reciting facts only, the way a robot would."

"That's just the way I learned. I didn't need to be constantly engaged or entertained to learn. My aunt would teach me something and then make me recite it back."

"Yeah, but now you act and talk like you're forty."

"You and your friends act and talk like you're fourteen."

"That's not our fault."

"How can your immaturity not be your fault?"

There was a certain level of comfort being around Natalia, but sometimes contempt accompanied comfort. "Oh, I don't know. Maybe because our examples of adults were less than stellar? My mom always thinking I needed her protection because my dad considers me a disappointment since I have no interest in sports. Or Kyle's parents sheltering him so badly that he needs medication to deal with even the slightest of anxieties. Then there's Cooper. His dad left when he was twelve, and he took it upon himself to be the *man* of the house and take care of his mother, who, by the way, completely checked out. For the last six years, she goes to her job as a tollbooth collector, hands her check to Cooper, and watches TV. No drinking or drugs or bad food, just vegetates in front of the television. Cooper pays the bills, does the shopping, cooks, cleans, maintains the house. He talks like a pompous douche because that's how he thought adults talked when he had to become one at the age of twelve. And Heston is the opposite. He has no idea how to cook or clean because his dad has no idea. His diet is pizza and fast food, because that's all his dad eats. He can't get a job because his dad makes him work for his landscaping company whenever someone calls off. Ever wonder why someone his size cowers so quickly?"

It was meant to be a rhetorical question, but Chad paused to catch his breath. Natalia handed him a fistful of napkins and whispered, "His dad beats him."

Chad dabbed his eyes and wiped his nose. He nodded, but his words lost the fervor they had seconds ago. "Not a lot, but every few months if Heston screws something up, it's a backhand and a twelve-hour Saturday of mowing lawns. Then add to all that being bullied at school ever since kindergarten. So, when do we grow? How do we mature? Our social interactions other than with ourselves have been limited, and we received no guidance."

"So your frustrations culminated into a string of bad decisions where you found yourselves as lycanthropes," Natalia said, completing his thought.

"Yeah."

"My aunt says you tried to take the easy way out. I say you took a risk. You tried to grow."

"Thank you."

Chad took her half slice of pizza and shoved it in his face to cover up the fact that he had nothing else to say. He turned to one of the three life-sized statues of the anthropomorphized eponymous rocket lizard. This one wore goggles and a scarf while pointing a bulbous barreled laser gun at anyone entering or exiting the men's room. He was a green lizard with small chips of paint missing from careless people knocking into him, and his name was Zaurn according to the discolored engraving at the base of the statue. Only those who visited the establishment enough would know that, Chad and friends were among those numbers. When the statues first arrived a year and a half ago, he thought they were cool, a way of bringing something from his imagination into the real world. A touchable dream. Now, he wondered if Viper could morph his body into a bipedal saurian creature. The plastic laser gun was fake, but the inspiration behind the statue was real. And deadly.

"What's so special about this place?" Natalia asked.

Chad wondered if he was exuding too much reverence while gazing upon the statue of Zaurn. "My friends and I came on opening day when we were six and immediately fell in love with it. It wasn't Rocket Lizard Pizza like it is today. Just a regular pizza shop that could be found in any town across America. But it was *our* pizza shop, you know? All four of us could walk here. Over the years, it turned into a haven for us. A place to meet with endless pizza and soda and a few video games against the one wall. One day we just declared this to be sacred grounds. Sanctuary for bad days. A court of sorts if anyone of us has an issue with anyone else in the group. Lying was forbidden. Not that we lied to each other often, but *here* we were never allowed to withhold the truth."

"You've been coming here since you were six? No wonder you don't know the pizza's bad."

"It's not bad. It's just what I'm used to and what I find comforting. It's one of the few constants in life. In the twelve years that I've been coming here, this place has had fifteen different owners, yet the pizza recipe has never changed."

"Interesting," Natalia said.

"It is if you think about it. And Cooper can name all fifteen iterations in sequential order. That's pretty amazing."

In the rare instance of a rabbit pulling a magician out of a hat, Chad's words made Cooper appear. "I do, indeed, remember every name that this particular establishment has adopted, and yes, I am amazing, but for more reasons than just knowing that this place first started as Vinnie's, then it became Vincent's, because the second owner who was named Vincent, but went by Vinnie, wanted to distance himself from the failure of the first Vinnie. Vincent's lasted only six months, then it became Sal's, coincidentally purchased by yet another gentleman named Vincent, but called it Sal's to avoid confusion. After nine months, the shop changed names with each successive purchase starting with Brothers Pizza, then Two Brothers, then Three Brothers, then Quatro Hermanos, then Six Brothers. Of course, to no one's surprise, it moved on to be known as Cousins. That didn't work, so the fusion fad came barreling through town and brought with it Wong's Asian Fusion Pizza, which lasted longer than the subsequent Holistic California Pizza. Shortly after that came the silly names of Dough Boys and Pie R Round and Slice N Dice, which caused mass amounts of confusion among those who thought it was vegan—as in dice up some vegetables—those who thought it was going to be an homage to slasher flicks, and those who thought it would be a haven for games where six-sided cubes of randomness were needed. Finally, an entrepreneur wished to create his own version of the mouse-singing kids' place, so he purchased the building we now visit in an effort to capitalize on that place's popularity. That is why we now have Rocket Lizard Pizza. Greetings, Natalia. As always, my lovely lass, it's my pleasure to behold your beautiful visage." Cooper concluded the announcement of his arrival with a deep bow at the waist.

Natalia took another crunchy bite of the pizza crust. "You're really fucking weird. And that's coming from a girl who grew up hunting lycanthropes and, apparently, learning too much about Transylvania."

Chad chuckled. It felt good to be on the inside of a joke like that with someone other than his three friends. It felt good to be able to vent in a way he couldn't with his three friends. Cooper cocked his head in confusion but opted not to interrogate. Instead, he ignored Natalia's comment and said, "So, what might be the reason to call upon me to join you within the sacred borders?"

"We need to get the band back together."

"Apologies need to be made and accepted, by all four of us, I believe, before we can be the group we've always been. I have faith it will happen, but it's going to take time. Some wounds are still fresh, especially with what Heston said to Kyle."

"I understand, but unfortunately, we don't have time."

Cooper grabbed the last slice of pizza and slouched back in his chair. He folded the slice and took two bites. Squinting like a thoughtful judge ready to pass a sentence, he asked, "Why is that?"

"The Ink Stains are trying to conjure the triple goddess Morrigan in an effort to get more Elder Blood."

Two more bites. Slow, deliberate chewing. "How do you know this?"

Chad turned to Natalia, and she nodded for him to share the information.

Cooper didn't move, didn't shift from his position as Chad told the stories of meeting with Wanda and his run-in with the Ink Stains at McClintock's grave. Cooper made no comments, asked no questions, simply ate pizza as he listened. Only when he finished eating, which coincided with the end of Chad's tale, did he move. Sitting forward and placing his elbows on the table, he pointed to Natalia. "The beautiful and deadly Kat is your mother?"

"She is."

"Now, I see where you get it from."

Blank stare.

"Well . . . ah-hem . . . sorry. Anyway, you two tangled with the Ink Stains last night, trying to thwart their plans from collecting the remains of the area's oldest soldier."

"Correct. We would have stopped them if Chad hadn't handed the remains over to them."

"Well, from the story I just heard, it seems like Chad saved your life."

"It didn't need saving."

"Let's put a pin in that for now and just agree to disagree. I think the one thing we should examine more is the fact that Chad recorded it on his cell phone? That's absolutely fantastic news."

"It was a bluff. He recorded nothing."

Cooper had the personality that some people could only handle in small doses, but one of his more endearing characteristics was his loyalty. He maintained an upbeat tone, but Chad could hear the frustration in his friend's voice. "But it was a great idea to get out of dying and to, you know, save your life. And the burner phone was real, though, right? You did use it to summon the police, correct?"

"The burner phone? Yes. My life needing saving? No."

Cooper huffed out a sigh and then turned to Chad. "Okay, so I've ascertained from the information given to me that they have two of the three components. Is this true?"

"It is," Chad answered.

"Okay, but it doesn't seem like that should matter much since you said the third ingredient is a mysterious plant called the Queen of the Night that grows in South America and blooms one night per year."

"Guess what?" Natalia said, a playfulness to her tone.

"Oh, fuck me sideways," Cooper moaned as he buried his face in his hands.

Chad put a hand on Cooper's shoulder. "We need to get the band back together . . . today."

CHAPTER 38

The meeting was going well per Chad's estimation. Awkward and uncomfortable, but everyone was here. In Tyler's barn yet again, sitting around the wooden spool table, knights of the round table as it were if the knights had to suffer through embarrassment.

Kyle's cheeks were pink while Heston's whole head was red. The slightest of smirks tugged at the corner of Cooper's lips while he absently played with a balled-up piece of hay on the table. Despite his predilection for making uncomfortable situations even more so, he kept his gaze downward and avoided eye contact with everyone. Chad felt that his cheeks held a blush, not necessarily for what was happening, but because Natalia sat at the table quietly, head down, her cheeks pink as well.

Rocket Lizard pizza became too crowded and noisy when a bus full of sugar-fueled children invaded the place. Tyler was gracious enough to host the impromptu meeting but said in no uncertain terms that he had plans and was going to focus on them, meeting or not. Chad, Cooper, and Natalia confirmed their understanding and got to work sliding spare hay bales around the table. Kyle showed up next and took a seat, aware that Heston would be in attendance as well. When Heston arrived, he was as quiet as usual but didn't turn away. Chad explained the situation, including the details of his meeting with Wanda, the three items necessary for the Ink Stains to call forth the Morrigan, and how they now had two of them. Natalia participated as well, adding details, her tone much softer.

Satan's Petting Zoo

Heston and Kyle both said they were sorry, but only time could get either of them to accept the apologies. They said the words, and that was good enough for Chad. He just wanted to disseminate the information and solidify the next steps they needed to take. "Guys, I just want to say that I'm really proud of you for apologizing to each other, and I'm really proud of us for meeting like this to prepare for what we need to do. I'm proud to call everyone at the table, my friend."

"Fuck me," a woman's voice came from Tyler's couch. Heston's face had started to lighten in shade until that outburst. Now it was full red again. Cooper's mouth twitched as he stifled a laugh.

The warmth in Chad's cheeks had yet to leave since Tyler started his "introspection" on his couch. Chad wanted to hurry through this meeting, but he also wanted to convey how he felt about everything. He continued, "This is a real coming together moment for us as we're endeavoring to move beyond our own limitations."

"Yes," the woman moaned, her words getting louder and faster. "Yes! There! Right there! Harder!"

Cooper snorted and brought his hand to his mouth to hide his smile. Kyle exhaled slowly and looked at the ceiling. Chad couldn't take this anymore. "Ummm, Tyler? Is there any way we could ask that you pause the . . . the what you're doing?"

Lounged on the couch, Tyler had his tablet in his left hand, a can of beer and a lit joint in his right. Without looking away from the screen, he replied, "You could ask. You could always ask. But I'm gonna say no."

"Could you maybe wear headphones?"

Tyler drew deeply from his joint, gulped a few times from his can, and then exhaled the smoke. "No. It would diminish the purity of the process."

Not knowing how else to shape his argument, Chad looked to his tablemates for any form of assistance. Everyone looked everywhere other than at him. Luckily, Cooper had enough wits about him to ask, "So, what is it that you're trying to do?"

"Trying to find a new addiction," Tyler answered, "Internet porn is the hot new addiction to have lately, so I figured I'd give it a try."

"So . . . why are you trying to find a new addiction?"

"I've always preached the twelve steps, used them to build a foundation for my clean living lifestyle. Ever since you've shown me the light about my GMO misunderstanding, I've felt like a fraud for using the twelve steps without having a legitimate addiction. I feel like if I don't have to struggle with something to warrant their use, then I've stolen them."

"What if you transcended addiction?"

For the first time all evening, Tyler lowered his tablet. Still lying on the couch, he placed it on his chest. "How do you mean?"

"The whole point of the twelve steps is to help manage addiction. Part of that process is finding a sponsor, and then potentially becoming a sponsor yourself. Maybe that's where you are on your personal journey? Look at what you do with us—you're our trainer, our mentor, our confidant. You're basically our collective sponsor already. Chad mentioned that you once implied to him that he was addicted to being a downtrodden loser."

"Hey!" Chad snapped.

Cooper dismissed Chad with a wave of his hand and continued, "If that's the case, then all of us at the table have the same addiction, other than the more than capable and confident Natalia. You've already given us a headquarters . . . nay . . . a sacred haven and you've made yourself available to us. You, Tyler, are working hard to make us better people, to help us conquer *our* addictions. You don't need an addiction to wield the twelve steps. You need to teach them to us."

Tyler arched his eyebrows as the corners of his mouth tugged downward. He nodded, contemplating Cooper's words. He then sat up and placed the tablet on his lap, face up so everyone at the table who opted not to look at the ceiling could easily see two naked women, each with a hand between the other's legs. "You might be right. I haven't thought of it that way. I'm like, your addiction counselor."

"Exactly!" Chad knew that Cooper was fighting hard with himself to keep from being mesmerized by what was happening on the screen by the way that his voice warbled.

Finishing his beer, Tyler stood up and made his way to the loft ladder. "I'm taking this upstairs to think about it. Anyone want to join me?"

Natalia gasped, and that felt like another punch to the dick for Chad.

"Nah," Cooper replied with a chuckle. "I think we're all good right here."

Tyler shrugged. "Suit yourself. If anyone changes their mind, come on up." He ascended the ladder and disappeared into the shadows.

The color of Heston's head lightened from inferno red to warm pink. "Sometimes, Tyler triggers my fight or flight."

"Yeah," Kyle said, finally looking a direction other than up. "With me, it's usually flight."

"Me, too."

Heston and Kyle laughed. Chad felt better now. His friends seemed to have moved past personal obstacles, and the constant distraction was no longer present. Well, for the guys, at least. Natalia continued to watch the loft. There was no noise, movement, or light from the space above, yet she continued to watch it as if she were stranded in a desert, and the last glass of water was up in the loft. Her jaw muscles flexed as if she was preparing for something to happen, or worse, contemplating going up the ladder. Before that could happen, Chad cleared his throat to get everyone's attention. "So, about the Ink Stains . . ."

Cooper found another stray piece of straw and twirled it around his fingers. "Well, boys and independent, self-sufficient woman of the twenty-first century, it seems that Berkman's Gardens has a Queen of the Night and is hosting a special exhibit for those who are anthophilous and willing to congregate at the wee hours of the morning to watch it bloom. Obviously, the Ink Stains will be there, which means that we should be there to do what we can to stop them. It seems like there's only one thing left to do."

"Game it out," the men said in unison.

"What are you talking about?" Natalia asked. She sounded annoyed, but Chad was happy that she finally stopped looking at the loft.

With the smarm of an aristocrat and a fake British accent reserved for the local Renaissance Faire, Cooper answered, "We're going to simulate what we have to do tonight by running it through a D & D campaign. Would milady care to join us?"

"I'm the DM," Heston added.

"No, thank you." She stood from the table. "I've got my own ways to prepare for tonight."

"Very good, very good," Cooper said, maintaining his fake accent. "Fare thee well, beautiful maiden of mystery. We bid thee good afternoon."

"Yeah. You, too." With a cursory wave to everyone at the table and one last glance to the loft, Natalia left the barn.

"She's so intense," Heston whispered.

Cooper stood and clapped Heston's back. "Ah, yes, my friend. Often the most beautiful of diamonds is also the hardest."

"Really? Aren't all diamonds the same hardness?" Kyle asked.

"Not at all. Don't forget the five c's of diamonds: color, cut, clarity, carat, and concreteness."

"Concreteness?"

"Yes. The hardness of the diamond."

"I really don't think that's a thing."

"Sure, it is. Come on. Let's reconvene in Heston's basement, and we'll look it up."

They all agreed to spend the night at Heston's. They left the barn and decided to head to their respective houses first for supplies. Chad stayed back and hid behind a nearby tree. So ashamed by his actions that he would deny them, but he waited for a half-hour to make sure Natalia didn't come back.

CHAPTER 39

The greenhouse was warm. Chad expected as much since one of the specialties of Berkman's Gardens was exotic plants that usually grew farther south and out of the reach of the potentially cruel winters of the Northeast United States, so he didn't look too out of place wearing nylon shorts, flip-flops, and a loose t-shirt. Kyle wore similar attire while Heston and Cooper opted to carry a change of clothes in the rucksacks slung over their shoulders.

Had he not been on a mission, Chad would have enjoyed what the greenhouse offered. Rows of sturdy tables bolted to the ground held all kinds of potted plants and flowers. Smaller, less expensive offerings were on the tables toward the center of the room while the larger, more costly ones were on the outer tables. Decorative trees that could act as a conversation piece for any office or upper-class suburban home lined the perimeter. All the aisles were wide enough for potential customers to walk side by side while discussing how beautiful the flowers were. Except for the Queen of the Night.

In the center of the greenhouse was the "stage." The stage was nothing more than a cordoned off ten-foot by ten-foot area with an ornate pedestal in the center. At least once a month, Berkman's Gardens held an event to display their most exotic flora. They tried to make it as lavish as possible—the stage barrier was a set of velvet-covered ropes while the presenter had the looks and charm of a professional actress—to make the viewers feel as if they were all part of a special experience, rather than merely marks here to purchase expensive flowers. On the pedestal tonight was the night-blooming cereus, or better known as Queen of the Night.

Three closed flowers stuck out in the beginning stages of their bloom. The tips of thin, white petals peeked out from a wrap of green. Chad chuckled at the necessity of a plexiglass casing around the plant as if a unicorn were about to hatch from a Faberge Egg. Sure, the Queen of the Night was rare, but it had a price tag on it just like everything else in the greenhouse.

Chad walked up and down the aisles, picking up a potted plant every now and again to be nonchalant. He adjusted his pace only if a sales associate entered his orbit. He was the designated rover, moving from team member to team member to share any data collected. So far, the only information to share was that the night-blooming cereus was classified as a cactus.

"It looks more like a vine," Cooper said. He stood in the north aisle. Heston and Kyle opted to take advantage of the foldout chairs by the south and east aisles. Natalia eschewed the chairs, choosing to stay on her feet, moving up and down the west aisle.

"The brochure says it's a cactus," Chad replied.

"I read the very same brochure. Since it's a mere two pages, I've perused it over and over and repeatedly."

"Yeah, I'm bored, too, but we need to remain vigilant. Have you seen anything out of the ordinary?"

"Negative. Have you?"

"No."

"Well, I have," Natalia said.

Both Chad and Cooper jumped, startled by her sudden appearance. Surprised, Chad blurted, "You're out of position."

Natalia nodded her head toward the far end of the north aisle. "Well, I wouldn't have to be if any of you numbnuts were capable of recognizing anything out of the ordinary."

Brick.

"What the literal fuck of all the holy and mighty fucks is he doing here?" Cooper asked.

"I have no idea. But I'm going to ask him."

"Do not engage, Chad," Natalia commanded.

"Yes, Chad, her suggestion is a very wise one. It seems like he's the only one of the football players here, so it should be of no great difficulty to continually traverse around the areas of the greenhouse where he isn't," Cooper added.

"I'm tired of being afraid," Chad said.

"This isn't about being afraid, buddy, this about sticking to the plan."

"You're right about the plan, but it will go better if we can remove any of the unknown variables."

"Dude, he's a *major* variable. We don't know why he's here, and we don't know what his plans are. If he kicks your ass right now, it will most definitely threaten the viability of our plan."

"Guys, trust me, I got this." Chad walked away from them before they could retort.

Brick noticed Chad, never taking his eyes off him. Chad made eye contact and walked toward one corner of the room. It was a bit darker, among a thick patch of hanging ferns, but not so far out of the way that Brick could murder Chad. Someone would notice. Chad shoved his hands in his pockets and waited.

The football player walked over, making no attempt at subterfuge. Stopping in front of Chad, Brick greeting him by curling his fingers into fists, tight enough to crack his knuckles.

Be calm, Chad reminded himself. *Remember Sensei/Sponsor Tyler's teachings. Stay focused.* "Brick."

"Nerd."

"What are you doing here, Brick?"

"I could ask you the same. Ah, fuck it. I will ask you the same. What are you doing here?"

"Like you said, I'm a nerd. I'm a nerd for flowers. I'm nerding out all over the place right now."

Brick snorted in amusement. "Yeah? I'm thinking it's something more than that. I followed you here to the Gardens, so I figured I'd follow you into the greenhouse as well."

Followed? Chad didn't like the sound of that. How long? What did he know? A big chunk of ice formed in his bowels, and he prayed that Brick didn't know about the barn, especially with his propensity toward arson. "So, you saw me at the practice field today and followed me here?"

Brick frowned, the furrow of his heavy brow, making his eyes darker. "Practice field? You weren't at the practice field. You came home in the afternoon and then went to Heston's house. You never went . . . aaaah. Clever. I sometimes forget that weak people are sometimes smart people. I'm not quick, but I catch on. You were fishing to see what I know, to see if I know something you don't want me to know. Don't worry. I'll figure it out. Starting with, why are you here?"

Chad exhaled, not realizing he had been holding his breath. Brick didn't know about the barn, so that was good news. Now he debated about telling Brick the truth, giving him the details about what the Ink Stains were planning, but he'd have to share that the Ink Stains killed Mason and the other football players. Brick would not react well to that news. He couldn't take that risk. "Brick, please listen. If you leave now, I will tell you everything . . . tomorrow."

"What if I say no?"

This was it. This was the moment Chad had been preparing for. He pulled his phone from his pocket just far enough out to for Brick to see. As soon as the large man looked down at it, Chad slid it back in his pocket. "Then, I'll have to use this."

Brick smiled; the lines that formed made his face look even harder. "So, you got a new phone. Surprised it doesn't have a unicorn on it."

"No, but it does have a rhino on it."

A series of tectonic plates shifted as Brick's smile crashed into a deep frown. He folded his arms over his chest, the thin material of his t-shirt doing nothing to hide the veins wriggling among his striated muscles. "You better explain what you mean by that right fucking now."

"The day we had our little one on one chat at the practice field. Why do you think I was concerned about getting my phone back?"

Brick growled, a bone-rattling rumble. The skin on his arms started to wrinkle and turn gray. "Brick, not here," Chad said, his words hushed and hurried. "Look, I know there is a way we can coexist. I know how you view me and what you think of me, but like it or not, you and I are a part of a very exclusive group. We're a part of the same team. It's obvious that my friends and I are here because of that team. But I can't tell you about it now. Something is going to happen here tonight that we need to take care of. For the good of our team."

"Tomorrow. You'll tell me the truth about why you're here?"

"Yes. Absolutely."

"And what happened to Mason and my missing teammates?"

If Brick was nowhere near the public, Chad had no issues letting him know about the Ink Stains. "Yes. I will."

Brick grunted as a goodbye salutation and left.

Chad exhaled slowly, trying to blow away the butterflies flitting around in his stomach. Once they were gone, a warmth bloomed within his chest. He just stood up to a man three times his size and convinced him to leave. He needed to tell everyone. Over the next hour, Chad made his rounds to his friends, retelling the entire story in detail. Kyle gave him a thumbs-up; Cooper smacked his back and punched his arm; Heston nodded his approval. Natalia got the abbreviated version because Chad still had no idea where he stood with her.

The flowers had opened more, tendrils of white spreading outward from the center. The presentation would begin in a few more minutes. According to the schedule, there would be a fifteen-minute introduction, a fifteen-minute history of the flower, a thirty-minute question and answer session, then the remainder of the night into the morning for observation. The seats were filling up fast, and Chad debated with himself about when to take one, or if he should. The Ink Stains were coming. But how?

Chad and his friends had debated about all the different ways the Ink Stains could attack. They could rush in as their animal selves. It would draw a lot of attention, but it was fast, so it seemed the most logical way for them to do things. Some more out-of-the-box ideas were bandied about, including creating confusion with smoke bombs and dropping down the from ceiling like they do in heist movies, or posing as smooth-talking experts about the flower and somehow stealing it right in the open, or hiring a different group of people to storm in and steal it, or wearing masks and waving guns. What no one thought of was Hunter strolling in by himself.

CHAPTER 40

A rock star ready to take the stage, Hunter was everything Chad was not. Confident. Imposing. Dangerous. A primal beauty found inside the deadliest of creatures. As his name implied, Hunter stalked his way through the greenhouse, eying Chad the entire way.

With the smirk of someone who knew the punchline to every joke, Hunter greeted him with, "Chad."

Not prepared for this, Chad simply replied with, "Hunter."

"So, why are you here?"

"Why do you think?"

Hunter's smile grew enough to expose pointed canines as he spoke. "Oh, you're going to play the 'answer my question with a question' game? Fine. Since you and Kat's daughter were at the McClintock grave and now here, I assume you know what we're trying to do."

"Summon the Morrigan to give you more Elder Blood."

"Correct. Since you tried to stop us from getting McClintock's remains, I'm going to assume that you're going to try to stop us from getting the Queen of the Night pollen."

"We have to."

"And why would you want to do that?"

"Because you want to fucking eat me."

"Not if you step aside."

"You shouldn't have that kind of power. *No one* should."

"Would you go to the Serengeti and try to strip the lion of his power?"

"If they ate nothing but humans, then yes."

"Humans. Please don't tell me that you still view yourself as one."

"I am one."

Hunter chuckled a throaty rumble that sent a chill racing down Chad's spine. He then placed his arm around Chad's shoulders with all the familiarity of two chums. Hunter turned Chad with ease to face the Queen of the Night. From this angle, Chad could see his three friends, all frozen in wide-eyed surprise while Natalia was nowhere to be found. With his free hand, Hunter gestured to two women seated close to the display case. "Do you really believe you're the same as them?"

Both women had short white hair, though one's was thinner. Both were overweight in the waist, arms, and legs while their wrinkled jowls flopped about when they talked. Their glasses were tragically thick, and the one worked on crocheting a scarf while the other struggled with the nonstop tremors in her hands. "No, but that's because I'm not an octogenarian woman."

"You're a funny guy, Chad. You know that's not what I meant. Ever since I've given you this gift, haven't they seemed different? How they move now, just clumsy and slow. Their words are muted. And their smell. You can't tell me that they don't *smell* differently now."

They did. Chad recognized it immediately. Well, when he was away from the persistent smell of pot and hay in Tyler's barn. Not that his parents and friends and classmates smelled any differently, just that he *noticed* their scent, almost to the point of recognizing who was in the room with him even if he didn't see them. "They do."

"Good evening, everyone, and welcome to Berkman's Gardens, home of the most exotic flora in the tri-city area," the presenter greeted the attendees with the soft, even tone of a golf tournament announcer.

Even though she was hosting a late-night event in a greenhouse, not a hair was out of place to frame the portrait of her face done by a professional make-up artist. Her pants suit clung to her curves, and her blouse was open far enough to make Cooper use his cell phone to find any and every picture of her once he had learned her name. She continued talking in soothing tones informing everyone about upcoming events as well as incredible, "can't miss" sales. Hunter leaned closer, shortening the distance between his words and Chad's ear. "How about her? When you were human, you probably thought of her as close to perfection, but now . . . Now you can smell everything about her. The powder of her caked-on foundation, the awful perfume she's bathed in, her desperate pheromones hoping to attract a mate, her fear that she won't be able to."

Chad couldn't smell her fear and assumed that prey animals couldn't smell fear. He still thought of her as close to physically perfect, but he did understand the intent behind Hunter's words. The smells clung to her like a miasma and made her less than perfect. Without being dramatic enough to attract any unwanted attention, Hunter pointed to other people in the crowd. "Her? Her? Them? Him? Do you feel any kinship to them? To these humans? Their concerns, their motivations, their boredoms? We are above them, Chad. We can do whatever we want with this gift."

"Gift? You gave me this 'gift' to make me taste better."

"To tap into your true nature and bring it out, to allow you to be more than you were. Yes, we wanted to eat you, but not now. You transcended your simple human nature and embraced what it means to be better. You used your gifts to survive."

"You turned me into a rabbit."

"*You* made you into a rabbit. I can make you into so much more. Just let us call upon the Morrigan, and we will make everything better."

More? The inference was Chad could move beyond being a rabbit. Into what? Could prey turn into a predator? That would solve so many problems. That . . . that was *the same* thought he had when he first accepted Hunter's offer! He wanted a quick and easy solution. He wanted to be the hero but ended up becoming the villain of his own story. "No. We will stop you."

Hunter moved in front of Chad and placed both hands on his shoulders and squeezed. His face twitched with slight distortions. The corners of his mouth pulled toward his ears. His eyes turned into black pearls while his jaw shifted outward. His canines were no longer the only pointed teeth. "Sorry, Chad, but that just isn't going to happen."

The lights went out as soon as Hunter released Chad's shoulders.

A dog barked.

A woman screamed.

The lights came back on, and Hunter was gone. So was the Queen of the Night.

CHAPTER 41

Confusion. No one knew what happened when the lights went off, only that when they came back on, the Queen of the Night had vanished, and a woman had been injured. Bitten.

Chad hadn't seen anything during the outage, but he knew exactly what had happened. Hunter had stolen the night-blooming cereus and left a message. The bitten woman was one of the older women that Hunter had used as an example of the inferiority of human beings. The one who had been crocheting. The bite marks on her forearm were noticeable but not deep. Blood pooled and flowed from only a few. Chad heard Hunter's voice in his head:

"See how fragile they are?

"Look at how easy that was.

"Such delicate creatures.

"I did that to her in mere seconds.

"We are better than them."

Most of the employees and a few of the attendees rushed to the woman's aid. The remaining staff helped escort the other visitors from the greenhouse while the voice of the presenter encouraged everyone to exit the greenhouse in a calm, orderly fashion and pick up a discount voucher at the front checkout as a form of apology for the unforeseen circumstances leading to this inconvenience.

Chad spun in a circle to get his bearings. Hunter wasn't the only one who vanished into thin air—Natalia was nowhere to be found. His friends looked as confused as he felt, but Heston led the way concerning their next move. He helped a shaky old woman with a cane to her feet and offered his arm as additional support. Even though the fear on her face showed that she moved as fast as she could, people still flowed around her. Chad had no better idea, so he went to an older couple that he had seen a few times at the mall before and asked if they needed help getting to the exit. Both being so stooped at the shoulders that it took a considerable amount of painful effort to see what lay ahead, they accepted his offer. Cooper stood by the door and asked everyone who exited if they were okay or needed any medical assistance. Outside, Kyle asked people if they needed help to their cars.

Chad and his friends decided there was no more good they could do once the familiar red and white flashing lights of the ambulance pulled into the parking lot. They scurried to Cooper's car, parked next to Natalia's in the farthest spot away from all the buildings Berkman's Gardens had to offer.

"Holy wow, Chad," Kyle said, wringing his hands together from nervous energy. "Hunter came right up to you. Face to face. What was that all about?"

"Yeah, Chad. What the fuck was all that about?" Natalia appeared from behind a group of nearby trees and stormed over to Chad and his friends.

"What was what about? Hunter tried to convince me that we should join him. I said no, and then he stole the Queen of the Night."

"Really? You said no? Are you lying to me?"

"No, I'm not lying to you!"

"Then why'd you let him go? Why'd you let him steal the flower?"

"Let him? What are you talking about?"

"He was right in front of you. You should have done everything possible to stop him, yet you did nothing."

"What the hell could I have done? He's twice my size."

"I came outside, expecting you to lead him to me. Instead, you're helping little old ladies out of a greenhouse."

Chad slapped both palms against his forehead. "What in the name of all that is holy is so wrong about helping senior citizens out of a dangerous situation?"

"It wasn't that dangerous of a situation. To them, the lights went out and came back on. What they came to see got stolen, and an audience member got bitten. They all would have made it to the safety of their cars without your help. You didn't need to expose yourselves like that. You four being at this event like this was suspicious enough and then prolonging your stay so everyone could see you and interact with you was stupid."

"No, it wasn't. We're nerds, so it's really not unusual that we're at a flower show and would have stood out more if we had left when the lights came on. Four men under the age of twenty running from a room full of senior citizens would have made us stand out and given people reason to suspect us of having something to do with the lights going out. Just remember, you're a suspicious character to cops only if you act suspicious. We did nothing wrong, so no one will suspect our involvement."

"Nothing wrong other than giving Hunter what he wanted and then distracting yourselves with the plight of the elderly."

Chad had enough. This overall situation was his fault. His quest for power, not understanding what it was, and not knowing what to do with it. He would take the blame for making rash decisions and dragging his lifelong friends into the quagmire with him. But he wasn't going to take the blame for this specific failure. "No! Tonight was *not* our fault. Helping these people is exactly what we should be doing. If more people with power helped those who didn't have it, then this world wouldn't be such a shitty place, and we wouldn't be in this mess. We helped those people because it was the right thing to do. And don't you dare tell me I fucked up with Hunter, Miss 'I'm going to shoot every lycanthrope with my crossbow,' because you did nothing more than I did. If you're as great of a lycanthrope hunter as you act like, then you could have killed him ten different ways before he even knew he was dead. The Ink Stains got the Queen of the Night because they outsmarted us and did something that wasn't on our list of possibilities, which by the way, is pretty damn extensive, but since you didn't bother to help us with that early this evening, you wouldn't know. So, instead of wasting everyone's time shitting on a plan you didn't help make, how about you be a part of this one—we know where the Ink Stains are, and we know what they want to do. Now either leave us alone or get in the fucking car and help us stop them."

Chad waited for neither rejoinder nor reaction; he got in the passenger seat of Cooper's car and slammed the door shut. After a few vision-rattling heartbeats, the other three doors opened. Cooper got into the driver's seat and popped the trunk as he started the car. He leaned to the side and whispered, "Dude, excellent speech."

Chad nodded his acknowledgment as he watched Natalia move her crossbow and bolts from her trunk to Cooper's. Heston got in the backseat first. Kyle and Natalia entered on either side of him. Chad felt like a jerk for saying what he said. She was just as much a social outsider as he and his friends; her lifestyle precluding her from the need to deal with others in a civilized manner. But the warm tingle of pride for standing up for himself flowed through his chest.

As Cooper pulled out of the parking lot, one thought continued to nag Chad. Something Natalia implied he had to do; the same thing Kat flat out told him to do—kill Hunter.

Could he do it?

CHAPTER 42

"What do we do now?"

Chad heard Heston's words, but offered no acknowledgment of them. He sat in the passenger seat of Cooper's car and stared out the window in silence. Now that they had parked at the top of the lot entrance to the abandoned coal depot, he had no idea what to do next.

After being played by Hunter at the greenhouse, Chad was fired up and looking for revenge. The worst aspects of all the events from the past couple of weeks culminated in a volcano's worth of frustrations. His emotions burned hot, but the lava flow cooled and left a useless chunk of stone in his gut during the drive from the greenhouse to the secret lair of the Ink Stains.

He wanted to regain control of his life, wanted this nonsense to stop. If he and his friends could stop the ceremony, then he could have the control he so desired for another year until the Queen of the Night bloomed again. However, there was one way to end it permanently.

Kill Hunter.

Kat had told Chad this was the solution. Natalia and Wanda had made it their life mission to do it. Chad knew very well that killing Hunter was a way to stop the madness. Could he do it?

Thirty minutes ago, he could. At least in the heat of the moment, he *thought* he could. Now? Now that the concept crept its way from anger-fueled fantasy to harsh reality, his fortitude had been called into question. Could he take the life of another person?

Hunter made it clear to Chad that he wasn't human, or at the very least didn't believe he was human. Chad reasoned that if this was true, then he wouldn't be killing a person, rather an unnatural creature that so many of his gaming characters had killed over the years. Unfortunately, if Chad could get himself to believe that, then logic dictated that he, too, was the same kind of unnatural creature. That made him even more special, more than human, just like Hunter had told him.

Even if Chad could convince himself that Hunter wasn't human, that he was merely an animal, he still wasn't sure if he could do it. His father wasn't a sportsman, so Chad never had the exposure to hunting or fishing. Once while mowing the lawn, he ran over a turtle and lost a week's worth of sleep and five pounds because of the accompanying guilt. Any roadkill larger than a squirrel that he saw while driving made him feel bad. Then again, he was a prey animal, the kinds of animals that end up being roadkill, or under a lawnmower, or unable to kill another animal when necessary.

Everyone exited the car, and Natalia readied her crossbow and checked her bolts. Cooper sidled up to Chad and asked, "So, you and Sisters Grimm have been in their lair. What should we expect? Will this be a dungeon crawl or an arena fight?"

Heston and Kyle moved closer as Chad answered, "A little of both. The building is huge, but old and burned out. There are large rooms with conveyor belts everywhere that lead from room to room, up, down, around, over, from one machine to another that do only God knows what. Huge metal beams are holding the whole structure together. There are second and third and fourth floors, but not in the traditional sense. Just stairs and suspended walkways leading to platforms and more stairs and walkways. It's as if M.C. Escher and Rube Goldberg collaborated on an amusement park ride and had this brain baby. There are some smaller rooms for storage and offices and stuff. In one of those rooms was where we found the Elder Blood."

"Do you think they'll have the Queen of the Night in that room? Or one like it?" Kyle asked.

"I don't think so. It's the third piece of the puzzle, so they're probably going to perform the ceremony tonight if they haven't started it already."

"He's right," Natalia said. "Hunter and my mother are not patient people, so I'm very certain that they've started the ceremony by now."

Cooper cracked his knuckles and rolled his neck. "Well, lady and gentleman, it seems that coming up with a plan isn't in our cards, so we'll just have to go all in."

SATAN'S PETTING ZOO

Using both hands to keep her crossbow at the ready, Natalia led the way.

The driveway in was long and curved down the hill to the massive parking lot. They stayed in the grass for as long as they could before terrain dictated that the last half of their walk be on the road. The crunch of gravel echoed from the mountain tops to the valleys in Chad's ears. They tried to be as quiet as possible with their approach, but they might as well be launching fireworks with every step. Chad pointed to the door he and the lycanthrope hunters had used the last time he visited this place. "There. We'll enter there."

As they got closer, they walked past mounds of long-forgotten shale; a few piled as high as a house. Their footsteps got louder, then Chad stopped in his tracks and held out his arms for everyone to do the same. The extra noise wasn't their footsteps; it was the figures sliding down one of the shale piles. There were only three of them, but once they hit the ground, Chad felt surrounded. Brick. Emmanuel. Orlando.

At first, the usual sense of fear made itself at home behind Chad's chest and lowered his body temperate to subzero, but he realized that the jocks showing up might not be a bad thing. He could finally tell Brick the truth, give him the one thing he had been searching for and falsely accusing Chad of doing for weeks now. For the first time in the history of society, Chad could broker an alliance between jocks and nerds. It'd be a national holiday, and there would be an annual parade in his name. If not for everyone else.

His companions were on edge, ready for a fight even if they had to start one themselves. Natalia shot a bolt from her crossbow at Brick while Kyle shifted into pheasant form and attacked. Brick turned into the same half-human, half-rhino mix that Chad encountered on the practice field, almost as if it were his default form, his natural self. The bolt shattered against his thick hide, and Kyle's beak did no damage no matter how hard or fast he pecked.

Cooper was quick to exact his revenge against Orlando. Or at least try. No matter how fast Cooper struck as a ferret, Orlando in greyhound form always seemed to be faster, jumping out of the way. Orlando snarled and barked, snapping his teeth, but Cooper had learned since last time and avoided every bite.

Heston was quick to turn himself into an ox but hesitant to attack. Emmanuel circled in his minotaur form, occasionally giving a head-shaking snort or hoofing at the ground. Heston remained on all fours and rotated to keep Emmanuel in front of him at all times.

Natalia shot at Brick again. Just as before, his hide turned the bolt into toothpicks. Squawking and flapping his wings, Kyle kept at Brick, unable to peck anything more than his arms. Finally, Brick backhanded Kyle, knocking him into Natalia. Fingers curled and ready to crush his attackers, Brick stomped toward Natalia and Kyle, both stumbling over each other, trying to get to their feet.

As much as he didn't want to shout, Chad had no other choice. "Everyone, stop!"

They did, all staying in their altered forms. "It's the Ink Stains."

Turning back to his human form, yet somehow still looking beastly, Brick walked to Chad. "What do you mean?"

"The Ink Stains. They're the ones to blame. I turned my friends into . . . whatever we all are, but The Ink Stains are the ones who turned me."

"So?"

"They're the ones who *killed* Mason and your other two friends."

Back in human form as well, Emmanuel and Orlando stood on either side of Brick, looking as if they were ready to kill the messenger. "Why?"

"To recruit me. To show me the power they had. But that was just to get me to turn into something tasty enough to eat."

The three men stood dark against the moon's light, looming statues of death, processing and judging Chad's words. Brick's fists clenched. "The Ink Stains killed Mason and Spence and Billy because you wanted them to?"

"No."

"You just said they did it to get you to join them. They wouldn't have done it if you didn't want them to kill my teammates."

No. This was not going to happen. Chad was not going to back down. He was not going to let someone tell him that he wanted something he didn't, twist his words, ignore what he was saying. "No! They wanted me to change because that's what they do—make people into something they get satisfaction out of eating. *They* killed your friends, *not* me. Yes, I wanted to have the power that the Ink Stains have. I wanted that power, and I wanted to use that power against Mason. I didn't want him dead; I just wanted him to *stop abusing me*. I wanted him to get the fuck out of my life, and since violence and power are the only things you people understand, then that was what I needed to get Mason to *leave me alone*. I didn't kill him. The Ink Stains did."

Eyes half shut, Brick stared at Chad. Black holes, voids threatening to suck Chad's soul from his body should he show any signs of weakness. "Then, why are you here?"

"This is where the Ink Stains live. Right now, they're performing a ceremony to summon the triple goddess, the Morrigan, their elder, to give them more power. They needed a few items, one being at Berkman's Gardens. I didn't want to tell you why we were there tonight, because I didn't know how you were going to react. Like I told you earlier, we're all a part of the same team now, so if you flipped out and turned into a rhino in public, it wouldn't have done anyone any good."

Brick took one step back and looked over each shoulder to his companions, teammates for so long that their communications were all but imperceptible to Chad. No nods, no shrugs, no discernable twitches. After a minute, Brick stepped closer to Chad.

All of Chad's friends tensed, crouched and ready to attack. Natalia had her crossbow loaded, but pointed at the ground. Chad pulled the familiar tingle of turning into a rabbit close to the surface, ready to jump to the side should Brick's next move involve his fists. Instead, Brick said, "You were right not to tell me at Berkman's. Now let's go kill those fuckers."

CHAPTER 43

On a cloudless autumn night, a full moon could be as bright as the sun. Chad had debated about bringing his cellphone to use as a flashlight, or to dial 911 if things didn't go the way of the righteous but decided against it. The moon's light didn't touch everything inside of the refinery and created more shadows than Chad was comfortable with, but it came through the broken windows enough to expose the bigger shapes throughout the building. Any light the phone could add would be minuscule at best, not worth the effort of trying to keep track of it when things went the way of fangs and claws and fury. And should there be a need to call 911, there would be nothing left but blood for the first responders by the time they arrived.

Brick and his friends took the lead, more than willing to be the first to encounter whatever terrors awaited in the darkness. In his human-rhino form, Brick walked in front of the group, chest puffed out as if his muscles would be enough to stave off all attacks. Emmanuel was to his right and a step behind in his minotaur form. He walked more cautiously, hands in front pulled into fists with his head down, allowing his horns to lead the way. Other than his hips being more human than canine so he could walk upright, Orlando stayed in greyhound form, a wiry Anubis treading upon the Earth.

Chad and his friends opted to stay fully human. To take advantage of an animal-human mix required a level of energy they would rather conserve. If the jocks wanted to be meat shields, then so be it. Chad was not going to try to talk them out of it.

The walls had been burned away or destroyed by vandals, but even without such encumbrances, it was impossible to see from one end of the building to the other. "Bigger than a football field," Brick mumbled. "Bigger" was definitely the right word for this place. Conveyers wider than sidewalks led to machines bigger than cars, some even bigger than trucks.

"Where'd you say you found the Elder Blood?" Brick asked.

"At the other end of the building," Chad answered.

"Of course." Brick was annoyed but still led the way. Machismo drove the rhino-man onward, but he did so cautiously. He was built to charge forward, but he took his time — small, quiet steps while looking around, even up. Chad kept his head on a swivel; everyone did as they padded along. But he found himself keeping an eye on Natalia the most.

Walking in a crouch, she had her crossbow ready, her every step precise as if each graceful movement was purposefully conjuring a form of magical spell to guarantee victory. Chad kept glancing her way to see if she was there. She didn't walk with the group, rather beside it, just close enough that he could still see her. He kept waiting for her to vanish, to find a better vantage point, or maybe even just to get away from those less experienced. The jocks thought they could handle themselves in any situation, but Natalia had done this before. There was no greater trump card than experience. Chad thought about sliding over a few steps to follow her instead of the jocks. Then she stopped.

The sound of something scraping in the darkness made everyone stop, which was followed by the clang of metal hitting metal. Chad snapped into rabbit form and jumped away from the noise behind him. Animal shapes rushed about as growls cut through the stale air.

Heston.

Cringing as if he tried to fold in on himself, he stood next to a table while holding a four-foot-long piece of rebar, scraps of fallen metal by his feet.

"Sorry," he whispered, the tip of Natalia's crossbow bolt an inch from his temple. "I just wanted a weapon."

"Had you been paying attention to Tyler's teachings, then you would *be* a weapon," Natalia growled. "Let's keep moving just in case you haven't alerted Hunter that we're here."

Heston kept apologizing, at least one, "sorry," for each person until everyone started to move again.

None of this looked familiar to Chad. He remembered being afraid. And running. He sprinted through the entire building and had no memory of the specifics. Had he seen that machine before? Did he remember that conveyor belt? He tried to glean clues from the floor, looking for giant rabbit footprints in the dust. The moon didn't offer enough light for such details. There had to be something to give him a hint of where he had been the last time he was here. Of course, he poured so much effort into examining the minutia that he almost missed the obvious. Not only did Chad not see the small fire in the middle of the next room they walked into, but he almost ran into Brick when everyone stopped.

Just like the other ceremony, the one from weeks ago that now seemed like decades, this one involved the four Ink Stains moving around a small area. They even used the same accessories: ornately framed mirrors, lanterns, a string of small lights dangling over their heads. And as before, they were in human form and naked, their bodies glistening.

Chad wondered how they should handle this, what plan of attack to use. Right now, they had the element of surprise. Should they work on a signal to have everyone rush the Ink Stains at once? Should they let Natalia find a good vantage point for her crossbow? All his questions were answered as Brick strode forward, separating himself from the others, and yelled, "Hey, douche bags!"

The Ink Stains stopped their ritual, and Hunter stepped forward. "Nice job, Chad. I knew you'd show up, but we didn't expect you to bring your lackeys."

"We're no one's lackeys," Brick said.

Kat scowled as the leader of the pack walked away. "Hunter! The ceremony. We're almost finished."

Not taking his eyes off Brick, Hunter addressed Kat. "Finish it up while I take care of Chad's minion."

Still standing on two legs, Brick became more of a Rhino. His skin thickened, the horn on his snout grew. Voice deepening, he yelled, "Not! A! Minion!"

"Hunter!" Kat snapped.

"You heard me, Kat. I'm gonna have some fun first."

Hunter demonstrated that he had been doing this longer than anyone else in the room by how effortlessly he shifted from human to werewolf. Not even two steps and his corded muscles were covered in fur; his fingers were razor-tipped claws. Lines of saliva flew from his mouth as he released noises that were somewhere between barks and growls. He dropped to four feet just long enough to launch himself at Brick.

Leading with his natural weapon, Brick lunged forward, but his bulk couldn't match Hunter's speed. The werewolf contorted his body midair to avoid the horn and swiped his claws at Brick's left arm. Brick winced, but there was no blood. Stumbling, Brick tried to halt his momentum and twisted to swing his fist. Hunter ducked and swiped again.

Chad wasn't sure who to cheer for. His brain told him that if somehow Brick killed Hunter, then they would all revert to being human, and all of this would be over. More importantly, it would stop Hunter from adding to the pack. It would be best for everyone, possibly in the world, if Brick won this battle. But in his heart, he couldn't cheer on a jock. Years of abuse took the form of a rhino, and his definition of uber-cool was fighting against it. Brick needed to win, but Chad just wanted Hunter to get a few good shots in. He almost clapped when that happened.

Hunter was so much faster than Brick. To deal with the speed, Brick stopped charging. A weapon that made no contact with its target was useless, and there was no hope of his horn connecting with his foe. The ratios between Brick's human form and rhino form changed; thickening his hide when Hunter attacked, dropping bulk to swing when the opportunity arose. Brick couldn't land a punch, but he did better at blocking Hunter's claws. But Hunter had been doing this for a lot longer than Brick.

Up until this point, Hunter only attacked with his claws, exposing his fangs from under his rippling muzzle, but never used them. He came after Brick with gnashing teeth, and the rhino over-defended for a bite that never came, only setting up for a different attack.

A claw swipe gouged Brick's horn. He bellowed and turned away, his hands cradling his face as it shifted back to mostly human. Three bloody cuts ran the diagonal of his gray face. The smell of blood must have excited Hunter because he became overzealous and leaped to finish off his meal. But Brick was no prey animal. He spun and knocked Hunter out of the air while shifting into full rhino. As soon as Hunter hit the floor, Brick charged. The werewolf rolled and tried to avoid the trampling feet, but Brick connected.

Coughing and spitting blood from his mouth, Hunter rolled over in his human form. In his hybrid form, Brick grabbed him by the neck and lifted him off the ground. Hunter coughed a ragged laugh, blood spilling from his mouth and over Brick's wrist. "Guess you don't want to be a rhino anymore?"

"What do you mean?"

"Put me down, and I'll tell you."

Brick let go, and Hunter collapsed in a heap on the floor.

"No!" Chad yelled. "Finish him, Brick!"

Coughing and holding his left side with both hands, Hunter stood up, legs unsteady. "Of course, your boss would say that."

Brick raised both of his meaty fists, his knuckles like burled wood. "Not my boss!"

"No? You're doing everything he's telling you to."

"You killed my friends."

"Because Chad wanted us to."

"Not true!" Chad yelled. "He's lying, Brick!"

"I'm telling you the truth. And did Chad mention why he wants you to kill me? Did he tell you what would happen?"

Brick took a step back from Hunter. "No."

"Think about why he did this in the first place, why he came to me and my friends."

"They came to me!" Chad shouted, but his words had no effect.

"Because he's weak," Brick said.

"Exactly." Hunter stood straighter and then bent to the side, stretching out his pained area. "His plan to become strong didn't work, and now he wants to reverse it."

"Reverse it?"

"Dude. Don't you watch any movies? Kill the one who started it, and everyone goes back to being normal. Is that what you want? To give up your amazing abilities? I'm impressed at how quickly you caught on to some of what you're capable of. Do you want to give that up already? Give all that power away? Why? Just because some kid . . . some *rabbit* . . . tells you to?"

Brick took another step back and regarded Hunter in silence. Like a scene out of Chad's nightmares, Brick turned away from Hunter and strode toward Chad. Emmanuel and Orlando joined Brick, their pace quickening.

They had changed sides.

CHAPTER 44

Natalia's crossbow was an easy pull, quick-load, complex mechanisms making three shots in ten seconds easy. Her aim was true, hitting the three targets she aimed for. She didn't count on her targets willingly taking the hits. Using their arms as shields, the bolts pierced the arms of Emmanuel and Orlando. They both growled in pain but yanked the bolts free as if they were annoying splinters. Brick thickened his hide, and the bolts shattered on impact.

"Brick! Stop! Don't forget that Hunter killed Mason and Billy and Spence," Chad pleaded.

"Can't make an omelet without breaking some eggs."

"But where will the omelets stop? The Ink Stains eat people! How long until they eat more of your friends? Your family?"

"You gonna eat my friends and family, Hunter?" Brick asked.

"We won't, as long as you tell us who they are," Hunter answered. He was still in human form, twisting at his waist as if getting ready for vigorous calisthenics. The blood flowing from his face slowed to an ooze.

Chad and his friends continued to back away from Brick and his friends. Chad and Cooper turned into the halfway point between human and their animal personas. Kyle went to full pheasant and stayed close to Heston while Heston remained in his human form and wielded the rebar like a staff with both hands. Knowing it would do little good, Chad continued to try to reason with Brick. "Did you even stop to think about why Hunter wants the Elder

Blood? It's to make more like him. More lycanthropes in the world, Brick. To eat people."

"Hey, Hunter," Brick said over his shoulder. "You mind if I use some Elder Blood for my friends and family?"

Hunter laughed. "Not at all. Make as many of us as you want, brother. Oh, it's also used to help us heal better. Those gouges on your face? Elder Blood will clear those up, no scarring."

"Good. I would hate not to be pretty anymore."

"Brick, you can't be serious," Chad said, the timbre in his voice getting higher as he and his friends continued to back away. "You can't want to turn your friends and family into what we are. How many people, Brick? Where will it stop? If there are too many of us—"

Running into Cooper derailed his train of thought. His friends had all stopped retreating. Behind them were Viper and Dylan in their animal forms. Scaly arms sprouted from Viper's body while Dylan raised his claws in the air. They both grabbed for Chad and his friends. Their attempts were lackluster, but it was enough to get everyone to scatter.

Chad went to full rabbit and sped away, but then looped around a vertical beam to return to the fray. Viper and Dylan made no earnest attempt to kill with their initial swipe, which meant their attitude hadn't changed one iota. They wanted to play with their food first. Hunt and chase, *then* devour. If ending up in their gullets was his ultimate fate, then Chad wanted to put up a fight at least. No one ever gave him credit for being anything more than a prey animal, one to be chased or ignored. Not again. Not anymore. Right now, they would acknowledge him.

Chad raced through the confusion as fast as he could, between the Ink Stains and the jocks, hoping to create a distraction for his friends and to get an idea of what to do next. Cooper attacked Orlando. Kyle dodged the swipes and strikes from Viper or Dylan. Chad wasn't sure if they were still toying with Kyle, or if Kyle was holding his own. Natalia continued to use her crossbow. Heston remained in his human form, even as Emmanuel, the minotaur, feigned his attacks, working to separate Heston from the herd.

Brick was the easiest to manipulate since he had only two emotions—anger and more anger. In full rhino form, he was also the one who could cause the most disruption if Chad could play his cards right.

Chad zipped in front of Brick, getting his attention and then ran a full circle around him, coming up on his other side. Brick turned his head to the right, but when Chad went behind him, he whipped his head around to the left, just as Chad stopped and kicked with his back legs, connecting fully with Brick's jaw. He ran another circle around the rhino and executed another perfect kick to his face. Back around the rhino, but this time he stopped and hopped onto Brick's back.

Spinning in circles, Brick looked for the rabbit that he couldn't feel through his thick hide. Chad felt like a meme with a pithy caption using a pun and alliteration to describe a rabbit on a rhino. He was sure Cooper could come up with one later. For now, he needed to figure out what the hell to do next. The answer came to him as Dylan in bear form growled, "On your back!"

Brick turned his head, but the physiology prevented him from moving it in any meaningful way. He dropped to one side as if he were about to roll over and shifted into more of a human shape to accommodate the act. Chad jumped off to the side and ran, but much slower this time. He wanted Brick to catch him.

Chad ran through the refinery, careful not to get too close to the machinery and equipment. He wanted nothing to get in the way, nothing to trip up Brick or slow him down. He ran just fast enough to go faster than Brick as a biped and then slowed down when he went to full rhino. That was all he needed.

Making a wide loop through the expansive room, Chad sped up a little more, just enough to encourage Brick to run faster. Right at Dylan.

The bear reared up on his hind legs, ready to crash down on the rabbit. Just as Dylan let out a roar, Chad slipped back into his human form and slid between his legs. He had plenty of momentum, and the concrete floor was covered in dust. As soon as he was behind Dylan, he switched back to rabbit and savored the fruits of his labor.

The sound of the collision echoed throughout the entire refinery.

The bear's body flopped to the floor and slid to a stop, arms and legs limp; his tongue flopping from his opened mouth. Chad wasn't sure if he were alive or dead. Everything he knew about the death of a lycanthrope came from movies, books, and gaming campaigns. In all of them, the dead lycanthrope changed back to human form. The crumpled form of Dylan was still a bear, so he might still be alive. Chad didn't want to kill him. He didn't *want* to kill anyone; he just knew that someone needed to kill Hunter.

Chad stopped behind a machine made solely from gears and belts to catch his breath. Hidden in the darkness, he couldn't help but feel a sense of pride that he took out one of the enemies and pissed off Brick in the process. "Fuck!" Brick yelled. "Chad! I'm going to fucking kill you, asshole!"

Okay, maybe Brick was *too* pissed off now. Chad wanted to stay hidden, but he didn't want to abandon his friends. Keeping his ears open, he snuck from this machine to a conveyor belt large enough to move entire cars. He stayed in rabbit form as he followed the whole thing back toward where he started. Almost there, he saw Heston.

Emmanuel forced Heston very far away from the rest of the group. Heston was *still* in human form, but he held the length of rebar like a sword. Natalia was wrong about Heston not being a weapon. He had been spending far more time learning from Tyler how to use a staff than how to fight as an ox. He had also been training solely in the barn, in a wide-open area.

Chad scooted from behind one piece of equipment to another, trying to get behind Emmanuel. The minotaur advanced, and Heston stepped backward. He glanced around and darted to the right. Emmanuel jumped to block his escape route, but he kept corralling Heston across the floor—to a wide-open area.

Heston wasn't retreating away from Emmanuel; he was leading him to a space in the building where he would be more comfortable. An open space like the area of the barn where he had been training. Chad hid behind a support beam, eyeing up options to sneak closer to Emmanuel, but stopped when he realized his friend, arguably the most timid person he knew, got one up on the bully.

Heston stepped to the right. Just as before, Emmanuel lurched quickly to block the path. This time Heston was ready. Gripping the rebar with both hands, he swung it like a baseball bat. The other end of the metal rod smacked into Emmanuel's bull snout with such force that Chad winced; a sympathy pain tingled at the tip of his nose. Blood poured from Emmanuel's nostrils.

The minotaur stumbled backward and covered his face with both hands. Blood splashed the floor as he pulled his hands away and clenched his fists. "You're dead. You hear me? You're dead!"

Heston replied by spinning the rebar like a propeller with his right hand, then flipped it to his left. A few more seconds of spinning and he tucked it under his armpit while getting in a ready stance, feet apart, knees bent. With his right index finger, he beckoned Emmanuel.

Emmanuel charged.

Worried that his friend was getting too overconfident, Chad readied himself to run at Emmanuel's feet to trip him up. He didn't need to.

Timing his actions perfectly, Heston shifted just enough to dodge the horns and then rolled around the minotaur, shoulder to shoulder, along Emmanuel's back. The minotaur crashed headfirst into a vertical I-beam. A gong sound accompanied a rain of dust and ash as Emmanuel dropped to one knee. He shook his head and spun around. Pushing off from the floor, he charged. This time Heston adjusted his grip on the rebar and spun. At the end of his circle, he crouched and swung, connecting squarely with Emmanuel's ankles as he ran by. A slap of skin against concrete, the minotaur rolled into a piece of machinery. Another clang of metal rang through the building as more dust and ash plumed into the air.

"I'm gonna kill you, you fat fuck!" Emmanuel yelled as he righted himself. He wasted no time in charging again, this time he did it as a bull.

Chad readied himself to jump from his hiding spot. He calculated a path to come from the side and use his back legs to kick at the feet of the charging bull. But just like the rest of the fight so far, he wasn't needed.

Heston transformed into his own form of minotaur.

The half-ox, half-human form of Heston lacked the defined muscles of Emmanuel's minotaur but had more than enough bulk to be imposing. Instead of sidestepping Emmanuel, Heston lowered his shoulder and charged as well. Meat against meat. Chad almost cheered when his friend was at the winning end of the collision. Emmanuel staggered, and Heston took advantage by jumping on his back, his full weight driving the bull into the ground. Flailing, Emmanuel kicked Heston in the shoulder, knocking him free and jumped to his feet. Snorting, Emmanuel readied himself to charge, but the crack of rebar against his skull ended the fight.

One shot wasn't enough to knock him down, but the next three in rapid succession were. And Heston didn't stop.

Slipping into his human form, Chad decided that now was the time to let his presence known and ran to his friend. Afraid of getting caught in his wrath, he approached while waving his hands. "Heston! Heston, it's me, Chad! You can stop. You got him."

Heston stopped hitting the bull, his whole body heaving with every gulping breath. "I got him?"

"You got him. You won."

"I won?"

"Yes." The growing pool of blood flowing from under Emmanuel's head concerned Chad, but he couldn't let Heston see it, or he might slip back into timidity. Just as Heston went to look at what he had done, Chad slipped into half-rabbit. He put his hand on Heston's shoulder and guided him away. "You won by a lot. Come on, let's go help the others."

They didn't get very far when a bristling ball of teeth and claws rolled in front of them. Orlando and Cooper were entangled with each other; Cooper as a full ferret, Orlando, in his hybrid form. Orlando snarled as he snapped his jaws at Cooper, each strike yielding nothing more than clumps of fur. Always in a constant state of movement, Cooper bit and scratched, but his attacks left only nicks and cuts. Orlando offered up his forearm, a target that Cooper sunk his teeth into. The canine hybrid sacrificed a moment of pain to land a solid punch, knocking Cooper away.

Chad readied himself to jump on Orlando, but as soon as he had knocked Cooper away from him, a crossbow bolt whistled through the air and sunk into Orlando's dog-like leg. He howled as he yanked out the projectile and looked up at the rafters.

There was movement above everyone in the darkness. Chad couldn't make out the details, but he knew it was Natalia, knew she wouldn't stay on the ground very long, and would eventually make her way to the catwalks above. Another bolt whizzed by. This time Orlando jumped to the side to dodge it.

More greyhound than human now, Orlando raced up the nearest set of stairs. The metal of the suspended walkways squeaked and rattled as Natalia fled from the pursuing lycanthrope.

Cooper jumped to his feet and ran up the same set of stairs. "Do not fear my dearest damsel and distress. I shall come to aid!"

Even over the clatter of Cooper running across the catwalks, Natalia's disembodied voice echoed through the building. "Not a damsel! Not in distress! Definitely not yours!"

From where he stood, Chad could see Kat dancing around the fire. Was she moving the ceremony forward, or was she stalling, waiting for him to kill Hunter? They were there to stop the ceremony, but Hunter needed to die. Did the sequence of desired events matter? Chad started to make his way to Kat when Heston grabbed his arm and yelled, "Come on! Kyle's alone with Brick, Hunter, and Viper."

CHAPTER 45

Chad shifted so his legs were more rabbit-like to keep up with Heston. His priority should be to stop the ceremony, but damn it, he wasn't going to sacrifice his friend's life to do so. They turned a corner just as Viper and Hunter slammed into each other, misjudging their attempts to grab the squawking pheasant. Kyle ran under a nearby bench. Hunter gave Viper a shove and then chased after Kyle.

Chad couldn't see Brick and hoped he was still wandering around other parts of the building looking for him. He also thought that he might not get a chance to fulfill Kat's request—Heston suddenly charged headfirst into Hunter. Still nursing wounds, Hunter shifted into his wolf-man form and fled into the darkness. Rebar in hand, Heston remained in his minotaur form and followed the werewolf.

Chad looked over to the fire. Kat was still there, still moving around it, orange and yellow reflections of the flame dancing across her naked skin glinted off her piercings. A flash of scales. Viper did not go to aid Hunter.

Chad dodged the claw swipe and punched Viper's face. The snake-creature shook it off.

Viper's face widened, becoming more snakelike as his jaws opened, impossibly wide even for a reptile. His entire torso opened, needle teeth gleaming in the slivers of moonlight, his forked tongue thicker than an arm. Chad ran.

Viper's was by far the fastest of all the lycanthropes. Chad had better eyesight, able to run circles through the refinery floor, but Viper was right behind him through each twist and turn. Chad assumed that his fear was like a neon sign for Viper's sense of smell, leaving a thick trail even through the stirred up dust and the oily stench of coal. He weaved among the beams, staying as close to them as possible, hoping Viper would misjudge a turn and smack headfirst into one. No such luck. He needed help.

Chad had no idea where Natalia and Cooper went. They could be anywhere in the building, and that was if they were still alive. Heston ran off to chase Hunter. Kyle and was Chad's only hope.

Across the room, a bench looked familiar, disturbances in the dust around it showed that someone had slid under it. Kyle poked his head out. Picking up speed, Chad decided to run past the bench and hoped that Kyle could assist. Then his world toppled.

A gray leg appeared out of nowhere so suddenly that Chad had to obey all laws of physics and trip over it. Feet colliding with each other forced him into violent somersaults, stopping when his back slammed into the bench.

"Chad!" Kyle scurried out from under the bench on his human hands and knees and stopped next to Chad. "Chad!"

Stars burst along the peripheral vision of his right eye, and the horizontal hold of Chad's world needed fixing. Kyle's face floated to the ceiling until Chad blinked, resetting it only for it to hover upward again. He attempted to lie, but his "I'm okay" came out as three raspy vowels.

Brick sauntered to Chad and Kyle, and Viper slithered next to him. Both in their hybrid forms, they took their time. Brick elbowed Viper and said, "You know who that kid's mom is?"

Viper grunted. "Who?"

"Betty Balloons."

A smile slid across Viper's human face, his tail twitching with excitement. "Oh yeah? I love her work."

"Me, too. Got a few blowjobs while watching her play with her tits."

Viper laughed, and they paused to give each other a high five.

Kyle stood up; fists clenched so tightly that his arms shook. "Shut up."

"Did she ever do any hardcore stuff?" Viper asked.

"Heard some rumors. Gotta' surf the dark web for that," Brick answered.

"Stop. Talking. About. My. Mother." Kyle's voice warbled as his whole body trembled.

"Ya know what I just realized," Viper said with a laugh. "If this is her kid, then she must be local. After we finish the ceremony tonight, I think I'm gonna visit her and those big titties of hers."

"Yeah? I'm gonna join you and impale her with my horn and not the one on my face."

Both half-human creatures laughed, and Chad's vision came into stark clarity just in time to witness a miracle.

Kyle transformed.

Chad knew little about pheasants. A wash of blue feathers over their heads and eyes rounded in a perpetual state of psychotic panic, not known for impressive talons or massive wings. If he made it out of this disaster alive, he'd do some more research into his friend's animal self.

Kyle had never been able to maintain a hybrid form. He was either human or animal. His attempts to stop somewhere in between usually ended up as a caricature of a person in a bird costume, just layers upon layers of drooping feathers. Now Kyle had finally nailed a hybrid form that was perfectly functional for the situation. Chad was terrified.

As Kyle's body morphed, he released an angry shriek that echoed through the building, knocking sprinkles of dust from the walkways above. Bones extending in uneven pops as skin tightened to keep up, he grew more than two feet taller than his original height. Wings jutted out from his back as if breaking free from a decades-long prison sentence, the feathers brown and tipped with a blue that shimmered in the moonlight. They didn't stop growing until each one was longer than he was tall. Growing and shrinking like the bubbles of a thick stew cooking, his muscles adjusted to accommodate his size. His chest widened. His arms and legs thickened. Fingers and toes grew into gnarled talons, each ending with a pointed claw. Round eyes frozen in a state of pain and madness, Kyle released another harrowing shriek, his pointed tongue twitching as if trying to stab the air.

Transformation complete, he slouched, weary from the ordeal and breathing in raspy gulps. No one moved, all eyes on Kyle, watching the calm before the storm. Like a bolt of lightning, Kyle struck.

Clawed hands out, he launched himself at Brick. The half-rhino grabbed Viper by the arm and used him as a shield. Kyle tore into the snake.

Viper opened his mouth but never had a chance to bite. Kyle drove his claws into Viper's chest. Screaming, Viper tried to push Kyle away. Taking chunks of flesh with him, Kyle ripped into Viper, using both his hands and feet.

Spewing profanities, Viper twisted and tried to push away from his attacker. Kyle refused to let go, raking his claws deep into the flesh beneath the scales. Changing into full snake, Viper's arms retracted into his body, but Kyle clamped down on one with his beak and ripped off. Viper screamed again as a spray of blood painted Kyle's face. The blood acted as fuel to Kyle's engine of destruction, and he tore into Viper faster, even after the screaming stopped. With one final strike, Kyle dug both hands and one foot into the flesh right below Viper's sternum and pulled. A balloon pop of gore, and Kyle was wearing Viper's entrails. Chad promised himself that he would never bring it up and would do his best to change the subject if the topic ever arose in the future, but he swore he saw Kyle tilt his head back and swallow.

"Fuck!" Brick yelled and shrunk back when Kyle turned his attention to him. Kyle left a trail of blood on the floor as he launched himself at Brick.

Having a thicker hide, Brick withstood the initial attack, crouching into a ball and covering his head with his arms. He went into full rhino form, but that didn't deter Kyle. Squawking in a bluster of feathers, Kyle sliced at Brick with both sets of claws on his hands and feet, using his wings to flutter around. Brick started to run, but Kyle kept at him, each cut more substantial than the last one. Brick swung his head from side to side, trying to stab Kyle with his horn, but his actions were impotent. Roaring, he went back to his hybrid form and flailed. One of his swings connected with Kyle's chest, knocking him away.

Kyle remained on his feet and screeched again, but this time he backed away. Stumbling, he turned and walked toward Chad, becoming more and more human with each step, turning back into the friend Chad had known all his life. He collapsed.

Chad caught his friend, his body slicked with blood. Right before he passed out, Kyle mumbled, "So . . . tired . . ."

"No worries," Chad whispered. "You were amazing."

Kyle was unconscious, and Chad had no idea where either Heston or Cooper were. He was alone with Brick. Gently, he rested Kyle on the ground and prepared himself for Brick to charge at him. He readied himself to turn into a rabbit and sprint away, leading him away from Kyle and through the refinery filled with potential traps for a large creature. He was ready. Instead . . . nothing.

In half rhino form, Brick hugged his waist with his right arm and squeezed his shoulder with his left hand. Blood flowed from all over his body, black and inky against his gray skin in the muted tones of the moonlight. Kyle did more damage than Chad originally thought.

Panting, Brick took a wobbly step forward and then dropped to a knee. A few more pained breaths, and he shifted his weight to sit down. He changed back to human form, his usually hard and angry face softened by fatigue and concern.

A noise from behind Chad made him jump and spin. Heston, in human form. "Kyle!"

Heston let go of his rebar weapon, and it clanged against the floor. He dropped to his knees next to his friend. "What happened?"

"Long story. I don't think he's hurt but may need some therapy later. Where's Hunter?"

"Don't know. I couldn't find him. I heard a loud shriek and came back here. Was . . . was that Kyle?"

"It was. He killed Viper."

"Whoa. Really?"

"Yep!" Hunter. He and Dylan stood over Viper's mutilated body, looking at it like two mechanics under the hood of a car, wondering why the engine wouldn't start. "He's all kinds of fucked up."

"Hunter," Chad said.

"Tell your fat friend I'm not done with him yet, but first we're gonna finish the ceremony. Shit's about to get real."

CHAPTER 46

"Shit's about to get real."

Truer words had never been spoken. Shit was indeed about to get real.

Even Brick seemed concerned. He used the nearest I-beam as support to get back to his feet and called out, "Orlando! Emmanuel! Get over here."

Orlando appeared out of the darkness in greyhound form but turned back to human and stood next to Brick. Pressing both hands against his bloodied face, Emmanuel lumbered in from the other direction, also in human form.

Still crouched next to Kyle, Heston looked up to Chad and asked, "Dude. Where's Cooper?"

On cue, the ferret skittered from behind a conveyor belt. Cooper slid to a stop as he transformed back into human, covered in minor scrapes and cuts. "I'm here. All good. What happened to Kyle?"

"He killed Viper and passed out," Chad answered.

"Oh, fuck."

Chad pointed to Kat and said, "We've got bigger problems."

"Oh, super fuck."

Kat circled the pit of fire, gesturing, chanting. The flames grew higher and changed color from oranges and yellows to blues and purples. The fire burned with no smoke, no embers or fuel, just flames blazing from the floor. Chad should have been able to feel some heat from it, at least a touch of warmth as it burned brighter, but nothing. Shadows danced with the flames, exotic twists of give and take, nonstop movement. Then the shadows flowed in unnatural ways, defying what the light of the fire told them to do. But they weren't quite shadows. They were something else. One sliver of darkness broke free from the rest.

"What's happening?" Chad whispered to himself. The undulating darkness was not from the depths or corners of the building, but something new. A new entity. A new being made from a collection of smaller things, creatures. Another sliver of darkness separated from the larger mass.

Chad tried to make out details from the pieces of darkness flying away like dandelion tufts on a windy day. He concentrated on one, followed it as it moved through the air. It didn't disintegrate like ash, nor did it float to the ground; instead it moved around the limited space with purpose. Wings. It flew; the sliver of darkness flew on wings. A bird. Each piece of darkness was a bird, black and aggressive. Crows.

The birds increased in number, some splitting apart into two birds, most coming from the mass of black flowing upward from the floor around the fire. Hunter growled in pain and scratched at his bird tattoo. It flapped its wings across his chest. He howled as the bird's head tore itself from his body. The wings bent at odd angles as if pressing against Hunter to pull itself from his skin. A moan of relief followed when the bird separated itself from him and flew into the fire. The same thing happened to the other Ink Stains as well.

The process didn't affect Dylan the same way, or if it did, he showed no hint of pain. The crow flew across his waist and freed itself. Kat doubled over in pain as the crow tattoo on her thigh, sprung free and flew into the fire. Squawking, a crow fought its way out from under the pieces of shredded meat that used to be Viper. Once free, it flapped the gore from its wings and took flight into the fire.

The flames continued to get darker, colors Chad never imagined possible. The fire soon bordered on black no longer resembling flames, rather wings. The fire turned into more crows.

The crows continued to multiply, an eruption of wings and beaks from a black geyser. So many crows. Would they stop before filling the building? Where were they coming from? What were they doing? The birds swooped and swirled, looping through the building. They flew into the darkness and back out. Small flocks formed, and then the birds flew tightly together. The groups started to form shapes. An arm? A head?

The roof was four stories above the ground, and this area of the building had no encumbrances to the ceiling. The flowing tower of crows was taking up every inch of that distance. Toward the top of the column, the birds tighten their formation, synchronizing their flying. A line of birds separated from the larger mass, flapping in unison, more and more pushing the arm shape into a hand, fingers. The top of the column rounded in the shape of a head. It turned, side to side, a behemoth being born and surveying its surroundings. More birds joined in to form hair while the ones on the front of the head adjusted and moved. Eyes, nose, mouth. A face. A woman's face.

"I feel as if we should do something, but for the life of me, I don't know what. What do we do?" Cooper asked, pacing in a short, tight line behind Chad.

Chad's nerves tingled, his fingers and toes itched. This ceremony was far more intense than the one to create lycanthropes. Had he known, he might not have placed so much trust in Kat. He hoped that someone would have killed Hunter by now, but that was just an unfulfilled fantasy. The reality was Hunter puffed out his chest and strode toward the fire. As he walked by Brick, he said, "Thanks for the assist, man. After we do what we need to do, we'll hook you up with as much Elder Blood as you need."

Brick didn't answer; just nodded to Hunter while he watched the gathering crows. Neither Emmanuel nor Orlando looked comfortable with the deal that they had made; Orlando shifting his weight from one leg to the other, Emmanuel holding his hands to his head while eying the woman formed by a murder of crows.

Hunter stopped in front of Chad. "And you guys. I gotta' say, I'm impressed with your efforts. Especially that wild motherfucker."

Kyle was awake and now sitting up. Heston helped him to his feet. Kyle asked, "What's he talking about?"

"Nothing," Chad answered.

"Nothing?" Hunter laughed. "Don't tell him that bullshit. He's one crazy bastard. So, fucking crazy, I'm not gonna eat him. As long as he tells me how he did what he did."

"What'd I do, Chad? What'd I do?" Kyle asked, his voice warbling from impending tears.

"You stepped up and really kicked ass. I will tell you all about it later," Chad answered.

Hunter sneered at Chad as he started to walk toward the fire. "Sissy."

"Now, Chad!" Kat called out. "You need to do it now!"

Hunter stopped. Frowning, he looked back and forth from Chad to Kat. "What are you talking abou—? Oh, I get it, you bitch. You're trying to get Chad to kill me?"

"Chad! Hurry!"

With a predator's swagger, Hunter sauntered over to Chad, stopping just inches in front of him. Chad felt small. He didn't have to crane his head back like he did with either Brick or Mason, and even though Hunter was pure muscle, he didn't have quite the size as either of Chad's other bullies. But Hunter was a machine designed for killing. Chad felt like the prey he was. They were both naked, a liability for Chad, an asset for Hunter. Their bodies were character sheets; Hunter rolled all twenties while Chad had nothing higher than a one.

"So, Chad, are you going to do it? Are you going to kill me?"

As black as the deepest shadows of the refinery, as black as the little demons that ate away at Chad's confidence, Hunter's eyes were all Chad could see. They weren't windows to his soul; they were mirrors into Chad's. Every moment in his life where he could have made a stand, but didn't, any chance to defend himself, yet he chose not to. He saw himself get shoved into lockers and trashcans. He saw swirlies and wedgies. He saw frustration and tears.

But what could he have done? For his entire life, his bullies were always bigger. Stronger. Faster. He *couldn't* stand up for himself. He *couldn't* defend himself. He *couldn't* run. He couldn't make the tormenting stop, so he had to take it. Hunter wasn't the biggest bully whoever threatened Chad, but he was the deadliest. It was too easy to imagine Hunter in werewolf form biting large chunks from his leg while being completely helpless. Broken bones. Pain he couldn't even fathom. It would be so much easier just to end it now. At least it'd be quicker.

Chad lowered his head and took a step back. Shaking and sniffling, he hugged himself and dropped to his knees.

Hunter laughed, a throaty noise of complete dominance. "That's what I thought."

"Chad?" Cooper whispered. "Chad, you can't quit on us, not now, not like this."

"You should think about doing the same, beanpole, 'cause I'm gonna eat you and make Chad watch." Hunter turned his attention to Kat. "But first, I got a bad pussy to take care of."

Chad never fought back in his life because he never thought he had any form of advantage. He was smarter than most people and certainly smarter than anyone who ever made his life a living Hell, but he never figured out how to parlay that skill into something useful for those dire situations. Until now. He was worried that Hunter would notice bad acting, or when he put his hand on

Heston's rebar after dropping to his knees. Grabbing the metal rod, Chad said, "Hey, asshole, my answer is yes!"

Hunter turned, and Chad slid into his hybrid form. Wielding the rebar like a lance, he pushed with his rabbit legs as hard as he could and drove the rebar into Hunter's chest.

The howl of pain shook the refinery, but Chad didn't let go. Hunter transformed into his werewolf state and grabbed ahold of the rebar with both clawed hands to pull it from his chest. He pulled, but Chad didn't back down. Driving his legs with all of his might, Chad pushed Hunter backward, stopping only when he pinned the werewolf to an I beam. Hunter let go of the rebar to swipe with his claws; Chad twisted the rebar, and Hunter howled. The werewolf thrashed and kicked, trying to find purchase to push away, but Chad didn't let go. In a last-ditch effort, Hunter leaned forward and tried to bite Chad. Bloody foam sprayed from gnashing jaws fractions of an inch from Chad's face.

Chad did not let go.

As the fury subsided, Hunter's werewolf form faded, eventually stopping as his human body went limp.

Chad dropped Hunter's corpse and backed away. Eyes wide, he looked around. He won. He had to kill someone to win, but it was someone who was evil, someone who wanted to kill Chad and his friends and many, many other people. It wasn't murder; it was self-defense. And he finally took control of his own destiny, finally worked to solve his problems. It was finally over. "Guys! We did it. We won. We can go back to being human and back to hanging out and back to not worrying about being eaten by lycanthropes and just be regular, normal people."

"Hey, numbnuts," Brick barked. "You're still half-rabbit."

Chad looked down at his fur-covered body and then over to his friends. Heston turned into an ox and then back to human. Cooper transformed into his hybrid state and shrugged his shoulders.

Kat was laughing, standing in front of the forty-foot tall woman made from fluttering crows. "You didn't believe Hunter, did you? *I told you* that's not how it works."

He did. He believed Hunter. He wanted to believe that by defeating the final boss, he'd immediately revert to human. Maybe he hadn't defeated the final boss. Maybe there was one more. "You used me."

"You made it so easy. I just needed to flash my tits, and then I could have led you from here to Hawaii by your dick."

"I'm still a prey animal," he mumbled to himself.

"All men are."

"Why? Why did you need me to kill Hunter? Why not do it yourself?"

"The Morrigan only grants an audience with the leader of the pack. With Hunter gone, that's now me. I couldn't do it because then I would go back to being human. Hunter wasn't completely lying. *You* would go back to being human if you kill *me*. Whichever one of your friends kills *you*, they get to go back to being human. You see how it works?"

"Because of the blood, isn't it?"

"You are a smart one, Chad. Hopefully, you're smart enough to know that me letting you live is a gift for killing Hunter for me. Of course, I can't make any guarantees what Dylan will do or any of the other pack members that I'll create. Now, if you'll excuse me, I have some Elder Blood to get."

Kat addressed the goddess made of crows. "Oh, great Morrigan, as leader of the pack, I beseech your wisdom, your courage, your blood so that we may grow in number."

A faint shade of red flowed from the top of the goddess all the way to the bottom, followed by a band of green, and then a band of purple. Chad realized that the feathers of the crows had very subtle differences in hue, only noticeable when a group of similarly colored birds flew tightly together. As the ribbons of color rippled, the goddess bent forward slightly and said with a voice the vibrated Chad's bones, "No."

CHAPTER 47

The flapping of thousands of wings was the only noise.

No growling. No yelling. There wasn't even breathing.

There was a hollowness growing inside of Chad, emptying him, dissolving his bones. He feared that he might float away should this numbness continue. The Morrigan said no. After confronting the Ink Stains to stop them from getting the necessary items for the ceremony to summon the great triple goddess of shapeshifters, she said no. After killing Hunter to help Kat, the Morrigan said no.

Kat stalked around the column of crows. Her fingers closed into fists and sprung open only to repeat the process as if they were so angry; they wanted to jump from her hands. "Why?" she yelled. "I performed the ceremony using totems of war, death, and earth to summon you. As the leader of the pack, I—"

"No," the goddess repeated. "There is more than one pack, therefore more than one leader."

Kat looked at Chad, and Chad looked at Brick. Blood still flowed between the large man's fingers from the wounds he clutched. He blinked slowly, and his face was slack from fatigue, but he still stood, still ready to lead his pack. Chad was the leader of his pack, and he wondered what costs and responsibilities came with the title.

"What . . . what do you mean?" Kat asked.

"We have been watching long before you summoned us. We are always watching. We are not in agreeance as to whom we wish to bless."

The top half of the Morrigan shifted, the red-hued crows congregating to make her shoulders wider, her head rounder but still distinctly feminine. Her body twisted and turned, extending to move her head and arms closer to Brick and his friends. "I, Badb, respect these warriors. Their desire to fight and win, no matter the battlefield, calls to me."

The body of crows moved again, taking the Morrigan's thinning torso to Chad and his friends. The green-tinted crows made a softer face. "I, Macha, wish to see more of this pack. They seek solutions within the confines of the world around them. They wish to learn more about the Earth."

All the crows flew away and reformed in front of Kat. The woman within this configuration was thinner than the other two while tinted with a deep shade of purple. "I, Nemain, have always admired your lust for blood. Your pack has always brought forth death, the best parts of war and earth."

The crows of the Morrigan shifted again, back to the constant change of subtle color. "We shall not decide who to bless. The pack leaders shall."

"How?" Chad asked, desperately praying that it wouldn't be determined by any form of battle royale where the last standing "pack" would receive blessings from the goddess of shapeshifters.

"By blessing you all."

The cryptic answer deserved more questions, but Chad already asked one and didn't like having a being powerful enough to be considered a goddess know who he was. Let someone else garner her attention; he didn't want it.

A stream of crows flowed from the center of the Morrigan's body, a tentacle reaching across the refinery to one of the back offices. The rope of birds returned, carrying nine empty vials. The Morrigan extended her arms and tilted her head back while her body broke apart into three swirls of crows, one for each of the individual goddesses. In the center of each spiral, a few birds squawked as other birds pecked at them. Blood splashed, flowed, filling the vials. In a whirlwind of feathers, hundreds of crows flew around the room.

Chad felt safe. He didn't know why, but he didn't try to duck or hide as the wind whipped around him from the maelstrom of squawks and feathers. None of the crows would hurt him. The commotion lasted mere minutes, and by the time all the crows returned to reform the body of the Morrigan, Chad was holding three of the vials. So were Brick and Kat.

"Each pack gets three vials to do with as they wish," the Morrigan said. "But the pack who uses the last of the nine vials shall receive my *eternal* blessing."

"Three vials," Kat said. "To make more of us."

"To heal myself," Brick said.

"To go back to being human," Chad whispered.

Making a sweeping gesture with her hands, the Morrigan said, "You may use the blood as you desire. If you save the last drop, I'll be yours to fulfill your desires; if you use the last drop, then you will never see me again."

Bit by bit, crow by crow, her body disassembled. The blackbirds shrieked as they jetted through the refinery. The whirlwind of feathers choked the air as Chad felt them passing over his skin, stinging his left shoulder. And then they were gone.

The crows.

The Morrigan.

Kat and Dylan.

Chad's shoulder stung, tender to the touch. Then he saw why. He had a tattoo.

A crow.

The bird's head was on his shoulder, beak facing forward. Its wings were spread, the left one just touching his upper arm, the tip of the right one stopping before getting to his neck. The tips of the feathers had a soft hint of green. Each of his friends had one, too. Kyle had one in flight over his heart. Heston's was on his back, between his shoulder blades. And Cooper's was on . . .

"My ass! The powerful triple goddess Morrigan, specifically Macha, the one who loves us, thought the best place to put a symbol of that love in the form of a tattoo *on my ass?*"

Chad would have to laugh about that later. The more pressing issue was that Brick and his friends each had a crow tattoo as well, theirs tinted red.

Brick popped the stopper of one of the vials and slugged it down. His bleeding stopped; his cuts faded. The gashes across his face closed up. Standing straighter, he rolled his neck and shoulders. "Well now, Chad. I think we have a few things to discuss."

Kat had called Chad smart. Now he needed to prove that. He hoped beyond hope that Kyle knew well enough to keep his mouth shut. "Yeah? Like how you used one of your vials?"

"Won't matter."

"No? Do you think we're just going to just let you kill us? You know what Kyle can do. Hell, you know what Kyle can do *to you*. Once he gets going, how long before you use your second vial? How long can you last not using your third? And what about Orlando and Emmanuel?"

With both hands over his face, bruises almost black in the moonlight, blood dripping from his chin, Emmanuel limped over to Brick and said, "Hey, let me have one of those."

"Fuck off. I might need one."

"Come on, man. My face is fucked up."

"I said, fuck off."

"Yes, Brick." Chad stepped forward, closer to a fear he needed to conquer. "You *will* need one. And that's if you don't kill Kyle. Don't forget, whichever one of you three kills him will go back to being human. Let's say you do kill us and trick either Orlando or Emmanuel into killing Kyle, there are *still* the Ink Stains, which . . ."

Chad gestured to where Kat and Dylan had been. They were gone. ". . . They can make two more and find you before you can heal."

Brick took one step closer to Chad to stare him down. Chad didn't flinch. His only move was to glance over to Kyle and then turn back to make direct eye contact with Brick. In the calmest voice he could muster, Chad said, "You *know* what he can do."

Brick growled, but then turned and walked away. Orlando and Emmanuel followed.

"Dude. I really think you should give one of those vials to him," Orlando said.

"You heard what she said."

"Come on, man. He's really bleeding a lot."

"Then get him a fucking tampon."

The trio disappeared into the depths of the refinery.

The only noise left was the blood flowing between Chad's ear, rushing along in the hastened rhythm of his heart.

"Hole. Lee. Shit!" Cooper said. "Can you believe what just happened? I can't, and I lived through the events in their entirety. Just like you and you and you. Okay, first and foremost, is everyone okay?"

"No," Kyle answered, hugging himself and shivering.

"Not really," Heston said.

"Me neither," Chad replied.

"Yeah. Yeah. Me too. Not doing so well. I mean physically, not too bad, but mentally? Emotionally? Spiritually? My world got rocked. Rocked hard, you know what I mean? Of course, you know what I mean. I mean, all of us were right next to each. Fighting and *kicking ass.*"

"Guys, I don't feel so good," Kyle said, arms still around his waist.

"That's understandable given the circumstances. Perfectly normal. Perfectly natural."

"There's nothing normal or natural about this," Heston said.

"You are correct, so very, very correct," Cooper agreed.

"Guys? Why was Brick scared of me? Why did Chad say to Brick that he knew what I could do?" Kyle asked.

Chad looked over his shoulders, looked up at the suspended walkways, looked deep into every shadow. The threats were gone. So was Natalia. "Okay. I think we need to head back to headquarters."

CHAPTER 48

Heston twirled the quarterstaff and slammed the one end down on a bale of hay. He then repeated his actions, spinning the staff in the opposite direction this time. With his bare knuckles, Cooper worked the heavy bag hanging from one of the barn's rafters. Kyle sat on the hay couch, curled in the fetal position. Chad wanted to comfort his friend, but there was nothing more he could say that hadn't already been said. All Chad could do now was mimic Tyler's Tai Chi moves.

"Thank you again for letting us store the Elder Blood here," Chad said.

"*Mi casa es su casa*," Tyler replied. "Your moves are getting better."

"They certainly came in handy two nights ago. For all of us, thanks to you."

"Glad I could aid your efforts to keep the world free from bloodthirsty beasts. I'm sure corporations and governments are grateful, too, since they don't like competition in that department."

With Tyler's squint and neutral tone, Chad still had a difficult time discerning between his dry sense of humor and his antiestablishment exposition. In this case, it might have been a bit of both. Then for the first time since meeting him, Tyler's eyes went wide.

Tyler stopped moving, and Chad turned to see what surprised him. Kyle. He got up from the couch and walked over to where Chad and Tyler were practicing. He stood behind Chad, placed his palms together, and bowed to Tyler. Returning the gesture, Tyler asked, "Are you sure you're up for this?"

"I . . . I really think I am. I killed and ate pieces of someone, which still freaks me out, but I don't remember it, so that helps. I've been so focused on what went wrong; I haven't thought too much about what went right. I mean, I turned into a big, badass bird creature that was strong enough to take out one of the Ink Stains. I had to kill him to do it, but he was trying to kill me and my friends. By every definition of the concept, he was a bad guy, a villain. And I beat him."

"Yes. Yes, you did."

"And I fought Brick too. I took one the largest person or creature I've ever seen and won. Right?"

"Also true," Chad said.

"We didn't stop Kat from summoning the Morrigan, but we came out of it alive. We held our own against the Ink Stains and the jocks, who could very well be just as crazy as the Ink Stains. I call that a win, and I'm going to focus on that. We won. You also said that Hunter wanted to know how I did what I did. That means I can do something that no one else can do; no one else knows how to do. That's pretty special, right?"

"Very," Chad said, smiling. There was nothing else to say. Tyler sensed that too, by continuing with his poses. Chad and Kyle followed along. After a few more practiced poses, Tyler asked, "So what are you going to do with the Elder Blood?"

Chad shrugged his shoulders. "We're not entirely sure. We're hoping that the jocks and the Ink Satins use all theirs so we can be the last ones left. We have no plans on using them, except for one that has your name on it anytime you'd like."

"I appreciate the offer, but I'm still going to decline."

"Just remember it's an open offer. As for the jocks and the Ink Stains, we'll have to keep an eye on them, but it won't be as urgent as before since they can't kill us if they'd like to gain the Morrigan's favor. We still need to keep peeking over our shoulder regarding Wanda and Natalia, though."

"So, Natalia just abandoned you guys mid-fight, huh? That's bad mojo, man. Bad mojo."

"I agree. We're hoping that they realize that we mean no harm, and they focus on the others."

"What about using the blood to change back to human?"

"Not right now."

"For the entire time that I've known you, you wished to go back to being human. You now have the chance, so why not do it?"

"We don't know how. Wanda knows how, but she and Natalia have gone incommunicado. I'm assuming Kat knows how, but it would be beyond insane trying to get that information from her. And we don't know if one vial can cure all four of us. If it's a one to one ratio, then that leaves one of us to remain a lycanthrope. We're all for one and one for all with any form of shapeshifting decisions."

Tyler stroked his thin goatee and nodded. "Understandable. Admirable."

"One of the things we discussed is seeing this through, whatever *this* is. None of us feel right just giving up and letting either the jocks or the Ink Stains have unlimited power. The Morrigan did say 'eternal' blessing. We need to step up and be the good guys in this."

Tyler nodded some more, but then shook his finger at Chad like a philosopher about to challenge the notion of God. "Or, what if you're addicted. Even though you weren't happy with your powers at first, you all still possess power. Any form of power can be addicting."

Chad almost laughed. Tyler was right about him having power, but he was wrong about it being addicting. He wanted to harness it and do the most with it, but he still wanted to get rid of it. That wouldn't be happening anytime soon. Right now he needed to sort through his emotions: the high of standing up to a bully and single-handedly defeating the big bad; the queasiness of having to kill a sentient being; the intimacy of bonding even more with his best friends; the fear of not knowing what pitfalls awaited them or what was going to happen next; the excitement of being a part of the unique adventure. Most importantly, he felt like he had a purpose—to defend the world against evils that it only speculated about. Having a purpose felt good.

It also helped him get a better understanding of Tyler. Despite having the coolest barn slash headquarters ever and the bizarre ability to abuse inhuman amounts of alcohol and marijuana, Tyler was looking for a purpose. Sure, he was doing an amazing job as their sensei, but it wasn't the fuel to rev the engine of his soul. When they first met, Tyler had asked about Chad's wellbeing. Tyler was a healer, not a fighter.

Chad waved the other three over and then placed his hand on Tyler's shoulder. He said, "I think you might be right. It is addicting. But, first, let's focus on our addiction to losing."

Tyler smirked and nodded. "Yeah. Let's focus on that."

Everyone cheered while Heston and Cooper worked on a new high-five, fist bump routine that incorporated moves they could only do in their hybrid forms.

EPILOGUE

Chad was feeling good, that perfect blend of excitement and soreness after a solid workout. Cooper drove him home from the barn and dropped him off in front of his house. Chad walked along the pavers of the flower-lined pathway to the front door but paused when he noticed the number of cars parked along the street. In this suburban neighborhood, potluck dinners and book clubs were not unheard of, but there was a concentration of cars in front of his house, many of them looking familiar. Were his parents hosting a party? On a Wednesday evening?

As soon as he put his key in the front door, it flung open. His parents greeted him with wide-eyed surprise. Their skin was pale, and his mother's bottom lip started to quiver, the harbinger of tears. She hugged him tightly and sniffled in his ear, "Oh, thank God you're okay."

Chad's father put his hand on his son's shoulder and squeezed. "I know you're an adult now, son, but we need to know where you are."

"Ummm . . . yeah. Sure. No problem. I'll start texting more when I'm out. What's going on? Did someone die?"

Chad's father gently separated his wife from his son. "Come on, Samantha. Let go of Chad. You're freaking him out."

She wiped away her tears with her thumbs. "You're right, Rick. I'm sorry if I upset you, Chad, but we learned some upsetting news. It . . . it might be easier if we just showed you."

They guided him to the living room, packed with people. Sitting on the loveseat were Kyle's parents, the Sedgewecks. A warmth blossomed within Chad's cheeks, this being the first time seeing Mrs. Sedgeweck since confiscating the posters of her being topless. He worked up an excuse to blame exercising should anyone notice his pink cheeks.

On the couch were Cooper's mother and a couple Chad didn't recognize, about his parents' age and rather nebbish. The woman looked exhausted while her husband had his arm around her, consoling her.

Sitting in the matching armchair, omnipresent beer can in hand, was Heston's father, somehow looking even more pissed off than usual.

The television was on; whatever they were watching paused on an image of a wolf's face. Chad thought about asking if they were watching a documentary about wolves until he realized that was no ordinary wolf. He recognized that face, knew whose it was, and stopped breathing when he saw Wanda and Natalia standing on either side of the television.

"I know you kids call her 'Whacky Wanda,'" Chad's father whispered into his ear from behind him. "Hell, most of the adults call her that, too, but she told us some things tonight . . . showed us some things that are . . . are . . ."

"Needed to be seen to be believed," Chad's mother finished. "Chad, this is Wanda Deveraux and her niece Natalia."

"Hi, Chad," Wanda said with a canary catching cat's smile. "I've heard a lot about you."

"I'm sure you have."

Natalia remained silent, simply glaring at Chad.

"The reason why Wanda and her niece are here is because of the disappearances of Justin Butera and the football players a few weeks ago, as well as the other disappearances of children," Samantha said.

The woman on the couch sobbed when Justin's name was mentioned, so Chad deduced that she and the man next to her were his parents.

Wanda and Natalia had told the people in this room, his parents and others, something about lycanthropes. How much information had been given so far? How much did Wanda and Natalia intend to tell everyone? And why?

Chad was tired of being played the fool and decided never to act that part again. Control. He controlled his breathing, controlled his non-verbal cues. Calm and still, he asked, "She says she knows what happened to the people who have disappeared?"

"I do, Chad," Wanda said as she limped to the center of the living room, a black leg brace hindering her movement. "I very much know what happens to the missing people."

Chad swallowed hard and hoped no one else heard the audible gulp. "What happened?"

Wanda smiled and picked up the remote control from the coffee table. No one spoke as she pressed the rewind button. The images zipped by backward, Chad catching glimpses of a wolf, a rhino, a snake. A rabbit.

Chad gulped again when Wanda pressed the play button.

It started with a downward shot of the Ink Stains walking through the forest, the camera holder high in a tree. The quartet wandered upon Mason and his friends. There was no sound, just the seven figures gesturing to each other. An eighth person could be seen scurrying away on the ground, but nothing distinguishable to indicate who it might be. No hair color. No gender. Then the Ink Stains stripped and metamorphosized into hybrid creatures to attack Mason and his friends. The video didn't capture the noises, the smells, the splashes of another human being's blood on Chad's face. But it did show four human beings turning into fearsome creatures capable of tearing apart three athletic young men. Before the Ink Stains finished their meal and conversation with Chad, the scene changed to the night Chad became one of them. The naked figures of the Ink Stains danced around a small clearing in the forest, shifting, changing completely into the animals they were. There was a fifth lycanthrope there that night, but he didn't make it onto the screen until the scene changed again. It was an overcast day on the college's practice field where a rhinoceros chased a human-sized rabbit crashing through a small set of bleachers. The scene changed one final time, to Hunter's dead and bloodied human body and Viper's shredded remains at the bottom of a rock quarry. Everyone else in the room gasped. Apparently, they hadn't gotten this far in the presentation until now.

Chad was never a good actor, but he wasn't acting when he gasped, too, just for a different reason. Everyone in the room was shocked by the existence of these creatures; Chad was shocked to see that the corpses of Hunter and Viper were not where he had left them. He so desperately wanted to ask Wanda what the fuck her play was, why she was doing this, and to what end, but he kept his mouth shut, afraid of accidentally saying something that would implicate him in the madness she had just shown to everybody.

"Chad?" his mother broke the silence. "Wanda and her niece are hunters, and they hunt these things, these . . . monsters. They're called lycanthropes—"

"Technically, lycanthrope refers specifically to werewolves," Mr. Sedgeweck interrupted, looking down at his phone, proudly reading the results of his impromptu research, "but thanks to many pop culture references, the term can apply to any form of human to animal shapeshifter."

"—thank you, Albert. These lycanthropes are real, Chad, and they're among us, living in The Bends, hunting us."

"I just can't believe it. I just can't believe it," Mrs. Sedgeweck whispered to herself, looking at the television screen. Mr. Sedgeweck held and patted her hands.

"Why not involve the police?" Chad asked, staring directly at Wanda.

"You saw the videos, Chad." He didn't like the way she emphasized his name, letting him know that she held all the cards. "What do you think would happen if I showed these videos to the police? They already call me Whacky Wanda, and then I show these videos to them? Anyway, they're already involved, investigating the murders of the two bodies in the quarry. They don't have much to go on. The only thing they know about them is what most citizens of The Bends know—they go by the names Hunter and Viper; part of a gang called the Ink Stains. Officially, they're both John Does. No one knows their real names or anything else about them. So far, the police have nothing to go on with these murders. No suspects, no weapons, no clues. They don't even have *anyone else's* DNA other than the victims."

She made it perfectly clear to Chad that it was she who moved the bodies, with the possible help from her niece. The refinery not only had the murder weapon used to kill Hunter but the DNA from the children of just about everyone in the room. Why? Did she do it to help Chad and his friends? Or was she setting up a nefarious twist that would ultimately lead to their downfall?

"So, why are you here?" Chad asked.

"My niece and I have been hunting the Ink Stains for a very long time. We were getting close to finally ridding the world of them when we were met with some . . . complications." Wanda tapped her leg brace as she said the last word, implying that the Ink Stains were the ones to thwart her plans, but Chad knew differently. He knew the truth—she blamed him for everything that had gone wrong.

The part that burned his insides, that twisted his guts to the point of literally clamping his jaws closed on his tongue to keep from speaking, was that he couldn't defend himself, couldn't express his feelings on the matter or tell his side of the story. The rest of the people in the room believed her to be the brave hero wounded in the line of duty, and Chad had to suck it up and pretend he believed her as well. "Your injury prompted you to tell us about the lycanthropes?"

"No. The murders of Hunter and Viper. The Ink Stains have always been a foursome. You've seen the video of them turning into a wolf, cat, snake, and bear. You also saw a rhino and a rabbit. There are more lycanthropes out there, Chad. *Who knows* how many? Natalia and I have been trying to keep track, but there seem to be too many for just the two of us. Now there are the bodies in the rock quarry. No human being could have done that do them. Whatever did that to them must be a *monster*. I mean, a purely *vile* creature to do that to their *own kind*. Well, this has now become too much for just Natalia and me. So, we tracked down Justin's parents and told them the truth. We're very sorry that we didn't tell them earlier. We then asked them about Justin's friends, and they mentioned that Kyle Sedgeweck was his friend. After talking to his parents, they told us about Kyle's three best friends."

"Now what?" Chad asked.

The crunch of a beer can commanded everyone's attention. Heston's father fought his beer gut to lean forward in his chair and say, "I got enough shotguns for each of us. Even better stuff once I can trust you all."

Chad had spent his entire life communicating with Heston's dad using only four phrases: "Yes please, Mr. McCurdy; No, thank you, Mr. McCurdy. Have a good day, Mr. McCurdy, Thank you, Mr. McCurdy." Never once did he feel comfortable or brave enough to deviate from the script until now. "Do you really think that's the best approach?"

"I hate to say this, son," his mother started, "but your father and I agree with him. We all do. That's the main reason why we're meeting right now. We're forming a sort of neighborhood watch, and we're going to have Wanda teach us and train us. The next step is to figure out who else we can trust enough to extend an invitation to."

Chad knew very well that his mother was speaking English, but the arrangement of words coming from her mouth baffled him. Never did he expect her to think such things, let alone say them in front of other people. "Mom?"

"She's right, Chad," Natalia said, putting the same contemptuous emphasis on his name as her aunt did. Arms crossed over her chest, she stepped forward. "We need to hunt these abominations of nature down and kill them all. Every. Single. One. Of. Them."

Once again, Chad's father leaned in from behind to whisper a message for him alone, "You see the way she's staring at you so intensely? I think she's into you, son."

Chad sighed, knowing very well that his father's perspective on the situation couldn't have been further from the truth.

Made in the USA
Middletown, DE
25 September 2024